P9-CQA-775

CRAZY BLOOD

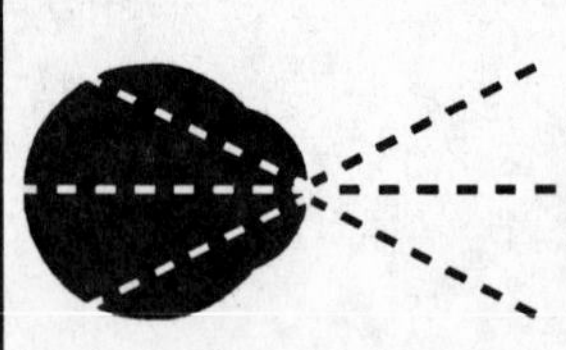

This Large Print Book carries the
Seal of Approval of N.A.V.H.

CRAZY BLOOD

T. JEFFERSON PARKER

THORNDIKE PRESS
A part of Gale, Cengage Learning

GALE
CENGAGE Learning

Farmington Hills, Mich • San Francisco • New York • Waterville, Maine
Meriden, Conn • Mason, Ohio • Chicago

GALE
CENGAGE Learning

Copyright © 2016 by T. Jefferson Parker.
Thorndike Press, a part of Gale, Cengage Learning.

ALL RIGHTS RESERVED
This is a work of fiction. All of the characters, organizations, and events portrayed in this novel are either products of the author's imagination or are used fictitiously.
Thorndike Press® Large Print Core.
The text of this Large Print edition is unabridged.
Other aspects of the book may vary from the original edition.
Set in 16 pt. Plantin.

LIBRARY OF CONGRESS CATALOGING-IN-PUBLICATION DATA

Names: Parker, T. Jefferson, author.
Title: Crazy blood / T. Jefferson Parker.
Description: Large print edition. | Waterville, Maine : Thorndike Press Large Print, 2016. | © 2016 | Series: Thorndike Press large print core
Identifiers: LCCN 2016000418 | ISBN 9781410487407 (hardback) | ISBN 1410487407 (hardcover)
Subjects: LCSH: Sibling rivalry—Fiction. | Ski resorts—California—Mammoth Mountain—Fiction. | Skis and skiing—California—Mammoth Mountain—Fiction. | Large type books. | Domestic fiction. | BISAC: FICTION / Literary.
Classification: LCC PS3566.A6863 C73 2016b | DDC 813/.54—dc23
LC record available at http://lccn.loc.gov/2016000418

Published in 2016 by arrangement with St. Martin's Press, LLC

Printed in the United States of America
1 2 3 4 5 6 7 20 19 18 17 16

A12006 681853

For all you sons and daughters and
the mountains you will face

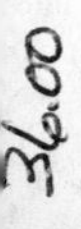

ACKNOWLEDGMENTS

Sincere thanks to the town of Mammoth Lakes for setting my muses free.

In particular, I'd like to thank Pam Lonza, Mammoth Mountain Ski & Snowboard Teams Administrator, for opening many doors and offering up so much of her valuable time to answer my questions.

Ben Wisner, Director of Mammoth Snowboard and Freeski Programs, showed me competitive skiing and snowboarding through the eyes of a coach. He also marked up my ski-racing scenes with an eye for verisimilitude that no outsider could have given.

Beat Hupfer, Mammoth Race Department Director, was generous with his time and very helpful with racing rules and regulations, politics and protocols, methods and myths.

Thanks to Mike Cook for always making me feel welcome in Mammoth Lakes, and for lending me his very real name for this work of fiction.

Many special thanks to John Teller, who grew up on Mammoth Mountain and was the sole American ski crosser in the 2014 Olympics in Sochi. It was a privilege to watch you race, and to see your sport through the eyes of a champion.

Last for Oakley Hall, who so beautifully ran these slopes before me in *The Downhill Racers.*

All truth contained herein comes from them; the errors are mine alone.

Why are you angry and why has your countenance fallen? If you do well, will you not be accepted? And if you do not do well, sin is couching at the door; its desire is for you, but you must master it.

— The Lord to Cain, Genesis 4:7

Chapter One

Sit down and I'll tell you a story.

I shot my husband, Richard, twenty-five years ago, right here in Mammoth Lakes, California. It was the first homicide in twelve years in this peaceful little town, and the only one for thirteen years after that. A justifiable killing, in my opinion, but not in the judge's. I shot five times. The prosecutor argued that I didn't fire the sixth cartridge because I'd planned to use it on myself, which by some loopy legal reasoning meant that I was sane and knew what I was doing. That lawyer badly wanted me sane because he was out for my blood, and they can't spill crazy blood. Only the healthy stuff. But he couldn't prove a "plan." I never considered using that sixth shot on myself. Not once. I told them so.

That's all behind me now, as much as anything is ever behind anybody, the past's not being even past and all that. Especially if you have children, which I do. Life's three great labors are to see what you've done, face the consequences, and adjust. People get stuck on those.

They will not look their acts straight in the eye.

They will not accept what they have coming.

They will not change direction.

I publish a weekly newspaper here in town, *The Woolly.* Woolly is our town mascot — a woolly mammoth, of course. I was a part-time winter-sports stringer when I was young. Even after all these years I still get a little thrill every time I see my byline: "Story by Cynthia Carson." This current work doesn't pay much, but the investigations and interviews, writing and photography, editing and layout (mostly electronic now, done right here on my red laptop) put me exactly where I want to be: in the real world. Which — being in the real world — is another thing that people have trouble with. They spend their whole lives trapped inside their own heads.

I've finished writing this week's edition of *The Woolly.* I've got the coffee poured and waiting. It's two degrees outside, but there's a strong fire in the stove and I'm going to sit close by that fire and edit my articles, then proofread and make them perfect before I put the paper to bed. That's what we used to say years ago at the *Mammoth Times* — "put it to bed." Which meant get it to the print shop. Always on Wednesday, so we could circulate early Thursday mornings. Now I just push a key or two and the printer starts to whir. This is my favorite time of the week, when I get my last look at what I'm about to publish. When I can change things to make my stories right. When I can think about what's been going on in town lately.

This week, my lead story is about the wave of ski and snowboard thefts — already up 300 percent this winter season over the last one, and it's only January. The thief/thieves are hitting all three Mammoth Mountain lodges, blending with the crowds, walking off with the rarely locked and often unattended items as if they owned them. He/she/they have a keen eye for quality. They do not take cheap gear or beat-up rentals. Last week's stolen skis and boards had a combined retail value of nearly eleven thousand dollars. The fact that six stolen pairs of skis and eight stolen snowboards are my lead story gives you some idea of what this town is usually like — a quiet village most days, a bit of Eden hanging on to a dome of volcanic rock ten thousand feet in the air.

I actually had to go to the Mammoth Lakes Police Department to get those stolen property stats for *The Woolly* — not easy for me to do after the unhappy hours I spent there, as you might imagine. They were courteous. I taught one of the sergeants to ski forty years ago, when I was fifteen, the year I was number one on the Mammoth girl's junior downhill ski team. I advised a detective to keep an eye on the Internet to find those skis and boards. Arrange a buy and you've got the criminals. He seemed to like the idea.

Chapter Two

Like when he was a boy, Wylie Welborn crunched across his backyard through the snow and started up the steps of the deck. Climbing, he counted backward from his twenty-five years, five for each step, so when he got to the top he was five years old again, bellowing and red-faced with hurt and cold, having just skied a blistering run down the hill behind his house, a little heavy on the throttle, and crashed into the toolshed. Now he turned and looked at that hill, shrunk by time, white and luminous in the moonlight. The toolshed was long gone.

The deck light glowed faintly, and through a jawbone of icicles Wylie saw movement behind the kitchen window. Then he heard his mother's yelp, followed by distant sounds that could have been war whoops or shouts of joy.

Kathleen threw open the mudroom door, flew into Wylie's arms, and braced him as if she were wrestling a bear. She dug her fingers in his shaggy dark hair and kissed his bearded cheeks, knocking his beanie to the deck. Wylie hugged back, assaulted on either side by two teenage girls, who pulled at him as if he was divisible. They pushed him toward the door.

"Come inside, Wylie," said Beatrice. "It's *freezing.*"

"My boy is back!"

"He's not *yours,* Mom," said Belle, handing her brother his beanie.

"He certainly is."

In the better light of the mudroom, they separated and faced one another, each trying in the sudden silence to comprehend what was what. Five years, communication but no notice of return, then this whiplash. Wylie saw the worry lines on his mother's face, more and deeper than before, and the new gray in her black hair. He saw that Beatrice, now seventeen and tall, still held her arms close to her sides, uncertainly. Belle, fifteen, had become pretty and now stood hipshot, with both hands resting on her low-slung jeans.

"You all . . . look great," he said.

"Oh, so do you, Wylie."

"He looks okay," said Beatrice.

"Okay plus," said Belle.

"Where's Steen?" Wylie asked.

"Delivering a cake," said Kathleen. "He'll be back any minute. You could have at least hinted that you were in the country, you know."

He nodded and looked at them in turn but said nothing. Belle put on her flinty expression, backpedaled partway into the dining room, then ran at Wylie and launched herself into the air, feetfirst, like a high-jumper. He caught her under the knees and shoulders, twirled her fast around twice, and set her down. "Still makes me dizzy, Wyles."

"You have five years to catch us up on," said Beatrice. "Skypes and texting don't count."

"I told you everything I was doing."

"Oh, *right,*" said Belle.

Each with a hand on Wylie, the women guided him through the kitchen and into the living room. The house seemed small and flimsy in a way he didn't remember. And dark. His mother helped him off with his jacket and hung it on an overloaded coatrack.

"You're just in time to see Robert race the Mammoth Cup," said Kathleen.

"Yeah, to watch him kick Sky Carson's sorry ass again," said Belle.

"Mammoth Cup sucks without you in it, Wylie," said Beatrice.

Wylie felt the extra chill in the house. It had always been a cold one. "Robert's not the only reason I came. I'm here to see all of you. I missed you. That's the truth." His smile was mostly lost in his beard.

"Are you staying, like, forever?" asked Beatrice.

"I haven't figured out forever yet."

"We could chain you up," said Belle.

"Five years all over the world and no *stuff*?" asked Beatrice.

"I've got a few things out in my truck. Maybe something for you."

"Afghani opium?" asked Belle.

"Enough of that, daughter. Wylie? Your room's full of file cabinets, outdated electronics, skis, and books. But the bed's still there, under all those boxes."

"Perfect. You guys? I apologize for just showing up out of nowhere. I've been loose in the world awhile. So I'm not used to being responsible."

"I'll bet the United States Marines loved that," said Kathleen.

"They taught me different for three years."

"I'm so glad you're not a marine anymore," said Beatrice.

"Right," said Belle. "Now you belong to

us again. I just heard Dad's truck pull up. It's like the old days! Let's belly up and chow down."

After dinner, Wylie gave Bea a necklace from Italy, and Belle a necklace from Peru, both gold. He gave his mother a gold bracelet in the shape of an elongated tiger, ruby-eyed, from Nepal, and Steen, his stepfather, an elaborately wrought gold shot glass from his native Denmark, made specifically for aquavit.

Kathleen let the girls skip homework and stay up until ten, rather than the usual nine, missing sleep they would regret missing when their alarms blasted on at 4:00 A.M. Before bed, Wylie hugged them and told them to hang in there, remembering how quickly four o'clock came, especially in winter, how black was the town of Mammoth Lakes at that hour, how bitterly cold was Let It Bean when he and Steen would let themselves in at 4:45 to prep the coffeemakers and steamers, grind the beans, form the dough, ready the counters, and bake the pastries that made the family its living.

With the girls in bed, the three grown-ups sat in the small, cold living room. Steen refilled their glasses with Aalborg and set another branch on the idling fire in the woodstove. The branch was pine, Wylie saw, surely scavenged from the forest behind the house. It would be punky and wet and burn poorly.

"So then, how many countries was it, Wylie?" asked Steen. Steen Mikkelsen was a trim man with an open face, white eyelashes, and smooth, almost whiskerless skin. He was a baker by trade and considered himself a pastry artist.

"Twelve, I think."

"All with mountains to ski."

"Most of them."

"And the war?"

"I did my tour."

"All of those lives. I am glad that you found a way to be both a healer and a marine."

Wylie gave his stepfather a look.

"Of course I understand. Robert Carson came to the bakery every week if there was news from you in Kandahar. You can tell us about the war when you're ready."

Kathleen went to the canvas log carrier, which lay open on the floor near the stove. She knelt and held up another twisted pine branch. "Steen?"

"We have the cut wood, honey. But the splitter is still broken, and the professionals want one hundred dollars per cord. I am sorry that I haven't had the time to split wood. But we made sixty dollars on the birthday cake tonight. You should have seen it. And our application for the vending license is near approval. Wylie, you will like my idea — to sell pastries outdoors in the parking lots of Mammoth Sports and elsewhere. From our own stand. It will bring income and promote Let It Bean. I am talking with the Mammoth Sports owners regarding placement. I have designed the stand. It will have bright paint, and handles and car tires for rolling."

Kathleen stood and rubbed her hands together histrionically. "We're trying to keep down the heating costs. It's scary how expensive everything is. Gas over four bucks again, and we still have to drive all the way to Reno for the Walmart. The girls hate to be seen in those clothes. But? It's that or the thrift stores. Life'll kill ya."

"We must always avoid that," said Steen.

"It's really good to see you, Wylie. You were a boy when you left. Now . . . look at you."

"You look good, too, Mom." Wylie noticed wear he'd never seen on his mother, a hint of hardness in her face, though she was only in her mid-forties and still trim and pretty.

"We work hard but we're poorer," she

said. "Gargantua Coffee came to town last year, and they're trying to run us out of business. It's working — our numbers are way down. The girls know it and they're scared. They take some pride in Let It Bean, you know? Even though it's hard work. Now a billion-dollar-a-month national coffee monster is after us. Imagine that. Next fall, we'll have a new landlord and lease to negotiate. Rent will rise, certainly."

"Don't be pessimistic, honey."

Kathleen sat back down on the nearly formless old couch. "Beatrice is unhappy a lot, and anxious. I found a hunk of hash in Belle's jeans when I was washing them. Her crack about opium did not amuse me. Both of them have been sneaking up to the old Burnside mansion at Eagle. Some Silicon Valley hotshot bought it so he could throw parties. He likes the racing and freestyle crowd. The youngsters in town call it 'Mountain High.' Cute. It's full of people like Sky Carson. So, I'm not pessimistic, Steen. I'm realistic, if that's all right with you."

"Yes, of course it is. But these are things all families must endure."

Kathleen swigged the last of her aquavit. "Let's give the mountain a rip, Wylie. Soon."

"You're on."

"I feel the need for speed."

"Still got it, do you?"

"You bet I do."

"Call of the wild, Mom. Me, too."

She smiled softly. "It meant the world to me that you called me every birthday. That couldn't have been easy."

"There was one from Kandahar that took a little doing."

"You're my prince."

Steen poured another drink and followed Wylie's mother down the hallway. Wylie put another soft branch and a few shards of kindling into the fire box. He left the door ajar to carburet the thing, turned, and let the faint heat warm the backs of his calves.

He looked around the old house. Same as ever. His mother had been renting it when he was born. She was a single mom then, and widowed in a sense — Wylie's father had been shot dead by his wife, Cynthia Carson, just minutes after Wylie's illicit conception. Back then, it was just Kathleen and her baby. Kathleen, getting minimum wage and tips at Bruno's Donuts, would never have survived without friends and family pitching in to help. Three years later, she married Steen, and they were able to buy Bruno's and make it their own. Then the girls came along. Kathleen and Steen had continued renting this house until they could make a down payment and get a mortgage.

Yes, they own it now, thought Wylie, his gaze roaming the water-stained ceiling, the cramped, dark kitchen, the knotty pine walls, the thinning carpet, the living room windows lined with old blankets behind the curtains against the winter cold, the drafts easing through anyhow. An orange plastic bucket in one corner caught drops of snow-melt coming through the roof.

He texted Robert Carson and Robert texted back.

Chapter Three

Wylie steered his truck up ice-slick Minaret toward Eagle Lodge and the former Burnside manse, now, apparently, "Mountain High." Before him, Mammoth Mountain towered, emanating its usual eerie, seemingly internal light. It was over eleven thousand vertical feet of volcano-spewed rhyodacite that would remain cloaked in snow until June, even into July in good years. The mountain brought Wylie the words of Rexroth: *There are rocks/ On the earth more durable/ Than the configurations of heaven.* The sky around the mountain was black, the stars fixed in shimmering clarity, their long-vanished light just now hitting Wylie's earthly eyes. His four-wheel drive was sure-footed enough to keep him in his lane if he went slowly and braked early into slow-motion turns.

All three floors of the old Burnside home were lit. Wylie saw maybe a dozen parked cars under the spacious, snow-crowned porte cochere — a fifty-fifty blend of swank SUVs, then the beaters affordable for young skiers and boarders. He heard music and voices and knocked on the front door, and a moment later it opened. A man towered over tall Wylie, who came to about the bottom of the guy's beard. "Wylie, man."

"Croft. You look bigger."

"I only stopped growing a year ago."

"Really?"

"It was a gland thing. But I can still fit in my truck."

"Robert's here, right?"

"Come on in. You gotta meet Helixon. And, you know, get his permission to be here."

From the dark entryway, Wylie was led into a great room, moodily lit, that was open all the way to the ceiling of the second floor. The vast interior looked to be hardwoods, warmly finished. Above, the second-story rooms sat behind the railed quadrangle of the atrium, like those of an old hotel. A wide stairway led to the second story, then swept up and over and out of Wylie's sight. Suspended from above was a behemoth chandelier of elk antlers and small flickering lights, graceful and complex. A faint veil of smoke hung within, cannabis and tobacco. Wylie heard music and saw movement in the second-floor shadows. Three young women came pounding down the burnished plank stairs, laughing and trying to balance drinks. A fourth, scantily clad but wearing a red elf's cap, slid down the banister on her butt. From somewhere above came a shriek, delighted and somewhat wicked.

"Third floor's kind of like forbidden," said Croft.

"That's probably good."

"Helixon's got more money than the Facebook guy and Bono put together."

"How is that possible?"

"He created this app that sees the future. I'm not exactly sure how it works. He also invented the Imagery Beast for training skiers and boarders. It's on the second floor, but only Helixon can open the door. This place is quiet tonight, but it'll be packed this weekend for the Mammoth Cup. Come on — that's Helixon over there, the one what looks like lightning struck him."

Bart Helixon looked to be in his early twenties, short and wiry, with a head of pure white hair. His mustache and Vandyke were similarly bleached, and it was only his unwrinkled skin that gave away his youth. He wore a window, positioned on its clear eyeglass frame like a tiny rearview mirror, his blue eyes studying Wylie from behind the chandelier flickers on the lens. Wylie shook his hand. "There's power in you," Helixon said.

"Standard-issue."

"No, nothing standard in there." Helixon broke the shake and wiped his hand on his lounge pants.

Wylie saw a phalanx of young men and women moving from the kitchen, bearing drinks and plates stacked high with food. With them came Wylie's half brother Robert Carson, smiling and clean-shaven and somehow bemused, which has exactly how Wylie remembered him. Wylie hadn't seen him in five years, but rarely had more than a week gone by without calls and texts when possible, letters and postcards when not. Robert was three years older than Wylie, equally tall but lighter. He had an athlete's body, the blue eyes and blond hair of the Carson clan.

Wylie and Robert hugged forcefully, measuring each other's strength and balance as they had been doing their whole lives. Wylie was startled by the great affection welling up in him now. It was so good to know for certain that not all of his heart was scattered throughout the Middle East and the cold peaks of Eurasia or the Andes, that a big part of it was still here in Mammoth Lakes. He hugged Robert again, then broke away and smiled as the gathered crowd hooted and raised glasses to them. Wylie clamped Robert's shoulder with one hand and accepted a beer from a woman in a short dress and black diamond-patterned leggings.

Suddenly, a wail pierced the room, loud and coming at Wylie. People scrambled out of the way, some stumbling, food and drink spilling to the floor. Sky Carson — Wylie's other half brother, born to Cynthia Carson just months before Kathleen bore Wylie — came powering through the crowd on a skateboard, wearing red swim trunks and red board shoes only, aiming straight at Wylie. Wylie foresaw the attack. Sky launched the board at Wylie's head and it speared through the burnished orange light of Mountain High, straight at its target. Wylie stepped aside and caught it. Sky landed, feet together and arms spread for balance, like a gymnast. He stared at Wylie. "Behold. Five years of peace on the mountain have come to this ugly end. Enter the demon, Wylie Welborn."

"Holy crap, Sky!" hollered Helixon. "These floors are Civil War reclaimed barn oak!"

Wylie lofted the board back to Sky, who snatched it midair, dropped it to the floor, jumped on with one foot, and pushed off. Sky carved across the reclaimed oak to the entryway, flipped the board up into one hand, then looked back. He aimed his free index finger pistol-style at Wylie, feigned recoil, then pushed through the front door into the freezing dark.

"Well, Sky's a bit up and down, as always," said Robert. "Come on. There's someone who gets to finally meet you."

Hailee Patterson had a good smile and steady blue eyes and her hand felt strong in Wylie's. Robert led them past a knot of frenetic dancers and into a theater with a large fixed screen and eight rows of seats descending like those in a lecture hall. The doors closed heavily behind them. Wylie saw himself on-screen, tearing down the X Course in the Mammoth Cup ski-cross final five years back, in which he had upset both Robert and Sky Carson, solid favorites, to stand on top of the box.

"Helixon insisted on showing this when he heard you were coming," said Robert.

"Look at you go," said Hailee. "Like you're stuck to the fall line."

Wylie watched his younger self glued high

would automatically go to the Aspen X Games the following week. The four finalists were *that* close in total points. The three others could advance only as alternates, at the discretion of the USSA selection committee.

"But either way, Robert's retiring after this season," said Belle. "To get married and work a job. Sounds horrible, doesn't it? With all his talent? With the Olympics only two years away?"

"He's going on to the next thing," said Wylie. "That's what people do."

"That's what you did," said Beatrice. "And at least Hailee is, like, moderately cool."

Belle just shook her head.

Glancing across the stands, Wylie saw Hailee sitting with Cynthia Carson — mother of Robert and Sky. Cynthia, his father's executioner. Hailee waved. Cynthia acknowledged no one, all her attention forward on the coming race, looking to Wylie, as always, commanding, indestructible, and frightening.

The stands were full. Wylie knew many of the people gathered here, but many he did not. The faces had changed in five years. It was an odd feeling to be remembered in your hometown but also to know that its

and tight on the narrow chutes known as Shooters, banking hard, then schussing past Robert and Sky on the final downhill straight. Sky got the silver and Robert the bronze. Since then, Sky had won once; then Robert had won the Mammoth Cup ski cross three years running.

"That last chute was the difference," said Robert.

"What a run," said Hailee. "What great snow that day, too."

Wylie watched himself on-screen, smiling rather goofily from the podium. What he'd thought at that moment was that his life was just beginning, that the world was his to see and he was ready to get this thing done. Now he missed his former clarity and wished for something like it again.

"Hey, Wylie. Hailee and I are getting married."

Wylie looked from his brother's pleased face to Hailee, who looked happy and desirable by any standards he knew. "I'm down for both of you. Truly."

"No more chasing dreams and Olympics. Grandpa's going to work me into the business full-time."

"Look at *this*!" Hailee flashed a diamond and gave Robert a warm smile. Robert hugged her and looked over her shoulder at

Wylie with pride and either contentment or resignation.

Chapter Four

Wylie sat in the start-gate stands with his mother and sisters for the Mammoth Cup ski-cross finals. The January afternoon was cold and clear and he could see through his binoculars that the upper X Course was still in good shape after two days of ski-cross racing. Ski cross was a young sport that pitted four skiers against one another on the same high-velocity downhill course at the same time. They raced one another, not the clock. Ski cross was one of the newest Olympic events, aimed at the new generation and considered by many to be equal to the fearsome downhill in peril and prestige. It was certainly rougher. For Wylie, winning this Mammoth Cup ski-cross event five years ago had been a defining moment in his life.

He explained to Beatrice the United States Ski Association point system, and how only the winner of that day's final

memory of you was already fading. At twenty-five, with a Mammoth Cup win to his credit and youthful indiscretions still trailing him, Wylie was a notable here, but old guard. The new hotshots were teenagers. Chloe Kim was good enough to have made the last U.S. Olympic boarding team but, at sixteen, was too young by IOC rules. There was much talk in town of half-pipe boarder Johnny Maines — not quite twenty years old yet and maybe the next Shaun White.

The women ski crossers went first. Wylie was struck by how much faster they had gotten in his five years away. They were stronger and braver. Sitting on either side of him, Beatrice and Belle fidgeted with anticipation. Beatrice was a slopestyle snowboarder and could make the Mammoth snowboarding team for next year. That was a matter of time and money. Five grand, roughly, Wylie thought. Belle was an up-and-coming ski-cross racer like him. She was fearless, even as the ten-year-old whom Wylie had last seen. They watched an eighteen-year-old out of Tahoe win the women's ski-cross finals, a full ten feet ahead of the pack. She skidded to a stop in the out run, throwing a wall of snow and a smile at the photographers.

Wylie felt the sun on his face and smelled

the sweetly noxious fumes wafting up from the waxing station. Nothing on earth better than a sunny morning with good snow on a mountain. He thought of the late bright mornings at the Great St. Bernard monastery in Switzerland, the sunlight on the mountains so precise and brief that long winter. There was never quite enough light at Great St. Bernard. Or the Benedictine monastery at Tegernsee, or the Monkey Temple in Kathmandu, or even in Lillehammer. Was there enough light in winter anywhere? Sometimes at dusk, he'd watch the last of that light dim down to no light at all and he'd have this squirrelly fear inside that it would never come again. But those were good years, alone and free.

Wylie's two years of wandering after Afghanistan were his way of shedding what he had been: boy, son, brother, baker, barista, ski-cross racer, marine. He had ditched himself as thoroughly as he could, believing that later he could re-collect the useful parts. He'd tried to simplify without oversimplifying: mountains, snow, and speed. He'd stayed at the monasteries because they were remote and beautiful and affordable if you labored. And because they were built on the promise of a God, whom by then Wylie had come to doubt. And because half of his fellow travelers were young women.

Now he took a hand of each sister and considered the X Course without the distraction of skiers on it. It was a good course, tucked into a crevasse between chairlifts twenty and twenty-one, both closed for this event. It had been designed by Mike Cook, Mammoth Mountain's longtime course setter. Cook was known for steep, fast runs, high ramps for big-air jumps, narrow banks, tight gates, and straightaways wide enough for passing. The X Course was smaller than that at the Sochi arena, but the jumps were higher.

With four racers on such a course, ski cross is a crowded, highspeed contest similar to downhill and slalom, but also related to motocross, speed skating, and roller derby. There is an element of NASCAR, too — high-velocity drafting only inches behind the skier ahead is an important technique. No contact between the racers is allowed, but "incidental contact" is expected, and ski-cross judges are known to be loose constructionists. Foes are occasionally cut off, shoulders thrown, bodies launched in desperation or team sacrifice, skis lapped over other skis, causing sudden explosive ruin, poles deployed. High-velocity wipeouts, known as "yard sales" because of the gear and clothing torn away and left spread all over a course, are common. Whoever leads controls the race; whoever would lead must pass. Race speeds reach seventy miles per hour.

Wylie had always loved the chariot race in *Ben-Hur.* His personal take on ski cross had essentially been a power game, big on mass and speed: E=mc2. He was burly for a ski crosser, bearlike at times, though not graceless. He wasn't quite quick enough to consistently make that first hole shot — right out of the start gate — to take an early lead. So passing was the heart of his game. Coming from behind, Wylie presented relentless threat; once in front, he was amply fast and stubbornly immovable. He worked his fall line — the shortest distance down a slope, the route your body would take in a fall — with a kind of adhesive velocity. His dark to-the-shoulder hair, full beard, and mustache reinforced his ursine air when racing.

Wylie watched as Robert, Sky, and the other two finalists loosened up. Robert was a classic skier with sound judgment and made few mistakes; Sky, a talented risk taker, high-strung, programmed for both winning and crashing. They were two of

America's best. In the years Wylie was away, Robert and Sky had both been racing the Federation Internationale de Ski World Cup circuit against the Europeans, who dominated the sport. The Carsons finished middle of the pack at best on the FIS-approved World Cup courses.

Watching the racers prepare, Wylie felt that edgy shimmer of adrenaline in his core. He yawned. He wondered what competition would be like again, after five years without it, unless you counted survival in combat as competition. Maybe that was the greatest competition of all. Certainly the most consequential.

"Robert's going to win today," said Beatrice. "He'll put everything into it for Hailee. He's romantic like that."

"God, look at Sky Carson," said Belle. "Doesn't he ever get tired of being himself?"

Sky Carson had gone to the staging area's barrier, over which he now rested his arms, helmet off, poles in one gloved hand, chatting up some girls and hamming for the cameras. He was trim and lithe, with a head of blond Carson hair, a sharp nose, and blue eyes. Like several of the many Carsons who had settled in Mammoth Lakes, Sky was a gifted athlete. Wylie had grown up with him and knew Sky as a high-energy egotist or sullen bully, depending on his mood. Meds were long rumored. Wylie and Sky had never gotten along, often much worse than that. A running public feud had begun in childhood. Same father; different mothers. Antagonists. Rivals. Bad blood.

Today, Sky had dressed in a pattern of exploding stars and stripes instead of Mammoth Mountain ski team blue. In a nod to the youthful snow-apparel industry, ski crossers — unlike USSA downhill racers — were allowed to wear casual clothes of their own choosing in competition. A race official trudged over on snowshoes, and Sky barked like a dog at him, then turned back to his audience.

The grandstands stood to the right of the starting gates, and the crowd could see down the course only as far as jump two, known as Goofball. After that, the start-gate spectators would view the action on a huge monitor perched across the course, opposite the grandstands. For those preferring to see the finish of the race live, more grandstands had been set up down the mountain, near the vendor booths and sponsor displays.

The racers finished their loosening-up routines and made short starts, then settled into their starting gates. Wylie's heart was beating hard and he yawned again, which he used to do incessantly before races to balance his oxygen/nitrogen mix.

A moment later the gates flew open and the four ski crossers dropped into the half-pipe start, war whoops sharp in the thin alpine air. Wylie heard the grind and hiss of the skis. Robert grabbed the lead out of the first right bank, held it down a short straight and into Launching Pad, jump one. Wylie could see his skis shuddering but tight together, his neat turn inside the first paneled gate, then his sudden burst of speed out. Robert had more hours on the Mammoth X Course than anyone, even his brother, and his home-course advantage was real. Sky hounded him, just a hair outside and behind. The two other men — one of them the previous year's X Games silver medalist, Bridger Burr from Colorado, the other a nineteen year-old racer, Trey Simms from Squaw Valley — formed a tight knot no more than two yards back. Wylie saw they were hitting fifty miles per hour on this first straightaway. In his gloved hands, his sisters' grips tightened.

The racers sped down the straight, bunching even more tightly. Wylie guessed if Sky maintained his number-two position in and out of the second jump — Goofball — he would try to pass his brother on Dire

Straights, which was wide and steep and had always been one of Wylie's favorite places to pass. Dire Straights schussed into Conundrum, jump three, the highest and most dramatic of the jumps, a Mike Cook signature. From there, the course then curved steeply into Shooters, where positions could be improved only at peril.

The racers launched off the Goofball ramp, dropping slowly through the air and out of sight. A thousand sets of eyes, Wylie's among them, rose to the video screen, onto which the ski crossers, now much larger than life, came floating airborne toward them in a tight multicolored formation in which each man, ski, pole, and rippling bib hung painterly composed and balanced against the pale blue Mammoth sky. Sky Carson landed a nanosecond behind Robert, but just as Wylie had foreseen, Sky precariously stole inside on gate 2 and passed Robert onto Dire Straights. Burr stuck right behind him, using Sky's draft to pass Robert, too. Trey Simms held fourth, back by twenty feet.

Heading into the next turn, Simms set too brash a line and clipped Burr from behind. It looked like no more than a brush, but Wylie knew better. Burr tore off-course and went down, smashing into the right-side netting, then somehow broke free to spin like a big eight-pronged child's top to a stop on the bank.

"Ugh," said Beatrice.

"*Scheiss* and a half," said Belle.

The three remaining racers ground out of the turn side by side, their poles feeling around them like the canes of blind men. They accelerated down the straight and launched off Conundrum as if linked. They soared identically, bunched and oddly still. Wylie's breath caught at this brief beauty.

As he landed, Robert's skis shuddered violently on a patch of ice. He rose from his crouch to check his speed, caught more ice, and — still going at what looked to Wylie like sixty miles an hour — shot off-course, scattering bystanders and flattening sapling pines, throwing snow high in an unstoppable ballistic calamity. Off the embankment he flew, rising higher and higher, pivoting slowly, then, on his descent, backstroking with his poles in a braking windmill.

The ski lift stanchion was set back from the X Course several yards, wrapped in padding. Safety padding could be thin, in some cases no better than a T-shirt pulled over a telephone pole. In Wylie's experience, and in ski-racing lore, stanchions drew you to them as if they were magnets and you a metal shaving, and the faster you were going, the less you could resist their pull. Their mojo was bad and strong. To Wylie, Robert's line of descent looked fated. Loudspeakers broadcast the amplified *whop* of him hitting padded steel, and he dropped to the snow like a bird having hit a window.

Thoughtless, Wylie was out of the stands, slipping and sliding fast down the snow steps for the lower course. When he got to Robert, there was already a small crowd. Wylie barreled through and knelt beside him.

Robert was unconscious and his head was turned acutely. His helmet lay nearby in two pieces, with the chin strap still fastened. Wylie found Robert's pulse and the rise of his lungs beneath the layers of his clothes. His skin was hot and slick, and when Wylie lifted his brother's eyelids, he saw uncomprehending black pupils set in their irises of blue. Spine, he thought, bone and nerves: Sgt. Lance Madigan, Kandahar, shot in the neck by a sniper.

Wylie stood and hollered "Away" to the onlookers so Robert could get some air. Unable to resist, and because racing is about winning, he checked the big screen, to see Bridger Burr cross the finish line inches ahead of Sky, nailing gold and his place in the Winter X Games the following week in Aspen.

CHAPTER FIVE

Adam Carson sat beside his grandson Robert's bed in St. Francis Memorial Hospital in San Francisco. The Carson patriarch was eighty-seven years old and feeling every second of those years. He disliked cities and their inescapable noise, and he had been here since Robert's accident two weeks ago. A big man, he sat forward on the chair, elbows on his knees, chin resting on the bulbous knuckles of his interlocked fingers. He had hands like driftwood. His hair was gray, straight, and cut unfashionably.

Finally, the endless Carsons and in-laws who had traipsed into this room today to sit and whisper and blubber over Robert were gone. Visiting hours were long over, thank God. But Adam had made arrangements for two of the most important of those visitors to return together for the first time, instead of separately. He heard footsteps coming his way.

Grandson Sky strode through the door first, followed a moment later by grandson Wylie. Neither seemed aware of the other. To Adam, it was wrong for young people to be sullen, with so much life still ahead of them. As a sympathy-inspired alternate at the X Games the previous week, Sky had done poorly, and that was surely eating at him. "You look like two fighters coming into the ring," said Adam more truthfully than he would have wished.

"Good evening, sir," said Wylie.

"Is he any better?" asked Sky.

Adam watched Wylie round the bed and stop opposite Sky. From this vantage point, Adam could see both of their profiles and trace the distinct Carson lines of jaw and cheekbone clear back to his paternal great-great grandfather, Theodore, born in 1848 in Portland, Oregon, and photographed in Union uniform after Vicksburg. These facial features had come all the way forward to the Carson-Fixx twins, Evan and Evangeline, born to great-granddaughter Leigh-Ann down in L.A., what, five years ago? The last five years of Adam's life seemed to have gone by in about five minutes.

Sometimes Adam drew comfort from the long years he'd lived, but sometimes he felt like he was just one more helpless observer.

He watched as Wylie lifted Robert's eyelids, looked down for a long moment, then smoothed them closed. Over the last weeks he had noted that, home from his five-year journey, Wylie seemed strong and humorless as ever. Wylie went to the foot of the bed, where he lifted the sheets to run a finger along the sole of Robert's left foot.

"He can feel that," said Sky, dropping into a chair.

"You don't know what he feels," said Wylie.

"There's another chair outside, Wylie," said Adam.

"I'll stand."

Adam looked at his favorite three grandsons, listened to the hum and shuffle of the hospital. "I asked you two to come here so we could have an honest talk. I have some questions that need answers. First is what to do with our beloved Robert. As you know, the doctors say he is beyond hope."

"The doctors are full of shit," said Sky loudly, aiming his voice toward the open door.

"In this rare case, I agree with them," said Adam. "However, inarguably, this room has been running me eighteen hundred a day for the last two weeks. Plus the meds, supplies, nutrition, et cetera. Cotton swabs cost eight dollars per. This isn't about the money, of course. It's about getting Robert to where he would want to be."

Adam caught Sky's impatient look and took a deep breath, reminding himself that forgiveness was divine, especially when it came to offspring. "And where is that, G-pa?"

"Mammoth Lakes," said Wylie. "Obviously."

"Yeah, but take him home? Or to a room at the hospital?"

"Neither," said Adam. "I think we should move Robert in with his mother. I think that would please her. The family can afford doctors and nurses as needed. But I wanted your thoughts before going ahead with that."

"Mom is Mom," said Sky. "But better for Robert than this dump."

"Wylie?"

"Not up to me, sir."

"I asked for your opinion."

Wylie thought a moment. "Robert's better off with his mother. So, yes, Cynthia."

Sky looked at Wylie impatiently, then shook his head as if Wylie were a simpleton. "So, G-pa — what did you really drag us down here for?"

"We need to talk about you two."

"Whatever."

Adam set his big hands on his knees, balanced his weight over his boots, and stood. His knees ached and his vertebrae clunked, but he straightened to his considerable full height. With his toe, he pushed his chair to Wylie and pointed at it. When Wylie had sat, Adam took a deep breath and looked down at his grandsons. "I believe in both of you."

"I believe in me, too, G-pa, although —"

"Shut up, Sky."

"Okay."

"Let me reassemble my train of thought. Good. Now. Twenty-five years ago, each of you was brought into this world with both advantages and challenges, as we all are. You are both parts of the larger Carson clan. Because of the death of my son, Richard, at the hand of Cynthia — and Richard's prior fathering of Wylie — you two half brothers have had a rocky time with each other. You were born less than six months apart. Innocence protected you at first. Then, through the years, you found knowledge, truth, suspicion, distrust, dislike, disrespect, and — for want of a better term — contempt."

"Don't forget his envy of my Carsonness," said Sky.

Adam looked down at Sky and rested his

gnarled hands behind his back, feeling his shoulder rotators grinding softly — an old man trying to keep from slapping his grandson across the face. "We are now set forth on a new direction. The one person who could sometimes keep you two at peace lies before us, unable to speak to you. So, on his behalf, let me try."

Adam relaxed his shoulders and let his arms fall forward to his sides, felt the blood surging back into place. "Robert loves you equally. He is never happier than in your separate companies and he looks forward to the day when all three of you can love each other as brothers are meant to. He is engaged to be married. If he could speak, he would ask that, in honor of that union, you forgive each other. The slights. The insults. The fights that spilled real blood. The hate. So I now ask you to forgive each other, in honor of Robert and Hailee. Move forward, apart in your lives but together in the spirit that Carson strength, excellence, and goodness shall not perish from the Earth."

"No shame in that game," said Sky.

"Wylie?"

Adam watched as Wylie continued to study Robert, as if Robert were a problem that could be solved. "What about Welborn strength, excellence, and goodness?"

Sky chortled quietly.

"Of course I meant to include them," said Adam. Now in the lengthening silence, he was lost for words. He'd outlined his address, of course, refreshing himself with his beloved Lincoln, but forgotten to write the clincher that would close the deal. It was time to improvise.

"Then please rise and face each other."

The young men did.

He saw their gazes lock, but he could see no emotion. They certainly were good-looking young men. For reasons he did not understand, Adam was prouder of these three than any of the others — even his own brothers and sisters, sons and daughters, other grandsons and granddaughters, great-grandsons and great-granddaughters — and the whole muddy slough of in-laws who were contributaries to the great river Carson. Of all, he loved these three troubled brothers most. Or, maybe, he was only most afraid for them. This idea was coming to him more often now, since tragedy had stolen Robert in his prime. Were the Carsons cursed? Adam felt his eyes welling and he willed it to cease. "Sky, do you swear in the presence of Robert that you forgive Wylie for all past wrongs? The words, the blows? Everything?"

"Yeah, okay."
"Wylie?"
Wylie waited a long beat. "Yes, I forgive all that."
"Embrace."
Adam watched Sky and Wylie come together briefly, then break apart with obvious relief. Still, hope lilted through him. "I'm not expecting instant miracles," he said. "But I do expect civil behavior from you men. This isn't for me. It's for Robert. He loves you both very much. I'll be making the arrangements with Cynthia to take him home. In the meantime, you two grow up. That goes especially for you, Sky."
Adam saw the anger flash in Sky's face. So much like his mother in that way, he thought; their emotions take them over and they do foolish things. Then, as Adam watched, Sky's anger changed to something more subtle. Sky looked to Robert and took his hand. "Robert, for you, I'll forgive this . . . man. But I'll do more than just that. I'll win next year's Mammoth Cup for you. I'll make you even more proud to be a Carson. I promise this to you more totally than I've ever promised anything to anyone."
Sky kissed Robert's hand and folded his unresisting arm back upon the blanket. To

Adam, the arm looked no more living than a shirtsleeve. Sky patted Robert's hand lightly, then gave his grandfather a look of satisfaction. Wylie left the room, and Sky followed. Adam sighed, very tired, and sat back down. He heard his grandsons outside:

"Wylie, I actually don't forgive you. I always hoped you'd die young and in agony. Still do."

"Back at you, brother."

"You're not my brother. I got the good blood."

"You can't win the cup next year, Sky."

"I can and will."

"No, it's mine."

"I'll do anything on Earth to prevent that."

"You can't beat me, Sky. The cup already belongs to me."

Adam took a cab back to the Monaco Hotel on Geary. He packed and had the bellhop take his bags to the lobby. He went downstairs with his Catton and got a glass of Napa cabernet from the restaurant. He sat by the fireplace and looked toward the street, exhausted by Robert's fate and by his two grandsons' unbending dislike for each other. Neither was at genuine fault. The true blame lay on his own son, Richard, and his wife, Cynthia, and the determined Kathleen Welborn. How many times had that story played out in the history of civilization — the married man of success and charm, the flattered young admirer, the shocked wife?

The wine was unearthly good. He pondered Sky's pledge to win the next Mammoth Cup for Robert, not sure what to make of it. Sky was certainly capable of winning it. But Sky had also always excelled at the hollow gesture. Sky, who, at age six, had wanted to change his name to White Ice Carson, to be more "marketable" as a skier. Who, at sixteen, had brought impoverished Croatian twins to live with him and Cynthia and train on Mammoth Mountain, then angrily turned them out when his interest in them dwindled. Sky, who had been engaged to and dumped not one but two women, practically at the altar. Sky, thought Adam — boastful and brash and brimming with inborn talent, but still afflicted by moods, like his mother, and by a sliver of fear on the mountain, like my beautiful Richard.

So, Sky as Mammoth Cup champion? Maybe. He would need to dedicate himself to it.

But Wylie could win it, too. He had comparable instincts and abilities. And Wylie was serious in ways that Sky wasn't, quite. He was strong and could summon will. He was both a skier and a racer — two different things. Wylie's Mammoth Cup win five years ago was the most impressive ski-cross run that Adam had ever seen on the Mammoth X Course. But Wylie would need to find desire. For Wylie, there had always been the next adventure, the next mountain, the next place where the grass would be greener and he could find whatever was missing. Like my beautiful Richard, Adam thought again.

Now, he thought, the cup stood equidistant between them like a gleaming sword that only one of them could grab first and employ. Which one of his grandsons would he really like to win that race? Well, legally, Sky was the legitimate Carson and therefore an heir. Spiritually? Bastard Wylie might have the edge.

Adam looked at the magnificent vase that stood in the middle of the lobby, at the elegant furniture, the beautiful marble floor. Through the front windows on Geary he could see the rain coming down and a bellhop with a raised umbrella escorting a woman inside. He thought of Sandrine, almost five years gone now, but he still often awoke in his bed believing that she was there beside him, as she had been for sixty-four years. Sometimes he reached his hand out, expecting her warm skin. Then that free fall into truth.

But surprisingly to Adam, what he found himself dwelling on in his advancing years were not the staggering losses in his lifetime — Sandrine, a brother, a sister, Richard, a granddaughter, several of his closest friends, and scores of people he had liked and loved — but, rather, the pleasures that carried him through each day. He had his home and his ATV and the Sierra Nevada to roam upon. He could still fish Crowley Lake and Hot Creek and the Upper Owens. He could still ski the more forgiving slopes. He had his reading and the eyes to do it with, thank God. He had the love of Teresa. He had Mammoth Mountain to manage — twenty-eight lifts, three lodges and a cross-country ski center, six restaurants, two bars, and an untold horde of employees — all subject to the vagaries of snow. Blessed, all-powerful snow. It had always been his life and love and fortune. Not that he was involved with the day-to-day running of the mountain anymore. It was time to sell, and he knew it.

In the early days, Dave McCoy had built the resort of Mammoth Mountain, most of it with his own hands. Young Adam had been one of his many acolytes. Eventually, through his family's commercial development fortune, Adam had bought controlling share of the resort, and it had been his for the last decade. But by now he had come to believe that, regarding what we love, we are all just janitors for allotted times. Adam had offers on the table from corporations in the United States, the UK, Germany, Japan, China, South Korea, and Dubai. He would make scores of millions of dollars.

Finally warmed by the fire, Adam surrendered his troubles to those of a darker time. He opened his beloved Catton, the finest writer on our great civil war, in Adam's not always humble opinion. Antietam was coming, still the bloodiest day in the history of the nation, a spectacle of profitless tragedy and waste. The first battlefield in the history of the world that was documented by a newfangled thing called photography. Brother killing brother. Adam read for half an hour, making occasional notes in the margins. When he was done, he riffled the pages quickly and smiled to himself. There were pen scratchings in his Catton going back sixty years!

An hour later, at exactly eleven, Mike Cook, friend and ally and Mammoth Mountain racecourse setter, walked into the lobby. He found Adam and rocked his shoulder, then sat with him for a while as the older man's mind began to fire again. It didn't take long. Cook had never seen such energy in a person. Sure, Adam was slower now, but once he got going he still had that unstoppability, that God-given combination of weight and gravity that took him places others couldn't get to.

Cook helped Adam get his luggage to the door, where a bellhop took over, setting the bags with care into the back of Cook's SUV. The rain had stopped. The bellhop asked about the current Mammoth Mountain snow level and Adam told him to the nearest quarter inch, adding that another six to eight inches were due on Thursday night. He overtipped the young man, as he did all gratuity-dependent service workers.

"Get me out of this city," he said to Mike.

Chapter Six

In the cold darkness the next morning, Wylie dug his old Chamonix Racing Saber Three skis from his bedroom closet. They were 180 centimeters long and slim-waisted, with acute, deep-carving edges. He propped the skis against the wall and ran his fingers along the sharp undersides. Dusty, and badly in need of wax, of course. He could hear his sisters banging around in the darkness, arguing over first shower while the hot-water pipe groaned and shuddered. He remembered what it was like getting up this early to get to Let It Bean, followed by ski workouts on the mountain, then school, then another hour or two at Let It Bean, then homework. Even with the special Mammoth School District programs for team skiers and boarders, Wylie had needed more than a little willpower to make it through four years with his 3.0 grade point average intact.

He arrived at Main Lodge just before 7:00 A.M., when the Mammoth ski team had its pick of the best runs. That gave the pros an hour of skiing and boarding before the paying public was allowed in. The morning was clear and cold, eighteen degrees, according to the lodge thermometer.

Wylie sat in the Mammoth men's ski team locker room, gearing up with the other skiers and boarders, some of whom he knew and some of whom he had never met. Ruled by the cold air of the locker room, their movements were efficient and their conversations brief. Most were younger, but some were his age and even older. As he bent down to clamp on his boots, Wylie could feel their eyes on him, sizing him up, gauging him against the young champion who had suddenly left here without warning. Boots on, he sat for a long moment in this room he knew so well, also gauging himself against the boy he had been those very long five years ago.

A boarder introduced himself as Daniel and said he was twelve and that he wanted Wylie's autograph.

"I was twelve when I joined this team," said Wylie.

"I don't have a paper, but can you can sign my cast?" Daniel gave Wylie a pen from his pack, then pulled up the left sleeve of his jacket. The battered and much-autographed plaster cast began just beyond his first row of knuckles and extended halfway to his elbow. Wylie scribbled his name amid the others and gave back the pen.

"How'd you manage this?" asked Wylie.

"X Course. Went off Goofball wrong and couldn't land. Hit a tree."

"That'll do it."

"Dislocated two fingers on my other hand but didn't say nothing. So I can keep skiing."

"Let's see." Wylie took the boy's hand and asked him to straighten the pinkie and ring fingers, then try to make a fist. The middle knuckles were swollen and scraped. Range of motion looked maybe half of what it should be. "At least tape them together. Keep them from getting worse."

"They don't bother me."

"You can be brave and smart at the same time."

"My uncle in Colorado Springs fought in the war, too. Aunt Maya says he stays in his room all day."

"Write him a letter or text or something."

"I do. Sorry what happened to Robert. He was a great guy."

"Yeah."

"You're going to race again?"

"With all my heart."

"You might want to lose twenty pounds first," said Sky Carson, throwing open his locker door with a bang. "Or you'll sink on those old skis." Uneasy laughter dwindled to a hush, and the racers' movements accelerated. One of the older skiers held open the door and half a dozen of the thirteen athletes tromped out with quick looks at Wylie or Sky, or both. "You'll sink like a pig in mud," Sky continued.

"Looks like you already have."

"I was at Helixon's 'til four."

The last athletes hustled out, and in the quiet the women's lockers banged dully through the wall.

"Beatrice was still there when I left. Looking mighty fine."

"She's seventeen."

"With her mother's genes."

"Shut up now, Sky."

"Okay. Silence while you walk on water."

Wylie carried his skis to the patio, where the men's freeski coach had gathered the team. Coach Brandon Shavers was in his late thirties and married to Andrea Carson, sister of Robert and Sky, a granddaughter of Adam. Coach Brandon studied Wylie from behind his sunglasses while condensation wavered up from his nostrils to the lenses. "Wylie Welborn. I heard you were back. But you can't just show up and get free practice time, man. You have to be on the team. You'll have to go back and buy a lift ticket. Just like the other tourists."

"I'd like to try out for the team."

"Everyone wants to try out for this team. So they get an appointment. That's basic respect for my time."

"You don't look overly busy right now."

"Seriously, Wylie, you want to use the mountain, you have to be on the team. There's an online application, and paper ones in my office. Take your pick. It's a hundred to apply, and five grand a year if we pick you. We're worth every penny. And who makes the team isn't up to just me anymore. There's a committee. It's a process. Not like before."

"Just let him ski today," said Daniel, the boy with the arm cast. "I want to see how he does it."

"Sorry," said Coach Brandon. "Okay, men — up we go. I want the u-twelves and u-sixteens up first, then the eighteens, then the old farts."

"Go Mammoth!" yelled Sky, brushing past Wylie and fitting his racing goggles up on his beanie.

Instead of skiing, Wylie once again helped his family through the 7:00 to 8:00 A.M. rush at Let It Bean. This was crunch time at the coffee pub, with scores of skiers and boarders impatient for their caffeine and pastries before the mountain opened at eight. His mother took the orders and Steen kept the pastries and breakfast burritos coming from the small kitchen; Beatrice and Belle jostled and made the coffee drinks while the steamers hissed and the shots of espresso gurgled into the paper cups, and the tourists watched with glazed anticipation. Beatrice looked pale and tired. Wylie wondered if it was the late night at Mountain High.

He went back to the kitchen and dropped the empty pastry racks into the big sink and drew the hot water. When his sisters left for school just after eight, he took over making the coffee drinks and tried to be chipper for the customers, but his heart wasn't in it. He felt that he had grown into a decent man, then returned to this place of his great launch, only to be enslaved again by the hospitality industry, needy tourists, and a pay grade just barely north of minimum wage.

He recognized some of the regulars, who'd been coming here for as long as the place had been open. It seemed less busy than in the older days. During a very quiet time, he sat with the regulars by the window, caught up a little. One of them handed him a sheaf of white paper stapled in the upper left corner.

The Woolly
A Journal of Mammoth Lakes
January 30

ROBERT CARSON IMPROVING
Story by Cynthia Carson

"Still bats but still at it," said a regular.

"You seen that hunter's camo she's wearing now?" asked another. "Can barely see her coming! Then all of the sudden, she's all over you, asking you questions."

The sitting area went quiet for a beat. "Awful about Robert, though. God, he was just . . . *here.* What a great guy. How's he doing, Wylie? Is Robert going to get better?"

"The doctors say no."

"You were a medic. What do you say?"

"Semimedic. But Robert is out of my league."

"I heard the break was at the vertebra where the hangman's knot goes."

Wylie winced inwardly, glancing at *The Woolly*. "I saw some guys make it I didn't think would. So, you know . . ." He suddenly wished he was far from here. He set the paper on one of the tables and went back behind the counter to clean out an espresso maker.

When the crowd failed to reconvene, he drove home and split the firewood by hand, something he was good at. The sledgehammer rang against the wedge, the logs cracked open and the air filled with the wonderful smell of fresh pine. Wylie imagined the ski-cross course on which Robert had met his end, and how he, Wylie, might handle the landing that had defeated Robert. Strange, thought Wylie, but Robert had made that landing what, over a thousand times? It was not a hard one. Not for Robert.

Hours later, he had stacked enough wood on the deck to last for two weeks, then covered it with a blue tarp. In the small family room, he turned on the old desktop and went online and found the Mammoth ski team's Web site and printed out the application. He filled it out and dug five twenties from his stash and clipped them to the sheet.

Ten minutes later, he set it on Brandon Shavers's desk. The coach at the men's freeski team regarded him with the same expression of wariness that most Carsons reserved for Welborns.

"Sky told me Robert is going to his mom's," said Brandon.

"We thought that would be best for him."

"I don't know why Adam puts so much faith in your judgment."

"You don't know a lot more than that."

"Adam is getting older."

"Just as sharp."

Brandon glanced down at the application, riffling the twenties with a thumb. "I can't fast-track this app. It's up to the Mammoth Racing Committee, not just me."

"That's Adam and you, like before, right?"

"Not anymore. We had to bring in Vault Sports and Chamonix. And Gargantua Coffee, big-time. Gargantua just stepped up as lead sponsor for all of the Mammoth ski and board teams, *and* the Mammoth Cup. So next year's race is now officially the Gargantua Mammoth Cup. You'll be seeing Gargantua's logo everywhere you look around town. Even in your dreams, my friend. And so will all your loyal customers at Let It Bean, which, of course, is the whole point. The Gargantua guy is Jacobie Bradford the Third, one of the coolest corporate weenies you'll ever meet."

Wylie recorded this bleak data with a sinking feeling in his gut. His mother hadn't been kidding about Let It Bean's getting run out of town. "So now three companies decide who skis for the Mammoth team and who doesn't?"

"Plus me and Grandpa. Money talks."

"Screams."

"Depends. If money ever comes your way, you'll think it has a strong, smooth voice." Brandon tapped the bills on the application and gave Wylie an amused look. "Sky says you've promised to win the *Gargantua* Mammoth Cup. To honor Robert."

"That's why I need to use the X Course."

"Wait just a minute. You win the cup five years ago, ditch us, then show up and expect to win it again? That's your plan?"

"It's become my plan. I have to get on the X Course, Brandon."

"I'll see what I can do." Brandon leaned back and crossed his arms and offered Wylie a tight smile.

Wylie managed to control his basic instincts, including the desire to strangle this man. "Fuck it."

"The usual Welborn answer."

Wylie snapped the money off the application and walked out.

Wylie looped back to Let It Bean to pick up his mother, as agreed. His nerves were still buzzing when he walked in.

"Okay?" she asked.

"Just thinking."

"You have that look."

"Even the marines couldn't beat it out of me."

They dressed out in the Let It Bean bathrooms and Kathleen collected her skis and gear from the kitchen. Steen smiled and waved as they headed out. At Main Lodge, Kathleen insisted on paying for the two half-day tickets that would get them the one remaining hour of skiing. The way we ski, thought Wylie, an hour will be enough.

They rode chair 25 to the black-diamond run at the top of Mammoth Mountain. With the cold wind in his face, Wylie studied the snow-covered Sierras cascading down toward the flat plate of silver that was Crowley Lake, and the White Mountains beyond, hunched in snow. From this perspective, there was no real vanishing point except the featureless pale sky behind the Whites. The immensity boggled him. Wylie felt his mother's gloved hand digging into his knee and saw that she was seeing what he was seeing.

They slid off the chair and gathered themselves at the top of the run. The earth knelt below them and the wind blew the snow against their backs. Wylie felt the sharp shards of it needling through his ski mask and he pictured Robert in his bed, life withdrawing from his body.

With a sharp cry, Kathleen dropped onto the Cornice. Wylie heard the rasp of her skis and saw the first burst of snow rise behind her. He counted five and launched. First came the sudden head-spinning pitch from horizontal to vertical, the brief second when the body senses free fall. The cure is commitment, so he leaned back nearly flush to the mountain, landed, and angled left, away from the trampled middle of the run. It was powder here and he found his rhythm, sweeping past his mom with a war whoop, but she quickly carved inside him and threw a rooster tail of sun-spangled crystals back his way. Wylie used the wider angles and kept Kathleen in front of him, and he was surprised at his age, his ponderous weight, his uncertain reflexes, and his general foreignness.

Down the mountain they braided. Wylie felt the altitude as a thin absence in his lungs, his pulse climbing, his respiration deeper and faster as he straightened out on a long, straight run and let the speed build. He heard the rush of his skis, felt the freedom, the magic of parting air. Coming out in a hard right carve, he drove his inside shoulder downhill and felt the crunch in his side. Kathleen was a blur at the far edge of his goggles. For a moment, he had everything right and felt like he used to, but then it was gone, and halfway through the mid-run moguls his thighs were burning and he sensed little joy between himself and the skis. The moguls almost did him in. Far down, the downhill run leveled into a wide expanse, at the end of which stood the lodge. Wylie saw the miniature figures streaming into the building, and more miniatures moving across the parking lot at this late hour, trudging for their cars, sun glinting off the skis and boards slung over their backs.

He stopped at the railing, breathing hard, and his mother swooshed to a stop beside him. "You might have to take things up a notch to win the cup."

"Roger that."

"You still ski beautifully."

"It's still inside me. Somewhere."

"How come you decided to enter the race?"

Wylie thought a moment. "To honor Robert and shut up Sky."

"Is it more to you than a simple grudge match?"

"I think so."

"You know the Carsons and us are fine. Finally. There's nothing that needs settling anymore. It's all over."

"It doesn't feel over to me. It's us and them, and most of them like it that way. It pisses me off."

"Oh, Wylie — I forgot most of that years ago. I had to. When you were gone, Sky seemed to get smaller and the others less obnoxious. But now, with the Mammoth Cup, there's a new . . . conflict."

"I'm going to win that race, Mom."

"It certainly has the town talking. I heard two customers making a bet on it this morning. Guys from San Francisco — bet each other five thousand bucks. One for you and the other for Sky."

"I'll bet on me."

"For myself, Wylie? I'd be happy for you to win. But I'm even happier that you're here. I know these last five years have been, well, challenging. I know you've seen good and bad, and I'd like to hear about some of that, when you're ready. But there's one thing I want you to know: If this little town gets to feel too little, or if for any reason you want to leave and go to a bigger world, I've got your back. I always saw you in the world, Wylie. Not necessarily in Mammoth Lakes, population eight thousand four hundred and thirty-four."

"I've got your back, too, Mom. And the girls'. I heard about Gargantua. All the stuff they're pulling on you."

"You are not responsible for us."

"I disagree with that."

"I want you to be free. To have something of your own."

"I'm getting something of my own, Mom. Jesse Little Chief and I are going to build a place for me to live. A kind of trailer I designed."

"Oh?"

"I drew up some plans last month at the monastery in Germany. A good idea — you'll like it. I got just enough money to get it started."

"Do what you need to do. Remember when we used to ski just to ski? Because it was fun?"

Wylie nodded. "Those were the days."

The PA system announced last lift. Wylie and his mother shoved off for the line, but it wasn't much of a line at all, just three adolescent diehards elbowing each other for position on the chair, and a young attendant with a sunburned face and her hair spilling from her cap, awaiting them with a smile.

CHAPTER SEVEN

The next day, after six hours at Let It Bean, then splitting another cord of wood, Wylie drove down the mountain toward Bishop. It was forty-five miles south, a metropolis even smaller than Mammoth Lakes. Once he got past Crowley Lake, the temperature rose ten degrees. His shoulder and back muscles hummed from the splitting and his hands still buzzed from the vibration of the sledge-hammer handle.

A slight smile crossed his face as he looked out at Round Valley, one of his several favorite places in the Sierras. The mountains above the valley loomed high in the west above Highway 395, eight thousand vertical feet of gray rock. The valley itself began to take shape at around six thousand feet, widening and pitching down to form a vast swale, dizzyingly steep. Looking out at it, Round Valley sucked away at his sense of balance the same way the mountains of

Afghanistan had. The valley lowered and spread toward the highway, laced by streams and dirt roads, dotted with cattle and willows and black cottonwoods, some of the land planted with hay or alfalfa.

Folded in his coat pocket were Wylie's sketches from the Tegernsee monastery and pretty much his entire savings from cheap living after the war — hopefully enough to get Jesse Little Chief going on the project. He'd done the sketches during the long, chill December nights at the eighth-century Benedictine site, which had been destroyed by the Magyars in the tenth century, then purchased nine centuries later by Maximilian I, who used it as a summer home. To Wylie, the monastery was surreal, scattered by time, ancient but modern, utopian and penal, seemingly part of another world.

In the Tegernsee dorms, the Europeans talked politics, the Irish argued, the Asians Skyped, the Americans listened to music and talked movies, and everyone drank the Tegernsee Spezial beer. It was here that Wylie had first sketched out his first rough design for the module, personal, portable, an idea he got in Kandahar. The MPP grew out of his thought that a self-contained, bulletproof, personal portable environment would naturally be great for war, but a peace-time version would be pretty darned good, too. Something like a tortoise's shell, but stronger. But he wanted it to be stylish, too. He went through many drafts to get a passable approximation, confident that if he ever made it home, Jesse Little Chief — a full-blooded Paiute, schoolmate, platoon buddy, and carpenter supreme — could pull off Wylie's elegant, almost nautical design.

The module was to be made mostly of wood, and it would be towed behind Wylie's truck. It would shelter two persons from extreme Sierra conditions, contain a small kitchen and bath, and have room for provisions, tools, ski equipment, and fishing gear. It would be roughly fourteen feet long and six feet four inches high. One axle, two tires. The general shape of the MPP was a gently rounded rectangle, like an unbaked loaf of bread.

"You should just call it a trailer, because that's what it is," said Jesse. He was a big man with shaggy black hair, a plate-round face, and still black eyes. He wore shorts past his knees, work boots, and a lined denim jacket against the January cold. They stood in his workshop, a metal building that shared the lot with Jesse's double-wide. Jesse lived north of Bishop, near the Paiute

Palace casino and gas station — reservation land rich in poor Indians. Beyond the roll-up door of the workshop, the sun was low and the mountains bathed in wholly orange light. "Straight right angles would save you money."

"But I want it to be . . ."

"Difficult?"

"Unusual."

"Gremlins and Pacers were unusual. Why not just buy a good camper?"

Wylie absorbed this truth but said nothing.

Jesse grunted. Then he spread out the drawings on a workbench and set cans of nails on the corners to keep them down. He ran a big finger along the curving slopes of the trailer. "Teak and maple weather good. I could weld a sloping frame, then notch and groove the planks for the curves you want. That marine hatch is sweet — views and ventilation."

"I'd hoped you'd like it."

"Oh, I like it. The whole design. But we could just do the smart thing, go with right angles and save you some bucks."

Wylie nodded, picturing the MPP as a simple rectangle. Nothing wrong with that, he thought, but . . . but he had been trying so hard to find his own true shape —

through racing, nature, reading, war, and travel. He wanted to fill his shape and fill it honestly. The idea of a *rectangular* trailer made him feel confined and ordinary. He wondered how he had become this fussy. Was he getting old? "For an Indian, you sure are sober-minded."

"Speaking of that, do you still enjoy a drink from time to time?"

"It's been a while."

"Let's have a drink and talk about this some more."

They drove to the liquor store for beer and bourbon, steaks and potatoes, ready-made salad, Funyuns, lotto tickets, and cigars. They bought enough food for Jesse's little sister, Jolene, and her friend. Jesse clapped the shoulder of the smaller man and they headed across the parking lot.

"Good to see you again, Wyles."

Jolene and her friend Tonya took over the second Wylie and Jesse walked into the house. Music was playing. The girls had dressed nicely, done their hair, and put on scent. Wylie felt as if he'd walked into a stage play. Jolene took the two bags that he held, pecked him on the cheek, and gave him an eyelash bat straight out of old Hollywood. "Jolene."

"You still remind me of a bear. Like your mom used to call you."

"It's good to be remembered."

"Look at me. I got beautiful."

"You did."

"I'm eighteen now, Wylie. Old enough to enter into a contract legally! You remember Tonya, but hopefully me more."

Tonya shook his hand matter-of-factly. Jesse looked at Wylie over the top of the open refrigerator, shaking his big head. Wylie grabbed two beers and Jesse found two shot glasses far back in one of the kitchen cabinets, slid the bourbon under one arm, and led the way back out to the shop.

At the workbench, Jesse placed Wylie's small drawings aside and positioned a large desk blotter of graph paper before them. He stripped off the corner-curled, doodle-choked top sheet and fished a thick carpenter's pencil from a coffee can filled with them. They touched beer bottles and drank.

Wylie loved the way the man drew so effortlessly and simply, as if his hand had eyes and a brain in it. Minutes later, Wylie beheld a rotated view of the MPP. The trailer was simpler and better than he himself had imagined — a graceful container with rounded transitions. It looked to be of one piece rather than pieces connected. Two portholes instead of one. And double doors for more and easier access.

"Beauty itself, Jesse."

"A bitch to build. What's your time line?"

"I want it badly. Spring? Early summer?"

Jesse studied him, nodding. "You specified an interior for two. Who's the lucky lady?"

"Can you build me one of those, too?"

"Just so you know, Jolene turns seventeen next month." Wylie nodded. "Tonya's even younger. I worry about them. You're only a kid once. . . . Look, I'll use scrap and salvage where I can, keep the cost down. Start with a junked trailer chassis, but a good one. I'll build this thing to last."

Wylie brought the wad of bills from the pocket of his coat. "Here's two grand down. I lived cheap and saved some."

They barbecued in the dirt yard between the double-wide and the haggard barbed-wire fence that marked the property line. The smoke rose into the cold night air and the Sierras hovered high and pale in the west. The stars were clear and close. Wylie refilled the shot glasses while Jesse prodded each steak with the tongs. "I should have stuck with you after the war," Jesse said.

"Should have traveled with you. I regret that now."

"You were right to come home when you did."

"Was I? I haven't accomplished one damned thing." Jesse looked at him, stepped back from the billowing smoke, and sipped from his glass. "Thanks for the news from your journeys."

"Least I could do."

Jesse added some mesquite chips to the fire and looked at Wylie through the shifting billows of smoke. "But I'm glad we ended up fighting together. After barely knowing each other at school, what were the chances of that? One of those coincidences that change your life. But the war wasn't what I thought it was going to be. Maybe I got what I deserved, after drinking all night before and signing my life away the next day."

"That's pretty much how I joined up, too. It's amazing just how dumb we were," said Wylie.

"Really, it is. But we did it. We made it out alive."

"When I hear about the war now, it doesn't sound like the war I was in."

"No," said Jesse. "Grunts shouldn't look back all the time like they do."

"No, they shouldn't. We did what we did. I don't think about it, but I'll never forget it, either."

Wylie and Jesse shifted positions again. The barbecue smoke seemed to follow them. "Have you ever told anybody?" Jesse asked in an offhand tone of voice.

Wylie was a fine compartmentalizer, adept at stuffing memories into imaginary boxes and setting them high on his mental shelves. There, they wouldn't fall down and hurt him, but he could find them if he needed them.

"Fuck no. I just say I was like a medic. That's good enough for most people."

"Sure. Yeah. That makes sense. And it's true: You were an unofficial medic. You did some real good when the corpsmen weren't around. Best tourniquet guy in the company." There was a long silence as Jesse prodded at the fire with the tongs. "I've told you a hundred times, but I want to thank you again for . . . sticking by me that day. It wasn't your idea, but you finished it for me. We could have got prison for that. It's a debt I'll always owe you."

"Look. That skinny killed Sergeant Madigan and was trying to kill us, Jess. And we did what we did and it's not changeable. Sometimes when you cross a line, the line goes faint, or even away. That can be a good thing, as in our case."

"Do you think we were right?"

"I don't think about it at all. Ever. Really. Except with you and some of the guys. I saw Lineberger and Carrasco in Germany. Lots of talk."

"Still, thanks."

"Jesus, Jesse — I've told you a hundred times not to thank me again, and here you go."

"I'm just a dumb stubborn Paiute."

"Me, too."

"That's what got us into all this!"

They laughed at this as they always did and drank a shot of bourbon; then Wylie refilled the shot glasses again. Jesse pulled the steaks away from the flame and got the platter ready.

"How many countries did you end up seeing?"

"Fourteen."

"Lots of ladies on your travels?"

"More or less."

"French the prettiest?"

"Tied for first with all the others."

"That's funny."

"True, even."

"And you always had mountains to ski?"

"Yeah. I never got that out of my system.

I still haven't."

Jesse turned the steaks and looked down at his watch. "Your sister told Jolene you're going to stay in Mammoth awhile. Going to win that Mammoth Cup thing again."

"I've committed to it."

"Why? You already won it once."

The breeze changed direction and Wylie stepped away from the roiling smoke. "To honor Robert and shut Sky up."

"And winning this race would do that?"

"I hope so."

"Robert's not going to get better?"

"He'll never wake up. He could live for years, though. It's just tubes, nutrition, and antibiotics."

"Shit, Wylie. I hardly knew him, but Robert was cool. He was a good guy. I saw that. Nothing like the rest of them."

"No one like him, Jesse." Wylie squinted and wiped his eyes with his jacket sleeve. Smoke and grief. It angered him that when he thought of Robert, he saw him paralyzed in a bed rather than flying down a mountain with sweet, beautiful speed. "Jess, there's another reason I want to win that race. I've been seeing a lot. And thinking a lot. I want something better for my family than them working their asses off year after year for less and less. It's worse now. Remember, back in the old days, when we were the only show in town? No more. Now Gargantua is in, and they're trying to run us out of business. It's working. They're price-cutting for market share, sponsoring the Mammoth ski team *and* the Mammoth Cup next year. All so Gargantua Coffee can rake in the tourists and run us out of town."

"Way of the white man."

"No shit. But here's the deal — if I can win the cup, then crank at the X Games, I'd have a shot to make the FIS World Cup circuit. And if I do well *there,* I just might make the Olympic team. And if I make the U.S. team and do well in Seoul? Well, then my family is set for life. That would be a dream come true. I've never actually had a specific, gonna-do-this kind of dream. Now I do. But *dream* sounds pompous and bourbony. I don't know. I'm thinking out loud."

Jesse nodded and stared down at the meat. "You a good-enough skier to do all that?"

"I don't know. That's a whole other question."

"That you can't answer until you try."

Wylie threw back the bourbon, set the shot glass on the barbecue deck and took up his beer. "Expensive to compete up at that level. Not sure exactly how to finance all that. But I'll tell you one thing, Jesse. I still love the speed. It's still in me. I'm happy flying downhill like there's a demon on my ass."

"That's what you looked like when you won the Mammoth Cup last time. I remember thinking, He's not chasing something. Something's chasing him."

They ate with the girls in the small dining room, with the TV propped up on the kitchen counter and a football game on. Jolene and Tonya tried hard to be adults — having set a nice table with somewhat matching flatware, quality paper napkins, and glasses of water with lemon twists floating on the ice. Jolene glanced at Wylie often and stopped talking a good full second before Wylie began a sentence.

Wylie felt the alcohol swirling through him. It loosened his memories and helped give voice to a story of what had happened while he was staying at the Great St. Bernard Hospice in Switzerland. Wylie confirmed that, yes, this was the place known for breeding the hearty rescue dogs. He gave in to the excitement of telling it, gesturing and raising his voice, which he rarely did. Waving his arms and using a thick German accent, he impersonated the panicked hospitality director, then dramatized their mad, half-blitzed scramble to get on their boots and skis and jackets to go attempt a rescue. He dramatized the rather dicey flashlight-illuminated extraction of three Swedish cross-country skiers who had fallen into a crevasse not five hundred yards from the hospice brewery. They had been on an after-dinner jaunt. Wylie revealed that the big rescue dogs did not carry casks of brandy on their collars, and that they had romped through the snow, barking uselessly while the men and women pulled the skiers up using ropes and a lot of muscle. Wylie capped off his tale by quoting each Swede after being snatched away from certain death:

" '*Tack!*'

" '*Tack!*'

" '*Tack!*' "

Much later, Wylie closed the door of the spare bedroom, stripped to his underwear, and climbed into the cold bed. Glancing through the parted curtain, he could see the western sky, black and dotted with stars that fell, then rose in unison, again and again, his vertical hold fully shot.

The door opened and Jolene, backlit by the hall light, stood in the doorway. She was motionless for a moment, then leaned against the door frame, pulled her blouse over her head, shook back her heavy black hair, and looked at Wylie. Her eyes were more stars, falling and rising. "You were showing off for me," she said. "My turn now."

Wylie saw the shiny plank of her hair and the curves and points of her breasts washed in the weak light from above. "You're beautiful, but I can't."

"Can't let me get in beside you on a winter night?"

"Can't be responsible for you."

"Then be irresponsible for me."

"Twenty-five and sixteen don't add up right."

"Yeah, with all those blondes falling over you up on the mountain."

"Nothing to do with blondes."

"Or maybe you'd rather go up to Reno for the professionals. With Jesse."

"You're beautiful, Jo. It's not that."

"Can I sleep on the floor?"

"Jo."

"I am not a child."

Wylie saw pinpoints of light in her eyes. She tossed back her hair again and it settled forward. "I do admit I was showing off for you," he said. "I wanted to feel like a big, important man. But I'd already made up my mind not to do this."

"Why not?"

"Then I would have to deny and ignore you, Jolene. I don't want to do that."

"When would you deny and ignore me?"

"Sooner than later."

"Why?"

"To keep us free. Which is how we belong."

"You're denying and ignoring me right now, Wylie."

"Maybe you'll thank me someday."

"Big doubts on that one."

"I'll see you in the morning."

Jolene stood still for a long beat, then waved her blouse at him. She yanked the door shut with a slam that shook the thin modular walls.

Just before dawn, Wylie stepped over her as she lay curled in a sleeping bag outside his door. She giggled. At the end of the hallway, he stopped and looked back at her.

"Have a good day, Wylie."

"You, too, Jo."

"Hi to Beatrice and Belle."

"I'll tell them."

"You'll get what you deserve, Wylie. Because you're good. I heard you and Jesse out at the barbecue. You'll win that race. And so far as the war goes, Jess told me what happened. I know it was his idea and he started it and lost his courage. So you finished it. For him. And it was a mess and it disgusted both of you. But I'd have done it, too, if the son of a bitch had killed one of my guys. I don't think what you two did was too wrong. You just got carried away. It happens."

Chapter Eight

Wylie Welborn is back. I saw him yesterday when I walked past Let It Bean. I was wearing my winter "snow bark" hunter's camo, so he probably didn't even notice me with all the snow on the ground. There he was, as if five years hadn't gone by, behind that counter like he always was, waiting on customers. He fought in Afghanistan, they say. He ski-bummed around the world after that, they say. They also say he's making a run for the Mammoth Cup next winter. They say it's a personal challenge to Sky, thrown down by Wylie in Robert's hospital room in San Francisco. Sky has posts about Wylie all over his social networks. Insults mostly. Wylie Welborn is back and their bad blood has stirred.

But I've learned to regard all information with skepticism, especially whatever comes out of the Welborn clan. I've never spoken to Wylie and have no plans to. I stare hard at him whenever we're in close proximity. Everybody runs into everybody else in a small town like Mammoth Lakes, whether they want to or not. But he's never had the courage to look back. Not once. I'd be afraid of me, too. But from a distance I do like to observe him, the way an epidemiologist might enjoy observing a virus, or a herpetologist a large python.

His mother, Kathleen, on the other hand, I've looked at directly many times. She'll look right back at you, that one. She did a lot of that from the witness stand, all sworn in and somber and ready to give the world her version of what happened to poor Richard Carson. At the time of his shooting, Kathleen was eighteen — another wannabe racer from San Diego, fast down the mountain and fast on her way to being a party girl, too. Those types all got drawn here to Mammoth back then. Or to Squaw or Aspen or Park City or Sun Valley or Jackson. Still do. By the time the trial got going, she was nineteen and her baby had been born. What a difference that year made in her. From snow whore to Madonna with child, in a heartbeat. I will admit that she was an attractive girl back then, and spirited, but without sound judgment. Easy to see what Richard saw in her. But Richard was without sound judgment, too. Thus, all that followed and is still following and will likely follow for many years to come.

I remember Kathleen sitting there in Mono County Superior Courtroom 1, Bridgeport, California, the cliché of a rosy glow on her, holding that bastard son of hers, rocking him like the gold medal–winning mother she thought she was, tears handy, looking down at me as if I'd robbed her of something that was hers, which I had not. Richard was never not mine. I felt contempt for her. After all, I had problems of my own. Such as the fact I'd lost the love of my life. Don't forget that, lady. In spite of his nonterrific judgment, Richard was more than a onetime inseminator to me. I adored him. There was even a tiny bit of worship in it. I had borne his children. Bore the last one — Sky, with whom I was pregnant on the night of the shooting — in a county jail hospital, where they flubbed the epidural. And let's not forget that I was the one she was helping send to prison. I was the one who wouldn't get to hug my own babies for thirteen years, unless you count hellos and good-byes on weekends and holidays at the Central California Women's Facility down in Chowchilla. You can bet I counted them. They were all I had.

Sounds preposterous, but what I missed most during those years was pushing my children around in strollers. So frustrating to have two children of stroller age and not be able to go outdoors and push them. When I first knew I was going to be a mother, I saw myself rolling the little one around Mammoth Lakes in a snuggly protective shelter, getting him/her outside into the beauty of the world instead of being trapped inside all day, looking up at what — mobiles or the ceiling or at me bending down to make funny noises at him/her? I knew it would bring both me and the baby great pleasure. I got to show Andrea the great outdoors. Then in an eye blink, Robert was three and Sky was an infant, but there were no strollers or sons or daughters in my loud, clanking, institutional world. You cannot imagine how long one day can be in prison. By the time I got out, my children were too big for strollers.

Adam brought Robbie here yesterday, as he said he would. Robbie looks better than he did over in San Francisco. More relaxed. What I see when I look at Robbie is the best of my children, broken by the life he chose to live. Literally, broken. Adam and Brandon and Mike Cook and Hailee Patterson got the hospital bed in here, and the paramedics did all the hookups, and the nurse gave us each printouts of how to care for Robbie, all the dos and don'ts. Like a new exotic pet. A creature from Borneo. It's going to be a full-time job. That's good. Idle hands and all that. I gave

them all the latest issue of *The Woolly.*

I couldn't wait for them all to leave so I could sit here by his bed and look at Robbie and remember. He was three when they threw me in the hole. I lost thirteen years with my children and I know there is no way to get those years back. What a terrible thought, me outliving Robbie. Maybe he will just . . . continue to live. Quite a few brain-damaged people do just that. My first goal toward his complete rehabilitation is to get him to move one of his eyelids in response to simple questions. One movement for yes, two movements for no. That is where we will begin.

I am more than pleased to have him here right now. He's not going anywhere and neither am I. Neither are Andrea or Sky. Finally.

Chapter Nine

Adam sat before the enormous fireplace in his great room, looking southeast down Mammoth Mountain. Looking through the wall of glass, he saw snow dropping off the branches in slow diagonals. Past the trees lay the steep flank of mountain and below the mountain sat the town. Smoke rose from chimneys almost too small to see. Gondolas and lifts climbed and descended. Toy skiers and boarders zigzagged down. Adam's house was perched on recessed caissons sunk into the steep rock, which allowed it to hover out from the mountain like a satellite in space. Some people coming into his home for the first time felt unanchored and afloat. He had actually had guests collapse to their knees with confusion and vertigo upon walking in. The two-track dirt road leading up to it was impassable for six months of the year — sometimes longer — leaving two gleaming silver funicular cars

for transportation.

Adam considered the newly expanded Mammoth Racing Committee, seated around the sprawling redwood burl coffee table: Jacobie Bradford III, the regional manager of Gargantua Coffee; Diane Dimeo of Vault Sports; Claude Favier of Chamonix Racing; and Adam's own grandson-in-law, Brandon Shavers, married to Cynthia's daughter, Andrea. Brandon coached the Mammoth freeski team.

He stood and began passing out copies of the revised *Racing Committee Bylaws.* Adam saw that Brandon handled the books with pride. Brandon had made no secret of how much work it had been to make so many last-second changes this quickly, even with the help of a very expensive attorney in Palo Alto. In Adam's opinion, the text was needlessly long and detailed, and the print almost impossibly small to read even though, for eighty-seven, his eyes weren't bad. These leather-bound editions had come in just yesterday, each cover embossed with the committee member's cursive signature in gold.

Adam accepted his edition of the racing bylaws, watching the lovely Teresa returning from the bar with another tray of beverages for his guests. She delivered a third Irish coffee for Brandon, which he took with a dopey grin. Adam could tell he was already jacked on caffeine and half-looped by the whiskey. Adam wondered for the thousandth time how his granddaughter could stand the man. He traded glances with Mike Cook, his closest friend and longtime Mammoth Mountain course setter, though not a Racing Committee member.

"Nice," said Jacobie Bradford, setting his bylaws on the immense planed and shellacked table. "But back to business, Mr. Carson — we really don't think that Gargantua banners at the start and finish lines for the Gargantua Mammoth Cup courses, and a smattering of verticals around town, would be unsightly at all."

"You said forty-six vertical banners, which is every streetlamp in town," said Adam. "And I didn't say 'unsightly'; I said 'piggish.' "

Jacobie chuckled. "Right. But Mammoth Lakes is spread out over —"

"I know how big my town is."

"Exactly. So with only forty-six eight-by-three verticals to hang, it's not like people will feel overwhelmed by them. The banners have full color *Mammoth-specific* nature scenes — skiing and boarding, cycling and hiking, all that. Not one pig! Each will have our Gargantua logo — of course — tastefully positioned."

"An ape's face," Diane Dimeo noted.

"But you should see what the design team has come up with." Jacobie said. He was thirtysomething, his head shinily shaven, and he sported a trim Vandyke.

Adam wondered what this generation of men had done with their hair. Traded it for smart phones? He raised his binoculars and watched a snowboarder wipe out way down on Ricochet. One second the boarder was carving downhill and the next he was a tumbleweed of snow.

"Grandpa? Sir?" asked Brandon. "I have to say I think we're getting a lot of buck from Gargantua. And I want them to get plenty of bang back."

Adam lowered the field glasses and considered several responses, but the moment passed.

"I think Mr. Carson is right to be skeptical," said Diane. Adam looked at her. She was slight, dressed all in black, with thin sheets of shiny white hair and dark brown eyes. He considered himself a good guesser of age, but couldn't get better than thirty to forty-five on Diane.

"Because Vault Sports wants to hang verticals banners, too?" asked Jacobie.

"Yes, we do. And because Vault doesn't want Mammoth Lakes to look like just another one of your many identical, metastatic coffee shops."

"Metastatic? As in cancerous? *Really,* Diane? I'm sorry we succeed so well. And employ twenty-six thousand people nationwide. Offer decent pay, good benefits, and donate millions of dollars a year to charity. God, am I so very sorry."

Diane set her soft drink on an end table and gave Adam a frank stare. "I still think forty-six vertical banners that advertise one company is overkill. We're sponsors here, not invaders. Mr. Carson, I ask you to allot the forty-six lamppost displays more equally among the three of us."

"But our patronage isn't equal," said Jacobie. "And it's not up to Mr. Carson anyway. It's up to his friends on the town council."

"They do whatever he tells them to," said Brandon.

Adam held his grandson-in-law with a look that silenced the room. Brandon smiled in discomfort. "Claude?"

"Of course it is the decision of the city," said the Frenchman. "We at Chamonix believe in winter sports. They are our life. Chamonix also believes in Mammoth Mountain. We will continue to sponsor young athletes here. We will continue to offer our best products at competitive prices in select Mammoth stores. We always advertise on the Mammoth TV channel. Chamonix is not made of money, but of passion."

"I suggest twenty-six banners for Gargantua and ten each for Vault and Chamonix," said Adam.

"That's completely disproportionate, sir," said Jacobie. He threw open his arms, raised his shoulders, and scrunched his head down.

"Share the mountain," said Diane. "Don't buy it."

"Gargantua has more than enough streetlamp banners, Jacobie," said Adam. "And you also have the start and finish signage for the half-pipe, the slopestyle, and X Course."

Jacobie sighed and shook his head. "What did I do?"

Adam lifted his binoculars and watched a very aggressive skier fly down Dragon's Back. Adam liked the straightforward power of the woman, the assured turns, the absence of hotdogging. Honest speed. "Brandon? What's this about Wylie Welborn wanting to join our Mammoth freeski team?"

"He's got it in his thick head to win the

Mammoth Cup. Him and Sky are hating on each other again. It's become some kind of loyalty thing to Robert. Like whoever wins the cup loves Robert more. But Wylie withdrew his app — snatched the money right off my desk."

"Wylie Welborn?" asked Claude Favier. "He won the Mammoth Cup ski cross very impressively five years ago. On Chamonix Saber Three skis!"

"He's older and fatter now," said Brandon. "I don't need him on the team. He probably couldn't afford it anyway."

Adam caught Diane and Jacobie trying to read his mind — not easy, he knew, given Wylie's divisive relationship with the Carson family proper. Adam understood that Jacobie wouldn't want Wylie on the team, given Gargantua's not-so-secret desire to claim pretty much all of Let It Bean's market share. Brandon was against Wylie because Brandon had never liked the Welborns and they had never liked him, and that was that. "Put him on the team, Brandon. I'll cover his fees."

"Why, Grandpa?"

"Because he's one of the best ski crossers I've ever seen." Adam raised his binoculars again. He hated committees, bureaucracies, democracies. Squabbles, strife, opinions.

Peering through the glasses, he watched some speed demon slicing down the black-diamond Head Chutes run. The equipment is so much better now than back in the old days, he thought. He remembered those heavy wooden skis, the bindings with minds of their own, the monstrous boots. Not a helmet in sight. Suddenly, Adam was sixty years back, helping his friend Dave McCoy build that first Mammoth Mountain rope tow — using a car engine and old tires! It was summer on the mountain and unusually hot, and they worked in jeans and boots. Dave's wife, Roma, was there, and Adam's beloved Sandrine, both so beautifully young and tan-armed in sleeveless blouses and shorts, and many others sweating and grunting and trying to get that damned V-8 rope tow to work without dragging them up the mountain at thirty miles an hour.

Adam could see Sandrine turn and smile at him. What a lucky man I was.

Now he watched the skier tearing down the mountain in a flurry of powder. And listened to the Racing Committee blather on.

Jacobie was agreeing with Brandon that Wylie should not be a part of the freeski team. Who could know better what the team needed than its coach?

"And if Wylie is on the team, think of those last few loyal customers who might stay with Let It Bean," said Diane.

"Jesus, Diane."

"But I agree with you. It's Brandon's team and Brandon's call."

"I believe we all would be fortunate to have Wylie Welborn on this team," said Claude Favier. "It would be good for Mammoth Lakes and the sport of ski cross."

"And you hope he rides Chamonix skis again," said Diane.

"Yes, I passionately hope for this," said Claude.

"But I win," said Brandon. "Three votes against Wylie. Only two votes in favor."

Then came a silence, during which Adam gazed down at the town of Mammoth Lakes.

"Wait," said Diane. "There are lots of moving parts here. So, yes, Adam, I'd be willing to give Wylie a chance on the team, if you would suggest to the town council a more equitable allotment of the streetlight banners. Say, fifteen each for Chamonix and Vault, and sixteen for Gargantua. As a nod to their much deeper pockets."

"That's a travesty," said Jacobie.

"Deal," said Adam.

"Sir," said Jacobie.

"The fuck, Grandpa?"

"Ah, excellent," said Claude.

Adam stood and made an underhand shooing motion toward the door. "Out out, damned spots. Mike, I need to talk to you a minute. You people hold the funicular for him."

The Racing Committee filed out, mostly arguing, Claude laughing, Brandon casting a hangdog look back at Adam before slamming the door. Teresa began the cleanup. Adam heard the funicular engine start outside. "Mike, has Brandon talked to you about the X Course for the next cup?"

"Yes. He wants two more gates, tighter banks, and flatter straights. For safety, after Robert."

And to favor his lighter-bodied skiers, thought Adam. Such as Sky. "And what did you tell him?"

"I told him to do his job and let me do mine. I always set the best and fairest course I can, Adam. And the safest."

"I know you do."

"And I want you to know that the padding on the X Course was very heavy, high quality, and correctly installed."

"I have no doubt."

"I'm crushed about Robert. I love him."

"I know you do."

Mike stood there for a moment.

"It's good to have a friend who tells the truth," Adam said. "Please let Wylie know he's on the team. Not to sweat the money."

"I hope those corporate pricks don't run his family out of business."

Adam considered this notion. He understood the value of prosperity for Mammoth Lakes, and he understood the value of family. This was about both.

"And did you hear? April Holly is moving to Mammoth to live and train, away from the spotlights in Aspen."

Adam had not heard. He'd never met April Holly, but he'd seen her image on supermarket magazines and on TV thousands of times. She had four World Cup Crystal Globes and a gold medal from Sochi. A snowboard wizard with a pretty smile and bouncy hair. America's snow princess. "Another Olympic medalist for our mountain. I'm pleased."

"I hear she travels with quite a crew. Private jets, custom Escalades with her picture on the sides. Bodyguards, coaches, and supermom. They say she creates a spectacle wherever she goes."

So much about snow sports has changed, thought Adam, suddenly back in his station wagon with Sandrine and Don Oakley and his girl, all packed in and barreling down the highway with eight pairs of skis on top, ski gear and cheap food loaded to the roof, music on the radio if they could get it, following the FIS circuit from Mammoth to Squaw to Aspen to Jackson to Stowe and then on through Europe. He'd never forget those days. Always trying to take down the Europeans, put America on the map for the downhill, slalom, giant slalom, and the combined. They hadn't quite accomplished that. But they'd gotten the attention of the USOC, and paved the way for Billy Kidd and Jimmie Heuga in '64.

A flurry of snow blew into the foyer just before Mike closed the door. Glancing out the window, Adam saw Mike's footprints multiplying in the snow, then Mike climbing into the silver funicular car. The thick steel cable lowered and the car started down.

Teresa took his arm and laid her head against his shoulder. "They want only what they want."

"Teresa, let's build a fire in the bedroom and lie down by it."

"It's built and I'm ready."

"You are a joy to these old bones."

"You are a joy to mine."

"Sandrine always said it wasn't how much

you love, but how much you are loved."
"That is what we do for each other."

Chapter Ten

Wylie dressed out with the Mammoth freeski team at the Main Lodge HQ, then caught the shuttle back to chair 24, which took him up the mountain to the X Course. Daniel, whose plaster arm cast Wylie had signed days before, sat beside him, steam wavering from the hole in his ski mask and forming clouds on his goggles.

"It's cool you get to try out," said Daniel.

"I haven't run the X Course in five years."

"But you skied all over the world after the war."

"Pretty much so."

"I saw you win the cup. My dad still talks about it. He's a cop. He thinks it's awesome I got to meet and ride up with you the other day."

The morning was cold and bright and the pure white Sierra peaks towered around them, dotted with rocks and trees. An hour ago, Wylie had left work at Let It Bean feeling guilty, but now even his family seemed a distant responsibility and his spirit felt lighter as the chair drew him up the mountain. At the dismount, the chair leveled off and Wylie and Daniel glided onto the snow side by side.

"Go forth and shredify," said Wylie.

"You, too."

Positioning himself in the X Course starting gate, Wylie's usual prerun yawns vanished, replaced by an odd adrenaline-fueled calm that he got only when racing, and, later, while on patrols in Kandahar. Now he heard the breeze in the trees and the distant creak of the chairlift and he was aware of the other skiers watching in silence. The thought crossed his mind how very small this X Course was within the context of Mammoth Mountain. Really, the X Course was just a little slash on a big map. So was the mountain itself. They had once seemed big to him. Five years, he thought. So we meet again.

He inhaled, ooo-rahed as of old, then launched off the half-pipe start and into the air. He landed balanced and shot the bowl, tucked for speed, and claimed his line against imagined enemies. He felt his heavier weight and took the first bank with some reserve, carving it mid-level, neither high nor low, weight mostly on the outside ski, poles touching down lightly, legs synchronous yet independent. The steep schuss into the first jump, Launch Pad, happened faster than his brain could fully comprehend. He launched into the jump and pressed it hard — weight forward and ski tips jammed down to keep the air from getting under and flipping him. He landed well, tucking into the long straightaway, then off the ramp at Goofball, landing well again, then carving hard through panel two into Dire Straights. He tried for the old velocity, but he couldn't quite find it, or be found. He tucked, jonesing for blankness of mind and shedding of thought, but all he felt was old, fat, and overpresent. He could hear the heave of his breath — a long time since he'd felt winded on the X Course.

He handled Conundrum well, pressing the jump hard again, soaring high and landing smoothly, hounded by the shadows of the ski lift stanchions and unstoppable images of Robert. Then through Shooters, a series of narrow rock and tree-lined chutes that opened to a long final straightaway and the finish. He tucked through the sprint, legs quivering as he braked and curved to a stop on the out-run. He glided to the orange mesh fence and draped himself over it, panting.

"One minute ten seconds," said Brandon Shavers, looking at his wristwatch, the walkie-talkie still held to his ear.

"Not bad," said Wylie.

"My guys *average* six seconds less. That's six long seconds, Welborn."

"I can be six seconds better in a month."

"I'm going to send you down against Sky."

"Anytime."

"How about right now? Get back up to the start. Maybe you'll wake up a little with some competition."

Sky Carson was already at the X Course start area, limbering up away from the rest of the team, which had gathered to watch. As Wylie slid to a stop two lanes across from him, Sky stopped mid-stretch. "I'll bet you a thousand dollars I win," he said, then cranked over at the waist and looked through his legs back at Wylie. "Payable tonight at Mountain High."

"I don't have a thousand dollars."

"And apparently no confidence, either." Sky smiled, completed his stretch, then turned to his teammates. "Friends, simpletons, countrymen — who is going to win this here shoot-out?"

"Kick his ass, Wylie!"

"Kick his ass, Sky!"

The team jostled along the orange security mesh, hooting and pushing one another for the best spectator positions, well back of Wylie and Sky.

On the count, Wylie launched with a grunt and found himself trailing Sky Carson's piercing war whoop before they had even come to the first bank. His legs still felt heavy from his first run and now he had Sky's snow and ice to eat. His jump at Launch Pad was weak and he tried to carve the first gate high, but the slush slurped his speed, and coming into the first good straightaway, Sky Carson had ten feet on him.

With only two skiers on the course, Wylie used the open snow to get uphill of Sky and away from his glittering exhaust. Harder work, but it paid off. He made up distance on the straight and more on the second jump, Goofball, coming high and tight into the next bank. Suddenly, Sky skittered and checked, and Wylie came nearly shoulder-to-shoulder with him. Wylie dogged him through the next gate, tight through the panels, and onto Dire Straights, where he locked in close like truckers do, drafting the soft air behind Sky, hounding him, close enough to hear the rasp of Sky's skis as well as his own. Sky trailed a pole in warning.

Dire Straights was Wylie's wheelhouse. Sky knew it, defending expertly, stuck close to his fall line, using his light quickness to deny Wylie the pass, keeping his pole points high and threatening. He took the next bank low and fast. Wylie cut above him, a shorter line through the apex but harder to make. Held it. Coming out, Sky again dodged into his path, backslapping his pole against Wylie's helmet. Wylie's ears rang and he crouched deeper and came even. There were no more than six feet between them. Ahead lay Traffic Jam, a tight series of turns whose entrance offered hardly enough room for two friendly adjacent skiers. But the leader coming out of it would carry real advantage into Conundrum — the last jump before Shooters, then the final long schuss to the finish line. A high outcropping of jack pine and reddish boulders marked the beginning of Traffic Jam, where the side-by-side racers could collide if neither man gave.

Instead, they sped like demons. Sky swept higher with his pole and Wylie heard the crack of it on his helmet again. They blasted into Traffic Jam dead even. This race was Wylie's to win now; he knew it was all right here, the moment he could take the lead. He dug deeply once, hunched his shoulders, and brushed past Sky into the valley and the lead.

Cut off from his line at fifty miles an hour, Sky crossed uphill behind Wylie, over the backs of his skis, hoping to overtake or trip him. Wylie hogged his line, blocking, his legs burning and losing strength. Behind him, Sky's skis clattered noisily over his own, and the strange drag made it feel as if he was braking. Then the clacking ruckus behind him gave way to a short, sharp yelp. Coming out of the turn, he checked and glanced back at Sky, who was badly off-course and careening through trees and boulders, still upright, slaloming precariously between the big rocks as if on fast-forward. Near the beginning of the Conundrum ramp, Wylie swept to a stop and looked down. Sky lay planted in the snow between two large rocks, arms and legs akimbo, not moving.

Already some of the freeskiers behind them were hooting and yelling and picking their way down into the gorge where Sky lay. Wylie saw Brandon sidestepping his way up from the finish area. Wylie took a deep breath and slid off the course and down into the ravine.

By the time Wylie got to him, Sky was up and leaning against a boulder, rubbing his left shoulder, watching his teammates working their ways toward him. Wylie saw them hustling down through the trees and snow. One of them had Sky's skis, another his helmet.

"You all right?"

Wylie studied him; Sky studied him back. His cheeks and forehead were scraped and his blond hair was matted with blood and pink runoff. "You shouldn't have knocked me off the course," Sky said calmly.

"I didn't. You lost your nerve."

"That's not what happened."

Wylie looked up the ravine at his teammates picking their way toward them, their voices caroming down the rocks. He pulled his goggles down to his throat. He was still breathing hard and he could feel dull pain where Sky had poked him with the pole.

"Wylie, you disrespect me. That makes me angry. It's a difficult emotion to deny. Ask my mother."

"This can't be about her."

"Everything is about her. Her blood is in me, is it not?"

Wylie considered his half brother. Sky had one face he gave to the world — cool guy, wiseass, extreme athlete, and champion. And another that Wylie had only seen when they were in private or nearly so, a darker thing, but with something vulnerable and hapless in it, too. Sky wore it now.

"What Kathleen did to my mother and what you just did to me are enormously disrespectful. This is a Welborn characteristic — disrespect."

"That's just nonsense, Sky."

"Then make our bad history good. Say you respect me."

Wylie did not. He heard voices closer now, heard the crunch of coach Brandon's skis climbing up the grade from the finish.

"Then at least apologize for running me off the course."

"I barely brushed you. Sky, did you hit your head after the helmet came off?"

"No — I did not hit my fucking head after my helmet came off. You should not have run me off the course."

"You should not have stabbed me or whacked my head."

"What do you propose to do about it?"

Wylie considered. "Forgive, I guess."

"But you ran me off the mountain and I don't forgive you." Sky's blue eyes were decisive and nonnegotiable.

The skiers converged variously and Coach Brandon huffed up the last few yards, breathing hard. "Carson? You okay?"

"Great, actually!" Sky held up his goggles, one lens thoroughly smashed in the wipeout.

"Though I'd like to state for the record that one Wylie Welborn cracked my goggles with his pole, like viciously. I assume there are witnesses."

"I saw him do it," said Platt. "Right before gate three."

"No!" said Daniel. "Sky poled Wylie. I saw him."

"Wylie knocked him off the course!" said Kosnovska. "I watched it happen!"

"Sky stabbed him, just like Danny says!" countered a junior whose name slipped Wylie's now-agitated mind.

"Maybe I'll kick both of you half-assed brothers off my team," said Brandon. "You're supposed to be leaders. Look at you."

"Chip," said Sky. "Chip, chip." He pulled the ruined goggles over his head and let them dangle at his throat. He pushed off the boulder and stood uncertainly, shaking his left hand as if his fingers had cramped. He stared at Wylie for a short moment, and Wylie saw the contempt melt into a smile as Sky turned to his teammates. "Any of you hair balls going to Mountain High tonight?" he asked. "Drinks on me!"

CHAPTER ELEVEN

Just before midnight, Wylie lay reclined in his boyhood bed, with blankets and a sleeping bag heaped over him to fight the cold, his head against the wall, reading Rexroth.

> The sun drops daily down the sky,
> The long cold crawls near,
> The aspen spills its gold in the air,
> Lavish beyond the mind.

He wondered why his own attempts at poetry were so consistently bad. His notebook lay on the nightstand beside him, unopened, a pencil still marking where he'd stopped. Did you have to be born with poetry in you? Which made him think of Sky and what he'd said about the blood of his mother being inside him, carrying a malice that today showed in Sky Carson's pale blue eyes. Sky had gotten to him. Wylie had never seen Sky so completely . . .

decisive. Wylie had never looked directly into Cynthia Carson's eyes, but he had seen her from a near distance, and studied her through binoculars once — scary — and found pictures of her on the Internet, and, yes, she had that same conviction in her eyes, the same certainty. *Everything is about her.*

His phone buzzed and he opened Beatrice's text: "Mountain Hi crazy. Can u come get me?"

The attached video had been shot from the first-floor great room of Mountain High. It was noisy and Bea's phone camera was aimed unsteadily upward at the second floor, where Sky Carson stood at the railing, wearing only boxers and the shattered ski goggles around his neck. He held a black book in one hand and a phone in the other, which he was using to shoot selfies of his injuries.

When Bea zoomed in, Wylie saw that the scrapes on Sky's face were a rawer pink now and his right shoulder wore a blue bruise. His left knee had swollen and the first two fingers of his left hand, which held the book, were splinted and taped together — white tape against a black leather Bible.

There were dozens of people in the big living room, all looking up at Sky, most holding phones. Wylie recognized Helixon and Hailee, a bunch of the Mammoth team skiers and boarders, old friends, local souls.

"Ladies and gentlemen, boys and girls," Sky called out. "Twenty-five years ago, something terrible happened here in Mammoth Lakes. A demon bastard was conceived and later born. He has haunted this town for one quarter of a century. We all know him. We have tried to forgive him. We have tried to forget him. But today the demon attacked me on the mountain during practice on the X Course. Behold." Sky scanned his phone over his bruised shoulder, then his fattened knee, then aimed it again at his scraped-up face and shattered goggles. The crowd murmured, then stilled. "I was attacked from behind and forced off the course and into the rocks at high velocity. I'm lucky to be standing here before you. And very happy to be. But this attack left me thinking about my responsibility to the mountain and to you people and to myself. How much more of this are we to take? What kind of man am I? When should wrong be battled instead of tolerated? After what happened today, I stayed up there on the mountain, asking Mother Nature, What should I do? I received an answer, and it was loud and clear. Mother Nature has asked me to accept an apology from Wylie Welborn for what he did today. To turn my other, nonbruised and nonabraded cheek. But she also tasked me to tell Wylie that if he ever tries to force me — or anyone else — off her mountain ever again, the consequences will be severe. Mother Nature was not specific, but she said *the consequences will be severe.* This, then, is my line in the snow. Apologize, Wylie Welborn, for what you have done. And for your own safety and well-being, promise never to do it again."

The crowd murmured again and someone offscreen slurred, *"Yeah, man, Sky, break the demon bastard curse. . . ."*

Wylie watched as Sky held the Bible to his heart. Sky held the phone out for a macro shot and the crowd went wild.

Wylie threw on a coat and started down the hallway. He knew his light-sleeping mother would ask him where he was going this late, and, in fact, from the darkness of her bedroom, she did.

"Out, Mom."

"Everything okay?"

"Everything is fine." Except not, Wylie thought. Except Bea's not asleep like she's supposed to be; she's up at Mountain High, watching Sky Carson make crazy threats.

He got to his truck. Letting himself in, he

thought he saw movement at the base of the little hill behind the house, in the trees and patchy snow, about where the toolshed into which he had crashed once stood. He paused. A deer, maybe. Too cold for bears. He saw nothing. If it was anything, it didn't move again. He slammed the truck door and drove to Mountain High.

Huge Croft, the Mountain High bouncer, opened the door. The music was loud and there were bodies in various motion behind him. "Wylie. Maybe you shouldn't come in."

"I'm here to pick up Beatrice."

"Sky's been extra weird tonight, so maybe just ignore him."

Wylie nodded and pushed past Croft and into the living room. The number of party people here this late surprised him. Many of them stood mute, staring at him as he scanned the room for his sister. He felt slandered and foolish and mad. He marched into the big kitchen, where the revelers fell silent and avoided eye contact with him. The counters were cluttered with liquor and wine bottles, both empty and full; platters of artful sushi and sashimi; dirty dishes. A guy burped and a girl laughed with exaggerated volume.

He checked the dark theater, where viewers sat beneath a dizzying big-screen Shaun White, tearing up his first Olympic Games. Wylie flipped on the lights and got cussed, turned off the lights and checked the library across the hall, where he interrupted a spirited argument about ski waxes while a pretty girl stood facing a wall of books, laughing.

"She's upstairs," said Croft from the doorway. "Not the third floor — don't worry. Just the second. Third's, like, forbidden and by invitation only."

"Yeah, Croft, you told me." Wylie took the stairs two at a time, feeling eyes on his back. He found Beatrice in one of the guest rooms, part of a circle of girls sitting cross-legged on a big bed. The smell of cannabis was strong and a haze of pale blue smoke hung in the ceiling beams. She looked up at Wylie. Her face was tear-streaked and her pale hair hung down limply. Two girls, sitting on either side of her, both had an arm around her. On her lap she held an overlarge schooner, the last inch of a lime green concoction slanting toward its mouth. "Thanks for comin', Wyles. I'm wrecked and I don't wanna hafta face Sky on the way out. Can you believe that shit?"

"Let's go."

"These are my best friends. I made them."

Wylie looked at each girl in the circle, not a one of them over eighteen, it looked, all with the glazed inward air of the stoned. "Ladies."

"Sky's just a random asshole," said one.

"Like, if we could just sell him to another mountain. He could be *their* mascot."

A pause, then giggles.

"In my opinion," said a freckled redhead, "you are not a bastard demon at all, Wylie. That's a, like, completely fictitional non-truth."

"Why, thank you. Bea? Let's hit it."

"Sky was, like, so bizarre tonight," said another. "When I got here earlier, I went into a bathroom without knocking? Sky was in there by the sink with a gun in his hand. Gave me this freak smile like he's trying to charm me."

"A gun," said Wylie.

"Don't ask me what kind or any of that. Medium-size and black."

"What was he doing with it?"

"I don't know, Wylie — holding it?"

Giggles.

"Let's go get more grasshoppers, girls," someone said.

"Beatrice?" Wylie asked. "Ready?"

She held out her hand. "So ready."

Bart Helixon marched into the room,

apologizing to Wylie, looking up at the ceiling through the window attached to his glasses as if puzzled. "This is best," he said. "You should go. You're welcome here, you're always welcome here, but tonight . . . well. Don't believe a word of what Sky said. Anything for attention. He's drunk and God knows what else. He'll probably forget about it by morning."

"He can't forget it now," said Beatrice. "It's been posted all over the world."

Helixon clapped a hand on Wylie's shoulder and leaned in close. His eye roamed weirdly behind the lens of his optical computer display. "And don't let him under your skin, because that's what he wants. He's just plain out of line with that kind of threat."

Wylie and Beatrice made it downstairs and almost to the foyer before Wylie heard Sky Carson yelling out behind him, his words booming from the second-story landing through the great room below. "I will accept that apology, Wylie!"

Wylie stopped and looked back at his accuser. Instead of the Bible and phone, Sky now brandished only a black semiautomatic handgun. It looked to Wylie like his own service M9.

When Sky aimed the gun at them, Wylie

got between Bea and Sky and pushed her hard toward the door. There was a second when Beatrice's hand fumbled off the knob and he nearly knocked her over. He looked back at the gun in Sky's hand, pointed straight at them. Suddenly, a string of water glittered from the barrel into the air, began to fall, then broke into diamonds that rained down toward him.

"Do not become a victim of your past!" Sky called down to Wylie. "I am serious, and so is Mother Nature."

Chapter Twelve

Sky helped his mother get Robert over on one side and hold him there so she could bathe him. It defied physics, how heavy an unconscious 180-pound body could be. The late-afternoon light came hard through the bedroom window of Cynthia's condo, through which Sky could see the peaks of the Sherwins white and jagged to the east. In the meadow out front, Mammoth Creek zigged and zagged, frozen at the edges.

As he leaned in to get a better grip on his brother's hip, Sky thought again about the night before at Helixon's. He had given Wylie a chance to apologize, but of course the bastard had refused. Turned it against him somehow. Which was unfortunate, because Wylie was the danger here, the threat. The asked-for apology was self-defense, Sky thought. How had it gotten turned around?

After all, Wylie had the proven record of

violence — a lifetime of scuffles and outright fights right here in Mammoth — often involving a Carson, usually Sky himself. A locally famous sixth-grade battle had landed them both in the hospital with bruised faces and broken bones in all four of their hands. They made a truce and posed for pictures with four black eyes and all four of their casts. The truce had lasted about two months. Now, thought Sky, Wylie is also a veteran of true war. God only knows what he did over there, what deadly things he learned, what impulses he had been encouraged to set loose.

So he had asked for an apology and Wylie had turned it around on him. Again. Wylie had always been good at that — being the aggressor but somehow rarely getting caught at it. A provocateur, a subversive. For example: Who was there to see the shove yesterday on the X Course? Really, no one but himself. Again, Sky pictured going off the course at sixty miles an hour, breaking up on those boulders and trees like some kind of doll, never to ski again. Like Robert.

Snow was falling. He held his brother while his mother bathed his flank. Sky stared out that window rather than look at Robert. He just couldn't look at Robbie for more than maybe one painful second at a time. His mother swabbed away with a sponge and disinfectant soap, her yellow-gray hair pulled into a tight ponytail, humming to herself. “I have a copy of the latest *Woolly* for you,” she said.

“Terrific. I liked the last astrology forecast.”

“I invent the predictions, based on my experiences with people and their birth dates.”

“Isn’t that what all astrologists do?”

“It’s not a hard science. But my readers love it.”

“The stolen skis and boards story was good, too.”

“Brave of the thief to just walk off the mountain with them.”

“He knows the good stuff, I guess.”

“Sky?” Cynthia gave him her chill blue stare. “That was quite a stunt you pulled last night up at Mountain High.”

“Well, I was drunk, but I meant it.”

“Do the injuries hurt?”

“Substantially.”

“You took a bad fall on the X Course, Sky.”

“No, Mom — Wylie shoved me off the X Course. Big difference.”

“You know, I’ve investigated a little, and

there's a split decision on that."

No surprise to Sky. His mother was a bold snoop. It amazed him that townspeople would actually talk to her, but they did. She was certainly direct and clear when asking questions. He knew that behind her back they made fun of her, and he'd heard plenty of jokes about her murderous actions of twenty-five years ago. Lizzie Carson took a gun . . . He'd actually cracked a few jokes about her himself, thinking that this was a fatherless son's right.

In a flash, Sky was back in the women's facility in Chowchilla, sitting in the hot waiting room, age four, Robert and sister Andrea on either side of him, Grandpa Adam and Sandrine there, all of them waiting for one of the stoic guards to lead them back to the visitation center. Sky saw again the tableau that played out over the thirteen years of his mother's incarceration: Mom sitting blue-clad and ankle-shackled to a big round steel loop bolted to the floor, sitting straight up in the immovable steel chair, her straight yellow hair pulled away from her pale face. Even as a four-year old Sky sensed that his mother's composure was requiring every drop of her self-control. Her strength was intimidating and inspiring. Sky had understood that his mother, Cynthia Carson, was a woman who had crossed a great divide. She was feared and lethal. A woman good to her word. A woman who stood and delivered.

"You can investigate all you want, Mom," said Sky. "But Wylie Welborn shoved me just past Conundrum. Where this happened . . ." He glanced at Robert, all he could endure.

"Oh, I believe he's capable of that, son." She looked up at him. "But what if it was your nerves kicking in?"

"It was a shove, Mom."

"Your father never had the nerve for winning."

"Not again, Mom. Please, not all that again."

"He *almost* had the nerve."

"That's not what G-pa says. G-pa says Dad *did* have the nerve but —"

"Of course, nerve is what separates racers at the highest levels, don't you think? My God, your father had everything else a racer could want."

Sky dared another glance at Robert. He looked peaceful and utterly relaxed, and Sky wondered if there was any awareness in him at all. He had seen a news report recently about these newfangled scans that could show brain activity not detectable before. Although the doctors were quick to say that this didn't necessarily mean the patients could improve.

"Robert had nerve," she said. "And he had good racing judgment, too. That's why this is a tragedy, not just an accident." Cynthia rinsed and squeezed the sponge, then patted Robert's temple with it. "I advise you against threats of any kind, Sky."

"Too late. I asked for the apology and promised punishment if he does anything like that again. I've stated my terms."

"You could forgive him."

"Why should I forgive Wylie for running me off the course? That is not right."

"My whole life, I've tried to explain to you the importance of consequence."

The Queen of Consequence, he thought: a lifetime of damnation in exchange for one squeeze of a trigger. Well, five squeezes. Sky had often wondered what his life would have been like if his father had shot his mother, rather than the other way around. But really, what was the point of that? "You've explained that to me maybe a billion times, Mom."

Sky looked out at the Sherwins. A snowplow clanked up Minaret toward the mountain. The top of the mountain was locked behind a white wall, which meant snow was falling there. In his mind Sky again replayed his race against Wylie the previous day, scrolled forward to Wylie ramming him on that high-speed, precarious turn. Wylie threw his shoulder, for sure. Why else would he have gone off-course? Nerves? No. There had been no pressure. It wasn't even a real race.

"More important, if you're going to beat Wylie in the cup, you'll have to train much harder, Sky. Off-season, too. And cut the drinking way back. Of course that was —"

"One of my father's weaknesses."

"Yes, it was. Of my three children, though, you are the one who is the finest *natural* skier —"

"Though I lack discipline and nerve."

"You're a better skier than Wylie Welborn, but —"

"He's a better racer."

"When you train harder, and learn to control your nerves, you'll be ready to beat him. For instance, you know you should be in Europe now, on the World Cup circuit, like you were last year and the year before that."

"Robert needs me here," he said absently.

"And you need to commit, Sky."

"You've told me that a billion times, too."

"Because you've never committed to anything that isn't easy. The way you race.

The way you drink and show off. The way you pledge yourself to people, then discard them. Especially women. You do what's —"

"Easy. I only do what's easy."

"Very much like —"

"My father."

"And yet the seeds of championship are in you. I was the hardest-working woman in my racing days. My body was very strong and sound. My commitment was never questioned. On your father's side is God-given talent. No one had greater nerve and commitment than your grandfather Adam. And of course a perfect body. You have that body, too."

He felt his blood heating up, that first tremble and bubble. "I can't be like them, Mom."

"But you can excel. I'll help in any way I can. And Robert can help, too. He's still here, in body and spirit, aren't you, Robbie? Robbie is in the prison of his body, but he can emanate blessings and advice, though he cannot speak outright. You have roughly one year until the race, Sky. But very much to do if you want to win it."

"I'm going to win the damned race and I'm not going to let Wylie run people off the mountain. If those are the first real commitments I actually stick to, fine. I admit my mistakes. I'm twenty-five years old."

"Old enough to grow up."

"I'm growing up, Mom. I'm growing up."

She hummed softly, dabbing the sponge on Robert's chin, as if he'd spilled a little formula on it. Sky glanced at the feeding tube that entered his brother through a round patch of gauze on his lower flank. It almost nauseated him. Made his blood feel sick. He looked at the little bank of monitors on the rolling table near the bed, the drip trolley backed into the corner for now. This is what Robert's commitment got him, thought Sky. Robert's reward. A hospital with no cute nurses. The only thing he hated more than hospitals were prisons.

Cynthia carried the buckets of bathing and rinse water into the bathroom. Still humming, then not. "Did you hear about April Holly coming to Mammoth?" she called out.

"Chip, chip," he muttered.

"*Did* you?"

"Yes, Mom. Great."

"Maybe our little town can learn from her," she half-yelled from the bathroom.

"Learn what? How to be a self-obsessed Olympic celebrity?"

"You know what I heard from Brandon? April is engaged to be married to her longtime boy, but her camp thought she was falling in with the wrong kind of people in Aspen. So they brought her here."

Sky found this to be very funny. "Wait 'til she gets a load of me," he said to Robert, smiling slightly.

"What did you say?"

"Nothing, Mom!" Sky summoned all of the determination that he so obviously lacked, according to his mother, and brushed a hand through his brother's freshly washed hair. Even unconscious, Robert struck Sky as truly good and deserving of his deepest love. Deserving of a lot more than that, thought Sky. But what else could he give Robbie now but love? He reached out and lifted Robert's left eyelid and looked into the clear blue emptiness. "I'll win that race, Robert," he said. "Mark. My. Words."

As usual this time of evening, Sky hit Slocum's restaurant for happy hour and ran into his group in the bar. The team skiers and boarders had claimed their high, round bar tables in the middle of the room. Thanks to them, the decibel level was very high. Johnny Teller and Greg Bretz and Tyler Wallasch were there, and so were Kelly Clark and Arielle Gold, which turned up the star power to eleven on a scale of ten. Local snowboard contenders Johnny Maines and Suzanna Scott were arguing loudly but with good humor. Sky joined the boisterous table talk. There was no better antidote than this to his mother and her dire pronouncements. Sky loved this part of being a racer, being in a room where every person knew who you were and what you'd accomplished and they just wanted to watch you being cool. And see exactly how you did it.

To his left, someone said, "Sage has got his whole routine so cold, every detail, man, right down to the way he holds the edge on his method, or the angle of his head on the back-side launch. It's, like, choreography." Sky immediately countered that Sage's whole style was "tweaked out because he has no idea what he's going to do next. It isn't planned out at all, dude — and that's why he looks like he just fell out of bed. And that's what makes him great." Sky knew little about board slopestyle — Sage Kotsenburg's gold medal Sochi event — but he couldn't pass up the chance to pontificate in front of an audience. He observed himself performing the Sky Carson act, pleased that he was so good at it.

Tourists and locals manned the booths along the walls, looking up with curiosity at

Sky and his young comrades enthroned on their higher pedestal tables. Sky knew that this audience was here because he and his friends were champions, or soon to be — the best athletes you would see up on this mountain, or anywhere really. Some would become Olympians. He and his peers pretty much ignored these onlookers because they were not ski or board professionals and did not take the risks of professionals, because, in fact, most of them skied and boarded badly, and looked fucking idiotic skiing and boarding badly in the expensive snow fashions they wore so they would look like professionals. Sky knew this was just his pride, but pride was all you had unless you went Olympic and podiumed; then you had fortune, too, so much fortune that it boggled the mind.

He drank two neat Stolichnayas. He couldn't be in that room with Robert and not feel disheartened. It took his spirit away. He wasn't sure that what had happened to Robert had really sunk in yet. It didn't have the finality of death. To grieve seemed disloyal. So Sky could not say good-bye to him. Was there really anything at all going on inside him? Or was Robert just a crude exhibit of what he had once been?

And two hours with his mother was punitive beyond words. She knew exactly where his psychological scabs were and she picked at them, over and over and over.

Ignoring his tablemates now — as a way to draw more attention to himself — Sky pulled *The Woolly* from his pocket, looked at the front-page headlines and amateurish pictures. His mother's head shot was on the front page, bottom right, as always, like a Realtor's, a picture taken thirty-five-plus years ago, when Cynthia was in her skiing prime. She was broad-faced and handsome and big-haired in the style of the day. She had been the number-five American woman on the FIS downhill circuit that year, as she had told him many, many times. He folded the paper once, Cynthia face-in, and set it between his stool and his butt cheek.

The thing that was really eating him, though, besides Robert and his mother, was the previous night at Mountain High. Why had so many people thought he was being funny? He was challenging Wylie, berating him, not joking with him. He hadn't meant it as even partially funny. An apology was the right thing for him to demand. He would stand by that. No choice now, since the entire world had seen him throw down the gauntlet.

Sky still had that blood-sick feeling he'd

gotten looking at Robert and listening to his mother. He watched the parade of vehicles coming down Main, their headlights moving slowly, dull slush spraying off the tires.

Luckily, Megan, the waitress, was cute as ever, and she had pulled herself away from Johnny Maines to deliver Stoli number three to Sky. He pointed to his abraded cheek. "How is it healing up, dear?"

She swung away the bar tray and leaned in for a closer look. Lovely dark brown eyes and hair. Shampoo like apples. "Kind of nasty," she said.

"Do you know any good remedies?"

"I always prescribe vitamin A ointment and TLC."

"Ready for that TLC when you are!" He gave her a smile. "I'll hang here until you're off tonight; then we can hit Mountain High."

"Maybe. I saw your selfie from there last night."

"And how did you like it?"

"You got pretty banged up on the X Course. I think Wylie should apologize. But the rest of it, it's all a joke, right? About punishing him? Just, like, comedy?"

"I meant it, Megan." Christ. He watched Megan size him up, likely trying to factor his mother's past violence into his own future capabilities: *What if he really is like her?* He never got tired of people wondering that, never got tired of wondering it himself. Sky Carson heartily disliked Sky Carson but thought he made for an interesting study.

"You're going to punish him if he runs you off the course again? Is that right?"

"Runs *anyone* off the course."

"But it's so not *you* to do something like that."

"I've been underestimated in the past."

"Put this on the tab?"

"Getting really sick of it."

"Of Stoli?"

"Cripes, Megan. Just put it on the tab."

Sky felt a sudden drop in cabin pressure. Without turning, he sensed a large party coming from outside into the vestibule behind him, where the hostesses waited. He saw the tourists' heads swivel in unison in that direction, and Megan's gaze, then those of his tablemates. When he turned, he saw three men — a guy even bigger than Croft, and a snowboard pro he recognized from last year's X Games in Aspen, and a fitness trainer named Andy he'd drunk under the table right here at Slocum's one night years ago. Behind them was a stocky, severely handsome middle-aged woman. And next to her stood gold-medal celebrity and snowboard genius April Holly.

Sky had never seen her in person. She was shorter than he would have guessed, and looked lighter. She had a thatch of blond curls held back in a black band, with her shampoo sponsor's logo up front, where no one could miss it. She wore striped lounge pants and a too-big, out-of-fashion peace sign–emblazoned flannel hoodie that looked like it came from a Mammoth thrift store two years ago. And she had the famously pretty face with the famously upbeat expression that looked, like, completely plastered on. She and her team stood in the vestibule while the hostess collected menus off the rack.

The hostess squared the menus and smiled at April. Sky watched April look around the room at the racers fallen quiet at the bar tables, and he was pretty sure she looked directly at him. Briefly. Then she turned and headed for the exit. Her mother closed in quickly behind her, followed by the men.

The big fellow held open the door until the rest had exited, and when a party from outside started in, he let go and the breeze blew it shut on them. Looking through the frost-edged windows, Sky watched April leaning into the snow, arms around herself, headed for the large black SUV parked in one of the handicapped spaces. It had a large likeness of her face on it, and *April Holly* written in a cursive, autographlike style above her mountain of golden curls.

"We're not good enough for her," said Megan.

"Yes," said Sky. "I am."

By the time Wylie came in five hours later, Sky had lost count of the Stolis and was halfway through the cowboy steak dinner. He had retreated into the back dining room, which at this hour was sparse of diners and gave him a view of the bar. It was still busy out there. He watched Wylie join a table of half-pipe boarders and skiers. No Carsons at that table, of course. The wallpaper in his booth had a detailed Victorian pattern that swirled and settled, swirled and settled. There was no proper way to leave the premises but past Wylie. Sky wondered if this was fateful. Of course he could go through the kitchen and out the back, but he was a man and a Carson. When he was finished with his dinner, he stood up straight, dropped some twenties onto the table, and walked into the bar.

The room was crowded and loud, football on all four screens, Sky keeping Wylie just in the corner of his vision. Sky could tell Wylie was watching the game, his bearded face uplifted and the TV light faint upon it. Sky thought he should stop and survey the room with some kind of propriety, just to project that he was in no hurry to leave, that he was champion skier Sky Carson, future Olympian, on his way to his next appointment. He looked around briefly and thought, I guess I should at least say hello to the bastard, if I'm to regain my authority and good name in this town.

He angled through the revelers, sidestepped through a tight spot, and brought himself to rest at Wylie's table. Wylie and the others turned to him and went quiet. Time to say something, he thought. "My line in the snow is fairly drawn."

"Beat it, Sky. I'm just so damned sick of you."

"Apologize."

"For what?"

"Foul play on the X Course."

"So, this is all about something that didn't happen?"

"It's about everything that has happened."

"Oh hell — not all that."

"Your ho mother cost my father his life

and sent my mom to prison. All I got out of the deal was you and your disrespect. You can apologize for that, too, while you're at it."

Movement. Sky threw a punch, but he was already falling backward under a blow. Smack and percussion, no pain. He was flat on his back, looking up at a thickly bearded face, Megan hovering, a chandelier, and a stamped aluminum ceiling, all interlocked and rotating like the pattern in a kaleidoscope.

Chapter Thirteen

I was five months along with Sky at the time I shot Richard. I was showing plenty, as a woman will do with number three. Thirty years old and my third child on the way. But I still had good strength because I was born strong, and I was extra stout in the legs from a lifetime on skis. Big-lunged, too. I could ski or run or swim forever and not get winded. I'd long ago given up racing to have my family, but I still got up on the mountain when I could. And ran and swam at the athletic club. And kept up with a three-year-old and a four-year-old. What I'm saying is I was a five-months-pregnant mother of two and I was still as beautiful and strong as I'd ever been, and I was there for Richard, all his for anything, willing, a good wife.

I was a prisoner when I bore Sky at the county jail hospital. The pregnancy really took it out of me. He was breech and I tried for weeks to coax him into turning around. I'd lie on the preg-room floor with my feet elevated and a little radio set up down by him, with music playing, trying to get him to just switch himself around inside me so he could hear the music better. The doctor said the music was an unproven folk remedy, and he was right about the unproven part, because Sky turned not one centimeter that anybody could determine. And like I said, when Sky finally came, the epidural didn't work right, so when it was over I felt like I'd died and gone to hell in the form of a county hospital staffed by tiny, grim nurses and one monstrous deputy sheriff wearing a shirt so tight that it pulled apart between the buttons, and, of course, a big gun.

They took Sky immediately, and I didn't see him again for one month. They did let me pump milk for him — to shore him up against allergies and worse — which went into a cooler that Adam and Sandrine ferried from the prison to Mammoth Lakes. Sky had a wet nurse, Teresa by name, who had lost a baby of her own. She used to wait on us at El Matador on Main.

Of all the infuriating things that got into me during those first months of prison, one of the worst was thinking about Sky suckling at the breast of another woman. Sure I was thankful he had something like a mother's milk. Sure I knew he'd be better off for it. But I had a recurring dream back then that I was standing on a cliff with Teresa and she handed baby Sky to me and I brought him into my arms and smiled at her, then placed my boot — a ski boot! — to Teresa's middle and pushed her over the cliff.

I healed up slowly. Never felt weaker or had less hope. Hell is a cage with you in it. Murder trials are time-consuming, for starters, and we had my pregnancy and the birth of Sky and a storm of pretrial motions to consider. I went through three lawyers. When we finally got into the courtroom, the DA went straight after me, and you can bet it was a free-for-all. Kathleen Welborn was one of the witnesses. The DA painted me as privileged Mammoth Lakes "royalty," which meant a Carson. Tried to make it a class thing, portrayed Kathleen Welborn as a penniless commoner who'd come up from San Diego and worked as a doughnut maker, then later as a ski instructor so she could try her luck on the mountain. Which is exactly what she was. Common.

The first time I saw Kathleen's son, Wylie, was in court. When she came in with him, it caused quite a stir, even though without a jury there weren't lots of people. The judge allowed it. Of course it was a naked ploy by the DA to steal any small sympathy for me that the judge might have in his heart. I didn't ask to bring in Sky. I would not stoop that low.

Even at two months, the baby Wylie had the hallmark Carson head. Same as Sky and all of them. Wylie had a hint of the Carson jaw, too, and I could see it would become more pronounced as he grew. So there I was, sitting ankle-shackled in the Mono County Superior Courthouse, room 1, helpless but worried sick about Sky back home in Mammoth, not to mention Robert and Andrea.

And being forced to look at my own husband's seed made flesh through Kathleen! That first time I saw Wylie was the closest I ever came to feeling like I might go crazy. I was never crazy. I was not crazy when I shot Richard. I am not crazy now. But for that first hour sitting in the courtroom with Wylie not thirty feet away, I feared that I might just leave my marbles behind and never be able to find them again. But I didn't. Instead, I stared. I stared at Kathleen and my husband's son, and resolved never to be defeated by them.

Earlier today, I got the wheelchair from the medical rental place by the hospital, even though Robbie's doctor said it would be impossible for me to get him in and out of it by myself, much less push him around town to do some sightseeing. He was quick to say that Robbie wouldn't be aware of anything that was around him. Nothing.

But — and this is interesting and I'll be writing about in *The Woolly* — when I pressed the doctor for a 100 percent guarantee that Robbie was not aware of anything, the sawbones would not give one. He admitted there was a small chance that Robbie was, in fact, aware of some things, just like it said in that newspaper article that Sky found. With the new scans, they can tell things they couldn't tell just a few years ago. So who is one nearsighted, itty-bitty little neurologist to seal my son's fate? Who is he to attempt that? I told the doctor I'd take Robbie out into the world regardless. I gave him a current issue of *The Woolly,* however. Certainly no hard feelings

It's a heavy contraption, that wheelchair. But I'm still very strong and patient and I'm going to get Robbie out there in the sunny, real world. As I would have done with him so many more times in his stroller if it weren't for Kathleen Welborn. Adam and Sky and Hailee will help, and we'll get the nurses if we have to. The way I look at it is, what could it possibly hurt?

Chapter Fourteen

Spring came and the racers skied and boarded the corn snow into June. Finally, the corn snow melted to hero snow — the slushy pack in which even beginners can carve deep turns. Eventually, the hero snow gave way to a thin mud-speckled carpet, and the man-made snow was too expensive to earn a profit for the mountain. So Adam Carson closed it. It had been a good year — 584 inches of snow, high visitation to the mountain, and high occupancy in the rental market. Restaurants were full and spending was strong, real estate inching back up for the first time since the Great Recession. No plane crashes, avalanches, ski or boarding fatalities, no tree-well suffocations, deadly fumarole collapses or earthquakes.

Robert's tragedy at the Mammoth Cup hung over the locals like a fog that wouldn't break, but the tourists who came and left and paid the bills seemed to have already forgotten. Wylie Welborn's one-punch knockout of Sky Carson in the bar at Slocum's was much discussed. Some said Sky had it coming. Some said Wylie was way quick to violence. For the most part, the town seemed empty and abandoned.

But by July, the bikers and climbers and fishermen and runners were back and Mammoth Lakes' second season was in swing. The sponsored and more prosperous snow racers were headed down to South America or New Zealand to board and ski. The less advantaged headed up to Mount Hood, or stayed in Mammoth to work the restaurants and sporting-goods stores, sometimes taking two or even three jobs at a time to pay rent, and do dry-terrain training. Snow was what they talked about, even though it seemed an eternity away. They rode mountain bikes and took classes at Cerro Coso College and hit the happy hours in the customer-shy bars and restaurants.

Wylie put in eight-hour days at Let It Bean, then went home and split wood, a lot of it. By mid-June, he had half enough for winter, all of it stacked neatly along the east side of the house. His arms, hands, and back became very strong.

He repaired the sagging rear deck and patched the roof with mastic and aluminum as best he could. But he saw that many of the old composition shingles were broken and the tar was dried and cracked everywhere he looked. He got two quotes for a new roof: twelve thousand dollars and fifteen thousand, and both roofers said to replace this thing before winter or it would be a wet one inside. Wylie gave the grim news to Steen, who cheerfully stated that they would find the money, as they always did. Wylie helped Steen finish his pastry cart, putting on two coats of bright red paint and, at Steen's delighted insistence, stenciling large yellow Scandinavian-styled letters that read *THE LITTLE RED PASTRY SHED.*

Every other day, Wylie ran distance with Bea and Belle, legs being the foundation of ski racing. Over the years, Wylie had been amused at the way ski and board racers — himself included — treated their legs as if they were special, privileged parts of the body. There were endless miles, ferocious sprints, hours of leg presses, lifts, lunges, and squats. A racer with a few moments of free time did in-place knee bends or one-knee bends. They'd have contests to see who could do most. Then came the stretches, rubdowns, liniment, ice, whirlpools, handfuls of glucosamine and condroitin pills for the knees and ankles, cortisone if it got bad.

Wylie didn't love the running, but he loved being with his sisters — so nice to learn what the young were thinking.

In the long afternoons and evenings, he fished Hot Creek and the Upper Owens and the East Walker up past Bridgeport. Sometimes he drove home, but often he slept out in the vastness of the Sierras, on the ground or in the bed of his truck. By lantern he read and composed poetically intentioned lines that amounted to nothing. He could not sustain a thought on paper. He ate his larger trout and drank bourbon in reasonable amounts.

By the time Jesse Little Chief called to say he had finished the trailer, Wylie had traded twelve pounds of fat for muscle, and the six combined miles he ran down Highway 203 toward Highway 395 and back up again were getting easier.

Now Wylie slowly circled the module, personal, portable, which stood outside Jesse's shop down in Bishop. The MPP was even more elegant than he had imagined. And so obviously capable.

Jesse had alternated bands of maple and teak, light and dark, and finished the entire module in a heavy spar varnish that captured the hot June sun. The oversized double doors to starboard were graceful and, when latched open, welcomed the world. There were real nautical portholes up on the roof for stargazing and ventilation. Jesse had gotten the portholes from a marine-salvage place in Morro Bay, and worked the brass into a potent shine. The birch interior, simple and beautiful, shortened Wylie's breath.

"I'm speechless. And I've got the next two grand, Jesse — I've been living at Let It Bean. Eight hours a day, seven days a week for three months."

"You need a Mexican."

"I am a Mexican." He thought of the agreed-upon fourteen-thousand-dollar roof job looming over the Welborn-Mikkelsen household. And the new lease on the Let It Bean space, which would surely be more money. And the heating bills to come in the fall, and the newly expensive health insurance. Good time to buy a custom-made trailer, he thought. Even the ten-thousand-dollar prize money for winning the Mammoth Cup wouldn't even cover the roof, let alone the roof and the MPP. But how could he have known back in January that the whole damned roof was shot? "I'll have enough by winter to pay it off."

"No worries, Wylie."

"You sure?"

Jesse gave him a look.

"I owe you more than I owe you, Jess."

A screen door wheezed open and slapped shut. Jolene hopped from deck to yard and picked her way barefoot across the dirt toward them, keeping to the cool of the shop shadow. She had a blanket over her shoulders and carried a large pasteboard box in both hands, the lid sections flapping. Her black hair shined. Above the box, her eyes were fixed on Wylie, and below the box, her legs were dark and trim. She arrived with an appraising look, then set the box on the front fork of the trailer chassis, which rested on a jack.

"Hi, Jo."

"Oh, it's you. Hello, Wylie. Here's some stuff you'll need." She slung the blanket and handed it to him and waited for him to do something with it. Wylie raised his arms and let it unfold. It was a Navajo-style print, acrylic, likely from the Paiute Palace gift shop up the road. "Fake Indian junk, but it will help keep you warm in this wigwam."

"I like it."

"You're welcome."

Wylie folded the blanket once over and set it inside the MPP. Jolene eyed him narrowly, reached into the box, and lifted out a battered and well-seasoned iron skillet, which she set on the blanket. In the skillet were paper dispensers of salt and pepper and a new Mag flashlight. Next from the box she brought two pairs of extra-heavy wool boot socks, a pair in each hand, wiggling them at him as if trying to interest an infant or a dog. She set them on the blanket. Then a handsome leather-bound journal with a jumping trout tooled into the cover, then the collected love poems of Kahlil Gibran, followed by a bottle of the bourbon he liked, and, last, an economy-size bottle of shampoo/body wash for men.

"I don't know what to say."

She stepped forward and kissed him on the cheek. "Stuff you'll need."

"This is really something, Jo."

"It's the next best thing to having me in there."

"Stop tormenting him, Jolene," said Jesse.

"Payback," she said. She squinted at Wylie once more, then strode through the shadows and back into the house.

Towing the MPP back up to Mammoth that evening, Wylie could barely keep his eyes off it in the rearview. The sun glanced off the varnish, and the alternating slats of hardwood made him think of the breadboard he'd made his mom in wood shop, grade seven at Mammoth Middle School, those beautiful runners like you'd see on vintage surf- and skateboards. That breadboard was still on the kitchen counter, he'd noted. He was happy with the substantial weight of the MPP, and wood was unbeatable for warmth retention and beauty. He pulled over at Tom's Place just to get out and walk around it again and see how totally sweet it was, hitched to his truck, waiting for him, for life, for adventure. He got a rag from the toolbox and wiped off the bugs that had met their Maker on the rounded edge of the bow.

Can't rub too hard or I might scratch the finish.

There.

He felt triumphant, idling at the first traffic signal in town. A guy in the crosswalk looked at the MPP and Wylie nodded coolly. He made the turn onto Old Mammoth Road, drove slowly through town, and pulled into one of the Mammoth Cycle parking spaces in the crowded Von's shopping center. Wylie was dying to show off the MPP, and his high-school buddy Chris, the bike maniac, was the nearest pal he could think of. Wylie found him in the service area with a bike up on the stand. Chris followed him out to the parking lot, flipping a box wrench end by end in one grease-blackened hand.

"Holy crap, dude."

"Don't touch it with greasy hands."

"Jesse Little Chief made this?"

"Every inch of it."

"I want one."

"Everyone will."

"How much?"

"Well, he'd have to run some numbers. Look at the way it just . . . *sits there.*"

Wylie kept staring at his trailer, not quite able to believe it was his. He was aware of someone coming across the parking lot behind him, more than one person, by the sound of things, although he was paying little attention. He turned and saw April Holly and a woman who had to be her mother, and a very large man, even larger than the bouncer Croft. They carried shopping bags from the market. April, in the lead, stopped at the trailer, set her bags on the asphalt, and studied it. There was a long moment of silence.

"Does it have a name?" April asked.

Wylie turned to her. "Module, personal, portable."

"So it's, like, military?"

"There could be a military application,

someday," he said.

"You're Wylie Welborn."

"Welcome to Mammoth Lakes, April."

April introduced him to her mother, Helene, and her bodyguard, Logan. They set down their bags and shook his hand. Helene had a deeply tanned, dour face. Her handshake was strong and brief, Logan's lingering softly with either gentleness or threat. The big man had a wide downward mouth and ears that tapered sharply. April's voice was soft and whispery, like a breeze in leaves, which made Wylie lean in closer to hear.

"I heard you joined the army," she said.

"I'm a United States Marine."

"And now you're back into ski-cross racing?"

"It will keep me out of trouble."

"Of what kind?"

"Those days are gone."

She looked at him frankly. She had a round, pretty face and looked smaller and older in person than on TV or magazine covers. Blue eyes and a sprinkle of freckles on her cheeks. Button nose, more freckles. Her hair was blond and curly and difficult to manage, according to shampoo commercials that Wylie had seen, and it now sprung up unmanaged from a pink bandanna.

He watched April considering the MPP. Helene checked her cell phone and Logan stared off toward the cop station. "I get claustrophobic," April said.

"Me, too. But check this out." Wylie swung out the elegant double doors, stepped inside, opened the portholes, and stepped back out. He fastened each door open against the MPP with the latches that Jesse had built in. He gestured at the trailer with both hands, like a salesman, to point out the surprisingly spacious interior of the module: the small table that would fold out to fit with the padded benches to form a bed, the two-burner stove, the yacht-size sink and john behind the sliding shoji screen. Jesse's birch caught the sunlight as if to banish claustrophobia.

April stepped in. "It's bigger than I thought."

She stood framed in the doorway, looking down at Jolene's box of presents on the table, then turned back at Wylie. "Hard liquor and poetry?"

"In moderation."

She looked down on him from her elevation just inside the trailer. "My people have prohibitions on almost everything, even moderation. Probably poetry, too, though I haven't been tempted by that yet. I don't think I'm smart enough to understand a whole poem. But can you recommend one poetic, dangerous, life-changing word that I should know?"

"Module."

She gave him a half smile. "You love this thing, don't you?"

"You can sit."

"No, thank you," she said, stepping back out. "But it sure smells good. Is it new?"

"Brand-new. A friend made it."

"It looks too shiny and perfect to leave outside."

"I agree, but it's made to be used. Very strong. There's insulation between the inside and outside walls. And real salvage portholes."

"For stargazing."

"And ventilation in summer."

She looked at him skeptically. "But no place for your skis and gear."

"This was my idea!" Wylie hustled around to the stern and unfastened two heavy stainless-steel latches. He pulled a substantial brass handle then stepped aside to let a long, heavy drawer roll out to its full length of eight feet. It glided with audible heft upon its bearings, burped a waft of redwood-scented air, then stopped. When he looked at her, April Holly had one hand over her mouth but couldn't staunch her laughter.

"Oh, that's just so funny!"

"How can a drawer be funny?"

"You are!"

"I . . ."

"Done yet, honey?" asked Helene.

"Oh, that made my day," said April. She gathered her bags, still laughing. "So nice to meet you, Wylie."

Wylie nodded compliantly. "Same here."

"Love the module! See ya on the mountain."

Wylie and Chris watched them cross the lot toward a black Escalade with her image on the side. While Logan held open the front passenger door for Helene, April glanced back at Wylie and Chris, waved, then climbed in the back.

"She's hard to figure," said Chris. "She seems halfway with it, then pretty random. And then cool and then only about herself. Did you know she gets two million a year for her headgear sponsor? The shampoo? Just that one little space on her helmet?"

"She liked the MPP."

"She didn't stay long."

"Not with her mom standing there."

"She's engaged. Did you see that ring?"

Wylie said nothing, rubbed his thumb over a tiny bubble in the finish.

"I sold her ten bikes yesterday. One-fifth of my stock. There're six people total on her racing team, counting the mom and her. But that Logan guy is too big for a bike. So April bought herself and the rest of them road bikes for asphalt and hard-tail twenty-nines for the bike paths. Pretty good ones. Thirteen thousand bucks. And another thousand for helmets and shoes and bibs and oh, man, every bike gadget you can think of. Most money I ever made in a day, by far. Maybe enough to buy one of these trailers from Jesse."

Wylie was again lost in meditation on the module. He heard the Escalade pulling away but couldn't look.

"April rented one of those big houses in Starwood," said Chris. "Six flat-screens and three hot tubs is what I heard."

"How many miles you think these tires will go?"

Later that night, Wylie retired from the Welborn-Mikkelsen house and got everything set up for his first night in the MPP. Beatrice and Belle helped him convert the benches and table into the bed, the thick pads making a firm mattress for his summer-weight sleeping bag. The battery-powered lantern gave off a good clean light. He read and made notes and sipped a short bourbon.

Later, Beatrice came back to hang for a while, talk about things. She lay down beside him in opposition, head-to-toe, using both packs of thick boot socks for a pillow. She told him she was thinking about maybe not spending so much time up at Helixon's — it was kind of a weird scene, with lots of pressure on girls to get high on drugs and go down on guys. And more. She wasn't sure if she wanted to do all that just to be popular. Wylie disliked the idea of his sister's having sex with someone he didn't approve of, which was just about everyone.

"Not a good reason," he said. "Popularity."

"You're a guy. Doesn't that like betray the guy code or something?"

"I kind of liked being unpopular," he said. "It was a form of privacy."

"I don't have that strength of character, Wyles."

"If you said you did, you would."

"That's like something Dad would say. Like positive but totally not verifiable." Bea ran her finger down the birch paneling of the wall, then picked a strand of her long blond hair and looked at it. "There's one guy at Mountain High I wouldn't mind talking more to. Kind of shy. He hasn't said one thing to me about either drugs or sex. And he's the most perfect dancer ever."

"Sounds like a start, Bea."

"It's cool. I can be in the same room with him and not have him all over me."

"You're the boss, Bea. Don't forget that."

"Okay. I won't. Wylie? I hope you're not disappointed, but I'm not much interested in competitive boarding anymore."

"I gathered that."

"I hope I'm not letting you down."

"There's a lot more than competition, Bea."

"I just don't have the nerves. I get so damned scared before every event. Now Robert. Jeez, Wylie. I'm so afraid of that being me. If it can happen to Sarah Burke . . ."

"Ride your board for fun, Bea. That's the beginning and end of it."

No sooner had Beatrice left than Belle showed up, and Wylie got an earful of what fifteen-year-olds were up to these days, not all of it comforting, either. He figured he must be getting old. Belle had a weak spot for getting high, and she admitted it and told Wylie she was fighting off the urge most of the time. But it was hard. Wylie set his glass on the other side of the bed, where she wouldn't be looking right at it, though he couldn't keep the smell from her. Can you keep anything from someone who really wants it?

Belle didn't seem to notice. She was talking fast about her ski-cross possibilities for next year as a sixteen-year-old, her good chances at making the team and maybe even a shot at the Mammoth Cup, and wouldn't that be the coolest to both podium in their events, both be top of the box with gold? Wylie had to agree. Belle had always been fearless and direct on the course, a lot like Wylie. With hard training and good luck, she could be a contender in the under-eighteen category. The u-eighteens were stacked with talent, so Belle had lots of competition.

She went quiet then, and Wylie caught her looking at him while pretending not to. After a moment, she gave up the pretense and speared him with her serious gaze. She had fierce concentration when she needed it. "Tell me about the war, Wylie."

"Not now. Some other time."

"When?"

"Later."

"You were a medic, right?"

"Unofficial. The medics were corpsman and I was a grunt. But I helped out some brothers when they couldn't help themselves. I seemed to have some knack for that."

She looked at him, half innocence and half suspicion. She had her mother's dark hair and eyes. "Were you on the battlefield?"

"Yes, a lot, Belle."

"Did you see people die?"

"I saw that, too."

"Did you kill?"

"No," he said, lying. In Wylie's opinion, this particular truth would be of no help to Belle as yet in her life. And no help to himself to confess. He felt the boxes containing his troubling memories jostling around, way up on the shelves of his mind. "No. I helped some wounded men survive. Nothing really dramatic, though."

"Oh."

"It's hard to think back, because you kind of have to live things again," he said.

"It's been two whole years."

"I'll tell you a battlefield story some other time, Belle."

"Maybe just a short one now? A really small one?"

Wylie sighed and shook his head. "We got lit up on a trail and there was nothing to hide behind. Which is why they hit us there. Some of it was mortar fire, and that comes from above and drops down on you and the shells explode in big rings of shrapnel. I hit the dirt and crawled like a bug to the nearest cover. It was a little pile of rocks maybe the size of a suitcase turned over on its side. I got myself up against it the best I could and buried my face in the sand and held my helmet on hard as I could. The shells kept landing and I was waiting to not be here anymore, and then they stopped. It was quiet for a minute, which seemed like an hour. I felt someone touch my shoulder, and when I cranked up my face from the dirt, no one was there."

"Who was it?"

"I don't know."

"How could they have gotten away that fast?"

"I don't know."

"Where was Jesse Little Chief?"

"A hundred feet behind me, half-dug into a low spot."

"Just your imagination?"

"Sometimes I think so."

Belle gave him an appraising look. "I'd like another story sometime."

"Okay."

"I'm holding you to that."

Then Beatrice was back and they lounged around in the MPP with the double doors open to the cool summer air and the fragrance of conifers all around. It was well after midnight when Wylie shooed both girls back to the house and stretched out and read through some things he'd written, shaking his head at the nonpoeticalness of them. Maybe there should always be something in your life you want but can't have, he thought. And I shall never write a good poem. He looked for a long time at the stars aglitter through the portholes. One of Wylie's mental boxes — the one containing the Taliban fighter — began to slide from its place on one of the high, orderly shelves in Wylie's mind. So he reached up and caught a bottom corner and pushed it back into place.

He went outside to view the MPP again in its entirety. Deep in the dark trees he saw movement, then none. He thought of the old toolshed he'd crashed into. And how the hill had seemed so high and steep to him at age five.

He went back inside and fell asleep. But that Talib sniper came back to life again in his dreams, shooting at him and the rest of his fire team through a murder hole in a mud-brick compound wall. And damned if

Sergeant Madigan didn't come back, too, just in time for the sniper's bullet to go through his neck one more time. And damned if Jesse wasn't there, the knife in his hand at a weird angle to the dead Talib's head. And damned if Wylie didn't take the knife and finish what Jesse had begun, in that moment conceiving the notion of mental boxes that could be locked and stored away forever, their secrets hidden, their devils screaming away unheard.

CHAPTER FIFTEEN

By the dawn's early light, Wylie let himself and the girls into Let It Bean. It was the Fourth of July. Even in summer the mountain cast its cold shadow on the town, and Wylie saw his breath in the air as he stepped into the still-unwarmed bakery. It smelled as it always did: of roasted coffee, warm cream, baked spices and yeast and flour mixed into a sweet, invisible, almost narcotic cloud. He flicked on the lights and set the thermostat and stepped into the walk-in refrigerator for a supplies check.

The girls worked by rote, too: Beatrice to the grinders and Belle to the steamers, then teaming up to make the breakfast burritos and get them into the electric warmer.

As always, all hands gathered side by side at the racks to appraise the pastries that Steen and Kathleen had created the night before. They were competitive about their baking — Kathleen self-taught; Steen formally trained in his native Denmark. Besides the usual staples, they found peach preserve/whipped peanut butter croissants; whiskey/apricot and Brie Danish; and a dozen dark chocolate/Tabasco-raspberry scones. Kathleen and Steen had arranged and labeled them.

"Mom thought up the peanut butter ones; you know that," said Bea. "And Dad the spicy raspberry."

"Maybe we could just split one of the croissants?" asked Belle. "I mean, three ways?"

Wylie ate his third in one bite, poured a double shot of espresso, just said no to the cream. He went to the front of the shop, which was just now growing light with the sunrise. The windows were festooned with posters for local events, the newspaper racks ready to be filled, the furniture straightened up by Kathleen and Steen the night before.

He turned on the baseboard heaters, lights and lamps, and suddenly he was twelve years old, doing this exact thing on his first official morning shift thirteen years ago, thinking that he would spend many hours of his life in Let It Bean. It was exciting to be part of the family business, though he had to get up awfully darned early. He was a quiet boy, serious, tall for his age and slightly rounded by the endless pastries that a two-baker family produced. He looked at his reflection in the window, watched it morph from a twelve-year-old to a twenty-five-year-old.

"Here we go again," said Beatrice, setting out the cup lids and napkins and insulators. "I hope it's a good day. I'm afraid what Gargantua is gonna pull on us next."

"Fear not," said Wylie. He wadded up some newspaper and set it in the fireplace, covered it with kindling, and made a tepee of logs on top. The cold newsprint resisted the match; then a good orange flame climbed up.

He knew that today would be busy in town and they should be able to sell coffee and pastries as fast as they could serve them. In a little over an hour, Kathleen would be here for the seven o'clock bulge. It would take all four of them to service their customers, if today went the way Fourths always did. Biggest day of summer, easy.

But Gargantua Coffee had launched their "Gargantua Froth of July Blowout," which was half off all purchases, with Gargantua paying the sales tax, too. Swag giveaways, drawings for snowboards, skis, mountain bikes, apparel. *Portion of Proceeds Benefits*

Mammoth Ski Team! They'd taken out ads in both local papers, and Wylie had seen the Mammoth cable channel and the Weather Channel running more ads for the Froth Blowout.

Not only that, he thought, looking out the window, but every streetlight stanchion in town was draped with banners, many of them featuring the Gargantua gorilla logo, writ large. What had riled Wylie the most was the cute yellow Piper Cub that had towed a Gargantua Froth of July Blowout sky banner back and forth over the mountain for the last three days running. Wylie had watched it, fairly sure he could shoot it down with his M16, so plump and slow and incredibly annoying it was.

"We took out ads in the *Mammoth Times* and *The Sheet,*" said Bea. "They were only six-by-six. I designed them."

"I saw them, Bea. I liked the way the steam became the words."

"Gargantua is gonna kill us."

"We're going to do what we do," said Wylie.

"Another of your random optimisms," Bea said. "Like Dad would come up with."

"I hope he slams a homer out there today."

This would be Steen's first day with the Little Red Pastry Shed, which he had gotten permission to set up in the Mammoth Sports parking lot. The lot was where all the store's bikes were racked for rental and sale, and plenty of tourists were sure to come by. Steen was expecting substantial sales, which would cover the time and material for the cart, and pave the way for profit.

A few minutes later, when Wylie opened the front doors of Let It Bean, it was to the half-dozen hale locals who met there every morning. He held open the door and greeted most of them by name, making small talk while scanning the parking lot to make sure there weren't more coming. He held open the door after the last regular drifted in. If you hold it open, they will come — but they did not.

Wylie's sisters had learned their regulars' habits by now, and set about filling the standing orders. Two customers did venture out for some of the new exotic pastries, one of them remarking that everyone would be at Gargantua today, trying to win prizes.

Kathleen came in at seven, but there was no bulge of customers at all, just a young tourist couple with twins in a double-wide stroller who told them Gargantua was too busy and the lines too long. The dad asked about fishing and the mom wanted to rent bikes that could pull baby carriers. They'd heard that bikes were being stolen in Mammoth a lot this summer. Wylie pointed out the Troutfitter across the street for fishing, and told them about Mammoth Sports, just up Old Mammoth — look for the Little Red Pastry Shed. He waited for them to make up their minds, looked back at Kathleen standing in the doorway to the kitchen. She was assessing things. Wylie hated the disappointment on her face.

The sun rose and the customers trickled in and out over the next hour. Only a few of the cutting-edge pastries sold — four burritos, some muffins. The customers just weren't there. There was usually a nine o'clock bulge, too, especially in summer, when there were no ski lifts to catch. So maybe at nine things would pick up. . . .

At one point, all four Welborn-Mikkelsens found themselves lined up with their backs to the rear counter, facing out toward the smattering of customers, with nothing really to do. Looking through the windows, they watched the vehicles coming in and out of the parking lot. Across the street, the pines were heavy and high and the sky was a chipper summer blue streaked with cirrus clouds. It would be dry and hot today.

"I used to think this was the worst place in the world," said Beatrice.

"Oh, why is that?" Kathleen asked.

"Because all winter it's so cold and so dark, and I have to be here so early."

"Well, *we* have to be here," said Kathleen.

"Yeah," said Belle. "Then off to school, with your clothes stinking like steamed half-and-half starting to spoil. You get there all sleepy and you're stuck all day. Classrooms too hot. Then home to homework, all afternoon. And in bed super early because the next day's going to be the same. Cold, dark, work. Cold, dark, work. Steamed half-and-half. School. Homework. Morning. And you can't work out early with the team when the snow is good, so you get stuck with slushy afternoons and weekend crowds. And you and Dad expect us to be great athletes. What a joke! Ask Wylie — he had to do it, too. No *wonder* he went to a war."

"I know it's hard," said Kathleen.

"There's something worse, though," said Beatrice. "It would be worse not having a here to wake up for. *Losing* Let It Bean."

"Oh, don't even think that, honey! We're doing just —"

Belle whirled around, turned her back to the customers so they would not hear. Her voice was a sharp whisper. "We're dead, Mom! The numbers have been going down for a year. You know it. You think because you and Dad keep the books, only you and Dad know. But we know! We feel it every day. We *see it every day!* Then Gargantua shows up. Now they have a line out the door and halfway to Von's. We've got this."

Wylie saw his mother's stricken look, watched her glance past Belle to the few customers.

"What we're saying is this is ours and we want to keep it," said Beatrice. "That no billion-dollar multinational has a right to take it away. And to make our dad have to go out and sell pastries from a street cart so we make enough money to live. And the new lease? And the roof at home? I hold Gargantua personally responsible even though he's a gorilla."

Eyes fierce but moist, Kathleen turned to the shelf of drink flavorings, fiddled with the bottles. "We'll talk about this *later.*"

"Sure, Mom," said Beatrice.

"Carry on, team," said Belle, stepping to the counter to service a couple of fishermen who were looking at the Let It Bean staff with uncertain expressions. "Welcome, anglers!"

Wylie caught up with his mother in the kitchen. She was slamming around the pots and pans harder than she needed to, anger frozen on her face.

"Mom, what gives?"

"Rent doubles in November, if we stay here. Stan over at Mammoth Commercial told me that Gargantua has made an offer for this space. And he told me what it will take to beat them. I don't know how the girls found out, but it's a fact."

Chapter Sixteen

Anger simmering, Wylie walked up Old Mammoth Road and saw Steen manning the Little Red Pastry Shed, and a line of customers waiting. Steen was gesticulating enthusiastically, and even from this distance Wylie could tell that he was retarding his own business. The only thing Steen liked more than baking was talking about what he'd baked. He could go on for an hour on a certain grind of cocoa. The Mammoth Sports parking lot was busy with tourists, some checking out the bikes and racks of postseason snow apparel, some eating and drinking in the warm July sun, some letting their children try to net a tagged prize-earning fish in the aboveground "Trout Derby Catch-and-Release Pool" sponsored by the Mammoth Chamber of Commerce.

From here, Wylie could also see Gargantua Coffee across the street, with its tethered balloons fluttering in the sky and its inflatable plastic logo large as a dirigible floating high, and of course the streetlight banners up and down the street with more ape-faced logos on them. There was a sun shade set up in the parking area out in front of Gargantua, and Wylie could see skis and boards and even a couple of bikes gleaming under it. A woman's amplified voice announced winning numbers.

Wylie and Steen were busy for the next hour solid. Wylie outsold his stepfather two-to-one due to Steen's yapping, but Wylie noted that the yapped-at customers just yapped right back. He didn't understand how people could be so happy buying and selling coffee and pastries. Steen had gotten the smart phone app to run credit cards. The change box had lots of twenties, some fifties, at least a couple of hundreds, and even several of the personal checks that Steen was always too cordial to refuse, though they almost never bounced.

Steen jovially blathered on. "Oh, yes, I have permission from Mammoth Sports to be here. They know I will bring in business for them!"

"No," said a young man wearing hiking shorts, trekking boots, and a Gargantua barista's shirt. He stood at the front of Steen's line, sipping from a *venti* Gargantua cup. His nameplate read JACOBIE. "I said the town. Did the *town* of Mammoth Lakes issue you a sidewalk vending permit?"

"We are very far from the sidewalk!"

"Funny," said Jacobie.

Wylie looked at him. "You're holding up the line."

"Pardon me." Jacobie stepped aside, turned to the people behind him, and swept his free arm toward the cart in an exaggerated gesture of hospitality. "I'm looking forward to the first Gargantua Mammoth Cup, Wylie. We're now the featured sponsors, as you might know. I'm Jacobie, regional manager."

Wylie looked up at the nearest Gargantua banner, then back to Jacobie. "I recognized you from the banner."

"Cute."

"It's unethical for you to undercut us like you did today. This used to be one of our biggest days all year."

"Are you calling unnecessary roughness? I feel bad now. But Froth of July is *national,* Mr. Welborn. Not just here in Mammoth. You don't take everything this personally, do you?"

"I take it personally when I see your prices cut in half and my store empty."

"To be honest, we're looking to win here

in Mammoth Lakes. But back to the Gargantua Mammoth Cup — good luck. I love it that you and Sky have squared off. Like a good weigh-in. Like the Rumble in the Jungle. It'll build the gate. Now that Robert canned up."

" 'Canned up' is disrespectful. Don't say that about Robert again."

Jacobie stared at Wylie. "So now Sky's the most talented ski crosser on Mammoth Mountain. Though you used to be a real bruiser."

Wylie considered Jacobie as he used to consider tactical situations. It always boiled down to consequences and what you thought they were worth. He tried to find that calm place inside.

"Are you judging something?" Jacobie asked.

"How far into that Trout Derby pool I could throw you."

"Violent bastard, aren't you?"

Wylie came around the cart. Steen squawked and tried to stop him. Jacobie held his ground with dissolving confidence. In the end, all he could do was drop the *venti* cup and raise both hands in frank capitulation. Like a strongman, Wylie jerked him by his belt and the scruff of his shirt, holding him high like a barbell, teetered a few yards, and pitched Jacobie into the fish pool.

The kids screamed and got splashed and the parents tried to gather them to safety. Some took pictures and video. Jacobie surfaced, throwing his head to shed the cold water.

"You'll pay," hissed Jacobie.

"You *should* pay," said April Holly. Her dour-faced mother was not far behind, bodyguard Logan towering next to her, and a square-jawed, clean-cut young man caught uncertainly between them and April.

"What do *you* want?" Wylie asked her. Right now, he was less angry at Jacobie for pissing him off than at April for seeing him this way.

"I want to know why you're violent. Why are you so violent?"

"This . . . he . . . okay, yeah, violent at this moment in time, but . . ."

"But why?"

"Ask the prick yourself."

"No call for language like that," said the clean-cut young man, stepping toward Wylie.

Wylie raised a hand and ordered Clean Cut to halt. It worked. Logan took a few steps Wylie's way, then stopped, too. Jacobie vaulted the shaky wall of the pool and plopped to the asphalt, soaked and dripping. He briskly brushed his hands together back and forth: a job well done. April was addressing Wylie and he heard her voice, but because of the water splashing off Jacobie, and the amplified voice across the street announcing the winning number, and the Trout Derby contestants bickering over whose turn it was next, and a teenaged girl now offering April a pen and a Gargantua T-shirt to autograph while she told April that her switch backside 540 was, like, epic, Wylie couldn't hear what she was saying. "*What?* Can't you speak up? I can't hear you."

April cleared her throat and projected with some effort. "I'm asking *you.* Why are you so violent?" She smiled down at the girl, signed the T-shirt, and handed it back. Clean Cut tried to help in this transaction but was too late.

Wylie tried to slow his heart and order his thinking. "Well, we've had this family coffee business for fifteen years and Gargantua's trying to shut us down so they can have all the business in Mammoth Lakes. And Jacobie, if you deny that or try to spin what I just said, I'm going to throw you back in that pool and hold you under."

Wylie cringed inside, tried not to show it.

Why, once he got riled up, could he not let a thing blow over? Especially a thing as underpowered and inconsequential as Jacobie? Escalation had always been his weak spot. And when his anger turned inward, as it had turned now, he became just plain stupid.

April looked at Jacobie. "Is that true?"

"Look across the street and figure it out for yourself," said Wylie.

"It's utter silliness," Jacobie said. "The reason he got violent is because I exposed him for the vicious clown that he is."

In hardly more than a flash, Jacobie was back in the pool, Wylie on top of him and holding him under. When Wylie finally let go, Jacobie came up gasping, fear in his eyes, and the men locked into a graceless waterlogged skirmish before two Mammoth bicycle cops waded in and pulled them apart.

Wylie got a holding cell with a homeless man, asleep and reeking of alcohol. Jacobie had the adjacent cell and they could see the rough outlines of each other through the perforated steel mesh.

Sgt. Grant Bulla sat on a folding chair outside the cages, with a laptop computer on his thigh and April Holly and her mother standing on either side of him. April and Helene had already stated what they'd witnessed, and Wylie had quickly confessed. Jacobie had gone from outrage to sullenness.

"Okay," said the sergeant, "I can write warning tickets and free both of you guys, if you both agree not to press charges. If you do press charges, it's arrest time, two calls and all that. So which will it be?"

Wylie and Jacobie declined to press charges.

"Okay. Next time, my gloves come off. I don't care who you think you are." Bulla opened the holding cells and the miscreants walked free. He took Wylie by the arm and held him back as the others moved along. "Get your act together."

"Yes, sir."

They walked toward the exit. "Those maple-bacon turnovers at Let It Bean yesterday were really something."

"Cops know their doughnuts."

Bulla smiled slightly. "I walked into that one. But good luck at the Mammoth Cup. The less time you spend behind bars, the more training you'll get in. My son is Daniel, on the freeski team, by the way. Thanks for being cool to him."

April was waiting for him outside. Wylie's

heart fell but bounced. He saw Helene at the sidewalk with Logan and Clean Cut, none of them speaking, all staring at him. Across the street, the festivities were still going on, though Wylie could see that Gargantua had given away most of their prizes by now. The big inflated gorilla logo swayed on its tethers.

"I'm sorry I had to testify against you," April said.

"I forgive you." Wylie felt foolish and repentant now and wished he could crawl into a hole.

"Have you always had that temper?"

"We go way back."

"I know the history here. And it looks to me like you've got a log on your shoulders, Wylie Welborn. Not a chip, a *log*. Why? Because certain people will not forgive you for being born. Or your mom for having you."

"What makes you a sudden expert on Welborns?"

"Tell me I'm wrong."

Wylie looked at her and nodded, felt all the old currents still running their unchanged courses, pettily violent and repetitious, channeled by the past.

"Wylie," said April. "There's a proven way to shrink that log down to a chip."

"How?"

"By hugging another person, or persons, at least four times per day."

"What?"

"It works. Give me your hands." He was too stunned not to. Hers were smooth and warm and small. She looked up at him, one corner of her mouth raised in a half smile, her eyes busily searching. He waited for her to erupt into laughter. Her voice was whispery, but it stayed on tune as she sang, "Four hugs a day, *that's* the minimum. Four hugs a day, *not* the maximum . . ."

Wylie felt his mouth part. "Mom sang that to me."

"Well, she was right. That song was written by Charlotte Diamond, who understood that hugs improve temperament. You can start by hugging me if you'd like."

She released his hands and slid her arms around him, leaning in and turning her face primly to one side. He placed his arms around April, but he couldn't commit because he wasn't sure if she was mocking him, so he bent at the waist almost formally and held her for a moment. Wylie smelled her hair and wondered if it was the shampoo she advertised. Glancing past her shoulder, Wylie saw Helene staring at him and talking to Logan, who leaned, hands on knees, beside her like a lineman in a huddle, nodding. The clean-cut young man looked eagerly to Helene, as if for a signal.

April stepped back and looked at him. "And?"

"I feel better."

"Of course you do. And are we getting negative vibrations from behind me?"

"Clearly negative."

"How come you don't shave?"

"I like my beard."

Her eyes scanned his face again. "What you like is distance between yourself and the world. I'd grow a beard if I could. I'd hide behind it. Then I'd make a million dollars doing an ad for a beard-trimmer company."

"I'd buy one. They haven't made a good one yet."

She smiled. "I'm going to Chile tomorrow for six weeks. Portillo. I'll get a good look at the next year's Europeans. Of course, we Americans invented my sport, so I've got an advantage."

"You're a beautiful slopestyler. I've never seen a triple cork like yours."

"It's all just amplitude on those triples." Her eyes were back in scan mode. "What you just said means a lot to me. My whole goal is to board beautifully."

"Good luck in Portillo, then."

"It's gorgeous there. You should think about heading down."

He nodded.

"Look, I only met him once, but I'm very sorry about what happened to Robert. I hope and pray he can recover. I've read about people coming out of comas like that. You must miss him very much." Wylie nodded, bracing himself for another hug plug regarding Robert. "Also, I don't like what Jacobie Bradford is trying to pull on Let It Bean. He denied it all, but I believe you. So you'd better watch that temper of yours, because all it's going to do is make things worse."

"That's all it ever does."

"See you later, Wylie. Four hugs a day. Minimum. *Not* the maximum."

She smiled at Wylie with all-American cover girl and Olympic gold medal wholesomeness, turned, and walked away.

Chapter Seventeen

In late August, on floor two of Mountain High, in a room behind a formidable steel door that only Bart Helixon could unlock, Sky Carson waited inside the dark, shiny belly of the Imagery Beast, Helixon's invention. The plasma glass enclosure housed him roundly on all sides as would an igloo. The glass was backed by black acoustic baffling, so it was always twilight in here, until the Imagery Beast came to life.

Behind Sky stood cabinets, glass-faced and filled with electronics. Red and blue lights pulsed or held steady. Six feet in front of Sky, an electric leaf blower was clamped to a ladder, eye level with him, the barrel of the blower aimed at his face. Glued into a hole in the top of the barrel was a large flared funnel filled with chipped ice and slushy water.

Coach Brandon Shavers's voice came to him from a small but powerful speaker mounted somewhere in the ceiling above him. "Ready, Sky? We don't have all day."

"The runs take approximately one minute, Brandon."

"But you'll be dripping sweat when it's over," said Helixon.

"I'm already dripping sweat and everything else." Sky thought that Helixon was the worst of dilettantes when it came to racers. Though to Helixon's credit, he'd invented the Imagery Beast to help racers train in the off-season. The Beast was really something. But of course Helixon insisted on hovering around and acting like he knew something about doing highway speeds down a mountain of snow with three other hell-bent maniacs.

"You should be," said Helixon. "I see on the monitor here that your pulse is still at a hundred and five. That last run was one minute, one and two-tenths seconds."

"My best."

"You can beat it," said Brandon.

"These shin bangs are bad. Much worse than on real snow."

"Eyes on the prize, Sky," said Helixon. "Your mind is a muscle and you are about to work it out again."

Sky couldn't see the video cameras that allowed Brandon and Helixon to see him, so he just flipped off the ceiling in general.

"Cute," said Brandon.

"Don't distract me," said Sky. He pulled his goggles away from his head to forestall condensation, then patiently fitted them to his face. The straps were soaked and the lenses flecked with bits of ice. He wore his baggy race pants and O'Neill jacket, which were pretty much soaked; his Head World-cup Rebel i skis with the Vöelkl rMotion2 race bindings; and his Head Raptor boots, cinched up tight. His poles were cut off short so they wouldn't hit the floor and actually move him off the sensors. He strapped his helmet and wiggled his fingers in his gloves.

"Ten seconds," said Brandon. "Nine . . ."

Suddenly, the dome around him brightened and Sky was standing at starting gate 3 on the Mammoth Mountain X Course. The course fully surrounded him in high definition, beautifully detailed. The snow glistened slightly, and downslope the branches of the pine trees dangled and swayed and cast moving shadows on the run. The tracks of prior skiers were visible. The blower roared on, huffing bits of snow and ice into his face, lightly now. He felt eager but calm, no nerves lurking inside, looking for a way to ruin this run.

Today they were focusing on flat light conditions, a treacherous combination of shadows and poor light that flattened out the course topography to the point where it was hard to read. Every racer hated flat light, especially when combined with hard-packed snow or ice. Helixon had constructed this virtual run beginning with Sky's Go-Pro videos of his runs down the Mammoth X Course. Stabilized and linked to Sky's skis through an intricate network of floor sensors, then streamed throughout the surrounding dome, the graphic course was visually authentic, and as close to being on the real course as anyone could get. Plus, Helixon could simulate different conditions of snow, light, and even wind. Due to his hours in the Imagery Beast, the Mammoth X Course — this time of year nothing more than a steep gash of rock and rubble through which mountain bikers bombed — had become more familiar to Sky than ever in his life. Much more familiar. Intimate. He was a full two seconds faster than he'd been the month before. By ski-cross standards, two seconds were huge.

The gate swung open and Sky launched and the half-pipe bowl rushed up to meet him. The shin bangs hurt, but he gave himself over in spite of them. He felt the chipped ice hitting his goggles and his racing buff, heard it tapping against his helmet. He tore across the bowl and down the first short straight to a hard right bank. He went in early and high, just above the track.

He let himself become lost, but not fully so, his mind mostly in the now but with one crafty corner of it thinking ahead to the next thing he would have to do. The clear, loud audio caught the movement of his skis with eerie verisimilitude — whispering on the powder, grinding through the ice, slashing through the turns. Even with his boots locked into his skis and his skis sensor-bound to the floor, Sky extended into the jumps and tucked into the straights, torquing his hips through Mike Cook's fast, narrow gates.

He finished the run panting hard, his heart thumping, his legs trembling. It was far more mental than physical, but still, four runs of the X Course every day, plus the exterior imaging that would come later, the weights and isometric exercises, the running and biking, all fueled by the Soylent diet, were making him faster and stronger by the week.

"One minute, three and eight-tenths

seconds, Sky," said Brandon. "Off the pace a bit."

"Chip, chip."

"Tired, Sky?" asked Helixon.

"One more run."

"Okay, animal," said Brandon. "One more, but that's all. Five a day is probably one too many. After that, we'll do some exterior imaging, then hit the weights."

"I love my Imagery Beast," said Sky.

His next run was a downhill scald, beating today's best by another one-tenth of a second, leaving Sky heaving for breath, his legs aching and his heart racing. Afterward, he knelt in the twilight to loosen his boots. The floor was opaque Plexiglas, and past his dull reflection he could see down into it like an aquarium. Sky studied the labyrinthine tangle of electronics built into the floor, which registered his slightest body movements and sent them to the computer. The boots were likewise fitted with microcomponents — a tiny motherboard in the sole, crowded with chips and capacitors and buses and wires he did not understand — and more within the walls of his boots, blinking and glowing when he stepped out of them.

He heard Brandon outside, speaking to Helixon: "So I guess they didn't arrest Wylie or Jacobie yesterday."

"I guess not."

"Wylie Welborn no longer exists," said Sky, stepping from the Imagery Beast.

"Still on that kick?" asked Brandon.

"It's not a kick, you cephalopods. It's the way it is. I'm starved."

"Weights, external imaging, then your wonderful Soylent supper."

"You're nothing but sadists living off my talent."

"Yes," said Brandon. "And we hope you have enough of it to win the cup next season."

Two hours later, Sky's daily workout was finished. Showered and replenished with chocolate-flavored Soylent and no longer hungry, his gear stashed in the Mountain High locker room, he biked back down the mountain to his place off Minaret.

It was a downhill glide and he got some pretty serious velocity. With the wind whistling past, he thought, I am large and in charge — one of Brandon's training slogans. Large and in charge is what Brandon wanted Sky believing when he went up against Wylie Welborn in the Mammoth Cup. Large was Wylie's thing, Brandon had explained. Or, Wylie *thought* it was his thing.

But in fact, nobody — not even Wylie Welborn — can own largeness, now can they?

So Sky was going to be large, too. He was going to remove Wylie's psychic advantage of largeness by becoming larger himself. In a very true way, Sky would become Wylie in order to defeat him. Sky wasn't exactly clear on all this. Brandon could get a little out there. Brandon had also suggested that Mike Cook might reconfigure the X Course into a tighter run that would favor a nimble racer like Sky and give Wylie fewer opportunities to pass. Sky wasn't sure what to make of that. The X Course had to be updated and reset anyway, so maybe Mike Cook should just do whatever he wanted. The wind shot through the slots in Sky's helmet and the tires vibrated up through his arms.

He carried his bike up the condo steps, propped it against the porch bench, and put his helmet and gloves in the outside ski closet. He thought of the rash of bicycle thefts so far this summer, way more than the usual. Of course, his mother had written about it, suggesting it was related to the sputtering Mammoth Lakes economy and the spree of ski and board thefts last snow season. He locked the bike to the porch railing.

Adam had bought Mammoth homes for most of his twelve grandchildren, and Sky's was this two-level at Sunrise. A dog shrieked inside. Sky waved to the mom who lived across the parking lot. Not many people here in summer. Most of the units were rentals owned by out-of-towners. He pushed the door open and stepped in. "Hey, baby, look who's home!"

Megan hopped off the couch and came across the room. Ivan the Terrier was already right there in the foyer, making a protective stand on stub legs, barking insanely, a Jack Russell on yet another mission.

"He's still getting used to you, Sky. You're still new to him."

"You're old to me," he told the dog.

"Don't hurt his feelings." They hugged and the dog continued his tirade. "How was it, Sky?"

"A minute one and a tenth!"

"You're amazing! Johnny Maines told me last night at work that the Imagery Beast is the best way he's ever trained without snow."

"Who cares what Johnny Maines said?"

"I sure don't!"

Sky kissed the apple-scented part of her shiny dark hair, broke away, and hung his backpack on a coat hook by the door. He looked around his home. It was sunny and tastefully decorated thanks to a former girlfriend. Sky thought it was cool, for the most part, to have a woman in his home again. His gaze settled on Meg and he smiled. She had surprised him with her sudden announcement last month — breaking off with Johnny Maines and confessing she'd always wished she was with Sky in the first place. Well, well. He liked her. She was straightforward, easy on the eyes, affectionate, and only about one-fifth as crazy as Sky was, in his estimation. She brought great desserts home from work most nights, though Sky could only watch her eat them because of his commitment to the Soylent diet.

Ivan the Terrier shot to the far screen door to get at a jay that had landed on the deck railing. Luckily, the dog understood something about the word *screen* and didn't blast right through it, though it seemed likely that someday he would.

In the moment of relative quiet, Sky met Megan's eyes again. "Good to be home," he said.

"Maybe later we can take Ivan for a walk in the meadow," she said. "But I could sure use a little nappy-poo first."

"Me, too!"

She took him by the hand and led him into the bedroom, shutting the door before Ivan could follow them in.

Chapter Eighteen

Wylie towed the MPP up the back side of the Sierras in four-wheel low, with slow, agonizing caution — the only way to finally arrive at Solitary.

This side of the mountains faced west and south, getting even more snow than the east side, where the lifts and town were built. Even now in August, the higher westside elevations were still packed with snow. But it was very steep country, heavy with boulders and conifers, slashed by sunlight and shadow, and there was only one primitive two-track road that, if you knew where it ran beneath the snow and you could keep your tires on it, would eventually land you in Solitary.

Adam and Dave McCoy had built the road with their own hands, cutting down the trees and bulldozing the rocks ten yards at a time to create the narrow passage. Used dynamite, too, Adam had told him. It took their "spare" time for the better part of three summers. Adam said that Dave McCoy had more energy than any person he'd ever seen. To young Adam, Dave McCoy had been a hero, a cross between Zeus and Paul Bunyan.

For Wylie's twelfth birthday, Adam had brought him to Solitary. Very carefully showed him the way in. They had spent three days and nights camping and fishing, birding and reading, glassing for bears, before packing up and skidding their way back down the mountain in first gear. Two flat tires. Over the years, they had camped at Solitary for a few days each October, around Wylie's birthday, weather permitting, until the war and his travels had taken him away.

Now, as his truck crawled up the mountain, Wylie's memory arced back to that first camp they'd made at Solitary. His tent had been green and Grandpa's yellow. He remembered stripping the lime green lichen off the kindling and the reluctant little campfires that took him so long to create. And fishing the creek for brook trout that darted for the banks like golden bullets. They'd hiked into backcountry so remote, it had been seen by a few scant handfuls of human beings. They had seen an eight-point white-tailed buck and a silver-faced black bear his grandfather guessed weighed four hundred pounds. They had dug for hours, hoping to find fossil bones, but found no bones at all. In his memory Wylie was light-headed for three straight days. Not only from the elevation, exertion, and the breath-snatching majesty of the Sierras, but — with his mother having told him about his conception — from realizing that Adam was closer to being his real father than any man could be.

On their last night at Solitary, Adam had told Wylie about his son.

You should know that Richard was a good-hearted man. He was generous. He was funny. He was handsome, and people were drawn to him. He was arrogant and vain, too. He had trouble maturing because I spoiled him, as I spoiled all my sons and daughters. That is my greatest failing. So Richard had little sense of consequence. He did not have the judgment required to be a sound man. He sensed this. To mask it, he tried to be lovable. To be admired. That's why Cynthia chose him — because she knew what he was inside and how to shape it. But he betrayed her, and that is part of why we're sitting here tonight, Wylie. Sometimes consequences are good. I won't dwell on Richard's flaws. He was a bright and shining star, more bright and shining than he knew. People loved him. Dogs loved him. He brought home a baby raccoon once and kept it in his room, and the creature was tame around him and violent toward everyone else. It acted like Richard was its mother. Richard loved to ski, but he did not love to race. He preferred being graceful to being victorious. He badly wanted to be like me, and to live up to my expectations and please me. I wish that on no son or daughter. When you think of him, know that your father had a good heart. And know that if he had lived, he would have brought his share of wonders into this world. Even beyond Andrea, Robert, Sky, and you. Inside, most everybody in the world is pretty much alike. Those who are different shoulder a load for the rest of us. And that load is not always light.

Now Wylie goosed his truck through a barricade of pine branches so thick he couldn't see beyond them. He was aware of the MPP fighting along behind. He prayed to God to deliver his trailer from scratches. And to be able to stay on the narrow, occasional path. So far, so good.

Three times he stopped and fired up the chain saw to lop off low-hanging limbs. He stood on the wall of the truck bed, careful of his balance as he swiped the heavy, smoking machine through the trees. The branches dropped and the air filled with the smell of gas exhaust and pine pitch and the sun felt hot and unfiltered on his upraised face.

When his truck trundled over the last, steep outcropping of boulders, he felt the vehicle starting to level. A moment later, he was on his first flat ground — nearly flat ground — in three hours. He could smell the clutch and his temperature gauge was getting up there. He looked out at Solitary, pulled forward a hair more, then cut the engine and stepped out.

The snow on the meadow floor was thin at this elevation. Up-mountain on the run, it got deep fast. Madman Run — Dave McCoy's and Adam's name for the slope — rose dramatically before him, still deep enough with snow to ski. Madman began above the timberline, a precipitous but wide run that narrowed to chutes through sudden stands of white-bark pine and mountain hemlock, lodgepole and red fir, then opened into a steep, unobstructed schuss that tailed out and gently flattened into the broad meadow in which Wylie now stood.

He looked down to the little alpine lake that Dave and Adam had named Breakfast Lake, for the many gullible brook trout they had caught there. Breakfast Creek wobbled into the lake, barely visible in the trees. Between the lake and Wylie's truck, the meadow floor was a mosaic of snow patches and wildflowers, mostly blue lupine and red snow plant, which gave the meadow a patriotic look. The air was sharp and cool.

He leveled and unhitched the MPP, then set up camp. He hoisted his cooler into a tree whose branches were strong enough to support it but not strong enough — hopefully — to support a black bear. He stopped to watch four deer in the cottonwoods lining the creek, looking at him attentively.

When he was done with the cooler, he stood a few yards away from the MPP and tried to fully appreciate it in this context. How could this svelte man-made confection even be in this wild place? It was the equivalent of one of Steen's perfect pastries, labeled and in its paper cradle, sitting atop Mount Everest. He shook his head at his good fortune, photographed the MPP from several angles, thought of the yawning aloneness and the huge exertion that were to be his for the next three days.

It was early afternoon by the time he was ready to set off for Madman. Enough time for two runs, he thought. He strapped on his snowshoes and started up the edge of the run, where the snow was shallow and he could sidestep confidently without sinking. He stopped and rested on his poles. The incline was steep, and the way was long. You asked for this, he thought. Within minutes he was breathing hard, but he timed his breath to his movement to make a rhythm, stuck to it, made some progress. He stopped and looked up again, panting now, not believing how far he had to go.

Forty minutes later, he was above the timberline, at the top of Madman, lungs dry, heart beating hard. He stepped up to the very edge of the cornice, snowshoes strapped fast to his back, ski tips in the air. He sipped from the nozzle of the hydration pack. Down-mountain the breeze in the pines made a long, distant rustle. He felt the familiar brew of fear and exhilaration jostling around inside like two ski crossers dueling for the best line, the brew more potent after Wylie's five-year absence.

He waited for a break in his thoughts.

The fire was hard to start, as usual. He set a small circular grill across the rocks and heated a can of stew. He watched the flames cast light and shadows against the MPP and felt his vast aloneness. Solitary was right. He thought of lovely Pilar at Great St. Bernard's Hospice and mysterious Juncal at Tegernsee and noted those lovers' great distance from here and now. But really, it was only months.

He wondered again if he'd done the right thing in coming home. To what avail? He'd regained his family but lost a brother. He'd resumed a pointless lifetime feud. He'd found a *possible* way to help the people he loved — and realized that he'd been avoiding just that for a number of years now. And maybe, in the same *possible* way, he could help himself. For the first time in his life, Wylie had a plan that included more than just a short-term future. That night at Jesse's, around the barbecue, he had described his idea to Jesse as a dream — his first official Wylie as a grown-up Dream — which at the time had struck him as pompous and bourbon-induced.

But now, bourbonless at ten thousand feet, *dream* still rang true to him. He felt confident he could win the Mammoth Cup. It would take training and luck. Then, close on the heels of the Mammoth Cup would come the X Games and an even higher level of competition. More training and more luck. But the World Cup tour? The Olympics? He almost scoffed, but he didn't. Why not the Olympics? Why couldn't that be his dream? Wylie Welborn, Olympian. *Olympic ski-cross medalist Wylie Welborn.* Were only certain people allowed to dream that? Which people? So what if he was almost twenty-six? So what if he couldn't afford to tour?

After dinner, he burned the paper bowl and towel, stashed the stew can in the cooler, and hoisted the cooler back into the tree. He set more wood on the fire.

He stepped into the MPP with irrational pride. By the light of an electric lantern, he made up the MPP bed, using Jolene's mock-Navajo blanket. He climbed in and propped himself up, closed his eyes, and imagined his first run down Madman just a few hours ago. Not bad. It was tentative enough to test the snow and find the hidden patches of ice and to avoid the lower trees and the potentially deadly wells around their bases. But tentative on Madman was still close to breakneck on most any other course.

His second run was made with heavy legs and a mind dulled by hours in a bumping truck and nearly two more hours of high-elevation climbing. Wylie could tell he was twenty-five and no longer twenty. But maybe he could overcome age with training. And this was the place for it. It always amazed him that he could find conditions like today in any but the driest and warmest of years. Solitary, Madman, and Breakfast Creek — all his. A private paradise to train in, Grandpa's birthday present. Adam had told him once that he'd brought Sky here for his twelfth birthday, too, but Sky had never, to his knowledge, come back. *It takes a certain mind-set,* Adam had said.

Wylie yawned and felt his energy all but gone and the sweet call of sleep. The box in his mind that housed the Taliban sniper from Kandahar had wandered to the edge of its shelf, where Wylie was now surprised to find it tilting in precarious balance. Sometimes his own tiredness allowed the boxes to spill. Sometimes they'd empty in his dreams when he was defenseless, and all he could do was wake up drenched in sweat, repack them, and place the boxes where they belonged, just so.

He lay in the module and looked up through the portholes at the bright pinpricks of stars and planets and the wide granular dusting of the Milky Way. These seemed indifferent to him, but not wholly different from him. He heard the steady sough of the wind in the trees and was for a long moment unsure where he ended and the world began.

That night, Wylie dreamed he was in Portillo, Chile, after having driven the MPP all the way there to see April Holly. In the dream, April was beautiful but skeptical of him. He had brought her some board wax you could get only in Mammoth. She made jokes about the trailer. In his dream, the MPP had sat silently, absorbing the jokes, riddled with bugs and dirt from the six-thousand-mile journey from California to Chile.

When Wylie woke in the early morning, the battery-hogging lantern had all but run down, but the sunlight was waiting just outside the portholes above him.

Breakfast Creek gurgled in the distance.

He made three runs that day and three the next. He timed each of the latest runs for the last minutes of light before thorough darkness closed on Solitary. The moon was right. In this final twilight, Wylie's reflexes had to be quicker, while operating on less information. He finished his last run on the third day in moonlit darkness, planes of silver and black rushing him in rapid overlays, guided half by his senses and half by faith.

Later, he bathed in Breakfast Creek, then bundled up in Jolene's blanket in the MPP. He put on Jolene's wool boot socks, too. He read and wrote by the freshly charged lantern. He drifted off to sleep, still believing that his idea of making the Olympics was not just a foolish indulgence. In the morning, he felt the same way. It was a quiet confidence, no swagger in it, just faith. The same faith that had guided him down the mountain in the near dark.

Chapter Nineteen

As promised, Wylie got back to Mammoth Lakes the next day in time for the town council meeting. Steen's application for a sidewalk vending permit had been contested, which required a public hearing before the council, where all sides could be heard.

The Town Council met upstairs in the Von's shopping center, Suite Z. Steen thought it would be a good idea to show pictures of the Little Red Pastry Shed, so he had two foam-backed posters made from Beatrice's photographs, and borrowed two easels from an artist friend in town. Wylie and Beatrice helped Steen set them up in the space between the town council members and the citizens. Beatrice kept adjusting them for good viewing angles. The photos were good, in Wylie's opinion, showing the bright colors of the shed and the beautiful blue Mammoth sky. The town hall seats were full when the meeting started at six.

Wylie and his family sat in the first row.

He turned and saw Jacobie Bradford III seated near the back, legs crossed and head down, thumbing away at his phone.

"Corporate swine, back row," Belle whispered in Wylie's ear.

He set his hand on the soft spot behind her knee and squeezed firmly. "Now now."

The mayor called the meeting to order and got straight to old business. He recapped the previous month's discussion of adding three waste-collection bins along Minaret, near the creek. All voted in favor.

Then they talked about the rash of bicycle thefts in town. Coming on the heels of so much ski and board thievery last season, the stealing of bikes was a real problem. The good news was that two suspects had been sighted by two separate witnesses on different nights, cutting bike locks with bolt cutters, putting bikes in the trunk of a car and then driving off. The perps were described as males, both bearded and wearing ski caps, somewhere between twenty and forty years old. Their car was an older model, and one of the witnesses had photographed the plates with her cell phone and turned the pictures over to the Mammoth

PD. Just as with the skis and boards last season, these thieves knew an expensive bike from a cheap one. The mayor's own son had lost a two-thousand-dollar Cannondale road bike Sunday night, left unlocked and pinched right off his front porch. The council voted unanimously to up the reward to two thousand dollars.

"Now, on to new business," said the mayor. He was a restaurant owner and had long been a Mammoth ski team booster. Wylie did wonder if a sidewalk vending permit for food and beverage might go against a restaurateur-mayor's grain. The mayor summarized the guidelines for sidewalk vending permits, took a long moment to study the posters, then asked Steen for input.

Steen went to the podium and nodded politely to the council and the full house. He pulled a sheet of paper, folded lengthwise, from his pocket, then began reading. "Thank you, friends and neighbors, for being here tonight. The Little Red Pastry Shed is in keeping with the town of Mammoth Lakes because it is handsome and well made. It will offer top-quality artisanal pastries and gourmet coffees at good value to both locals and guests. The shed provides its own power by generator and solar panels, which you cannot see in the pictures, but they are located . . .”

Wylie listened, but his mind was back on Madman, third run of the second day, the most difficult because of the falling darkness. Still, somehow he’d been allowed into that privileged place where his body was working almost on its own and his thoughts were able to skip ahead just enough that nothing on the run could surprise him, nothing could even come at him in any real hurry, although this was his fastest and tightest run of all. The final schuss had left him wired by adrenaline but utterly at peace.

“. . . and it is my dream to move the pastry shed from location to location in town as a moveable feast, so that everyone will get a chance to buy our wonderful pastries and coffee.”

“How many times have you done business from the shed without a permit?” asked the mayor.

“On July the fourth and three times after. For a total of four days.”

“Is it profitable?”

“Not greatly, but yes. In those four days of operation, we made approximately four hundred dollars. This is revenue enough to cover our rent at Let It Bean for five days.”

"Not bad."

"Of course, we have the cost of time and materials to build the shed. And we do need a new roof at home, which will be very expensive."

Wylie flinched at Steen's admission of family financial troubles.

"Why did you proceed without a permit?" asked another councilperson. He was a real estate agent, whom Wylie recognized from his picture in the local listings, but he'd never met the man. Wylie realized now that the photo was probably two decades old. His nameplate read HOWARD DEETZ.

Steen nodded contritely. "I . . . didn't know if the shed would earn us even one dollar. And the application is expensive. For us."

The councilpersons shrugged, traded glances back and forth, and sat back in odd unison. "Open to public input now," said the mayor. "The mike is open."

Steen headed for his seat and Jacobie made his way to the podium. Wylie saw that Jacobie was not dressed for Gargantua Coffee, but for fly-fishing. The cleats of his wading boots clicked on the floor. Wylie had heard from a friend at the Troutfitter that Jacobie had paid in advance for one hundred half days of guided fishing over the rest of the summer and fall. At full retail, the bill would come to approximately $25,000, not including tips. Jacobie's face was absurdly tan and his long-billed cap sat at a cheerful uplifted angle. His caped, vented, multi-pocketed shirt was a pumpkin color, and his sleeves were rolled and buttoned up.

Jacobie introduced himself and stated his position as the Gargantua Coffee regional manager. He said he'd grown up in the Bay Area but loved the Eastern Sierra and aspired to own property here so he could visit often. In fact, he was now actively looking for a home to purchase. He joked about how the locals had kept fly-fishing a secret from him for so long, and said he was making up for lost time. He stated that he actually felt like a local when his road bike had been stolen the previous week. He had ridden it to work at Gargantua, locked it up behind the shop, and when he'd come out ten hours later, the bike was gone. He made a show of looking at the pictures of the Little Red Pastry Shed, then cleared his throat.

"I contested Mr. Mikkelsen's permit application because my company's toughest competition in Mammoth Lakes is his very wonderful Let It Bean. I make no secret of this. From our point of view, this Little Red

Pastry Shed is an extension of the Let It Bean place of business. Now, as you all know, according to Mammoth Lakes code, sidewalk vending is restricted to special city-sanctioned events. No full-time permit exists. With good reason. Mammoth Lakes is the jewel of the Sierras because it has strict but fair codes with regard to nonadjacent sidewalk and out-of-doors vending that does not coincide with city-approved events. That's a mouthful. But it's really pretty simple. No such permit exists. And we want Let It Bean to play by the same rules we do."

Belle stood before Wylie could stop her. "You hypocrite! You've been trying to run us out of business for almost a year now! Now you won't even let us fight back!"

The mayor fumbled around for his gavel and finally gave it a good three raps on the tabletop. "You are out of order, Belle."

"Damn right I am." She dropped back into her chair and sat glaring at Jacobie.

He looked at her with his eyebrows raised and his hands open. "There's no such permit. You don't expect the town council to invent one for you. Do you?"

"Give them *some* kind of permit!" someone called from the back.

"There's no permit to give!" someone else replied.

The mayor slapped his gavel and ordered the citizens to come to the podium or be quiet. "Jacobie? Is that all?" Jacobie thanked the council and started back to his seat. The mayor solicited comments from the council, but all declined, apparently having decided. There was a brief off-mike exchange, and the nodding of heads. Howard moved to take a vote and someone seconded. Four no votes were cast against the mayor's aye, and the matter was settled. "Sorry, Steen," he said. "Too bad. Okay, we've got Mammoth Park dog-waste stations to talk about now."

"Do the dogs need permits to use our sidewalks?" Steen shouted out. Wylie saw by his smile that he was trying to be funny, but the councilpersons and mayor shot him looks as he stood there red-faced. Wylie helped him collect the exhibits.

Chapter Twenty

Adam and freeski team coach Brandon Shavers stood at the head of the Mammoth X Course. The August morning was warm for the Eastern Sierra, and a wildfire burning to the northwest had spread a blanket of gray-white smoke over the mountains.

Adam looked at his watch. "Mike Cook is never late," he said.

"Actually, I told Mike ten o'clock," said Brandon.

"But you told me nine," said Adam.

"I wanted to go over a few things. This Gargantua Cup is keeping me up nights."

The X Course was snowless and the boulders stood exposed. Adam picked his way down the course for a look from the first jump. So easy to picture this run in its full bloom of snow, and to see himself not sidestepping down the rocks as a rickety octogenarian, but carving youthfully through the turns, throwing rooster tails of snow behind him. At eighty-seven years old, he wasn't quite up to the X Course, though the gentler Mammoth Mountain runs were still heaven on Earth for him. What really made him aware of his age wasn't his skiing, but how damned slow he had become at the mundane daily tasks: getting his socks on, tying shoes. He could go crazy, waiting for old Adam Carson to get out of his way.

Beyond the physical, Adam was also now suffering what all serious skiers and boarders suffer in late summer — the dread that it wouldn't snow again until almost next year. Adam and people like him talked snow and thought snow and dreamed snow. Their bodies craved it. The young people called this "fiending," and Adam kind of liked that word. Plus, in Adam's case, since his livelihood was snow, he felt a businessman's practical fear that another terrible warm winter was surely coming. Adam had lived the Sierra snow for most of his life and he saw that the snow came later and left earlier now, that the averages were down and the ski seasons were shorter, and he believed that only a fool could deny that the world was heating up.

Brandon caught up with him, breathing a little quickly. "Grandpa, what I'm hoping to do is reconfigure this course for the best

Mammoth Cup ever."

"You can't. You're not the course setter."

"Well, yes, I know that. But Mike is open to reason, and I'd like to talk to you about some changes."

"Fire away, Brandon."

Adam looked at this grandson-in-law, then back to the course, and in a heartbeat he was back in the United States Army recruiting center in San Francisco seventy years ago, just turned seventeen, thinking about signing up for the war. A sergeant who looked a lot like Brandon looked now — upright, blockish, and somehow untrustworthy — said he would do his best to get Adam into some action in the Pacific. The Japs were on the run. Adam expressed interest in the European theater, because of the mountains and the snow. The recruiter had said that of course, with the German surrender, Europe was slowing down but that he'd see what he could do. It was August 3, 1945, a Friday.

The following Monday, Adam was on foot in the weirdly cold city, headed back to the recruiter to sign up after a weekend of soul-searching, when he heard that the United States had dropped an atomic bomb on Hiroshima. He signed up anyway. Very difficult, saying good-bye to Sandrine. Aside from Sandrine, Adam had no direction in life except to go down mountains of snow on heavy wooden skis, faster than anyone else, but there was no place to sign up for that.

"I'd just like to tighten up this course a little," said Brandon. "I love Dire Straights and Shooters and the schuss to the finish. I love Goofball and Conundrum — you know how many magazine shots we get taken on those? But what I'd like to do is *add* two new gates. And maybe consider flattening out Dire Straights a little."

"Why?"

"I want to slow the whole course down, just a hair. Grandpa, the USSA and boarding brass are all leaning this way for the other courses, mostly for safety. I mean, what happened to Robert was just a terrible accident. And, you know . . . Nick Zoricic dying at the World Cup finals. There's going to be backlash, and I want to be ahead of it. I honestly think a more technical course would be safer and help the Mammoth team."

"Specifically, Sky."

"Well, him for sure — and Scotty and Trevor, and for certain Maria and Becky. Pretty much all of them."

"But not Wylie Welborn," said Adam.

"No. Not him. He's more of a straightforward downhill racer."

"Whereas ski cross is supposed to be a combination of downhill and slalom."

"Right, Grandpa, and BMX and motocross and NASCAR and speed skating all that other stuff they say. And that's not just PR talk. There's something very . . . primal about ski cross." Brandon smiled knowingly. "You'd have torn up this course in your day."

The U.S. Army recruiter had given Adam the same fraudulent smile when he said he might be able to get Adam over to the French Alps, or maybe Switzerland.

"Brandon, my gut tells me to let Mike make whatever adjustments he sees fit. We've talked about the extra padding on the lift poles, of course. What we had was sufficient, but he wants to double up on it, out of respect for Robert, and to admit that bad luck can defeat good plans."

"I know Mike listens to you."

"I'm not going to ask him to change one inch of this course."

"I thought you'd like to give Sky a more level playing field."

"Sky and Wylie grew up on this thing."

"With all due respect, Grandpa, sometimes it seems to me that you favor Wylie over your own."

"He is my own."

"You know."

"He's got the Carson blood, Brandon. He didn't even have to marry into it."

Brandon blushed and his mouth tightened like a plastic coin purse. Adam was surprised to see him so taken aback. "Maybe I overcompensate," Brandon said.

"You make Andrea happy."

"I try very hard at that. I've never so much as raised my voice to her. She's my . . . priority. We gave you three beautiful great-grandchildren. They are Shavers, and I'm very proud of them. But Grandpa — I have a problem here. Wylie badly embarrassed the team by throwing our biggest sponsor in the fish derby pool. Twice. After embarrassing the team by coldcocking Sky at Slocum's that night. He could have really hurt Sky. And you know what gets me most about all of it? Not one *word* of apology out of Wylie."

"I wouldn't think so."

"What kind of a team player does that?"

"I'm aware that you and Wylie have some history."

"He called Andrea a 'fat twat' when she was a sophomore in high school. That hurt her feelings because she was insecure at the time. And somewhat overweight."

"Wylie was in sixth grade, wasn't he? And you broke his nose for it."

"I had to do something. Now I'm the coach. I have to do *something* again. So, here's the deal, Grandpa. The other night I decided to reread the bylaws. And I realized that the selection of the ski and board team membership is up to the committee for each team. But as I read further, I found out that the, well, *deselection* of an individual team member can be done by each team coach, respectively. The term *gross misconduct* is open to interpretation, but I think Wylie's qualifies."

"So you can throw Wylie off the ski-cross team."

"Correct. It's section three point four, paragraph G."

Adam studied his grandson-in-law. Even with the blackout wraparounds hiding his eyes, Brandon appeared nervous, if not just plain guilty. "I just had a funny thought," said Adam.

"Oh."

"Yes. The idea came to me, right out of the blue, that you and your lawyer friend from Palo Alto added paragraph G just after Wylie came back and wanted to try out for the team. One of your last-second changes.

And I got this other funny idea that you had the draft bylaws printed so small, your beloved grandpa Adam wouldn't have the patience to read them before he signed off."

Adam watched as a two small crescents of condensation crept upward from the rims of his grandson-in-law's sunglasses. "None of what you're implying is true."

"The last part sure is — I *didn't* have the patience to read them before I signed off. So don't be silly, Brandon — I'm just stating self-evident truths."

"Good God. All I'm trying to do is coach a team."

"You do that. And leave the course to Mike."

"Adam — I'm going to kick Wylie off the team if you don't get Mike to make the course adjustments I need. For the good of the team. I have no choice."

"I won't ask, and Mike wouldn't anyway."

"But if Wylie's not on the team, he can't use the mountain before the tourists swarm in every morning. A half-day ski pass, five or six days week? It would cost him half of what he makes at Let It Bean. So he won't be able to train properly. Which means his results will suck and the USSA won't help him get on the World Cup circuit. No Europe means he won't see the real competition. The USSA can afford to send only the top two or three — you know that. If he's not on the team, Wylie won't even get skis or boots or bindings or the Volcom gimmes or the damned free breakfasts at Gargantua. He won't get squat. It's simple as that, Grandpa. So talk to Mike. Please. Wylie's future is on you."

"Make your own mistakes, Brandon. You appall me."

"Then Wylie's off. Fuck it, Adam. He's off my fucking team."

Later Adam, Cynthia, and Bruce, the nurse, made sure that Robert's temporary reconnections were properly made, then got him dressed and settled into the wheelchair, strapping him upright. It was tiring, time-consuming work. Cynthia brushed Robert's healthy blond Carson hair, fluffing it up and patting it down with her free hand. Then she worked onto his expressionless face a new pair of sunglasses with stars-and-stripes frames and dark reflective lenses. "You look good, Robbie. Very handsome indeed."

Now it was Adam's job to push the chair down the walkway from Cynthia's house and muscle it over the curb to the dark, pine-shadowed street. Once they had gotten to Main, the bike path was wide and smoothly paved.

This first stretch was slightly downhill and Adam let Cynthia take the helm. She smiled to no one in particular as she took the grips from him and lengthened her stride. She wore forest green camouflage pants and a long-sleeved T-shirt, green camo hunting boots, and a wide-brimmed green camo fabric hat. The clothes were cut for women, and Adam thought she looked stylish in a very strange way.

It pleased but didn't surprise him that Cynthia had become happier in the six months that Robert had been with her. For some years he'd thought that the widow needed more to do than skulk around Mammoth Lakes, asking questions and making notes for her weekly "newspaper." He'd been right. For one thing, she was trimmer now, with all the wheelchair exertion. Her complexion was ruddier with the almost daily time outside, and she moved about now with a good carriage instead of her old hunch-shouldered, I'm-not-really-here posture. There was a good-size piece of Adam that still loathed Cynthia for what she'd done to his son, but a larger piece felt empathy with her. They had all lost their beautiful Richard. Son and husband and father.

"This camo contains odor neutralizers so game can't smell me," she said.

"Yes, I've read about it in the catalogs."

"I bought the winter versions back last year. In the 'Snowy Bark' hunter's pattern, I'm virtually undetectable in snow."

"You could wear regular clothes and let people see you."

Cynthia nodded. "I've never gotten used to my own celebrity."

The afternoon had grown hot and the gray-white underbelly of smoke hung closer in the west. Like droughts and weaker winters, wildfires were another thing Adam had seen increase in his lifetime. Cynthia stopped and pulled her hat back on its strap and shook loose her yellow-gray ponytail. "I think Robert's beginning to become aware of me, Adam."

"How can you tell?"

"First, it was the eyelid flutters. Now it's his breathing. When I talk to him about certain things, his respiration speeds up. Such as skiing. Or Hailee. Or Sky, or even Wylie. There's this deeper inhale? And I believe it to be a precursor of speech. Like he's trying to get enough wind up to deliver a word. Or even just a sound."

Adam wasn't sure what to do when she talked like this. Who was he to question her hopes? Or to endorse her misconceptions? "I have to believe that he feels the sun on his face right now," he said.

"Darned tootin' right he feels it. I know what being inside without sun feels like, just like Robert does."

They went into the liquor store for refreshment. Cynthia removed Robert's sunglasses. Adam got one of the newish energy drinks, which tasted great and dispatched a heavy dose of caffeine through his old system. Expensive. He wondered what Teresa was doing right now. Teresa, thirty years ago the waitress with the raven black hair and the beautiful smile, now a mother of four grown children and long widowed. Now thirty pounds heavier, her hair half gray. But — and this was the part that sometimes made Adam dizzy with happiness — she was just as preposterously beautiful as she had been way back then. Maybe more. Beauty was all about perspective. It came from you. He felt lucky to have had her in his life. First as an attentive waitress, then as a trusted employee who — when she'd lost her firstborn and Cynthia had begun her prison term — became a wet nurse for Sky. Now as a most dear companion.

Robert's head bobbed gently as Adam pushed him from the cooler to the cash register. Cynthia was asking the clerk about upticks in shoplifting in the summer months, due to the cooled tourist economy. In fact, the clerk had seen an uptick: Just last night, he'd called the cops on two young men who ran out with a bottle of rum and a twelve-pack of cola drinks. Cynthia had already taken the small notebook and pen from the book bag she hung on one of the wheelchair handles. Now she made notes.

Adam set the wheelchair brake with his toe, put his drink on the counter, and dug out his wallet. Cynthia traded in her notebook and pen for a folder. She carefully removed the latest issue of *The Woolly* and handed it to the clerk. "Let me know if the shoplifting continues. I think it's an important local story."

"Yes, Mrs. Carson. Hello to you, Robert."

"Robert is sending his regards. See, his eyelid is fluttering."

Adam set the bill on the counter and glanced down at his grandson. Robert's face was serene, his hair was just right, and his right eyelid was quivering. Adam told himself it meant nothing. Told himself again. But he thought, I'll be damned.

Outside, he drained the drink and tossed the can into a recycle bin. "Shall we do this thing, Cynthia?"

"I'm kind of dreading it," she said, working the star-spangled sunglasses back onto her son.

"You look fine, Cynthia."

"Well. It's not about how I look, Adam. Why did we agree to do this?"

"Sky's deal. It means something to him. Look, he's already there."

Chapter Twenty-One

They arrived in the Footloose parking lot a few minutes later, where *Adrenaline* had arranged to shoot the interview. As Adam pushed Robert toward the store, he saw Sky talking to the host, Bonnie Bickle. *Adrenaline* aired on Extreme TV and was one of several shows about young daredevils doing crazy things and living to tell about them. On the show, Adam had seen young people kite-sailing in a hurricane, wriggling through tunnels a mile below Earth, towed by Jet Skis into fifty-foot waves. It reminded him of when he was young. They had had the same crazed bravery, but less imagination. Or was it more imagination? Either way, he liked the show.

Sky waved and continued yapping with the host. Adam was getting a little tired now, but with help from Cynthia, he pushed the wheelchair toward the set. He had had a premonitory bad feeling about this interview and the feeling had grown stronger. Too late to get out of it now. Bonnie Bickle shouted and pointed his way, and a videographer hustled over for this human-interest moment, tracking three generations of Carsons as they rolled along. Finally, Sky came over, and Rialto, the director, got them seated, then clipped on the mikes. Someone moved the light towers closer, and Adam could feel the extra heat on this already hot day. He helped Cynthia get a cap emblazoned with MAMMOTH FREESKI TEAM onto Robert to shield his face from sunburn.

Bonnie introduced herself and shook their hands. She looked as on TV, but smaller and more serious. She had a quirky smile and large teeth. She knelt before the wheelchair and withdrew one of Robert's hands from the blankets. "Robert, with all respect, thanks for doing this. Do you understand me?"

"Don't underestimate him," said Cynthia.

"I won't." Adam watched Bonnie look into Robert's face as she pushed his hand back under the blankets. By the way that Robert was strapped upright in the chair, the way the new cap sat on his head, and the way that you could tell the eyes behind the sunglasses were seeing nothing, Adam realized that what he had hoped might be a dignified program about his family might well become something else. "Thanks to all of you for being here," Bonnie said. "Sky, special thanks to you for pitching us this story. It's going to be a good one. We're calling it 'The Carson Curse.' "

Adam's heart dropped.

"That wasn't my pitch at all," said Sky.

"No worries," said Bonnie. "It's just a handle for the sponsors."

"But this show is supposed to be about how we're turning bad fortune *around,*" said Sky. "And me winning the Mammoth Cup for Robert."

"Exactly. Rialto?"

Bonnie seated herself and Rialto arranged her mike, then got back to his camera and counted down. Adam looked at Robert's serenely empty form, then at Sky's dubious, eyebrows-arched assessment of Bonnie. She looked down, took two deep breaths, then turned to the camera with a smile and introduced the Carson clan.

Bonnie started with the beginning of skiing in the Sierras, when Dave McCoy envisioned the first ski lift here on Mammoth Mountain, and couldn't get a business loan to buy one, so Dave and Adam had built one with their own hands from a car engine.

Adam's mind shot back to the day that Dave had invited him to test-ride the first lift once again, after days and days of it failing — too fast, too slow, the ropes snapping, the cable threatening to decapitate someone — and Adam took hold of the crude handle and let it pull him five hundred feet up the mountain. Sitting here in the Footloose parking lot now, Adam didn't feel the artificial light and the hot August sun, but, rather, the cold breeze in his hair as he gathered himself for that first run off the new lift. He felt the heft of the wooden skis and the cumbersome bindings and the eager thump of his heart. He saw Sandrine and Dave and Roma down the mountain, their small faces turned up to him. And again he felt that sweet drop of stomach as he launched.

"You're best friends with Dave, aren't you?"

"Yes. He was my best man."

"And together you took Mammoth Mountain from just a mountain with snow on it to the third-most-visited ski resort in America."

"Dave did that. I just helped."

"Adam, you helped build a town that a lot of people think is paradise. You had children make the U.S. Olympic ski team. You made a lot of money. You have had a charmed life, haven't you?"

"I always thought so."

"Until tragedy struck for your son, Olympic downhill skier Richard Carson. Now, our viewers should know that this *Adrenaline* segment is the very first time that Cynthia Carson — Richard's widow — has spoken publicly about that tragic night. Cynthia, welcome to the show. And I know this might be difficult, but can you tell us what happened?"

"Hey!" Sky called out. "Hey, Bonnie Bickle! This is fully uncool."

"What is?"

"This story was supposed to be about the Gargantua Mammoth Cup and me against my rotten half brother!"

"We'll get there, Sky. I'm backgrounding. Now, Cynthia Carson — tell us about that night here in Mammoth Lakes, in January of 1990. You were married to former U.S. Olympic downhill skier Richard Carson, you were thirty years old, a mother of two, and you were pregnant with Sky. You went to a party. Take us there. . . ."

"Well. Don't forget that I was an Olympic skier myself. I competed in Sarajevo, as did Richard. The downhill, slalom, giant slalom, and the combined. Neither of us made it to the podium, though I finished higher than he did."

"Fantastic. Now take us back to that night."

"Oh my gosh, where to start? There was this rich man's house where all us racers went to have fun? Richard went there early, as he always did. I stayed home with the children, as usual. Andrea was four and Robbie was three. They finally went to sleep. . . ."

"And you went to the party?"

Adam looked at Sky, flip-flops propped on the footrest of the director's chair. He was looking down and kneading his right thumb into his left palm. "Leave her alone, Bonnie," Sky said, cutting her a look.

"This is an interview, Sky."

"The story is not that night!"

"I'm okay, son," said Cynthia. "But thanks for your concern."

"I can't believe this shit," he said.

"Say whatever you want, Sky," Bonnie said cheerfully. "We'll beep out the too-naughty stuff."

"Okay, then — I can't believe this fucking shit."

"You're funny, Sky Carson."

"Mom, you don't have to talk to this doorknob."

Adam watched Sky consider Bonnie for a long moment; the boy's coldness surprised him. Adam had never seen *that* look from his grandson. But he recognized it. It was Cynthia's, when you thought she was going to fold up or go to pieces. When you thought she'd been defeated. Then, suddenly, she was absolutely certain and capable. As Sky was now.

"Let your mother continue," said the host.

"I'm okay, Sky," she said, but Adam heard the tiredness in her voice.

"Bonnie?" asked Sky. "Are you aware that you're exploiting a family tragedy for entertainment and a paycheck? Can you formulate this concept in your small ornamental brain?"

"I'll work on it," said Bonnie. "So, Cynthia, Richard was at the party and you were home alone that night, and?"

"Oh, well, of course I got bored. So I called some friends to come sit with the children. I drove over and went in and got myself a diet soda from the fridge. Had some potato chips and pretzels —"

"And was your husband, Richard, there?"

Cynthia's voice sounded thoroughly weary when she spoke again. Adam wondered if she'd be able to continue. "I thought I'd made that clear."

"Where was he? Where was your husband and what was he doing?"

Adam heard Cynthia clear her throat. She looked at him. At first, he saw the tiredness in her eyes, the worry, and maybe even panic crouching quietly in there. But he watched all of this slowly give way to an expression of wintry calm, forged from something pale and hard. Like a time-lapse film of water freezing, thought Adam.

She turned to Bonnie Bickle. "Richard was down in a basement bedroom with a very young woman named Kathleen Welborn and they were engaged in S.E.X. Under the covers, somewhat. They were so involved, they didn't even know I was there."

"That must have been awful."

Sky hissed something incomprehensible.

"It was for me," said Cynthia. "Not for them. But what happened after was awful for everyone."

"Which was?"

"I went home and got my gun, then came back to the party and shot him. Five times, up close. He was in the game room by then, playing beer pong. The first shot went through his heart and he was dead not long after he hit the floor, according to the coroner. Of course I didn't know that, so I made sure. Five shots, total. I came *that* close to getting first-degree, because of the leftover bullet and the time between what I saw and what I did. Prosecutor said I was a manipulating wife and a calculating killer. Those lies hurt me more than the truth ever did. It came down to the judge. He felt sorry for me. And by then, he was probably sick of the whole pathetic mess. Wouldn't you be?"

A long silence. Adam listened to the cars and the crows cawing over the trees and the mutterings of the crowd that had gathered.

"Wow," said Bonnie Bickle. "So. Thirteen years in prison?"

"No, thank you, I've had quite enough," Cynthia said politely. Adam watched her snug down her hat and slip on her sunglasses. He set a hand on her arm, which was trembling.

"Bonnie," said Sky. "Maybe we could discuss extreme sports. Like this show is supposedly about."

"Certainly, Sky. Let's talk about Robert, and how the curse of the Carsons seems to be continuing."

"Robert's not a curse; he's a blessing."

"But can you take us back to the last Mammoth Cup ski-cross finals, when Robert — in the lead — lost control? We're going to show that clip now, so you take over and call it for us, will you?"

Adam tried to watch the miserable clip. He'd seen it too many times. What if Robert was aware? Adam looked out at Highway 203 heading out of town, at the cars winding down the mountain, and an eastern sky untouched by smoke.

"You can see for yourself what happened, Bonnie," said Sky. "What's important is that Robert is a great man and a great brother. He is the finest ski-cross racer I've ever seen. So I'm going to win the Mammoth Cup in January for him. And he's going to stand on that podium and help me accept the trophy. I don't say this as a publicity stunt. It is a fact that you will witness."

"Does Robert have a chance of recovery?"

"His doctors are, of course, utter fools. But Mom has been getting Robert out into the sun almost every day. We're seeing that the stimulation has started to rebuild the damaged neural pathways in the nerve bundle. He's already using his eyelids to signal certain . . . recognitions."

"Really? Can he, like, blink once for yes and two for no?"

"We hope to be there by the fall."

"Okay, Sky, you don't want to believe in a Carson curse, but tell me about your half brother, Wylie Welborn. Most *Adrenaline* viewers know about Wylie Welborn, but for you people out there who don't, Sky — your father, Richard, was Wylie Welborn's father, too."

"That's insightful of you, Bonnie."

"And your mother, Cynthia, as she just told us, killed Richard in a jealous rage — after catching him in the act of, well . . . *creating* Wylie Welborn. You and Wylie were born one hundred and forty-four days apart. Looks like the beginning of bad blood to me. In fact, you and Wylie have a history. You recently posted serious threats against him on social media. You called him a 'demon bastard.' That's a quote, Sky. So tell us, is Wylie Welborn part of the Carson curse?"

"He is the curse incarnate. That's why I'm going to beat him in the cup."

"Wylie Welborn won the cup five years ago on his first attempt. You've won only one time in eight tries."

"Oh ye of little faith. I'm training well. Eating well. I have a new girlfriend, Megan Brown, and she's totally into me. I've cut way back on the partying. I'll win. You can bet on it in Reno or Vegas if you're so inclined. Robert and I will stand on the podium with our gold. Wylie Welborn will not."

"What if he runs you off the course, like you claim he did in practice?"

Adam saw Cynthia's look of calm come to her son's face again. It wasn't quite as strong or thorough as hers, but it spoke of the same resolve. Sky leaned forward toward the camera. "Chip, chip, chip, Bonnie — you're part of the curse, too. And we Carsons are out of here."

Adam stood slowly and readied himself behind Robert's chair. His knees and back were stiff after sitting this long, and his sudden memories of Sandrine and Dave and those early days had left him wistful. Yes, he thought, I want to be young and strong again, but I cannot. So let Sky be young. And Robert. And Andrea. And Wylie. All of them. I have appointments to keep.

Camouflaged Cynthia came over and dug into the book bag hanging from the wheelchair handle. "I could have been an Olympic medalist," she whispered to Adam. "But I chose to raise a family for your son instead. These half-wits understand nothing." She got her folder from the book bag, extracted this week's edition of *The Woolly,* and walked it over to Bonnie. The host smiled politely and gazed at Adam with a questioning look.

Maybe there's some truth in the Carson curse after all, he thought. He'd had that idea before. And he'd wondered more than once, Have I made it better or worse?

Chapter Twenty-Two

Richard had more than his share of women, and this was no secret when I met him. Soon after, I found myself in the same condition that Kathleen would find herself in years later. But Richard wasn't married when he made me pregnant. I lost the child later, but Richard had already committed to me — a late spring wedding here in Mammoth, then a long summer honeymoon in the Andes of Chile — and I wasn't about to let him off the hook. He didn't struggle much. We were happy. And hell-bent, as all good ski racers are. We had mountains to conquer and medals to win. Marriage? Oh, why not? We were young and talented. The Sarajevo games were coming.

So the idea of Richard straying from me was there from the start. I told him once, just once, that if he betrayed me, I would punish him. How, I didn't say. But I was very clear as to degree — it would be serious. Extremely so. But the precise idea of doing what I did was never in my head until that night. And then it seemed like the only thing I could do. I didn't agonize over the decision. I've taken longer deciding on a sweater. I just saw that I needed to do what I'd said I would. It was as if I had one line in a play and now it was time to step out and deliver it. Only then did I know what I was going to say.

Oh, and I was furious.

After Adam and I got Robert home from that difficult *Adrenaline* interview, we bathed Robbie and Adam left. He was very tired. I was buzzing with the energy I am known to have for long periods. Years ago, the meds were useful, but I've outlasted them. I really don't like other people's hands inside my head.

We who live on mountains learn never to waste one second of summer, so I went back out late that afternoon with my green camo still on, hat and all, and headed for the Welborn household, which is less than a mile from my condo.

I kept to the trees, of course, so as not to advertise myself. This is where the camo comes in. We have so many lovely old pines and firs in Mammoth, you can almost always find yourself a cool, fragrant pool of shade in which to rest and observe. That's why we have so many fine bears. So I came upon the

Welborn household from behind and found just such a cool place in which to hunker, and so I hunkered.

Their home is an unremarkable wooden structure near downtown, off of Cornice Bowl, with a gambrel roof and dormer windows, painted pale green, very typical 1970s mountain construction. It sits in a little swale and behind it is a slope on which Robbie and Sky would occasionally ski with Wylie, I am told, during their brief détentes when they were all very young. You know how children veer from enmity to affection so quickly. I remember how in prison my body would recoil at the thought of my sons playing with my husband's bastard child. It was a very raw feeling, and a helpless one. There is nothing that takes away hope faster than a cage. I very much enjoy the popular women's prison show on TV now. It gets the crazy energy that cooping up people produces. It gets the fact of contraband and how the COs are not necessarily better than the inmates. They get some of it wrong, too, such as the fact that in a real prison, nobody inside thinks they deserve to be there. Every last one has an excuse or maintains innocence even with reams of evidence against them. The emphasis on sex is exaggerated, for certain, though I do remember three women — one small and the other two large and mannish — who were physically/sexually intimidating to the others. I messed up one of the big ones with the heel of my hand once, broke her nose like it wasn't even there, stomped her, too, badly. They never bothered me again. I think they mostly had sex with one another, a deserved punishment, if you ask me. Personally, after I shot Richard, I never wanted to have sex again with anybody.

Today my timing is good, and from my spot here in the trees I see Wylie and his sisters come from the house and get into Wylie's truck. That cute little wooden trailer is hitched to the back. They make the turnaround and swing right past me, but they don't see me. I wear nothing reflective and I close my eyes as the windshield lines up with me, so they can't see even a twinkle of light from my cornea. Watching is a lot like sitting in a cell, so far as your options are concerned. But I know I can stand up and walk away when I'm finished. Belle is pretty, like her mother. Beatrice is tall and still slender and she moves self-consciously. I suspect she lacks a solid view of herself. I know from my investigations that she is a near-regular at Helixon's party house. Any seventeen-year-old girl with wobbly self-assurance entering Helixon's place is marked for trouble. The party mansion where I shot Richard was just like it — same booze and drugs and reckless abandon you find anywhere there are promising young people and pandering leech-dilettantes living vicariously off them.

You would be right to ask what I'm doing here at the Welborn-Mikkelsen home, what I'm trying to accomplish. I have an answer: I am here because I am related to these people. I feel somewhat responsible for them, too.

Of the three most important things to learn in a life, I have managed only the first two.

I look my deeds straight in the eye.

I see what I have coming.

But that third, most important thing is the hardest by far and I have not learned it.

I have not changed direction.

This, because I have not forgiven Kathleen and Wylie Welborn for what they did. So I watch. And wait, related and responsible, looking for a way to forgive them.

I move on to Mountain High. I park short of the mansion by a few hundred yards, get out, and hike up to the house by way of the tall stands of conifers lining the road.

There's a good evening lie for me on the southwest side of the house, recessed in the trees but about eye level with the spacious deck. I'm backed into it and pretty much invisible from the house. The partygoers have drinks and appetizers out here, watch the sunset. Tonight, I have jerky and an energy drink waiting in my satchel, along with my 10 × 32 bird-watching glasses. In the warmer months, such as now, Helixon's guests stay on the deck well past nightfall and they're easy for me to glass, illuminated by the fire from a big central pit built of stone and copper right in the middle of the deck.

Peering through the binoculars, I see the Mikkelsen sisters talking with Johnny Maines, and Jacobie Bradford approaching them right now in the orange-black flame shadows. As he draws near them, it's easy to see how strongly the sisters dislike him, how they stiffen, determined not to back away, not back down, not let him push them around. I'm momentarily proud of them, given Gargantua's multinational muscle versus a tiny coffee pub run by the two teenage daughters of an aging Mammoth Lakes party slut. I almost laugh at the symmetry here, slut and slutlings, history repeating. Jacobie hands each of them a drink with an umbrella in it, bows humbly, and gets guarded looks from them. I see this very clearly in the binoculars. Then the Mikkelsen sisters, in unison, hand their umbrella drinks back to Jacobie and walk away. A minute later, I see them and their two friends, way down on the street, getting into an old Chevy.

Sky and Megan come onto the deck from inside. He's got a beer and she a glass of wine and there's a sense of calm about Sky that I like. He's every bit as up and down as I am, always has been, but he's never given in to the meds idea, and I do not blame him. These days, he seems not too high and not too low. He and the girl have a nice thing going. I've never seen him focused so intently on anything as the Mammoth Cup. Ever. More to the point, he's doing all the right things to get ready. Making commitments. Trying to follow through.

It's interesting to watch your own children when they don't know you're there. Sky behaves differently with me than with the rest of the world, of course. He's got more swagger when he's away from me, and, oddly, more humility to go along with it. I like those things in a man. Richard was extreme swagger, but underneath it was a swamp of self-doubt. I knew what that meant, knew what he was asking for. Sky's asking for it, too. They're asking to be loved. And that's how you get them to do what you want.

Later, I see Bart Helixon come out to the deck with a woman dressed as Tinker Bell. She spins off his arm and throws her fists toward the fire. Her hands open and the fire erupts into a swirling mass of bright green flame. When Sky goes inside, I get up and sneak from viewpoint to viewpoint, all around the perimeter of the house, moving higher and lower but always deep in the trees, hitting the good viewing angles through blindless windows and doors left ajar and sliders open to the fresh, cool air. When I can't find Sky anymore, I'm on my way.

Town is quiet. I place some current issues of *The Woolly* in the stands for free newspapers outside the Do It Center and Let It Bean, then on to Mammoth Liquor and back around to Von's and the Booky Joint, my favorite small bookstore. I note the police station across the street, where I spent some inglorious time after the shooting. I see that Gargantua is busy, even at this hour. They are staying open later and later, with light dinner items on their P.M. menu, and all manner of decaffeinated coffee and tea concoctions. They are clearly trying to run Let It Bean out of business and I think they will succeed. Maybe it would be good for the Welborns and Mikkelsens to make a fresh start somewhere else. They could find their own mountain. Quit dwelling on the past. This is a Carson mountain and always will be. And don't get any big ideas: I may have been born a Boyle, but I can out-Carson any Carson. Ask anyone.

I head down Old Mammoth Road to Main and stop at the light. I see a man loading a bicycle into the trunk of a long, older car in the Do It Center lot. He's in overalls and a beanie, bearded, and moves quickly and nervously, like he just can't wait to get that thing into the hole and away. The driver's a bearded guy, too, and he looks straight ahead through the windshield, as if nothing unusual is taking place. I read about these guys in *The Sheet.* They've been spotted stealing bikes around town. I've seen them before, too. I can't make out the license plate number from here. Binoculars are no good in the dark.

Abruptly, their car lurches, makes a 180, cuts across the lot, and bounces onto Main without stopping, heading up toward the village. The cop house is less than half a mile from here, so these guys have some real stones. Or real stupidity. Of course I must follow. I can't run the red light with a Boar's Head delivery truck lumbering down at me. When the light changes, I try to catch up, but by the time I make the signal at Minaret, I can't tell if the bike thieves have gone right, left, or straight.

That's okay, because I have an idea where they're headed. I saw these two malingering behind a big empty house up near Canyon Lodge just three weeks ago. Up to no good, it looked to me. Their old boat of a car stood out in that tony 'hood, I can tell you.

So I head up Main, cut through the village on Canyon Boulevard, cruise all the way down to Canyon Lodge, and sure enough, I see the old car pulling around behind the same home as before. Twelve Madrone. It's a big river-rock and wooden Craftsman, two stories. Always one of my favorite styles. It's got a FOR SALE sign out front. A light comes on inside. I drive past and around, and looking through the trees, I see the old car now parked in the garage of that big almost-mansion, and the garage door going down and one of the thieves lifting the trunk lid.

I loop back and park and watch for a few more minutes. Pretty soon the house light goes off and the garage door rises and the old car backs out. As it makes the slow reversing turn to exit, I catch, in the driveway motion-detector lights that suddenly spring on, a glimpse of the thieves. They look so different from the way they did just minutes ago, when they were stealing that bike. I rub my eyes and the old car rumbles back down toward town.

Chapter Twenty-Three

On a Saturday morning in early October, in the fragrant interior of Let It Bean, Wylie knelt behind the counter to clean the inside of a lower refrigerator. It was something to do. The place was almost empty. Not only was presnow autumn the slowest time for tourists but Gargantua had launched Y-Not? Days, which meant half-off prices from 6:00 A.M. to 8:00 A.M. "On Any Day That Ends in Y!"

Some of the locals were sticking it out with Let It Bean, but Wylie saw they were doing half the business they'd done in early summer, which was half of what they had done five years ago, when they were the most popular gourmet coffee shop and bakery in town.

With the Little Red Pastry Shed now history, and the fourteen-thousand-dollar roof job looming, and the lease here on Let It Bean soon to be doubled by a new landlord,

Wylie felt the same cold undertow of shortage that was part of what had pushed him away five years ago. Again he wondered about his nontriumphant return home. Toil and trouble. Now he wanted to stay and make things right. He wanted to help his sisters, mother, and Steen get a better shot. He knew he had a chance at the cup. After that, the X Games and FIS circuit and the Olympics were higher levels. Could he be good enough? All of that was technically possible, but another part of Wylie wanted just to light out for new territory, get back into the bigger world that lay beyond this mountain.

Now Beatrice was banging around in the kitchen and Belle was tucked into one of the leather chairs by a window, reading her world history textbook.

Wylie, still crouched, heard the bell on the door chime and sensed incoming customers. He kept at the fridge, giving the newly arrived patrons a minute to read the wall menu. It was amazing how much time some people took to figure out what size coffee to buy.

"What's a person have to do for some service around here?"

He recognized the voice and stood. "You have to want it badly."

"I badly want a pumpkin scone and a double nonfat latte."

"Welcome back from Portillo."

"Thank you."

Wylie watched Belle look up from the book as if surprised, then wave coolly. He knew Belle idolized April Holly by the offhand and often dismissive way that she brought April into conversations over and over.

"Looks like some serious homework there, Wylie's sister," said April.

"Like I need to know when the First Crusade left Constantinople."

"One thousand ninety-nine. You should see Rhodes. It's beautiful, and their coffee is Turkish — almost as good as yours. Wylie, you've lost weight."

"Been training hard."

"How's the module?"

"Personal and portable."

April was tanned from the Andean sun and snow and she wore an Inca-style knit sweater with a band of characters holding hands across a white background. The figures all wore gloves and caps and boots. Wylie watched her curls dangle as she unsnapped a colorful woven coin purse.

"This is on us," said Wylie.

"But —"

"If Gargantua can give away skis, I can give a coffee and a scone."

"Please accept our gifts!" called out Belle. "Is Portillo, like, the best resort ever?"

Beatrice peered in from the kitchen and April smiled at her. "It's unbelievably fantastic. You should go there sometime. Not to train. But to have *fun.*" She pushed a couple of bills into the tip jar and hooked a bouquet of curls behind one ear.

"And you should come here every morning," said Wylie. "You'd get great coffee and pastry and you'd bring us more customers. And I could give Gargantua the finger."

April snapped the coin purse shut and dropped it back into her bag. "What? Still no inner peace? Haven't you evolved at all in the last two months?"

"No. But they threw me off the Mammoth freeski team, if that makes you feel better. I'll have to battle the tourists for X Course leftovers."

She frowned. "Because of what you did to Jacobie and Sky?"

"I think there was some politics, too, but I don't know for sure."

"That's an awful thing to do to you."

"I'll keep up my dry-terrain training program until the snow."

"Splitting wood and running?"

"Correct." Wylie bagged the scone and handed it to her, then moved down the counter to make her coffee. The previous week he'd spent another three days making his secret vertiginous moonlit runs down Madman. He felt right. Legs and eyes strong, spirit firm. But still no snow on this eastern slope. The earlier it came to Mammoth, the better. As he'd discovered on that first run down Madman back in August, he was twenty-five now, not twenty. He needed more time on snow. There was no invitation to the Imagery Beast from Bart Helixon. And when the snow finally did come, having to share the X Course with the tourists would be an expensive handicap, but he'd have to make it work.

"Where's your mother and the dwarf?" asked Wylie.

"Gave 'em the slip. I've got a day to recover from South America, then hit the gym and pray for snow. Nice to be free for a whole day."

Wylie steamed the milk into the espresso, sprinkled some cinnamon on the froth, and worked on a plastic lid.

"I'll drink it here," said April. "Unless you're trying to hustle me out."

Wylie gestured to the empty chairs and couches. There was a nice little fire going, though, and magazines all about skiing and boarding and fishing. What more could an Olympic gold medalist want? He poured the drink into a big ceramic mug and set it on a saucer in front of April.

"Manners, Wyles!" Belle whisked around him, picked up the saucer and mug, and took them to her favorite table, near the window and the fire. After April had settled into one of the red leather chairs, Belle moved the saucer just a skosh closer to her, gave Wylie a look, and headed back across the room.

With no more customers, Wylie knelt down and went back to work on the refrigerator. When he stood again, Beatrice and Belle were both seated in red leather chairs at April Holly's table and the three were tightly engaged in conversation. They all stopped talking and looked at him at once, his sisters proudly defiant but April smiling.

Wylie went about his work, looking over at them now and then from various inconspicuous angles. April caught him once, or did he catch her? A couple came in and headed toward the counter, faces raised to the wall menu.

She stayed almost two hours, talking with the girls, signing autographs, and posing for pictures with the steadily growing stream of social-media-informed fans. With her around I really *could* give Gargantua the finger, he thought. To Wylie, she seemed earnest, asking questions, considering her own answers. He kept a weather eye for falseness but saw none. But when the rush was over, he saw April sit back and let out a big sigh. Her face looked a little slack. He offered to see her out.

They walked up Meridian toward the Starwood homes. The golf course grass had gone pale and the tractors were already taking up this year's turf. Wylie shortened his stride to match April's, though she was a brisk walker. The sunlight lit her hair and freckles and bleached the blue of her eyes. When she smiled, April looked almost impossibly happy, and he wondered how much of this was her act. It certainly brightened magazine covers and sold shampoo. But now, up close like this, her face looked puffy and tired and older than when she'd left two months ago. "You must be thrilled to see me again," she said.

"I am. I thought about you."

"Thought what?"

"There's this run we call Madman. It's a secret. Adam Carson showed it to me years ago, a good steep run, and you have to use snowshoes to get to it. I've been hitting it hard. I think of you when I go down it. Think of you boarding it, I mean. It's not a slopestyle course. Just a straight alpine schuss."

"No one else was there?"

"Deer."

"And what do you do at night?"

"Grill up the catch. Read and make notes. Listen to music. Sleep like a rock."

They continued slowly up the gentle grade. Wylie felt proud and privileged for the chance to walk alone with April Holly. Like he'd won it in a contest. He was hoping a carload of friends would come by, just to witness this.

"That sounds fun," she said. "The second I turned pro, they tried to take the fun out of boarding. I had to fight to keep it. Still do."

"How old were you?"

"I had sponsors at eight, Mom and an agent lining things up. Pressure. You?"

"Sixteen, I got skis, boots, and bindings. And free breakfasts at Main Lodge after workouts. I loved those."

"We athletes live weird lives. Sometimes I think we're born to do what we do. Other times, I think we get a notion in our heads because it's all around us when we're young. But then they make a pro out of you and everything changes. They, like, melt you down and pour you into these body molds so you can reanimate and become a champion and make money."

He smiled at this, but she did not. "You're the best there is," he said.

She looked up at him. Her standard public expression of permanent sweetness seemed far away now, replaced by something somber. "Wherever I go, I see two kinds of people," she said. "Mammoth? Aspen? Portillo? It's all the same. There're the ones who love what they do. They're at their best when they're doing it. Then, there're the ones who want to be the best in the world at something. And to prove it by winning."

Wylie had come to the same conclusions. There were two basic paths: to be *your* best or *the* best. "Which are you?"

"I live for it, Wylie. Launching into the sky at high velocity, doing impossible things? That's my best me — doing something beautiful in the air. It's what I care about most. What about you?"

It took Wylie some time to put words to the complex brew inside him. "The other. I need the Mammoth Cup for a shot at the X Games. If I can do well at the X Games, I'll have a shot at the World Cup tour and the

U.S. Olympic team. I don't know if I'm good enough, but if I can get to the podium in South Korea, my family is set for life. I'd get endorsements and job offers and who knows, maybe another Olympic shot when I'm thirty-two. I could buy the space for Let It Bean instead of Mom and Dad leasing. Hire some help. Get the girls out into the world. Give a rest to Mom and Steen. This is my first official dream. So, I have to win."

"So you want fame and riches."

"Sure. Sign me up."

"So skiing is a job?"

"If I win, it is."

"Oh, man. No pressure, Wylie!"

They walked on. On the flanks of the Sierras, the aspens had burst into orange and the cottonwoods were coined with yellow. The meadow grasses glimmered white in the sun. Wylie felt a sudden desire to talk. "And there's Robert. I want to win for him because I love him and he loved racing and now he can't even walk. That sounds corny, but it's true."

"That's not corny. It's love, looking for a way to show itself."

They continued up Meridian and along the golf course. Wylie successfully stole another glance at April. He thought back to when he and his friends had sneaked onto the golf course to steal golf balls and seen a large black bear digging a gopher out of a fairway, and the clots of good green turf flying through the air.

Now, loading up ahead, Wylie saw the forest that surrounded Starwood. Mammoth had still not recovered from the recession and real estate crash, so many of the beautiful Starwood homes now sat locked and empty. They slowed their pace. "So, Wylie, you have to beat everybody in the world to get what you want?"

"Every one of them."

"It must be scary, saying you're going to do that. Because if you fail, the whole world will know you've failed at what you wanted most. They'll know and you won't be able to hide it. And they'll use your pain against you."

"You must feel that pressure, too."

"Oh, yes, I feel it."

"You board for yourself, but there's got to be a part of you that wants to blast the opposition off the snow. Just being out there says you want to win. And you know those other slopestylers think the same, teammates or not. No friends on the mountain, as John Teller told me once."

April nodded along but said nothing for a

long moment. She stopped and gave him a half smile. "I love winning. But being on the podium isn't as good as being in the air."

He tried to steal another look at her, but she was studying him closely. "I love skiing, too," he said. "When I'm coming down Madman, there's no one to even beat!"

"Don't let racing be only work. It can't be only that. Mom and the coaches always say, 'It's your destiny and your job.' And I keep trying to fight off that job idea." She was still looking hard at him, blue eyes roaming his face as if searching for something. She reslung the bag strap over her shoulder and they continued up Meridian. "Why did you give it up? You were at the top of your game."

"I had to launch."

"Meaning that we athletes live narrow, self-obsessed lives and have no idea of the real world around us?"

"I saw that happening to me."

"Most of us pros don't have an idea of the world."

"You knew about the Crusades."

"I got lucky and had some good tutors."

Wylie could see the Starwood houses huddled in the trees now, and the black Escalade with April's face and the yellow

Team Holly logo on it. Helene Holly and extra-large Logan climbed into the vehicle and slammed the doors. "Here comes your posse."

"Mega crap."

"We can cut across the golf course and hide."

"I'd feel childish."

"Me, too. We never ran from the skinnies, and they were trying to kill us."

"I've never thought of my mother as Taliban."

"She has that look."

"Do you want to blast Sky off the mountain in the Mammoth Cup?"

"Positively." Wylie watched the SUV turn onto Meridian and start toward them.

"Everybody's heard about his pledge to beat you. And I saw his selfie threat, what he'll do if you run someone off the course again. I also got the gossip, Wylie, even way down in the Andes, and what I heard is that half the freeski team saw you run Sky off the X Course, and the other half saw him try to do that to you."

"Vote Wylie. I barely touched him. I forced him off his line and he lost his nerve."

April stopped mid-sidewalk and gave Wylie another long assessment. The Escalade whooshed past them and Logan made a U-turn. "You idiots should wake up and make up. Lose an enemy and gain a brother. It would lighten both your loads and you'd ski better."

"Would I have to hug him?"

"That's a shitty comment." The SUV came to a stop behind them. April looked back, then at Wylie.

"April? April!" Helene's voice cracked sharply in the warm Sierra afternoon.

"I apologize then, April. But I don't have anything to make up with Sky. He makes messes; then other people have to clean them up."

"April, we are late for the two-thirty! Please? Now!"

"Four hugs a day happen to *work,* Wylie. I was about to start my hugs today with you. But you can wait and I can, too."

"It's my loss."

"I hate your detached sarcasm."

"But I meant it."

She wiped a sudden tear from each eye. "I broke my engagement. His name is Timothy and we've known each other since ninth grade and he is a good, good guy. It was the hardest thing I've ever done in my life."

"April!"

April turned. "Shut up, Helene! Just shut

the *fuck* up!" Then she wheeled on Wylie. "Don't you say one word."

An Escalade door opened and slammed, and looking over April's shoulder, Wylie saw Helene marching toward them.

"Look me in the eyes, Wylie." April's voice was a hurried whisper, almost a hiss. "I thought about you every day in Portillo. It was *ridiculous.* I texted you every day, and deleted them. I couldn't wait to get back here and see you. There's no order left inside me, and I don't like it."

"I dreamed I drove from Mammoth to Chile to see you. Slept in the MPP."

"I wish you had."

Helene stopped short of them. *"Honey?"*

"I dreamed it twice."

"April — we just really can't leave ESPN waiting, can we?"

"Come ride Madman with me," said Wylie. "We'll stay a few days. Adam and Teresa will be there, too. For adult supervision."

"You really do think I'm a sheltered child, don't you?"

"Nothing childish about this."

"I can't do something that foolish."

"Sure you can. Soon, while the weather holds."

She looked at him unreadably, then turned

and walked toward the vehicle. Helene came to Wylie. "Stay away from her. She's very vulnerable now. She has no time in her life for you or people like you. April wasn't born to lose, Mr. Welborn. Surely you can see that."

Chapter Twenty-Four

The evening of that same October day, the Black Not began creeping down on Sky Carson. He happened to be with Megan at Mountain High. What terrible timing, he thought. Just when he was feeling healthy and strong and optimistic.

The Black Not — Sky's name for it — was a black shapeless thing that slowly draped itself over him, tarlike. He could never get a good look at it. While it lowered and began to seep into him, it talked to him in his father's voice — a voice he'd actually never heard except in recordings. The Black Not made him feel bad about things, very bad, and it brought him pain, surely as a poison. He could keep it off him for a day or two at most. Then it would have him for three, maybe four days. Those days were hell on Earth. He had been free from it now for nearly seven months.

He sat there in Helixon's theater with

Megan, nursing along his second beer of the whole night and watching *Fight Club* for the forty-eighth time in his life, trying to prepare himself for what was to come.

"I want to go home," he said.

"All right. Okay. Though this *is* one of my nights off."

"I hope Ivan hasn't torn apart the other couch."

"He's still just a puppy."

Sky lay in his bed in the dark with her, Ivan locked out but scratching inquisitively at the door. Sky looked through the blinds at the ragged outline of the Sherwins, darker than the sky and topped by stars. "I love you," he said.

"I can tell something's wrong."

"Uhhh . . . yes."

"Is it the dog?"

"It's in addition to the dog."

"Talk to me."

"I get low sometimes."

"I heard. That's okay. We all do."

"Okay."

"Dangerously low?"

"Very low, yes."

Ivan scratched at the door with vigor, growling softly.

"Is it me?"

"No, it's not."

"I'm good for you, Sky."

"I'll need to be alone for a while."

"It's me."

"I swear it isn't."

"For how long?"

"A few days."

"Let's have sex."

"God, yes."

By now, Ivan was tearing at the door with industrial strength. There were odd pauses, then the sound of the dog rending wood with his teeth. Sky turned to Megan and wrapped his arms around her and pressed his body against hers. His desire, urgent and whole, blocked out the dog, and, for a moment, even the Black Not. Megan's mouth was warm and her taste was sweet. And those apples in her hair! Then the Black Not found him and Sky sensed its blackness easing closer and he heard his father's voice again, the one that as a boy he had played over and over and over on video to save in memory, now telling him, *You'll ruin love, Sky. Like I did. And it will be the end of you.*

"Harder," she said.

Later, Sky rose and let in Ivan, who flew onto the bed and defended Sky's place as his own, backed into the pillow, his butt hitting it with each bark. Two weeks ago, the dog would have bitten Sky, but Ivan's ferocity was waning and now he allowed Sky back into the bed with only warning growls and barks. Megan turned the pillow and patted it and Sky lay down next to her. They looked out the window at the stars, always good in the fall. "You don't have to leave here, Meg. I have a safe place to go. It's kind of a regular deal."

"How regular?"

"Once a year. Maybe twice."

"Is this the first since we've hooked up?"

"Yes, it is. I have a favor to ask before I go. I'd like to take Ivan with me."

There was a silence. "He's my dog. I'd miss him."

"I know, but I want him with me."

"Why? He's not . . . sold on you yet."

Coming down from the lovemaking, Sky was aware of the Black Not having moved closer. He felt the first little burst of pain in his stomach, always in his stomach, left side and low. Like a bee sting, but deeper. Followed by a hard ache that would grow in area over time. Until it had his whole body — the quick of his nails, the nerves of his teeth, the arches of his feet, even his testicles. "Ouch."

"What?"

"Nothing. I want to take Ivan because I like Ivan. And he'll distract me."

"You can have him for your trip. Can you call me?"

"No bars out there."

"I hope you're not just playing me like your next dumbass chick. I'm trusting you, Sky, but I don't tolerate disrespect. Zero tolerance. Take care of Ivan. You know what he means to me."

"I should get a move on."

He hit the market and the gas station on the way out of town, got his usual provisions, and for Ivan a box of chew sticks designed to clean his teeth. The dog stood on the passenger seat with his front paws on the window frame, watching the world go past.

Three hours later, Sky was down south and west of Randsburg, in the high desert, wind whistling through the hard arroyo of rock and scrub where the cabin stood. His truck bounced up the last half mile of two-track, Ivan managing to keep his balance and a weather eye on the rock-strewn, sparsely vegetated, faintly moonlit desert.

Sky came to the cabin and parked. It sat in a loose stand of Joshua trees, which shivered spikily in the wind. Dug into the western hillock above the arroyo was a long-abandoned copper mine. The tailings formed a pyramid at the base of the hill and the tailings glowed blue in the moonlight. Sky got out and stood a moment and looked at the blue light surrounding the mound like a halo. Ivan waited at his feet, still, nose to the wind, ears cocked.

The cabin belonged to an acquaintance Sky had given ski lessons to one winter, and who was willing to replace the window glass the vandals broke, and keep it locked and baited against the kangaroo rats. No water or electricity, which suited Sky fine. Inside, it had a picnic table and benches, bunk beds with thin mattresses, perfect if you had a sleeping bag.

The important thing was the privacy, being able to confront the Black Not without having to worry about the commotion. You couldn't go through a battle like this with people around. People trying to help. People watching you unravel. Straitjacket time. He hoped Ivan could handle it. Dogs were forgiving. Years ago, he'd come here with Tyrell, a formidable pit bull/rottweiler mix who had kept a silent eye on Sky through the rantings and ravings. More than once. Tyrell was big enough that Sky hadn't worried about the coyotes here. The dog had met his end against a speeding driver on Minaret one evening, and Sky hadn't yet found the heart to get another. Which had left him vulnerable to Ivan's charms.

Before unpacking, Sky poured two fingers of añejo tequila into a coffee mug and took that first promising sip. He was still living almost totally on Soylent, which had ground a few pounds off his lean frame but allowed him greater strength and stamina in whatever he did. Earlier this week, his runs on Helixon's Imagery Beast had been nothing short of amazing. Even Brandon was impressed. Brandon had taken a run on the Beast himself, just to see if maybe the clock was off, but no. What else could Sky attribute those times to, other than Soylent and clean living? And aside from two weeks of excessive intestinal gas to start out, the Soylent was absolutely agreeable, once you got used to the idea you no longer got to enjoy conventional food. Sky flavored his Soylent with chocolate or vanilla and sometimes cheap Kool-Aid-like products from the market. He'd never gone through an encounter with the Black Not while living on Soylent. He figured the lack of substance — once mixed with water, Soylent was more of a goop than a liquid, but certainly far from solid — might make the effects of alcohol even more dramatic with the Black Not upon him.

That first night wasn't too bad — just a lot of trembling and not much sleep, and night sweats that soaked his T-shirt and briefs. Then the eerie awakening to a new day with the Black Not fully within him, tightening down his vision, tensing up his muscles, multiplying the pain. And the worst of it, really, wasn't the pain, but the hopelessness the Black Not brought. That was the *Not* part — the utter impossibility of all that was good. The Black Not poisoned all his hope and optimism, all his dreams and wishes. All in his father's voice.

Not.

No.

Never.

That morning he walked Ivan into the desert on his leash. It was easy to imagine the dog taking off after a rabbit and never coming back. Terrier fearlessness was a threat to their survival. Megan would be crushed if something happened to Ivan, and Sky loved Megan. The October weather was mild. He poked around up on the hillside, where the copper ore tailings shined in the sun. Picked up a few warm pale blue rocks for Megan.

He smiled to himself bitterly while the Black Not told him in his father's recorded voice how poorly he would do at the Gargantua Mammoth Cup in January. Sky imagined Wylie sending up a victorious rooster tail of snow in the out-run. The Black Not asked him why he thought that Soylent and the Imagery Beast and clean living would be enough to defeat destiny. Was it pride? And wasn't that what ruined every man? The prideful attempt to deny one's fate? And was it not true that Megan would take up with Wylie after he won the cup? She was a very attractive woman who would need more from a man than losing, noted his father. Of course she will take up with a winner, he said. Yes, Sky had to agree: Of course she will.

The pain had spread. While standing on a low hillock, the arches of his feet suddenly cramped, as they often did, just knotted right up, like fists. Sky gasped and dropped to his butt and tore at the laces of his hiking boots. How could a foot arch hurt that much? When he'd gotten the boots off, he used both hands to unclench one cramp, then the other. It was like trying to unbend metal. Then the first arch locked tight again.

Ivan seized the opportunity and ran. Sky foresaw coyotes. He ordered Ivan back, but the dog tore off along the bottom of the hillock, leash bouncing along behind him, apparently fixed on something that Sky couldn't see. Sky tried to run a few steps, but the rocks were brutally sharp, so he high-stepped back and plopped down and got the boots on as fast as he could, but the long laces kept falling out of the "speed hooks," so by the time he finished, the boots looked like they had been laced by a chimpanzee.

Sky ran around the base of the hill. Ivan was out of sight, but Sky heard his barking and understood that the dog was soon going to die here in some painful and gruesome way. It was the only thing that could happen. He slipped and fell, and this did not surprise him, because the Black Not only allowed him pessimism, defeat, pain, and death. Even an appreciation of beauty, like a sunrise, say, or gratefulness for sudden good luck, or the genuine joy in a glass of cold, clean water — all this was forbidden by the Black Not. Banished. Only *Black.* Only *Not.*

Sky rounded the hillock and saw Ivan out a hundred yards ahead, barking furiously at a pack of bony stray dogs closing in on him in a rambling, low-snouted fashion. But Ivan's leash had miraculously caught between some rocks! Without this restraint, he would probably have already raced to his own death, but Sky saw no good fortune in the snagged leash. All he could envision was Ivan stuck there and unable to run, soon to be torn to ribbons and devoured by the marauders. *Torn to ribbons right in front of you,* said his father.

Sky didn't think he'd ever get there. Then he *was* there, grabbing the snagged loop end of the leash without stopping or even slowing down. But when he took up the leash, a weird slackness greeted him and the collar came hopping back along the rocky ground toward him while newly freed Ivan sped in the other direction, toward the dogs.

"IVAN! NO!"

Sky put everything he had into the sprint. Running was such a crude, slow thing compared to downhill skiing. He yelled as loudly as he could, hoping to frighten or confuse the dogs. Ivan was fast, but suddenly he stopped, cocked his ears, and looked silently at the pack moving up the arroyo toward him. Sky dug in, knowing he'd trip and fall on the sharp rocks, cut his knees badly enough for stitches, maybe even lacerate or crush both patellas, which would ruin his workouts for weeks and reduce his

Mammoth Cup chances from slim to none. Of course he would fuck everything up.

Before Sky knew it, Ivan was in his arms, solid and squirming wildly. Sky tucked him against his side like a football and kept charging toward the pack, hollering. The dogs stopped and waited a moment, ears and tails up, before splitting off in half-hearted, sideways retreats. Sky stopped, clutching Ivan fast and watching the dogs, which watched him and Ivan as they blended into the desert.

He spent the rest of the day inside the cabin in light, sporadic sleep. Ivan prowled the interior for vermin. Then night came, and with it an eternity of waking hallucinations arranged in the maddening nonlogic of dreams. He lolled on one lower bunk, sweat-drenched and shaking, stripped of will-power, his muscles aching like the flu he'd sometimes had as a child, but much worse. In these flulike fevers, the world was black-edged and huge, and Sky was minuscule within it. Powerless. Helpless. The bunks across from him appeared to be immense ramparts of frame and fabric, and Ivan, on the other lower bunk, seemed the size of a bison. A huge snake with scales the size of Sky's head appeared outside all four cabin windows at once, as if preparing to constrict it. A naked, wizened crone threw open the door, smiling broken pillars of teeth, curling a come-hither claw at him. And all the while, the voice of the Black Not goaded him. *You cannot. You will not. You will never. You are not.*

So he closed his eyes, but this was worse. He became a small whirling thing, plummeting through a bottomless, black sky. At first, he was small as a pea, but the velocity of his fall rubbed away at him, sanding him down to the size of a mote of dust, then to a thing even smaller than dust, until he was nothing but nerves and senses, helpless in this huge and tactile world. Then he wasn't there at all, and this was not a bad thing. A goddamned relief, actually. He was gone but the world went on. Fine. So good to feel no pain. He lay there trembling.

Ivan never took his eyes off him.

Sky pulled himself up and off the bed and stumbled to the picnic table and his boxes of provisions. He dug down into the first box but couldn't find it, though he was sure he'd put it there. So he upended the second box and out tumbled the snacks and the teeth-cleaning biscuits for the dog, more Soylent, the bottled water, another bottle of tequila, some underwear, socks, his iPod and computer tablet, and, finally, the handgun!

It was a trim little thing, a .38-caliber autoloader with nine shots. It was here for times like this, when he seriously considered trading the Black Not for the much kinder black forever. He stared at the weapon while he tore open the box of dog treats and, without looking, dropped one into Ivan's mouth.

It would take only a few seconds, he thought. Already loaded. You check the chamber. You unsafe it. You hold it to your temple and close your eyes. No pain forever.

The Black Not had gone quiet now, as it always did when Sky got out the gun.

The implication was, *Of course you can't do it.*

Because he was Sky Carson, who lacked nerve, just as his father had lacked nerve, according to Cynthia. Who knew everything. Every single thing. And clearly did not lack nerve.

Because he was Sky Carson, a mid-pack ski crosser forever trying to catch Robert and Wylie and whoever else was racing well on any given day.

Because he was Sky Carson, royally born and genetically gifted. But assaulted on his own X Course by Wylie. And what had Sky done about it? Nothing. He had responded with a threat that people saw as comic but had taken no real action at all. Made no defense of his honor. If that wasn't lack of nerve, what was?

Because he was Sky Carson, knocked out cold with one punch by Wylie that night at Slocum's. In front of his friends and fans and the waitress he liked, and half of Mammoth Lakes.

Because he was Sky Carson. Of course he couldn't pull the trigger.

He couldn't even pick up the thing.

Sky poked at it with an index finger, as if trying to see if it were alive. Vision off, he kept missing. Then his fingertip caught the front sight and the gun spun and came to a stop with the barrel facing away from him and the grip waiting for his hand, just inches away, an invitation.

He still couldn't pick it up.

Because Sky Carson couldn't even answer an invite from God.

Dad, what should I do?

Pick it up, you fucking coward.

He went to the open bottle on the kitchen counter, tilted it up for a long swallow of the añejo, then veered back to the bed and fell in.

■ ■ ■ ■

The next two days were similar, but without Ivan trying so hard to get killed by a pack of wild dogs. Sky tightened up the dog's collar and got him outside every few hours on the leash to do his business, then pretty much dragged him back inside the cabin for the next assault from the Black Not. Sometimes Sky argued with the voice, denying the terrible emotions the voice made him feel. Sometimes he yelled. In quieter moments, he fed the dog. Threw a wadded-up sock for him. Drank Soylent. And tequila to blunt the pain.

By the third evening, he was exhausted. Then late that night, after several hours of torment that left him looking down on the gun once again, sobbing at his lack of courage, Sky fell into a sleep that lasted well into the next afternoon.

He woke up and drank a double helping of Soylent flavored with powdered raspberry mix. Downed some pretzels, too. He washed himself with bottled water and a little tablet of motel soap, rinsed with fistfuls of the water, air-dried in the sun and put on clean clothes, then headed north for Mammoth Lakes.

Coming up Highway 203, Sky looked out at the forest and the mountains looming high and he felt that strange sense of newness that always followed the Black Not. As if he was seeing things in a fresh way. Familiar but different. Old but new. It made him feel as if he'd been away a long time. The afternoon had turned cool and the sky beyond the mountain looked gray and solid as granite.

He caught the light red at Old Mammoth Road and watched the cars coming down from the village. He saw Johnny Maines roaring down Main toward him on his yellow motorcycle. Sky was always kind of impressed by how Maines could control the big Harley on tight turns even when the weather was bad. He'd seen Johnny slide through ice on the bike as if he were snowboarding it. Sky saw the fly-rod tubes that were strapped to the back of the motorcycle, vibrating with the speed; then he saw a flag of brown hair waving behind Johnny and realized he had a passenger. Even with the helmet and sunglasses she was wearing, Sky recognized Megan, for sure, holding Johnny tight around his middle, and damned if Megan wasn't smiling as Johnny ran the red light and turned the loudly farting Harley right in front of him.

No Harley out front when he got home. He led the dog up the stairs and let him in. It looked like Megan had had a party — cans and bottles and open bags of chips everywhere. A sleeping bag lay on the floor beside one slip-on canvas sneaker. He looked into the bedroom, cringed when he saw the unmade bed with the sheets all twisted up and every pillow on the floor.

He sat down on the bed with his back to the door, looking out the window to the sharp peaks of the Sherwins. The Black Not, never fully absent, piped up: *Of course she's with Johnny Maines. Cat away. Probably learned it from you. What did you expect?*

He heard the pounding of someone starting up the outside stairs, soon joined by a second person. Ivan launched into a tirade of barking and ran to the front door. Sky heard voices, male and female, something being discussed, the male voice louder and more forceful but the female agreeing. The front door opened and shut and a moment later he felt eyes on his back.

"I'm sorry, Sky."

"Just get out," said Sky without turning around.

"Yo bro," said Johnny Maines.

"You get out, too."

"I want Ivan," said Megan.

"Take him. Go. All of you."

"I tried," said Megan. "But the Sky Carson show just wasn't working for me, once I saw it a couple of times."

"It's the best I have. Leave your key."

"Can you at least turn around and look me in the eyes?"

"There's nothing to see."

"Don't blame you, dude," said Maines. "See you around. I'm all about you for the cup."

"Yes. Godspeed, you regicidal toddlers."

Chapter Twenty-Five

Five-fifteen A.M. October air cold and thin, mountain darkness close.

Wylie unlocked the front door of Let It Bean, to find April Holly waiting outside in that darkness.

"I'm ready," she said. "Sorry for the short notice."

His heart hopped to. "Come in. I need to do some things."

"We should be fairly quick about this."

At the counter, Wylie wrote his address on a napkin, sensing eyes from the kitchen on him. "Park under the blue tarp by the pastry cart. It's up Main, left on Mono, then left on Cornice. Put all your stuff on the deck. Steen will help." She took the napkin and her eyes searched his face as they had done before, and in this Wylie saw fear and determination.

"Please hurry," she said.

"I'll be there soon."

His sisters and mother were in the kitchen, at work in glum silence, the girls dressed for school, the radio low. Since Gargantua had begun opening at 5:30 each morning, the Let It Bean staff was getting up half an hour earlier to open at 5:15. At 4:00 A.M., those thirty minutes of sleep were sorely missed.

Wylie told them he was taking off for a few days; not to worry, Steen would be here by 7:30. All three of them gave him knowing looks. "If that was April Holly's voice," said Belle, "then that must have been April Holly."

"Where are you two going?" asked Beatrice.

"Solitary," he said. "Madman."

"Adam, too?" asked Belle. "For your birthday, like you used to?"

"We'll see, with the short notice."

"I'd go with April Holly on *no* notice," said Belle.

"Happy birthday almost, Wylie!" said Beatrice.

A moment later, the girls hugged him and his mother handed him a paper bag. Wylie hustled across the parking lot in the cold dark, slipping and sliding on the ice, risking a half lutz as he got close to his truck, landing the jump nicely.

■ ■ ■ ■

April said nothing as they charged toward Highway 395 from Mammoth. She kept her eyes on the side-view mirror, and Wylie felt her nerves. They ate the pastries and drank the big coffee drinks. He was surprised how small the cab of his truck became with her in it. Much smaller than with a sister or Mom or even Jesse Little Chief aboard.

He used the phone just once — it was going to take Adam and Teresa two days to get up there. This gave Wylie the thrill of having April Holly to himself. *To himself!* He would be cool and courteous. He would be April Holly's host. Her driver, guide, protector, and companion. He would be Helene and Logan and Clean Cut and himself, all rolled into one. That was funny.

This late in a snowless autumn, the faint two-track path was easier to find and follow. Wylie happily goosed his truck up the front side of the Sierras. Aspens shivered against the gray flanks of the mountains and gold medallions rained down. The gorge was a furnace of red and orange flames in a cloudless blue sky, the breeze-blown leaves swirling like embers. Jays squawked at them while two big hawks circled in the updrafts precisely as clockworks. Glancing in the rearview mirror, Wylie cast an appreciative eye at the MPP, then let his gaze linger on April's profile.

Her voice was faint and seemingly distant. "Last night they arranged to have Tim stroll in with an armful of red roses and tears in his eyes. I'm not a hard person. I'm not. But I'm furious because . . . I'm just furious."

"I understand."

"Please don't. I'm exhausted by it. I hope I brought the right stuff for out here. I used to camp, but it's been years."

"We've got everything."

"Where will I take a bath?"

"Breakfast Creek. You'll be clean and very awake. We'll heat up water on the fire."

"Let's not talk about a single thing."

"Okay, not one."

"I'm never sure if you're making fun of me."

"Sometimes I am."

"Can I be not me for a few days?"

"I'll call you Mae. I like that name."

She sighed. "Yeah. Sure. Old-fashioned, like me. Twenty-one going on ninety."

"Not talking might be good."

"Don't you shush me."

"We're going in circles, April."

"Triple corks."

"Always imaging."

"Snowboarding is the only thing I'm not sick of. And I don't want to know what that says about me."

They parked in the middle of Solitary, away from the canyon walls so the sun would be on them, but not too far from the young tree upon which he'd been hoisting the food away from the bears. Wylie got out and threw open the door of the MPP and the tailgate of his truck. April walked off.

Wylie arranged the folding chairs facing each other across the fire pit, set his ground pad and sleeping bag on a flat spot near the tree, propped the skis and boards against the trailer tongue. Kept an eye on April. He wrestled the MPP off the hitch, then leveled it, cranking and uncranking the handle until the bubble was exactly equidistant between the level lines. He watched April walk into the meadow and stand in the waning wildflowers, looking up at Madman.

Wylie was suddenly unsure of what to do. He rechecked the level of the MPP. He fussed over the boots and bindings and poles and snowshoes, arranging them under the tree twice. Back at the trailer, he carefully wiped the road dust off the portholes.

Short of counting the change in his pocket, he was out of ideas. So he rearranged the stones in the fire pit. April was still out there catching the sun, sitting on a round boulder, a singular woman alone in the world. Let her be, he thought.

Two hours later, they stood panting on the precipice of Madman, snowshoes fastened to their backs, ski and board tips in the air. "Take this first one slow," he said.

"My heart's beating everywhere."

"Good luck."

April launched. She vanished in freefall, then landed with a hard rasp and carved right. Wylie dropped in and went left, gained speed, made a wide turn back toward the middle and crisscrossed April coming the opposite way. The snow was softened by the afternoon sun, but it was last year's snow and far from powder. He heard the edges of his skis cutting into it, felt the surge of speed when he ran through tree shadows and shot into sunlight near the right side of the slope. He swung back and they crossed in the middle again, Wylie letting out a war whoop and April opening her hands in a bring-it-on gesture as she flew past him.

They essed down the mountain in a loose weave, each holding back, feeling for the ice and the softer holes. Wylie was truly impressed by her ease and economy of motion, her lightness and promise of speed. Such easy transitions from goofy to conventional, he thought. Fluid. Thoughts played out on snow. How does she do that? He put his weight into the turns, legs powerful from the miles on Highway 203, upper body staunch from splitting cords of wood. On the last few hundred yards, he pulled up next to her and they fell into a rhythm determined by the course, reading the snow, anticipating and approximating each other. They stopped at the downslope end of the natural out-run, both breathing hard, Wylie's poles dug in for stability and April with a hand on his arm for balance. "Oh. My. God."

"I thought you'd like it."

"Planet Amazement. Again?"

"Let's go."

Their second run was freer and faster, Wylie out ahead, coursing through late-afternoon shade and sunlight, trying to find that place where he was present but absent, where his body skied while his mind oversaw. Maybe it would come. He was strong enough, but he didn't feel limber. Power without feel. Twenty-six years old tomorrow. Not twenty. Not bad. Just different. They figure-eighted down, two signatures on one mountain.

At dusk, they made a fire, using good split wood brought from home, then put on the steaks, asparagus, and rolls they'd picked up in Big Pine. The folding chairs were actually comfortable. Wylie poured her a very small bourbon in a coffee cup, which she casually sipped, then spit into the fire. "That's just awful."

"Practice."

"Forget that. I like red wine."

"Let me check the cellar."

He got a bottle from under the sink and a wineglass from the tiny yachtlike galley cupboard. He felt worldly and important as he handed her the wine. He saw the flames flickering in her eyes and the dusting of freckles on her cheeks. He checked his watch, then turned his attention to the steaks, touched one of them with a fork. Four minutes. Asparagus and rolls, aluminum-wrapped and off the flame, would be ready about then. He sat down across the fire from her.

"This is the only part of the trip I've been dreading," she said.

"Yeah. It's dark by five and there's really nothing to do."

"You read a lot?"

"Sure."

"I was impressed when I saw a book of poems in your trailer that first day I met you."

"It's in there, if you'd like to try some."

"Maybe. The wine's good. My trainers say one glass a night, max."

"That's reasonable."

"What about you?"

"Overall, I shoot for somewhat reasonable."

"Your definition of somewhat reasonable."

"Of course!"

Wylie got the food onto two plates and the plates onto the small table in the trailer. With the door and windows and portholes open, it didn't feel cramped. The screen door kept out the bugs, which were few tonight. A squat votive candle burned between them. He had pictured April Holly sitting across from him in the MPP, but his imagination paled against the real thing. In his imagination, she hadn't been this close.

"I'm still waiting for the terrible awkwardness to arrive," she said.

"Me, too. I imagined you here, so maybe it's helping."

"I imagined myself here at this table."

"We could say things like 'Pass the salt.' Or get more serious, like 'That next government shutdown could be a bad one.' "

She smiled and drank more wine, her shoulders forward in the small space and her voice a leafy rustle. "Or I could say 'How do the planets look through the portholes?' "

Wylie's turn to smile. "And then I could say 'Mars rocks, but Venus is always my favorite."

"But then I'd think you were flattering my gender."

"And you'd be right."

"So then I might say, to distract you, 'Great asparagus tonight, Wyles.' "

"This conversation just keeps getting better and better, April."

They were leaning toward each other, and Wylie could feel the heat from the candle. Her lips were red from the sun and dry alpine air. Golden hair. Her eyes were blue, with little orange flames in them, and they considered him side to side, skeptically, searching again.

"I like our conversation," she said.

"I like you."

"It's awfully hot in here," she said. He blew out the candle. "That won't make a big difference."

He leaned in and kissed her lips, lightly, briefly. She did the same back. "Walk me to the creek."

"It's going to be cold."

"Hot, cold," she said. "Let me get a few things. Could you put some more wood on the fire?"

April got into her duffel bag in the bed of his truck and came back with a bundle of clothing, a bath towel, and a lidded plastic box. Wylie set three big logs on the fire, then found a towel and a bottle of body wash. He led the way through the aspens to the creek, holding back the branches. Yards apart along the stream, they stripped down and spread their clothes on the boulders.

"Fast in, faster out," he said.

Wylie felt the shock of the water, heard April gasp. In the good moonlight, she was pale and solid, like ivory or alabaster. Wylie was impressed that she waded in, squatted down, and went under to her neck. She held up her hair with one hand and splashed her face with the other, then rose dripping silver beads. Under the water, he rushed his hands through his hair and under his arms, came up and got the body wash lathered up. The cold went from skin to bone in seconds.

"I've never been in water this cold," she said. "You wonder how anybody gets used to it."

"I've got this body rinse stuff."

"I've got soap, but I think it's frozen solid."

A few minutes later, they were standing as close to the fire as they could get, hopping in place as they dried off, teeth chattering, skin raised with goose bumps. April ran into the MPP and came back heavily dressed. Then Wylie went in, put on clean clothing and a good fleece jacket, stowed the dining table within the benches. He looked out at April shivering by the fire. He smiled to himself while folding out the bed and unzipping the two-person sleeping bag. You are Wylie Welborn, he thought: protector, provider, lover, luckiest man on Earth.

"All yours in here," he said, stepping out. "I'm going to hang the food so the bears don't get it."

"Where are you sleeping?"

His heart stumbled, but his words did not. "By the fire. I do it all the time."

"But that's a two-person bag in there."

"So let me know if it gets lonely."

"Oh, it won't. I'm a sprawler. Need help hanging the food?"

"I've got it, April."

Wylie washed the dishes in the creek, then packed them with the food and lugged the canvas bundle over to the lodgepole pine.

He got the rope up and over the right branch, third try, tied the bundle tight, and hoisted. His spirit had fallen with April's sleeping arrangement and he felt rejected and ashamed of the rejection, then angry at the shame, but at least he could be man enough not to show his disappointment. He tied the rope fast to the trunk, smacked his cold, stinging hands together. Wylie Welborn, he thought: *Man.*

Back at the MPP, Wylie knocked, then stepped inside. It was dark. He opened one of the storage hatches to fetch his single sleeping bag, which he had anticipated needing. The self-inflating bedroll was there, too. He could smell the soap she'd used, and the faint aroma of her much-advertised shampoo. In one of the commercials Wylie had seen, April smiled and shook her head — after shampooing, it was implied — which threw her hair into curls that stretched and retracted in slow motion like golden springs.

"Good night, April."

"Good night, Wylie. Four hugs today?"

"Three. Mom, Beatrice, and Belle hugged me when I left Let It Bean."

"You're one short. So get in here!" He heard the soft rustle of her laughter, a laughter that seemed to Wylie to hold no malice at all. "You didn't really think I'd take over your bed without you in it, did you?"

"You had me going, all right."

"Hurry up, please — my teeth are still chattering and I'm extremely naked."

In the darkness, he could make out the shape of her lifted arm, the pale fold of the sleeping bag waiting open. He undressed in record time and got in as lightly as he could. She turned into his arms.

"Does the beard keep your face warm?"

"It froze off once."

"Do I get to see the hidden face someday?"

"I don't know if you could handle it."

He felt her fingers cold and small on his face. They kissed. He felt his clarity diminishing and thought, *Onward.* All he knew for certain was the immediate pleasure that was April Holly — the taste of her, the slick bumps of her teeth, her hot tongue prodding his own. He slowly ran his hand down her smooth, warm flank and onto one haunch, still oddly cool, then back up again. He spread his fingers on her cheek and drew her face even closer and she shivered and groaned and they kissed deeply and long.

April rolled back and Wylie climbed on. "I have raincoats," he croaked.

"Let it rain. We don't need them."

He entered her slowly. He ordered his sensations to check themselves, which didn't quite work, so he bit the tip of his tongue sharply and thought of their first run that day.

"Does it bother you that you hardly know me?" she asked.

"I love that I hardly know you."

"What if we're different?"

"Please be very different."

"You got inside me weeks ago. Now you're inside me for real. Where'd your lips go?"

Wylie kissed her again and, without willing it, everything went big picture: Earth from space, turning on its axis, jet stream white and wispy left to right above rugged land and vast blue sea. Next he was falling dizzily, North America rushing up at him as he steered west, angling for California, coming in fast now, the northern and southern counties peeling from his vision, which left him hovering right here over this meadow, almost close enough to touch the cute little trailer sitting not far from a creek that looked good for trout, beneath a steep chute of snow carved top to bottom by human beings who, by the look of the tracks, must have had a really good time making them.

Then, there was April Holly again. He felt

the clenched commotion in her, wave upon wave, then her release. Followed by his own, crazily, electric and full, and announced with a roar. After a brief, shallow doze, they roused each other again, and this time things were longer and slower and Wylie proudly outlasted her five to his one by his count. His whole body trembling, he withdrew and rolled over. He felt like a rubbery tortoise that would never be able to right itself. His heart began to slow. She ran a finger over his face for a moment. Then she worked herself out of the bed, brought a jacket to her chest, and jumped up and down, counting out loud to twelve. Wylie looked up at the bouncing girl, pale flesh, arms and elbows and her crown of curls unfurling to just short of the laminated ceiling of the MPP. She smiled down at him, then tossed the jacket and landed hard on the bed, crawling quickly back under the covers.

I'm surrounded by beauty, he thought.

They made love again once before sunrise and once after; then Wylie got the fire going for coffee. Later they took the fishing rods and meandered down to Breakfast Creek arm in arm, like adolescents. Wylie rigged a short one-weight fly rod and showed April how to flick out the fly and let the riffle take it along. He used his two-weight with a black ant pattern. The brook trout were famished, as always, and they put back the small ones and in an hour had enough for breakfast.

Before lunch, they made two runs down Madman, then ate and slept like the dead in the MPP, then made another two runs before sunset.

Near sundown, they sat on rocks at the top of Madman, considering separately the vastness around them, snowshoes strapped to their backs and ready to go. Wylie tried to admit his emotions in small quantities because they were far from normal for him. The setting sun burnished the western face of the mountains above them with a light promising darkness.

"I've never boarded at night without lights," she said.

"You know Madman by now. Be the snow."

"I'm happy, Wylie. A new kind of happy. All I can think about is this snow, and that I don't have to compete on it. And that I've got this man who is my secret and friend. And this hidden place. I'm not April Holly wearing a medal. Or April Holly for Salonne. I'm April Holly doing what I love to do."

"I like that."

"Or maybe I'm just April Holly, loved into idiocy by a large bearded love bear."

"I like that, too."

"Dark enough yet?"

"Yes."

"Do we have to go back?"

"We've got provisions for four more days."

"And guests arriving tomorrow."

"You'll like Adam and Teresa."

"I want to put out the No Vacancy sign. Do you have one?"

"We could carve one up."

"God knows what they'll think of me. But I have one more day of invisibility with my secret mountain man. I'm going to devour it."

"Ready? I'll lead this time."

"I want to lead."

"Madman is all yours, April."

The next day — Wylie Welborn's twenty-sixth birthday — was the best birthday of his life. He and April skied and napped and cooked lunch. They hiked a steep escarpment and sunned themselves on a flat boulder. By the time they came back to the MPP, Adam and Teresa had made camp.

They sat under the bear-foiling lodgepole pine, each with a fat book open. It was still warm for fall, but when the sun went down, the temperature fell like a dropped rock.

That evening, Adam cooked ribs and corn he'd brought up from Bishop, and Teresa made drinks, and Wylie and April built a fire and kept it fed. They ate and talked late around the fire and had birthday cake made by Teresa. At one point, pleasantly drunk and feeling less weighted than he had felt in his adult life, Wylie looked at April. He smiled at her across the rippling flames and she smiled back. He saw otherness and strength and beauty and he marveled that two of the same species could be so different. He felt nothing to hide. He wanted to declare.

"Wylie," said Adam. "I saw two of your runs down Madman today. You looked fast and relaxed. If you win the Mammoth Cup, that's an awfully good beginning and a pass to Aspen for the X Games. I'm offering to send you there, then on to Europe for the FIS World Cup tour if you can make that cut. And, of course, the spring qualifiers back stateside, for Olympic selections. There's no use getting ahead of ourselves, but I want you to know that money won't be a problem for any of that. Happy birthday. I've made the same offer to Sky, of course. Just so it's all on the up-and-up."

Wylie had to tell himself that he'd heard the words, not dreamed them. Or conjured them in a bourbon haze. He felt April's hand squeeze his leg. He was aware of Adam and Teresa watching, their eyes four distant orange windows. And he thought, This is what it is to be in love, and to have a living father who is well pleased by you. "Honored, Grandpa."

"Are you sure you want to do this?" she asked.

"I'm sure."

"Why, again?"

"To show you the real me."

"I hope they're sharp."

"I keep them that way."

In the dimmed lantern light inside the MPP, Wylie leaned forward toward the mirror. He raised the utility shears and went to work on his beard. It took several minutes of cutting, the fat clumps of whiskers landing audibly on the open sheet of newspaper he had pressed into the small sink. Behind him, reflected in the mirror, April watched him in attentive silence. Two inches dwindled to one inch, then an uneven scape of angled tufts and divots. The face beneath was pale and smooth. He used one of her pink disposable razors to take the whiskers down to the skin — three slow passes through thick shampoo lather to accomplish this. He rinsed and dried, pulled the rubber band from his ponytail, and turned to her.

April ran a hand down one cheek, frowning. "I liked it better before."

He smiled.

"I'm kidding. You look so young. You're a beautiful man. Sorry, but I'm not going to be able to keep these hands off you." She pulled him back into the bed and they brought the sleeping bag over them. "I gotta tell you, Wylie. When Adam said he'd sponsor you on the World Cup tour, I got goose bumps up and down my back. Because you're good enough. You're good enough to do that."

"You really think so?"

"I've been watching you up there on Madman, boy. I've seen a lot of skiers, and you got it. I can see that you've got it."

Two days later, Wylie steered the truck up Minaret toward Starwood. He felt fully triumphant but tried not to show it. April had her hand on his knee and he felt her grip tighten when she saw the uplink news vans parked outside the gate, the Mammoth

Lakes police cruiser, and a smattering of vans and SUVs with radio or TV logos emblazoned on their flanks. There were a few loitering locals and some kids on bikes.

"Mom ratted me out," she said.

"She'll be happy to have you back."

"She'll be furious. If you don't want to get into all this, you can drop me here and just keep going."

"I'm all in."

"Brace yourself. Please don't do anything like to Jacobie or Sky. Just . . ."

"I understand."

She pulled off her beanie, leaned out the window, and looked at herself in the side-view mirror as she shook out her hair. "What they want from me is Little April Sunshine. And they're going to get her."

He pulled past the gathered vehicles and bystanders and up to the gate. April told him what numbers to punch as a posse of photographers and videographers hustled around to April's side of the truck, firing away. She shook her curls again. Wylie could hear the clatter of the motor drives and he watched as one of the women barged in and pointed a large mike toward April. "Monika Silver from ESPN — are you okay, April?"

"Hi, Monika. Just terrific! I've been camping in the mountains with some friends. I can't tell you how *great* it was to get away. I boarded down a beautiful run and washed my hair in a creek. Salonne shampoo works beautifully in Sierra creek water, I can tell you that."

"April! Newell Yost with City Cable — why didn't you tell anyone where you were going? Your mother filed a missing-person report."

"You know, I just forgot! And the phones don't work up there. And . . . I'm so embarrassed to have caused all this trouble. Can you let us through?"

Wylie saw that the gate had rolled open. A Mammoth Lakes cop rapped on his window and Wylie rolled it down. "Welborn?"

"Sir."

"Everything all right?"

Some of the reporters had come to Wylie's side of the truck now, squeezing around the cop to shoot. "Yes. Just camping, sir, and she forgot to tell her mom."

"Helene was worried. She'll be happy to see April alive and well. You? Not so sure."

"I'm prepared."

"For what?"

"To behave myself."

"Wylie, we can go now."

They wound through the pretty neighborhood to April's rented house and parked in the drive. April took a deep breath but said nothing. They got out and Wylie saw the worry on April's face as Helene and Logan came through the front door. Helene was in the lead, arms swinging wide as she advanced on Wylie. "Get off my property, you bastard. *Now.*"

"I'm going to help April unload first, ma'am."

"She does mean now," said Logan.

Wylie said nothing, but Helene got so tight to his face that he could smell the coffee on her breath. "I forbid you to see her again."

"You can't, Mom. I'm twenty-one. I like him."

"We were just camping with friends," said Wylie, stepping back as Logan came closer.

"Get back in the truck," Logan said softly.

Helene whirled on the big man. "Can't you do more than that? Can't you do *anything* but cook and cash your paycheck?"

Logan dropped into a wrestler's crouch, arms outstretched, fingers prodding the air slowly, tarantulalike. Even with Logan crouching, Wylie had to look up at him. Logan ambled forward weirdly. Wylie heard April scream *"No!"* and somehow the sound of her voice became a breath-robbing clinch and takedown that left his arms splayed helplessly, his shoulders crushed to the concrete, his body twisted and writhing, and his neck feeling like it could snap anytime now.

"Don't kill him," said Helene. "Just make sure he doesn't come back."

"Let him go! Stop!"

Wylie couldn't draw breath and he knew to tap out. He sent the signal to his hands and it seemed to take a full second for them to respond. But he found nothing solid to tap out on, so his palms just waved aimlessly in the air. . . .

He woke to the sight of his hiking boots. There they were, one canted to the right and the other to the left, way, way down at the ends of his legs. The edge of his vision was dark, like binoculars poorly adjusted. He could feel his back and shoulders and head propped against something rough and hard. Through the dark perimeter of his eyesight, a face came at him, distorted as through a peephole or upon a Christmas tree bulb. A pretty woman. Behind her hovered two more figures, these unfocused also. Their voices came to him more clearly than their faces.

"Logan, call the paramedics. Now. I don't want a lawsuit on my hands."

"Yes, Mrs. Holly."
"Wylie? Wylie? Can you see me?"

Chapter Twenty-Six

The first snow of the season fell overnight in early November, lowering a thin white blanket over the town. That morning, Wylie sat in his truck outside Cynthia Carson's home, looking up at the mountain and watching the snowflakes still wafting down from above. His truck engine was running and he had the heater cranked up. Yesterday's text from Cynthia Carson was more an order than an invitation: "Be at my home at 8:00 A.M. Wednesday — C. Carson."

He looked again at Cynthia's front door. He had rarely felt such dread. He had never actually spoken to her before. Never really looked her in the eye. Soon, he would have to do both. Sipping the last of his coffee, Wylie remembered first hearing the whispered gossip about Sky Carson's mom shooting his dad before Sky was born. She was in prison. One of the other kindergarteners had a folded newspaper picture of her walking into court. Sky was suddenly different to him, but how? Was this the reason why Sky was either funny or sad? No kid talked about any of it when he was around, that was for sure. As a kindergartener, Wylie had thought a lot about all this. Wished it hadn't happened. Wished they could all wake up from it, like from a bad dream. He'd lost his own father to a bad illness, so he understood growing up without a true dad around.

Wylie drained the coffee, dropped the container into the holder, and suddenly it was fifteen years ago, his eleventh birthday, and he and his mother were walking along Mammoth Creek. It was a beautiful October day. Atop a lookout point with a breath-stealing view of the White Mountains across the valley, Kathleen told Wylie that she wanted to set a few things straight. "I think you're old enough now," she said. "I don't want you hearing half-truths. I hope you don't judge me too harshly."

"I wouldn't do that, Mom."

In fact, whatever she says is okay with me, he'd thought. He'd heard some very strange rumors. Maybe she could clear things up.

"When I was seventeen and just out of high school in San Diego, I moved here to Mammoth Lakes to become a pro skier. I was brave and naïve and I had some talent. I worked three jobs to pay rent and to buy my ski passes. I made the team. And . . . about a year later, Wylie, I became pregnant with you."

"This was when Dad was alive."

Kathleen took his face in her hands and looked tearfully into his eyes. He had never seen such an emotion from her and he was afraid. "Wylie? Your father was Richard Carson. He was my coach."

He felt light-headed and took a knee. He had no idea what to say or do. Sky's long-dead dad? How did that happen? Kathleen had continued talking, though her voice sounded far away. She said that when she got pregnant, Richard had been married to Cynthia Carson. Cynthia had then killed Richard in anger, so, yes, some of those rumors Wylie might have been hearing were, in fact, true.

By then Kathleen was crying and trying to blot up the tears with a pink-and-white paisley bandanna that flapped in the dry alpine breeze. *"You were my baby, Wylie. My baby, and Richard's. . . ."*

Suddenly, he had felt something heavy unfurling inside him, like a thick curtain trying to separate the complexities of what his mother was saying from the simple truth he had always known, that his father — William, a good man — had loved Wylie but died of natural causes just two years after Wylie had been born. Yes. Truth. And that Kathleen had married Steen years later, with Beatrice and Belle coming along soon after. Yes. Truth again. Then Wylie was aware of his mother kneeling beside him, and of her arms strong around him, her voice cracking, and her tears smelling somehow tropical.

"But I saw pictures of Dad. You showed me."

"The man in the picture was an old friend. He was not your father. His name was not William. I lied to you. And I'm so very sorry, Wylie."

Wylie had stood and walked away from her, back down the dirt road toward Mammoth Park, slowly, his ears roaring and his vision shrunken and blurred around its edges. He could hear her footsteps behind him, keeping pace but not coming fast enough to catch him. He wanted badly to be going fast down a snow-covered mountain, so incredibly fast that it would tear all the bad things away and leave only the good and the happy and the true. He ran for home as if he were running for his life.

Two years later, Cynthia Carson was back

in Mammoth Lakes. She was shorter and thicker than Wylie had expected. Her hair was white and her face was pale and her eyes were the blue of lake ice. When small-town coincidence brought them into proximity, she would stop what she was doing and stare at him and say nothing, as if daring him to look back. He couldn't, because he was terrified. Did she hate him? Why? How was it his fault that she had killed his father? Shouldn't he hate *her*? Did she still have the gun? Wylie, age thirteen, was overmatched.

Now as the first snow of the season came down, he looked again at Cynthia Carson's front door. It opened and a white swatch of human face appeared. He checked his watch. Crap. Let's do this. He turned off the engine of the truck and got out.

She watched him approach, but when he made it to the door, she made no effort to open it farther. He stood before her. He watched her lake-ice eyes roam him, summoned his will not to look away. "With your face clean-shaven, you look more like a Carson," she said.

"If you say so."

"Finally you've looked me directly in the eye."

"You used to terrify me."

"Now?"

"A little less."

"Close the door behind you."

He followed her through a short foyer and into the living room. The town house was warm inside and smelled of coffee. The walls were crowded with ski posters, their frames aligned to form perfectly symmetrical rows both up, down, and across. There was a faux-leather couch faded by sunlight, and a recliner with a bear and pinecone blanket draped neatly over the back. A card table and one folding chair were set up near the woodstove. A red laptop computer, closed, sat centered on the table, along with a printer, a yellow legal pad open to a clean page, a stapler, and a Mammoth Woolly coffee mug stuffed with pens and pencils. Wylie's guts were in a sore twist. He wondered if Cynthia was crazy enough to shoot him dead, too.

"Do you read *The Woolly*?"

"Now and then."

"I'll give you the latest edition."

"Why did you call me here?"

"I want you to see Robert. Come."

Robert's room was dimly lit. When Cynthia turned the rheostat, Wylie saw the hospital bed and Robert's sheeted body propped upright at the waist. His still-handsome face reclined in pillows.

"You may have heard about his progress," she said.

Wylie looked from Robert to Cynthia. "Really?"

"He can move both eyelids in response to questions. One blink means yes and two mean no. It can be either eyelid. He's equally fluent with both. His respiration rate also changes in response to my questions, as if he's trying to answer. Right now, he's either asleep or opinionless. Robbie? Wylie Welborn is here. I'll bet you never thought you'd see the day I'd let *him* into our home. Are you awake, Robbie?"

Wylie stepped closer to Robert, touched his half brother's forehead. Robert's skin felt thin and cool and there was no movement of his eyelids. "Hello, Robert. It's Wylie. I'm in your home, all right. I'm not really sure why. But I'm standing here with you."

Wylie saw Cynthia at the edge of his vision, canting her head keenly toward Robert. Robert's eyelids did not move. "He's asleep," said Cynthia. "Clearly."

Wylie found Robert's hand under the covers and took it. His experience in combat had taught him almost nothing about this kind of neurological damage. In combat, Wylie could perform the four lifesaving steps: restore breathing, stop bleeding, protect wound, treat for shock. It was bloody, adrenaline-crazed work, but only once had a man died right there on him. Sergeant Madigan. The others were alive when they got CASEVAC'ed out. Some made it and some did not. Early in his deployment, Wylie had been amazed at how badly a man could be mangled and still survive. The medical corpsmen were good, the CH-46 evacuations were swift, the doctors at the field hospitals were excellent, and the drugs were strong. Thousands of lives were saved that in other wars could not have been. A couple of them were partly due to him.

But he felt more helpless with Robert now than he had ever felt on the battlefield. Wylie had no tools for this — no tourniquet or QuickClot or even a roll of gauze, no gun to shoot back with — and no hope, either. He watched Robert's eyelids intently for a long moment, hoping he was wrong about Robert. He'd never wanted so badly to be wrong. He almost envied Cynthia's delusions. Almost. Which was worse — no hope or false hope?

"Well," he said. "Maybe he's asleep. Like

you said."

"April Holly will not be true to you. True champions are never true."

Wylie turned to her. The light coming through the cracks in the blinds lined her face, and he saw Robert and Sky in her. "Why did you bring me here?" he asked.

"Life is made of three great labors. The third is learning to change direction. By that, I mean I want to apologize for what I did to your father. My husband. But now that we're standing here so close together, I can't apologize. I cannot form the words."

Wylie looked into the pale blue eyes trapped between the slats of light. "Maybe someday."

"I've certainly looked my deed straight in the eye. Even then I saw what I had coming. But I cannot change direction with you and your mother because first I would have to forgive you."

"Forgive us for what?"

"For taking Richard from me, of course."

"Have you forgiven yourself for killing him?"

"Never. The consequence is mine. My burden through eternity."

"And mine is to not have my father."

"Things circle outward from the act. As from a rock thrown into a still pond."

"Not much stillness here, Mrs. Carson. On this mountain. For us."

"Toil and trouble."

Wylie looked at Robert again. "Well, then."

"Well then, indeed."

"You still scare the shit out of me."

"You cannot imagine my dreams."

Before he could think of anything else to say, Wylie was outside in the lightly falling snow, unaware of having passed back through Cynthia's town house and out the door. He started up his truck. His heart was racing and sweat ran down his flanks and he couldn't get the picture of Robert's beautiful, unconscious face from his mind. He closed his eyes against it and let the defroster roar.

He heard the rapping on the window, saw Cynthia's fist coming at the glass again, and her eyes open wide. "Roll down the window!"

Wylie hit the down button, felt the cool gust of air, saw a strand of Cynthia's white hair blow across her face. "You forgot this!" She pushed a copy of *The Woolly* through the window. He set it on the seat beside him.

"I can't apologize to you for what I did," she said. "But I can commit a small act of kindness on behalf of someone you care about. And give you a piece of practical advice."

He waited, locking eyes with her again. "Kindness and advice? From you? Commit away, Mrs. Carson."

"Make them show you number twelve Madrone. Up by Canyon Lodge."

"Who? Why?"

"Your sisters. Twelve Madrone. Make them take you there. And here is my advice — beware of Sky's threat. He has the blood to back it up."

Cynthia turned abruptly and headed back inside.

Chapter Twenty-Seven

Wylie found Beatrice and Belle at the dining room table, bent over their studies. Kathleen and Steen were still at Let It Bean, tangling with a plumbing issue in the kitchen drain, which had been aggravated by the freeze the night before. Outside, it was snowing lightly and the house was cold. Wylie brought in wood and kindling and got the stove going.

"What's with twelve Madrone?" he asked as the flame crept up the logs.

Belle looked at him briefly, but Beatrice did not. "Isn't that a street?" asked Beatrice, more to her book than to her brother.

"A street up by Canyon Lodge."

"So what about it?" asked Belle.

"I asked you what you know about it," he snapped.

A beat of silence, then Beatrice said, "I'm kind of trying to keep my GPA up in the stratosphere, Wyles. And you're talking about a street I've barely heard of."

He watched them attempt casual eye contact and saw the worry on Belle's face, played off as boredom.

"I drove by twelve Madrone today," he said. "For sale. Looks empty. Maybe I'll just call the Realtor and get a tour."

"And buy it with what?" Belle asked. "We lost money again last month, if you haven't heard. Lots. Third month straight."

"Fall is tough in Mammoth," said Wylie.

"Unless you start dating April Holly," said Beatrice.

"We'll be bankrupt by March," said Belle. "Mom does the numbers. We don't make them up."

Wylie took away Belle's *American Experience* textbook and set it on the breakfast counter. Then Beatrice's *The Tortilla Curtain.* "I can smell your bullshit from across the room, sisters. Now talk to me."

"We know nothing about that house," said Belle.

"Totally nothing."

"Fine."

"Who told you what?" asked Beatrice.

"Anonymous tip. I've got a Realtor friend who can let me in. I can check it out my own. You know I'm not bluffing."

This time, their anxious faces met Wylie's

without any pretense at casualness. Belle turned to her sister. "No."

"It's time," said Beatrice.

"Be strong," said Belle.

"We'll show you," said Beatrice.

"We're doomed," said Belle.

They stood in tall pines beside the garage of 12 Madrone Street. The house was part of a small development that shared a common patch of forest, with a tennis court, pool, and barbecue area scattered within the trees. Several had FOR SALE signs out front. Light snow fell from a gunmetal gray sky. Beatrice took the key from the fake rock hider, set the hider back among the decorative river rocks arranged along the driveway, then slid the key into the side door of the garage.

"You've done this before," said Wylie.

"Kristy and her family moved out last year," said Belle. "She told me about the key. In case we needed to get in."

Wylie's imagination went a little south. "Why would you need to get in?"

"We didn't know why until later," said Beatrice.

She pulled open the door and Wylie stepped inside, followed by his sisters. The windows were small and the light was dim.

It was a big garage and empty, the floors stained with motor oil and tranny fluid and coolant. A gas can and snow shovels sat in one corner. Large plywood cabinets had been built along one wall. Wylie saw that they were secured with the cheap combination locks used by high schoolers, the pink ones favored by some girls.

Beatrice went to the cabinet nearest the door of the house, turned the dial of the lock, and pulled it off the latch. She swung out both doors and hung her head. Wylie saw the neatly arranged skis, ten pairs — expensive skis in good condition. Beatrice opened the adjacent cabinet. Ten more pairs.

"There're six cabinets with ten pairs each," said Belle. "Sixty pairs."

"Wow. From the lodges," said Wylie. His heart beat heavily, seeing how his sisters had fallen, knowing that so much had changed. He'd foreseen drugs and alcohol and maybe early sex for them, anger and truancy and rotten grades. Growing pains. Not grand theft.

"Do you carry snowboards and bikes, too?"

"Right this way," said Beatrice.

She unlocked the door to the house and stepped in and found a light. When she turned to him, Wylie saw the resigned expression on her face.

"Go ahead, Wylie," said Belle.

Wylie went into a laundry room that smelled faintly of detergent, then passed down a hallway into the darkened great room. The blinds were closed and Bea hit the lights. His heart fell further. The bicycles stood in rows — good bikes, Wylie saw — and the girls had wiped them shiny and sprayed the tires with dressing and arranged them by type: road bikes in back, then mountain bikes, then various hybrids and specialties. Snowboards were propped up casually against the great room's walls.

"How many boards, girls?"

"Forty-two," said Beatrice.

"Bikes?"

"Forty-six," said Belle. "That white Colnago C fifty-nine with the disc brakes went for sixteen grand new. The S-Works Epic was ten grand retail. It's all either good or great stuff. Total bike retail is thirty-nine thousand, not counting those two. And fifty grand more in boards and skis."

"Did you steal them yourselves?"

"Every single unit," said Belle.

"How many have you unloaded so far?"

"Not one," said Beatrice. "That's the beauty of our plan. The deal goes down

Sunday morning. One transaction and out. Clean."

"How much are you getting?"

"Fifteen thousand for the lot. As is. We just have to get everything down to Bishop."

"Who's your buyer?"

"A friend of a friend who does this kind of thing," said Belle. "A pro. He started at twelve thousand, but I was extremely firm."

"You two have truly fucked up," said Wylie.

"We don't see it that way," said Belle. "At least I don't."

Wylie looked at each in turn. "First off, this stuff cost people hundreds of dollars. Some, thousands. Dollars they probably earned, like we do. Maybe they get up at four-thirty in the morning, too. Maybe they work overtime. Did you ever think of that?"

Belle looked down, tapping something invisible on the floor with her boot toe. Then she turned back to Wylie. "We did it for rent, heat, insurance, and a new roof. We did it to keep Let It Bean alive. Not for clothes or makeup or drugs or a custom trailer to go *fishing* in. Don't get holy on us. We did it for us. Which includes *you.* Fifteen thousand, Wylie. That's a good roof over our heads. You have any better way to get that money?"

"I'm working on it." Wylie walked between the rows of bicycles, his mind bouncing from one dire thought to the next. All it would take right now was a Mammoth cop to see his truck parked in the driveway of this empty house and follow his curiosity. Grand theft. Both juveniles. Detention, expulsion, lawyers, court, bargains, punishment. God knew.

"Is Jolene Little Chief the Bishop friend in question?"

"No," said Belle.

"No," said Beatrice. "Actually, could be."

"Fuck!" Belle snorted. She kicked over one of the hybrid bikes, which toppled down three more. "Why don't you just hold your hands out for the cuffs, Bea?"

Beatrice went to the nearest wall, slid her butt to the floor, and buried her face in her hands.

"Wylie?" asked Belle. "Maybe *you* truly fucked up. Without you, we'd have fifteen thousand Sunday morning and nobody'd know squat about squat."

Beatrice sobbed. "I'm so unbelievably . . . exhausted."

"Shut up, Bea. Who ratted us out, Wylie? Who knew?"

"It doesn't matter."

"Does to me."

"To take these bikes, you had to make some changes in your appearance. Can you show me to wardrobe, Beatrice?"

"It's back in the garage," she blubbered.

"You two pick up these bikes and meet me there."

Wylie stood in the middle of the garage, trying to think, watching the shadows of his sisters moving faintly over the floor stains. From one of the cabinets, Bea brought him a big plastic storage bin containing two costume beards, two pairs of overalls, assorted hats and beanies. A pair of long-handled bolt cutters lay on top. She set it down at his feet. Belle put the pink combination locks back on the two open cabinets, spun the dials, and gave Wylie an unreadable look before coming over to him.

"Whose car were you using?" he asked.

"Claire Hobbs's," said Beatrice.

"I thought she'd died," said Wylie.

"She's ninety-nine and doesn't mind us borrowing her car once in a while," said Belle. "She can't drive it anymore anyway. We sort of trade out for pastries, delivered. She fiends on the whiskey/apricot and Brie Danish."

He sighed. "Didn't you know that the second someone snapped a picture of the license plate —"

"We got Nevada plates off a junker up in Bridgeport," said Belle. "We strap them on with rubber bands, then take 'em off when we're done."

Wylie nodded. "Tell Jolene the deal is off. Don't explain, don't apologize, don't negotiate, and do not change your mind."

"But we —"

"Zip it, Belle. I give the orders and you follow them."

"What are we going to do with all this stuff?" asked Beatrice.

"I'll handle it."

"What if you get caught with it?"

"I'll blame it on you two."

"I doubt you would," said Belle.

"I know you wouldn't," said Beatrice.

"Do what I told you with Jolene," said Wylie. "And never say anything about this again. Even in the privacy of your own home. Never, anyone. You know what this would do to Mom and Steen?"

Beatrice sighed hugely and hung her head again.

"How are we going to keep Let It Bean going and keep a roof over our heads?" asked Belle.

"We'll figure something."

"I've already *figured* that double the lease

and a new roof will bankrupt us by March," said Belle. "It's pretty simple math, Wylie."

"We'll figure something," he said. "My first idea is to send you two idiots to Mammoth PD and let you explain the whole mess. Mercy of the court and all that."

"After all this effort? Go ahead, Judas!" Belle threw open the side door and slammed it behind her. A moment later, Wylie saw her through one of the small garage windows, trudging down Madrone toward town. He watched her, seeing himself — the same strong body and will, the same talent for escalating a bad idea into a worse one.

His phone buzzed in his pocket and he checked the text from April: "Took Snowcreek cuz you liked the view. Gate code 1015."

Bea gave him a knowing look as he put the phone back in his pocket. "What are you going to do, Wylie?"

"I don't know yet."

"I'm so sorry."

"We'll find a way."

"It started with the skis, like, can we get away with this pair of Head five twenties? It looked so fun and easy. And it was. Then it got out of hand."

"Way of the world, Bea."

"I don't want to grow up."

Wylie looked after Belle again, but she was long gone. He wished he could run her down and hug her, make it all go away. His head and heart hurt. The snow fell harder. He saw a white Mercedes SUV coming up Madrone in the snow. The asphalt was black where the tires rode and white on the edges and the middle. The SUV pulled into the development entrance and, to Wylie's mounting anxiety, came down the street toward 12 Madrone.

"Stand away from that window," he said.

"Nobody ever stops or looks."

Wylie yanked her to the wall with him. The Mercedes pulled up behind his truck and parked, and the exhaust lingered in the heavy air. Looking through the tinted, snow-dusted windows, Wylie could make out a driver and a passenger. The driver got out and Wylie recognized him as the Mammoth councilman/Realtor, Howard Deetz. His apparent client, Jacobie Bradford, dropped from the passenger seat to the ground, looked up from his phone, then gave 12 Madrone the executive once-over. Howard noted Wylie's truck and trailer. He motioned to Jacobie and headed toward the front of the house.

"That perv Jacobie," said Bea. "You

wouldn't believe the crap he pulls at Mountain High."

"They'll use the lockbox on the front door," whispered Wylie. "As soon as I say, I want you out that side door and lost. I mean lost *fast.* Do you understand?"

"Not without you!" she whispered back.

"You obey me, Bea, or I swear you'll regret it. Okay, *go*!"

He watched Bea zigzag through the tall, dense pines. She ran up a gentle rise, down into a swale, and then vanished, footprints dark ovals in the white.

Wylie waited, imagining the entrance that Jacobie and Howard were likely making. When he thought he'd allowed the right amount of time for Howard to open the lockbox, unlock the door proper, hold open the door for Jacobie, who would then enter and pause in the entryway for an oh-wow moment before beginning the tour, Wylie slipped quietly out, shut the door, and strode to his truck, keys in one hand. His fingers touched the door handle.

"Yo! Wylie Welborn!" called Jacobie. He stood at the railing on the near side of the porch, holding his phone out from his ear. "What are you doing? Burglarizing this home?"

CHAPTER TWENTY-EIGHT

"I'm bottom-feeding, Jacobie, just like you! Looking to buy up some recession-blasted Mammoth real estate."

"These puppies are a steal, aren't they?"

"From what I've heard."

Jacobie lowered the phone. "I thought you were shacked up with April Holly."

"We're good friends, and that's absolutely untrue."

"Don't get violent again."

"Don't make it so tempting."

Howard Deetz came to the porch railing, holding up both lockbox and house key. "Finally! Wylie? What are you doing here?"

"Waiting for my Realtor — what's it look like?"

"Oh, hell, come in out of the snow. I'll split the commission with your agent if Jacobie doesn't buy it first."

"She's late. I'll try her again."

Wylie dug out his cell phone and got into

his truck. His heart was pounding hard in his ears and he was having trouble coming up with any solution other than the lame bluff he'd begun. He called an old high school friend who sold real estate. She happened to be at her desk at Century 21, with really not much going on. He told her he'd been interested in 12 Madrone for quite some time, would love to look at it.

"Set you back a million six," said Dawn.

"I still want to see it. Can you be there in five?"

"Okay, okay. Hey, is that true about you and April Holly being an item?"

"Just friends, Dawn."

"Hmmm. See you in five."

Wylie got out and crunched across the driveway to the front of the house. It was a large Craftsman style with timber columns footed in river rock and a big front porch. He climbed the steps, feeling as if he were about to enter a prison, which, it occurred to him, might well be in his future.

He entered the great room, in which Jacobie Bradford and Howard Deetz stood slack-jawed and speechless amid the warehouse of bicycles and snowboards. "Jesus," said Wylie. "The stolen ones?"

"What else could they be?" asked Jacobie. He was shooting video with his phone, sweeping down one row and up the next. He wore a fleece-lined flannel jacket and shearling boots and a knit cap in Rasta black, red, and green.

"This is the weirdest damn thing I've ever walked in on," said Howard, taking out his phone, too. "I've found homeless families and drunks and fornicating teenagers, even a bear, but never an entire bike and board shop."

"These are good products," said Jacobie. "Those bearded bike thieves know their stuff." With this, Jacobie lowered the phone, looked at recently shaven Wylie, then back at the bikes. "So, who's your Realtor?"

"Dawn Loe."

"Yes, hello, Officer, this is Howard Deetz, town council. Can you put me through to Sergeant Grant Bulla?"

"Where is your professed Realtor?" asked Jacobie, walking down the first row.

"Running late, she said."

"You've been here awhile, then?"

"Grant, Howard Deetz — hey, you gotta get someone over to twelve Madrone. You won't believe what's in the living room!"

"I was early, waited in the garage, out of the snow."

"My NielPryde!" said Jacobie, running a hand along the top tube of a beautiful road bike. "Oh, baby, baby, I missed you." He stopped caressing the frame, as if interrupted by an idea. "You look good without the beard, Wylie."

"You look like Mr. Clean with that shiny head."

"Here we go again."

Jacobie positioned himself defensively, with two rows of bikes between him and Wylie. "Humor me, Wylie. I watch too many TV cop shows, I admit it. Helps me escape. But they always tell you that in a crime, there's no coincidences, you know? *No coincidences.* So, the sharp cop arrives on the scene and you're already here. No biggie, but of all the houses for sale, why are you at this particular one? Then the sharp cop goes inside and sees the loot. So he has to figure it's at least possible that you knew the stolen goods were here. After all, you're a local, and the sharp cop knows the criminal tendencies in you. Then he thinks, Heck, this yokel might have stolen the damn things. So he thinks that maybe when the Realtor, Howard, and the legitimate house hunter, Jacobie, pulled up, you were already right here in this great room, maybe adding to your latest haul. And you heard them and sneaked out to the garage and tried to get to your truck and out without being seen.

Fail. In fact, you didn't look happy a minute ago when I called out to you, as captured on my phone. You still don't look happy. Of course — and we learn this at the beginning of the episode — a few weeks ago you shaved off your beard *after* witnesses described the bike thieves as bearded. So that's my plot. Think I can make it in Hollywood?"

"If someone doesn't pinch your head, just for the fun of it."

"There you go again, like you're stuck in the sixth grade or something. Don't you think anything's funny? Can't you use your words, like an adult?"

Howard's voice drifted through the silence. "How would I know how they get in and out? All I know is the lockbox was locked, just like it's supposed to be."

"Maybe a local Realtor is in on it, too," said Wylie. "The key to the lockbox, right? Maybe it's Howard."

"Maybe what's Howard?" asked Howard. "Grant's on his way."

"Wylie here was conjecturing that you're part of the bike thieves' ring, Howie," said Jacobie. "Because you have the lockbox key."

Howard shrugged with apparent disinterest, started taking pictures with his phone.

"Sorry, Wylie," said Jacobie. "I'm not a bad guy."

"You're annoying and insignificant."

"I've done okay in life, for having no talent and an abrasive personality."

"You'll learn the hard way."

"I wish I'd served my country."

"But you have a reason you couldn't. People like you always do."

Jacobie nodded and glanced over at his bike. "You know what's interesting, though? Back on the 'no coincidences' theory? I saw Belle trekking down Madrone in the snow when we drove up. That is to say, heading away from this house. Walking fast and determined, like she was upset. Or maybe in a hurry. Or both."

"She's at home doing schoolwork right now."

"I can certify that she is not. Think I should tell the sergeant my theory?"

"What exactly is the theory?"

"You and some bearded buddy are the bike thieves. Belle does the cleanup here, gets the product ready for market. Somehow you guys got yourselves a house key for this place. You keep the beater car somewhere out of sight when you're not using it. You shaved because you'd been spotted. Probably your partner shaved, too. So now you think you're one step ahead of Johnny Law. But you've got a flaw in your alibi. Namely, that a doughnut shop employee/ski bum gigolo is in the market for a house listed at a million six. Unless April Holly wants somewhere to play house with her boy toy."

Words failed Wylie. He gauged the pleasures of strangulation against the consequences, kind of liked the way it penciled out.

Jacobie eyed him with a small smirk, as if he'd spotted a stain on Wylie's trousers, or a weakness in him. "Maybe I'll just tell the sergeant what I saw and let him figure out the details."

Wylie's old friend Dawn Loe pulled up a moment later in a silver Suburban. Wylie parted the blinds and watched as one of the vehicle's side windows went down and the heads of two curious golden retrievers filled the frame, snouts lifted to the air. Next came a Mammoth PD slickback from which plainclothes Sgt. Grant Bulla stepped. He stopped to pet the dogs. Howard came from the house to greet him.

"I'm not going to say anything about my theories, Wylie," said Jacobie. "At least not yet. I'm still putting the pieces together."

"Let me know what you come up with."

"You can bet I will."

■ ■ ■ ■

Wylie sat in the living room of April Holly's furnished rental in the Snowcreek development. It was a spacious town house, richly appointed, with views of the mountain. April had a fire going by the time he got there. It was mid-evening. Wylie looked out to the fading profile of Mammoth Mountain, the stilled lifts rising like toy structures, their cables bellied between them.

On late evenings like this, anywhere in the world that Wylie happened to be — in Mammoth or Solitary or in Kandahar or the Tegernsee monastery or the Great St. Bernard Hospice — he always tried to leave the lights off and the lanterns and candles unlit to enjoy the simultaneous fall of outside and inside darkness. Such a slow and subtle transition from day to night. A reminder to slow down. To reflect and maybe give thanks. But that was impossible right now, because April was buzzing from room to room, doing what someone always did — cranking up house lights in advance of sunset. Let there not be light, he thought.

But this was her home. Wylie shook his head at his own pissiness, told himself to put one foot in front of the other. Be cool anyway, he thought, house lights or not. He'd been nearly silent for an hour. He felt stymied and useless and wanted to be alone and was only here now to please April, who delivered to him another light bourbon on ice. He took it without looking at or thanking her.

He thought of Robert and his eternal stillness. Would he ever move again? Was he aware at all? Did he want to be alive?

He thought of Belle and Beatrice running off into the snow. He thought of the diminishing returns from Let It Bean and the snow soon to be melting through the ceiling into plastic buckets at home, and the fourteen thousand dollars it would take to replace that decaying roof, and the rent going up another $2,200 a month in January if they signed the new lease. He finally decided to list his MPP on eBay — the proceeds could pay for something, even if it was only the balance for the MPP itself. He'd thought long and hard about selling it just the other night, and now he saw no real alternative. He felt small and horrible.

And he saw himself here, holed up in this tidy luxury chalet with America's darling — a beautiful girl who was momentarily stuck on him for whatever reasons, who just also happened to be the most gifted aerial snowboarder the world had yet seen. A millionaire several times over. Which made him feel even worse. It might simplify things just to walk out on her right here and now. Let her get on with her career, and him with his. Pop the fantasy and get real again. Back to Earth. He turned and looked at the door. Where will I go when my plans betray me?

Suddenly, he felt his inner boxes shifting around and heard the thumping within them. Once they started sliding, he was never sure when one might topple over, hit the floor, and spill its contents. Some of them housed relatively minor things, such as the small square one that now crashed and spilled out the beating he'd given Sky Carson when they were eight. Wylie saw his little fists flailing away, landing often on Sky, who squirmed flat on his back on the playground grass, trying to cover up. What shamed Wylie now wasn't the beating, but the satisfaction he had taken in it, how good it had felt to silence a tormentor. He could have stopped sooner but didn't.

Down fell another, this one rectangular and long, as if for roses, rocking end to end before it settled. This contained Ellen Pelleri in their sophomore year at Mammoth High School, whom he had spurned bluntly, and who not long after had veered into an express lane of heavy recreational drugs and promiscuity. Two years later, she had committed suicide. He'd always known it was his fault, or at least partially his fault, so, what percentage exactly, and to whom did he owe restitution? No word on that from anyone. So there she was.

Before Wylie could get Ellen back where she belonged, Sergeant Madigan landed hard on April's hardwood floor, neck-shot and blood-drenched and knowing he was dying, and really, what more could Wylie have done? A team of surgeons couldn't have saved him. QuickClot and tourniquets versus a blown carotid, severed vertebrae, and a ruined spinal cord? Wylie was helpless. Then why was Sergeant Madigan still up here? War was war. How was Wylie supposed to make it up to him?

Next tumbled free the Taliban sniper who had shot Sergeant Madigan from a murder hole in a shot-to-shit abandoned hillside compound. Wylie's B squad had patrolled past that compound nearly a hundred days running, checking it coming and going every time. But suddenly it was not abandoned at all and the sergeant was down in a blast of blood. Then came a barrage of enemy mortar fire. Wylie had done his best for Sergeant Madigan as the rounds rained down upon them. Hopeless, and they both knew it. Jesse thought he hit the sniper with a very good shot through the sniper's own hole in the mud-brick wall. Later, Wylie and Jesse had clambered against the rocky hillside for cover, then worked their way up to the compound to see if Jesse had hit his target.

Now Wylie saw the dead fighter splayed out in his man dress on the dirt floor of the compound, Jesse kneeling over him with the big knife in one hand, working away at the top of his head. At first, Wylie thought Jesse was taking a lock of his hair. Then he heard the grind of the steel against skull, and the rasp of parting scalp. And saw the in-and-out motion of Jesse's elbow. Then, suddenly, Jesse went still. He looked down at his blood-sheathed hands. When he finally lifted his gaze to Wylie, it was in helplessness and wild shame. Wylie took the knife and pushed Jesse away and finished the awful act. It was the hardest thing he'd ever done. But the reason for it was good and true, was it not? To help his friend and take some of the shame and guilt for himself, to prove to Jesse that he was not alone, that they were in this together. Always faithful. Always. He would do it again.

Wylie sat in the brightly lit room for a long

while, waited for another box to fall, but none did. His mind wandered now, fatigued.

"It's Bea and Belle," he finally said.

"Can you tell me?"

"That could put you in a position. They may be in some genuine trouble. I might not be able to fix it."

"Then I'll stay out of it, Wylie. My plate's plenty full, too."

"With Helene?"

"Only by phone. But I spotted Logan today, cruising by here in one of my Escalades. Imagine a six-nine gargoyle in a beanie hunched over the steering wheel. I was standing out front and he looked straight ahead when he went by, like I wouldn't notice it was him."

Wylie smiled at this.

"I got you to smile."

"I know all this is hard. Helene. Everything."

"It's been coming for years. Now, finally. There's no good time for it."

"Is it as difficult as a triple cork?"

"Harder. But, I have an idea." She offered him her hand, which was warm and strong. "Let's turn off all the lights and put on some music and dance to the last of the daylight."

He rose and began turning off lights. He

willed his spirit to rise, too, but it seemed to be trapped in a concrete room with no door or windows. He watched her plug in a speaker no larger than a tennis ball and hook her phone to it. A tearjerker came on. Wylie caught April in the near dark and put his arms around her and they moved to the music. He felt her heart tapping away against him.

"I feel good, Wylie. No matter all the stress. No matter what happens. I know we'll catch some hell for this. They'll try to give us hell. But I feel free and strong for this season. I like our chances for the Mammoth Cup." She brought him closer. "However. What I don't like was the look on your face a minute ago."

They danced and Wylie's nerves began to unjangle. Images of head-butting Jacobie into the Grand Canyon dissolved as the small of April's back moved warmly against his hand. "I want to be as good for you as you are for me," she said.

"You're very good for me."

"Four hugs a day good?"

"Or five, or six."

"What else is eating you? Besides your sisters? You're almost strong enough to hide it."

"Just the usual."

"There's a hot tub in the bath," she whispered. "And the master bed's a four-poster I just made up, and they have a fake bearskin rug by the fireplace. Fire's all lit."

"Your choice."

"Up to you."

"Where we stand?"

"Oh my, yes. Good as middle podium, you beautiful, haunted man. Kiss me now."

Chapter Twenty-Nine

Sky guided his new love, Antoinette, into one of the wing chairs in his grandfather's great room, trailing a hand across her shoulder on his way to the other chair. Adam sat opposite them at one end of the old leather couch, the hefty burl coffee table between them. Snow-streaked Mammoth Mountain waited just outside the window glass, looking close enough to touch. Sky tried to focus on the steep boulder and snow carapace of that mountain, then on the chairlift towers staunch against the silver sky, but his eyes kept drifting back to Antoinette, and hers to him. She was petite and stylish, black-haired and brown-eyed.

Teresa came into the room from behind him, but Sky sensed her before he saw her, as he often did. She swept by and mussed his hair. "Such bright colors," she said. He'd always liked Teresa, even as an infant, he'd been told. To Sky, it was nice that she was with Grandpa often now. They seemed comfortable and right together. Sometimes love was easy. And sometimes it was a high-adrenaline blur, like a ski-cross race. Which is how he felt around Antoinette. He stood and introduced the women, watched Antoinette rise and Teresa move forward for a brief handshake. Teresa then sat down at the opposite end of Adam's couch and crossed her legs.

Sky stood. "Grandfather, Teresa. The news I want to share with you is that Antoinette and I are engaged to be married."

"I thought so from that rock on her finger," said his grandfather. "Congratulations to both of you."

"Yes," said Teresa.

Antoinette held out her left hand, smiling and blushing. Then she briefly bowed her head, as if acknowledging great and undeserved fortune. Sky watched the curtain of black hair fall, aglitter in the light from the deer-antler chandelier above.

"I have never in my life, sir and Teresa, felt this way about a woman," said Sky. "I feel like I've awakened from a quarter century of sleep. You're looking at a new Sky — the Commitment Guy."

Antoinette hooked a section of hair behind one ear and looked at Adam as if prepared for judgment, then to Teresa.

"How long have you known each other?" asked his grandfather.

"Twenty-two days," said Sky.

"Twenty-three days," said Antoinette, simultaneously. They smiled at each other, raised palms in a high five, though they were seated some eight feet apart. They had joked about this time discrepancy before, whether it was a Tuesday or a Wednesday that Sky and Antoinette had met at the Rock 'N Bowl. He clearly remembered that it was the Wednesday two-for-one local brews beer night — two being his max while training for the cup — and Antoinette clearly remembered it being the Tuesday ten frames, ten bucks night, which, as a true bowling nut, brought her to the Rock 'N Bowl every Tuesday.

"We've agreed to disagree," Antoinette said pleasantly. She had a bell-clear voice and she articulated precisely, which Sky found refreshing after a lifetime listening to loose-jawed snow bunnies. He liked her sophistication, too: trim-cut clothes instead of baggy pocketed stuff, fashion boots instead of snow boots, dramatic full-length coats, not bulbous down-filled parkas. She was not afraid of a little makeup. And, God, those eyes.

"Antoinette grew up in New Jersey," said Sky. "She snowboarded in the Poconos and Catskills when she was little and learned to ski here when she was fourteen. Guess who taught her here? Robert! Antoinette fell in love — with Mammoth, I mean. She moved here six weeks ago with her cosmetology degree in hand and a job waiting for her. She's got a chair at Hair It Is and she's a certified level-three color consultant for Redken. I've always liked hairstylists. They're curious, good conversationalists, and often pretty. I can't believe it took me six weeks to discover her."

Sky's grandfather nodded. "And that's why your hair is now bright red on the left and bright white on the right?"

"Correct. It's just a marketing thing, G-pa. Mammoth speed demon goes patriotic."

"Not to be an old man about this," said Adam, "but don't you think an engagement is kind of soon, after only three weeks?"

"It certainly is," said Antoinette.

"I agree," said Sky.

"But the sheer wrongness of it," she said, "is what convinces us it's right."

"And the logic in that is where?" asked Adam.

Sky was ready for this. He scooted to the

edge of his chair. "It's nowhere, Grandfather. We know that. That's why the wedding will be after the season. After I've won the Gargantua Mammoth Cup and the X Games in Aspen, there's going to be the long FIS World Cup circuit in Europe, then the U.S. Olympic team selections in spring. All of which you have generously offered to finance. So . . . we're thinking of a classic June wedding. By then, we'll have been together for almost eight months. And if we're not still together . . ."

"We're both trying to go in with our eyes open," said Antoinette. "Although I will admit that I am completely, blindly in love with your grandson. And I feel that I always will be."

Sky noted that both his grandfather and Teresa were sitting unusually still.

"Doubt us all you want," said Sky. "But give us time. I ask you for that."

"I will believe in you," said Teresa.

"You make my heart glad," said Sky.

Antoinette bowed her head again.

"Well," said Adam. "You're twenty-six, Sky. I *want* to believe in you. I am ready to believe. I want you to find a good woman and settle down. But there is a much more urgent concern. Namely, the Mammoth Cup. I expect to see your good character and steady nerves in that race. I expect to see you on the podium."

"I'll be there, sir."

"And if you and Wylie run afoul of each other on the X Course that day, I expect sportsmanship out of you — in spite of your empty and theatrical threat."

Sky absorbed this body blow with a nod, vowing to reverse its sharp thrust and, like a hapkido master, convert its power to his own. It was all in the plan. "No, sir. My threat is not empty."

"Focus on the race," said Adam.

"I have done that, G-pa. You'll see."

But Sky knew that words would not satisfy his grandfather. Not after so many wasted ones. So many false starts, broken promises, bold declarations that amounted, in the end, to nothing. Which is why he was looking forward to G-pa's reaction when he won the cup. That victory would wipe the doubt from G-pa's face once and for all. *Wipe it right off, Sky. I never could.* With the Gargantua Cup victory, Sky would step forth into the world as a fully emerged man, a man respected, a man whose word was his bond. Sky breathed slowly and deeply, banishing all negativity, or most of it. He was surprised to hear the Black Not lurking so close by, so soon after their last episode.

"Sir, may I say something about Sky's alleged threat?" said Antoinette.

"Of course you may."

Antoinette stood and clasped her dainty hands together in front of her, like a student preparing to give a speech. "Sky and I have had some long talks about Wylie Welborn, and the . . . promise that Sky made at Mountain High that night. Sky's public vow was to punish Wylie if he knocked Sky — or anyone else — off the X Course again. It was a promise to the mountain and to any person on it." Sky watched Antoinette's hands release each other as she looked at Adam and Teresa in turn. "But — and this is what everyone seems to forget — in one wonderful, beautiful, gracious moment, Sky Carson followed up by saying he would withdraw his threat if Wylie would apologize for what he had done. Sky was willing to forgive Wylie, and he said so, publicly. It was the moral thing to do. But no apology came. Instead, Wylie sucker punched Sky in the restaurant for no reason, and they've not said a word since."

Antoinette swung back her shiny black mane and cast a firm look at Adam. She had delivered comparable speeches to Sky, though on differing subjects. He loved them. They were always truthful and persuasive. And in that clear voice, they were tonally beautiful, too, like a Sierra creek or rain on a roof. Antoinette's speeches seemed to run on their own fuel. Now she walked around the wing chairs and the big couch, circling back to where she'd started.

"So," she continued. "What we came up with was that Sky and Wylie should sit down together alone and talk it all out. The sooner the better. Wylie can apologize in private, and Sky can retract his threat without losing face. Because — and here's the heart of it, sir — Sky doesn't need this hanging over him before the race. It's a burden. He loses sleep over it. He obsesses. It eats away at him. Sky doesn't want to 'punish' Wylie at all. He only wants the apology and an acknowledgment of truth. It doesn't have to go viral, or even be public."

"So the threat *is* empty," said Adam.

"No, Grandpa," said Sky, summoning calm. "I mean what I said. I mean it . . . thoroughly. Shouldn't you be trying to talk me *out* of it?"

"But the whole point is, Sky will retract it for the apology," said Antoinette. "This is a mark of good character, sir, and Teresa. And a way to get this thing off his back and win the cup. That's all he wants for now. So, with that in mind, we were hoping you could bring them together, sir. Sky and Wylie. Maybe right here in this beautiful room. They'll talk if you order them to talk. You alone. They respect you more than anybody on Earth."

Sky watched his grandfather pry his gaze away from Antoinette, glance at Teresa, then slowly rise. It took him longer and longer these days. He certainly was tall. The room was quiet enough for Sky to hear his grandfather's joints crack. Adam walked slowly and steadily toward Antoinette, who stood waiting for him in the middle of the room.

Adam nodded and offered his hand and she shook it.

For Sky, the next hour of conversation was a pleasure. He mostly listened. His grandfather and Teresa prodded Antoinette with questions about her family and childhood, and Antoinette responded with all her natural charm and easy grace. That voice of hers was so clear and bright. He learned some more things about her, too — that her community-college-speech-teacher father spoke four languages; her eldest sister had died at birth; her mother, a trial attorney, ran triathlons and was now on her fourth marriage. One of the things that Sky first loved about Antoinette was her reaction to the fate of his father at the hands of his mother. "What a terrific loss for everyone," she had said, brown eyes becoming wet.

Sky gazed down the mountain to the bustling little village. The eastern sky looked like powdered lead and he'd heard that more snow was on the way. He could feel his own inner barometer lowering in response to this minor snowfall and the promise of more on the way. When he smelled something markedly appetizing wafting into the room, his grandfather asked, "Are you still eating that slime instead of real food?"

"Sir, yes, sir. It's called Soylent. I'm supernaturally strong now. I've clocked a fifty-nine-second X Course run on the Imagery Beast. The first ever."

"But not on the real X Course."

"There's no snow on the real X Course."

"Under one minute?"

"Fifty-nine point seven five."

His grandfather nodded. "Well. Nice. Teresa has made us up some venison chili that is excellent, and ready to be served. Please stay for lunch."

After lunch, Antoinette wanted to see Robert again. Sky was intrigued and impressed that she had developed such a lasting affection for Robert, having taken ski lessons from him five years ago, when she was fourteen. Cynthia let them in, touched Sky's newly colored hair, and reported that Robert had been communicating more clearly these last few days — sometimes by fluttering an eyelid, sometimes by subtle changes in respiration. Robert's fiancée, Hailee, was there, too, and to Sky she looked disheveled and dispirited.

They stood in the warm bedroom, the blinds open to let in the autumn light. Sky greeted Robert cheerfully, touching his hair and face. Antoinette reintroduced herself as one of Robert's students from five years ago. She recalled that her first run with Robert had been down Schoolyard. She told him she still loved to ski. Hailee stared wordlessly.

Then Cynthia bored in close, face-to-face with Robert, and told him about the last snowstorm — which had dropped six very nice inches — and the storm forecast for later that night, which was supposed to be heavier. "I know how much you love the snow," she said. "Don't you, Robbie?" They waited a long moment in silence for either the eyelid flutter or respiration-rate change.

"Might be asleep," said Sky.

"Quite certainly," said Cynthia.

"You're beautiful, Robert," said Antoinette.

Sky watched Hailee turn, hugging herself, and leave the room.

"No room onboard for the unhopeful," said Cynthia. "There, did you see that? Left eyelid. His response is not always immediate."

"Yeah," said Sky. "Pretty sure I saw it."

Sky drove Antoinette back to her apartment. They stopped off at Von's for a few things she needed. As they were crossing the parking lot Megan and Johnny Maines and Ivan the Terrier all paraded past.

"Mahalo, bitches!" Johnny called out, waving. "I've got money on you for the Mammoth Cup, Sky! Don't let Wylie Welborn butt you off that mountain again!"

Sky and Antoinette walked to Sky's car, each holding a plastic shopping bag and the other's hand. At the mention of Wylie Welborn's name, Sky's expansive mood seemed to deflate and fall again. He heard the Black Not cackling faintly in the background. He took a deep breath.

"Are you okay, Sky?"

"More than okay."

"Was it what Johnny Maines said about the race?"

"Indeed. I'm trying to control my emotions."

"Adam will arrange the meeting. You can get to the other side of this thing. I so believe in you."

"You're the only person in the world who does."

"I almost never hear self-pity in you."

"That was factual, not self-pitying."

They walked the rest of the way to the car in silence and Sky took another deep breath. *You can do this.*

"What do you guess Adam and Teresa think of me?" she asked.

He looked at Antoinette. It startled him that someone with so much intelligence and good grooming could be so uncertain of herself in the eyes of others. "I think they were impressed but worried that we're hurrying things."

"Well, we kind of are."

"Totally. It's part of the rush. But, Antoinette, I'm nonbudgeable in what I feel for you. I've made up my mind. So it is written. I love you very much and want you to be my wife."

They put the bags in the trunk of the Subaru; then Sky held the passenger door open for her. Before climbing in, she stepped up close to Sky and kissed his lips lightly. "I'm proud to be your woman. I'm going to be the best woman you've ever had. I'm so sorry about Robert. I still remember the day I skied with him. You reminded me of him the second we met."

"We were — *are* very different."

"Less than you think. And he didn't have your disadvantages."

"It wrecks my soul to see him," said Sky. "But I try to be strong for Mom."

"You're a good son."

"I'm not sure what to do with crazy people."

"Just love them." She hugged him tight. She was small and slender enough to practically disappear. Her voice came from almost behind him now, disembodied, like his father's. But Antoinette's voice was invariably positive, not negative. Not *not.* "You don't feel the Black Not coming, do you?"

"A presence but not a threat."

"It'll pass. You can beat it! I'm with you, Sky."

"I feel like I was raised by a gigantic ghost with a face bigger than the whole town of Mammoth Lakes, and she hovers just above the tree line and watches everything I do. Do you think Wylie will talk?"

"For Adam, yes."

"But not for me."

She broke the embrace, sat down in the car, and looked up at him as she swept the shoulder restraint into place. "You two are half brothers. You're going to figure it out. Just remember to stick to your facts and your ideas when you talk with Wylie. We'll write out the main points on four-by-six note cards you can take with you."

"Awesome, Antoinette. You are awesome."

Chapter Thirty

Then, as in a movie smash cut or in a dream, Sky was sitting in the same wing chair in his grandfather's aerie without Adam or Teresa, only Wylie heavily seated where Antoinette had been, seemingly moments ago. It was night, and in the expanse of the outdoor lights Sky saw the thin carpet of boulder-strewn snow, and beyond that the blackness of the slope, then the distant twinkling Christmas globe of a town far below.

"What's with the hair?" asked Wylie.

"Antoinette did the color. What do you think?"

"Well . . ."

"I may grow a beard and have her do it sky blue."

Wylie nodded in his superior way, Sky noted, or was it pure disdain? "I'm glad you showed," Sky said, looking down at the note cards. Antoinette's handwriting was neat and as sweet as her voice. *Clear air first.* "I want to clear the air so we can have a good clean race."

"I'm good with you, Sky."

Recap facts of the attacks. "Not so fast. You forced me off the X Course last January. And knocked me out at Slocum's."

"To clear the air, you have to let go of those things."

"Exactly."

"I can't let go of them for you, Sky."

Politely restate request for apology. "But you can apologize for running me off the course. Then I can let go. Really, that's all it would take."

"Are those note cards?"

Wylie looked at him for a long beat and Sky returned it. Without his beard, Wylie looked less bearlike and less intimidating to Sky. With the long hair, Wylie could have a Jesus look going, if only he could bring spiritual credibility to his face. Sky could see their father's bones in him, at least what bones he could extrapolate from photos and video. Sky also noted the skeptical, show-me stare that nearly every Carson had. And, as always, Sky saw something of the brute stubbornness that ran through the river Carson like a deep, wide undertow. Wylie still held his gaze.

"Sky. I brushed by you. I took the line and you lost it and canned up. I won't endorse your lie. And I won't apologize for what I didn't do. Why would I do that?"

"Because I'm asking you."

"I won't. You can't revise something once it's done. You don't get to. Nobody does. You have to see things for what they are. Not what you want them to be."

"But you, Wylie, can change things with a simple apology."

"No. I can't change things at all, with anything. That's the whole point, and you don't get it."

"I knew you'd be too stubborn and self-righteous to apologize." There was a long silence, until Sky spoke again. He watched the snow slanting softly down. "And there's the threat I made."

"Right."

"I won't retract it."

"I let it go, Sky."

"Big mistake. I gave my word on it. And my word is something I don't retract. Not anymore."

"Right."

Right. The inflection in Wylie's voice hit Sky like the X Course rocks he'd busted up on that day. It was a revelation. He dropped the cards to the floor. He sensed the Black.

Not nearby, eavesdropping on all this. He heard his father's soft cackle. He tried to blot it out so he could hear Antoinette's clear, logical, persuasive voice. "You don't take my warning seriously."

"No. I never did."

"Never?"

"Not after I saw the water come out of the squirt gun."

"Not even a shadow of doubt?"

"A very occasional one, maybe."

"What if the gun had been real?"

"There you go again, trying to change what can't be changed."

"The realness of the gun is changeable. Didn't you learn threat assessment in the war?"

"From the second I signed my name at the recruiting office."

"Then how can you ignore this? You're making a terrible mistake, Wylie." Sky leaned forward, rested his arms on his knees, and stared down at the note cards splayed on the floor before him.

Accept apology with graciousness and retract threat sincerely.

Remember that your mutual love of Robert is behind all of this.

If no apology, withdraw threat ANYWAY to remove obligation and clear conscience.

Withdraw?

No, he thought. I won't do that. Not again. As I have so many times before. I'm sorry, Antoinette, but that was the one card you wrote out that I didn't agree with. I spoke very clearly, but you talked over what I was trying to say. Your clear, beautiful voice went right over me. But you can't talk over me now. And I have to speak for myself.

"Don't try to force me off the mountain again. *Anyone* off the mountain. The consequences will be severe."

"You are a man with red hair on the left and white hair on the right," said Wylie.

"Don't confuse showmanship with lack of conviction."

"Got it." Wylie looked at him, shaking his head, but said nothing more.

Sky squatted, collected the cards, and stood. "You're a belligerent mongrel," he said. "If you don't run a clean Gargantua Cup, you won't be able to change the consequences and I won't be able to help you."

"I've let the threat go, Sky."

"As I stand before you, I can't overstate the danger you are in."

"Let it go. All of it. I have."

An idea then came barreling into Sky's mind, straight into the gap between his defeated diplomacy and his stymied plans. He sized it up and found it promising. "But . . . maybe there's another way to make you see. I may just try one more time." Sky saw that he finally had Wylie Welborn's full attention.

"Let it go, Sky, whatever it is."

"Don't worry about anything. I've got the idea."

Sky brooded late into the night, turning over his idea every which way, looking for the downsides. Antoinette had chosen to sleep at her place, which was fine with him, though he already missed her. Small amounts of time apart were good for lovers. And without her, he could wander his little condo, nip the tequila as needed, and mutter freely to himself.

Unable to concentrate or sleep, he turned on the TV. Whereupon — as if through Satanic intervention — an XTV *Adrenaline* interview with Wylie Welborn was in progress. Sky watched, at first affronted that Wylie could just take over his TV like this, then fascinated.

Apparently, the interview had been recorded not long after the "Curse of the Carsons" piece. Wylie, fully bearded, looked to Sky like the Wolfman on Xanax, a hulking, resentful hominid with plenty of axes to grind. He talked about his Mammoth Cup and other races he had won way back in the dark ages; his impatience with being only a ski-cross racer and a desire to "grow up"; his service to his country in Afghanistan; his "wandering around the snowbound world," which was a kind of "spiritual journey" — sheesh! — his eventual "realization" that he needed to return to Mammoth Lakes to see if he could become "somehow more complete, or maybe even neccessary." Sky had never heard such self-referential bullshit delivered with such a straight face. Of course, Bonnie Bickle prodded him on with all her toothy prettiness.

Adrenaline then showed Wylie's semifinal and final victories at the Mammoth Cup. Sky watched intently, having to admit that there was some good speed and a cagey use of body weight in Welborn. He'll need it, thought Sky, reminding himself of his 59.75 second run on the Imagery Beast. It was the fastest time Helixon had ever recorded. After, coach Brandon had told Sky that Wylie's best time trial on the X Course was not only five years ago but a ho-hum 1:2.20 minute run under perfect conditions. Sky was almost three seconds faster!

Next, Bonnie asked Wylie about the curse on the Carson family. Wylie tried to defend the clan, which, he said, had no curse that he was aware of, just the same ups and downs of any family, and maybe some things had happened, but the Carsons helped build Mammoth Mountain, along with Dave, of course, so no, if anything, the Carsons were blessed, not cursed.

Bonnie reminded Wylie of his long-running competition, feuds, and literal physical fights with several Carsons — most often Sky — and of forcing Sky off the X Course during training for the upcoming Gargantua Mammoth Cup. Wylie smiled way back behind his beard, shook his head, and said nobody bumped anybody off the X Course, that it was just a routine accident on a fast course — he'd busted up on that part of the course lots of times himself. Bonnie asked about Sky's "line in the snow," got a shrug from Wylie, then showed the entire video monologue delivered by bruised and battered Sky in his shorts at Mountain High that night. They played the part about Wylie being a "demon bastard" twice, which led Bonnie to recap the whole miserable nativity of today's guest — Wylie Welborn — using clips of Cynthia.

But by the time *Adrenaline* went on to its

next segment — attractive young women in swimsuits zip-lining over a crocodile-infested river in India — Sky felt energized and motivated by Wylie's self-serving interview. Wasn't there a flicker of doubt back in that hairy face, some worry in his eyes? How could there not be? Especially now that the entire racing community in Mammoth Lakes — Wylie included — knew about Sky's unprecedented under-one-minute run on the Imagery Beast. Take that, W.W.!

Although, actually, what had Wylie shown tonight at G-pa's, other than his usual arrogant stubbornness? How was it even possible that Wylie could have dismissed Sky's solemnly sworn challenge, publicly offered? Could Wylie no longer see? Had Afghanistan taken away his senses? His courage?

Time to wake him up, Sky thought. You might be doing him a favor.

Chapter Thirty-One

"What was he like, Mom? Dad."

Kathleen set the croissant on the baking rack and looked across the worktable at Wylie, her face flushed and the great vertical worry lines setting in her forehead. Wylie had been waiting for days for a private moment to ambush her. Now they were doing the morning prep at Let It Bean, the girls were sleeping in on this Saturday, and Steen was home putting tarps over the worst parts of the roof.

She picked up another handful of dough and began forming the next croissant. Her face was still red, but Wylie saw that the worry lines had let go, and he thought he saw the suggestion of a smile on his mother's face. "He was . . . impressive."

Wylie nodded, surprised by this, though he'd had no idea what his mother might say about Richard Carson. He cut the dough, got the wedges a little big. He'd always been an earnest but untalented apprentice.

"Of course, I was seventeen when I met him. To me, he was a god, and my coach, and I fell for him. The Carson men — they have that . . . *quality.* Then as I got to know him over the weeks, I discovered that he wasn't the cool king he pretended to be. But he did a great job of faking it. He wanted to be liked. He was polite, but provocative and charming. Under the influence of alcohol, which was often, he became unpredictable. Never mean or morose, but hyperenergetic and out of kilter. Alcohol or not, he was funny in a goofy, boyish way. He made fun of almost everything and everybody, including himself. The general feeling on the mountain back then was that his lack of seriousness about racing was Richard's Achilles' heel as a competitor. He also doubted his nerve. He was serious about his students, though."

"How old was he?"

"Twenty-nine. He'd had a good Olympic showing at Sarajevo in '84 but broke a leg six weeks before Calgary. When I met him, he'd retired from downhill racing, but you wouldn't know it to watch him ski. Out there first thing, every day, carving his name on that mountain. He said skiing was more fun than racing. He was very dedicated to his students, though. I think he was trying to make something sacred for us that was never quite sacred to him. It worked on me. He taught me to love skiing. And I wanted to race. He told me I could be good enough, that it would take training and luck. I felt that I was a born racer. I had the speed need, courage, and cool, good eyesight and reflexes. I wanted to race and win, then have a family. Like Richard. I wanted to do what he had done."

Wylie mulled this over. He had over-handled the dough and had to start over. "He was married and had two kids, Mom."

"Ouch. Yes."

"I'm not criticizing. I'm just —"

"Stating the facts of the case."

"Exactly."

Kathleen kneaded and pressed and shaped the pastries with nearly automatic precision. Wylie had always been impressed that her hands could do one thing while her mind did something else. "Really, one of the hardest things has been what to tell you and what not to. And how to give you the truth in the right amounts. When you were eleven, and we took that walk, and I told you that William was made up and that your father was Richard — I saw I'd hurt you. Your face changed in that moment, and I swear there's a part of that expression I still see sometimes. It about killed me when you ran. It wasn't right, what I told you then. I thought I'd ruined you."

"I made it to twenty-six, Mom."

She looked at him across the flour-dusted stainless table, her hands working away as if without the rest of her. "Tell me what you want to know."

"Did you have sex before him?"

She reddened again and shook her head.

"Then Richard Carson was your first?"

"Yes."

"Was it really at a party?"

"Yes. Such a perfect storm that night. Everything hit me right at once, Wylie. All my admiration for him and my commitment to what he was great at. All my tingling attraction and desire for an almost but never before . . . thing. All my youth and reckless courage. The damned alcohol and Richard's total attention. That basement room was so welcoming and private. Another world. I knew he would never be mine. Never leave his wife or children. That made him more perfect. I knew he'd had other girls. I didn't care. To me, at that moment in that place, he was what I wanted. He was there and I took him. I knew it was wrong. That didn't matter."

Wylie understood what she was saying, but he found the visuals troubling. "Did . . . when Cynthia . . . were you and Richard still in the bed when she . . ."

"No. Richard was playing Ping-Pong in the game room and I was out on a deck, looking at the stars and wondering what I'd just done. I was crying because I was afraid, then crying because I was sad. Utter confusion. Total regret. I heard the shots. Not loud. Five. I wasn't sure at first what they were. Then the screams. Looking through a sliding glass door I saw her marching across the room, people flying from her path every which way. Pregnant and showing. She looked very purposeful and focused. Not in a hurry, but not taking her time, either. I could hear the door slam when she went out. And somehow I knew what had happened and that she'd seen Richard and me, or been told. I made my way to the game room and through the crowd and finally saw. It was so terrible, son. He was so beautiful and peaceful and all those holes. Torn up so badly. I still see him like that. I'll never get it out of my head."

"Wow."

"Is right."

"Jeez."

"That, too. Cynthia got prison and I got you."

Wylie worked a long while in silence, his croissant dough suddenly fascinating. He finished it and began another. The secret was the force: too much and the pastry would toughen when baked. "Why not adoption or abortion?"

"I thought about them, but not for very long. When I knew you were in there, everything changed. The world had flipped and then it flipped again."

"You gave up skiing? Dreams. All of that?"

"Racing, not skiing."

"But you gave it all up?"

"I changed. This will sound . . . well, I'm not sure how it will sound — but what I did with Richard was the most destructive and most wonderful thing I'll ever do. I ruined lives. And gave you yours."

Wylie felt a shudder pass through him. Like a seismic tremor, he thought, or a swell or a wave of sound. I am a simple moment in the rush of time, he thought. So much does not depend on me. So much is given and nonshedable, no matter the wars you fight or the miles you trudge or how fast you go down a mountain. I showed up. I am innocent. And I am connected, separate but part of. "Was I worth it, Mom?"

"You will never know . . ." Wylie watched the tears well in her eyes and an impossible-seeming smile come to her face. Still, her hands continued forming the thing to which they were devoted. ". . . how much I love you."

Then he was tearing up because she was, and they met at the halfway point of the table and embraced. Laughter followed, soft and complicit within the smells of flour and coffee, steamed milk and tears.

Chapter Thirty-Two

After his mother had gone home and Beatrice and Belle had come in for the afternoon, Wylie traded his street clothes for sweats and running shoes. The weather had cleared and warmed slightly and there was still daylight enough for the long run down Highway 203 and back.

He jogged out and across the parking lot, to find Claude Favier standing on his tiptoes by the MPP, looking through one of the portholes. Since putting it on eBay, just seeing the MPP sank Wylie's heart. It was as if there was a bright red for sale sign on it, even though there was no such sign. Pride kept him from parading his need around town like that.

"Is he in there, Claude?"

Claude turned quickly. "Ah, Wylie! You have escaped. It looks very small inside."

"Table for two," he said, immediately regretting the pleasantry. He caught the knowing sparkle in Claude's eyes.

"Why do you pull this vehicle around the town with you?" asked Claude.

"Because I like it." The MPP had but thirty-four hours left on the eBay auction block. Midnight tomorrow. The best offer was $4,800, which was still $2,200 short of the seven grand that he would end up paying for it. Sometimes the big offers come in fast at the end, he thought. Right? His secret hope of getting half enough for the new roof seemed frankly ridiculous now. He wiped a smudge off the door with the cuff of his sweatshirt. He wondered again how he could have been so loose with his money. He could have bought a used minitrailer for a few hundred dollars and called it a day. Jesse had told him as much.

Claude gave him a puzzled expression but kept his Gallic nose in the air, as if he might soon understand.

"What's up, Claude?"

"I have brought something for you."

Wylie looked to the posh silver Mercedes SUV parked beside his trailer. Claude smiled and raised his hands for Wylie to wait, then went to the SUV and touched the liftgate handle and up the liftgate rose, motor humming softly. "I have been thinking about the Mammoth Cup," he called.

"The *Gargantua* Mammoth Cup, I should say. And because of this, I went back through my many computer files to five years ago because I wanted to know precisely what Chamonix products were helping you to victory."

"They were the CR Saber Threes, one eighties with the seventy-eight waist."

"Yes! And what are you skiing now?"

"The same pair."

"No! The Chamonix Saber racers have evolved since then, Wylie. Edges are slightly harder for the carve but not too hard for our Mammoth snow. So, for the arc to be proper, these skis require high skill. And body weight is factored, too, which you have. I truly believe the new Saber Five is the ski that you will prefer. Please, look at them."

Claude stepped back from the SUV, drawing out the new Chamonix racers. They really do look like black sabers, thought Wylie — slender and elegant and purposeful. The Sabers were part of the Chamonix racing line, made for groomed but slightly softer western snow. Chamonix's traditional red race trim was now splattered bloodlike across the lacquered black, reinforcing the saber idea. Pure aggression. Claude stood the skis beside him, one in each hand, then leaned one out. Wylie took it, registered the slightly greater heft of the racer compared to his earlier model, shook it sharply to gauge the flex.

"Stout," he said.

"It has speed greed," said Claude. "Yet you feel *ee-pox-ied* to the snow."

"Same length as my old ones. Narrower in the waist. Nice."

"You are holding nearly eight decades of history in your hand. We will launch them to market in December."

Wylie slowly turned it to catch the pale autumn sunlight. "How much will Chamonix be asking?"

"Eleven hundred twenty-five."

"I'll stick with the threes."

"Of course you must. But try these fives."

"I'll just ding them up and not be able to pay you for them."

Claude waved his free hand, as if shooing a mosquito. "Wylie. I know you cannot afford them. But take these skis. Chamonix is proud that you win on our equipment. All we ask is that when you are posing for photographs, you turn the ski so the Chamonix name is highly visible. If you don't like them, use the old Saber Threes. But still keep Chamonix highly visible!"

Wylie looked at the Frenchman's weathered, sharply chiseled face and delighted light blue eyes. "I'm suspicious of gifts."

"Then this is a flaw in your character. If you are worried about the USOC, this we consider to be a testing pair for you. As such, no retail value. Not a gift and not a sponsorship. Most legal. Although I ask you not to tell Brandon Shavers about this gift — I have not similarly equipped the Mammoth team."

Claude held out the other ski and Wylie accepted it. "Thank you, Claude."

"Thank Chamonix. Chamonix is passion."

"That's a good slogan."

"Yes. Passion opens wallets."

Claude smiled again and brought a cigarette from a silver case and offered it to Wylie, who declined. The silver case was also a lighter. Claude slid it back into his jacket pocket while the smoke slowly mingled with the heavy air.

Wylie carried the skis to the MPP, knelt, unlatched the equipment drawer, and let it roll out. He slid the beautiful new Sabers into the carpet-lined compartment, smiled slightly at them, then pushed the drawer closed. When he came back around the trailer, Claude was leaning against his SUV. "You are at an interesting place in your life," he said.

"It's interesting all right."

"Are you ready to race?"

"I could have used Chile or New Zealand this summer. But I'm ready."

"You have lost weight."

"Same as five years ago. Well, three more pounds, actually."

"The Saber Fives will use your weight well. Tell me of your plans, Wylie. If you are to be winning the Mammoth Cup on my skis, I want to know where you will be going. I want to share in your plan. I want to help."

Wylie told Claude that he was putting his all into the Mammoth Cup, and if he did well enough, he'd go to the Winter X Games later in January, and if he did well there, he'd do the FIS ski-cross circuit in North America and Europe.

"You have the backing of Adam for this travel, yes?"

Wylie nodded.

"And then?"

"I want the Olympics, Claude. I need them. I can build a life on them."

Claude looked at Wylie through the loitering smoke. "Yes, as we all can. And for you, what is this life you would like to build?"

Wylie told him about buying a place for Let It Bean, and maybe sending his sisters to college, giving them a chance for more than a small-town bakery. He crossed his arms and looked down at the asphalt and saw rows of stolen boards and bikes, cabinets filled with skis, Jacobie Bradford's shining head and combative face.

"They are doing well in life, your sisters?"

Wylie looked up at him. "They're young is all."

"Yes, when youth is wasted."

"I never believed that."

"Not quite."

"Can I speak to you as a friend?" Claude looked at the end of his cigarette and tapped the ash to the ground. "Wylie, of course you know this, but I should remind you that you have no chance of placing in the Olympics. The Europeans are several years ahead of you and every other American ski crosser. Why? Because their mountains are better. Their courses are better. Their programs are better because skiing is much more important there than here. So, because of this, there is always money for training. But more than the money — in my native France, for example — ski racers are heroes. They are athletic gods. Here in America, your ski racers only exist every four years for the televised Olympics. One or two stars are made and quickly forgotten. They are not gods, but only celebrities. The rest of you compete when you can, and work in bakeries and bike shops and restaurants. How are you to compete at the highest level?"

Wylie nodded, pondering this. "Well, fuck, Claude, I guess I'll have to prove you wrong."

"Please, Wylie, do not take offense. I am trying to help you, as a much older man, by being practical and realistic. Yes, you may win here in Mammoth if you can beat Sky Carson. And even yes, perhaps you can do well in Aspen. But on the World Cup circuit, you will be up against the very finest in the world, and these men are younger than you and trained professionally, and have single-mindedness bred into them. Look what the French did in Sochi ski cross. Gold, silver, and bronze!"

Wylie shrugged, felt his usual useless anger begin to boil. "Then why did you give me the skis? Pity?"

"I want you to win the Mammoth Cup on Chamonix skis! That is all."

"That is not all. I'm going to win more than that on them. I have to."

Claude drew on the cigarette and looked at the ember philosophically. He studied Wylie for a long time. "You want to win for your family? And perhaps as a sentimental gesture to Rob —"

"Yes, Claude — I just said all that."

"But is there more? Is there another motivation for you that is larger even than those? I sense there is. I want to see if you will confess it."

Wylie nodded. He felt pried open. "Me. I want good fortune for me."

"Of course you do! All champions want this. I had no idea your dreams were so big, and so serious."

"Now you know."

Claude gave him another long, squinting assessment, then a subtle nod. "But you must still be realistic. So, let me suggest a simultaneous plan, in case your FIS and Olympic goals do not fall into place. You yourself mentioned a table for two. My advice is: Do your best to make April Holly a happy woman."

"Leave her out, Claude."

"Leave her out? Why be childish? Be as honest with me as I am being with you. You should tie your life to her if she will allow it. Tie it tightly. Let her be the one to go to Korea. She is nearly a certainty. Let her become an even bigger celebrity. Let Salonne shampoo and the many more lucrative endorsements to come be your security, too. She has more than enough for two. She has the singular talent, the gift. You do not. Sky Carson does not. What happens on this mountain is small compared to April Holly. And someday, all of this heated competition and striving to be champions will pass. You and April will both be too old for racing and aerial trickery. And she will want children and you will give them to her and care for them. She will want a ranch near Aspen and an apartment in Lillehammer and a chalet in New Zealand or Chile. She will want her sisters-in-law to have every opportunity in life, not just a bakery. I think this is a beautiful future for you, and any man in the world would accept it happily. You could be most eagerly replaced."

"I've thought of all that, Claude."

"So?"

"It feels wrong."

"Do you love her?"

"Yes, I do."

"If you love her, then what is wrong with wrong? You really are suspicious of gifts, aren't you?"

"Good should feel good."

"So to feel good, a man can take no gift? He must do it all himself? Alone and on a white horse?"

Wylie nodded. "Some of it."

"But where did he get that strong white horse? Or the sleek black skis?"

Wylie looked at Claude but said nothing.

Claude drew on the cigarette again, then flicked the butt away. "Wylie? Wylie. I see something in you that I did not see before. You have no rational right to your dream, and yet you surrender your heart to it. All right. You have the smallest of chances. But in your smallness of chance is the seed of heroism and glory. You know I have spoken to you out of respect, not malice. I hope the Saber Fives land you on the podium in Seoul. And if they don't, you have my respect and best wishes as far as my skis take you. I have seen you race many times, and I have watched every video made of your races. And I offer this advice for the Mammoth Cup: You will not make the hole shot off the start. That will belong to Sky. He is under one minute now on the IB — the only one under a minute. But once he leads on the real X Course, he will expect extreme pressure from you. Apply it thoroughly but patiently. Do not try to pass him too early. Do not force yourself. Let the pressure eat his nerves away and he will surrender according to his nature. You will see your moment. Be like a lion upon a gazelle."

Wylie breathed deeply and exhaled,

watched his breath condense in the air before him. "Thanks, Claude. I'll try the skis. I'm off and running now, just like a big lion."

"Excellent, Wylie. And just so you are aware, upper-level representatives of the U.S. Olympic Committee and the USSA arrived together here in Mammoth just yesterday. The main purpose for their visit is to speak to Adam about you and April Holly. They have great concerns about your love affair coming at such an important time for April and for the sport. . . ."

Wylie heard the last few words trailing off from behind him as he chugged across the parking lot toward Highway 203, one foot in front of the other.

Just past the gas station, Wylie ran past Cynthia Carson, sitting still and barely visible in the trees and patchy snow, dressed in green-and-white camo. She stared right through him. Wylie's heart jumped and he sped up to catch it.

CHAPTER THIRTY-THREE

The next morning, Wylie guided his truck up the steep rocky road that led to Adam's aerie on the mountain. The MPP bounced along behind, stable but nimble. Wylie parked near the funicular landing, looked at the sleek silver car waiting beneath the tall pines with a futuristic air.

He helped Adam load in his fishing gear, again checking the sky for signs of the big Alaskan storm due to arrive later this Friday evening. The streets of Mammoth Lakes were already buzzing with weekend vehicles, and the ski shops had their rental banners out, and the young go-getters who sold and installed snow chains for incoming tourists were already staking out their turf. Traffic on Highway 203 was steady for late November, an inbound stream as Wylie and Adam headed down the hill toward Hot Creek Ranch.

As they came down into the basin at 395,

Wylie saw that the sky had the hard white heaviness denoting a storm. Such skies had been one of his early pleasures as a child. He clearly remembered his first runs down the hill behind their house, executed on flattened pasteboard boxes. Then later the plastic snow dishes, and after that a sled. Then his first pair of skis and boots, a birthday present when he was four. He'd slid around the house on them and slept with them beside his bed for a month, anticipating the first snowfall. Something in him clicked when he was on skis. A gift. He never felt like a beginner.

"I met with brass from the Olympic Committee and the USSA yesterday. Their hero? April Holly. Their villain? You."

"Claude said as much."

"Their position is easy to see."

Wylie headed to the airport/hatchery exit and followed the dirt road past the hatchery to Hot Creek. He turned onto the private ranch. Hot Creek was exactly that — a creek partially fed by thermal springs, which kept it relatively warm year-round, much to the delight of aquatic vegetation, insects, and trout. The fish were many, some quite large, most of them experienced at telling artificial flies from real ones.

Wylie parked by the lodge and the manager came out and talked to them while they rigged up. He liked the MPP, touched it lightly. He was an old friend of Adam and let them fish here for free. There were no other fishermen today and the manager said there had been *Tricos* mayfly hatches mid-morning and pale morning duns when the sun hit the water. "Use the lightest line you can still see and lots of it," he said with a smile.

Wylie saw Adam's curt nod — the old man disliked jokes about his age from anyone but himself. Adam was ready to fish before Wylie had even gotten his line through the guides. Wylie tied on a PMD and mashed down the barb with his hemostat and they walked downstream, looking for rises.

"So I've been tasked with talking some sense into you," said Adam. "What are my chances?"

"Good as they ever were."

Adam smiled. "I told them to talk to you themselves. But there's no end to the mess they can make, dealing directly with an athlete. Who knows what you'll say or post? And they stubbornly profess to believe you'll listen to me. I told them no young man in love is going to listen very closely to anyone."

"I'll listen, sir."

"I like this run."

They stood well back and watched. The long, glittering run came hard downstream, dropped over rocks, and tailed out, pooling against the far side. It looked deep. The water was nearly black under the pale sky, and the aquatic grasses swayed beneath. Wylie knew that the fish loved the vegetation for cover and for the healthy bug life it engendered. People from all over the world came here to test their skills. Wylie had seen trout thirty inches long in here but had never caught anything much longer than twenty. These were the pickiest and most annoying fish in the Sierras. Adam decided to change flies, and while he studied the contents of his dry-fly box, Wylie checked his eBay auction. The high bid was now five thousand dollars, with fifteen hours until midnight. Damn.

Adam cast upstream and mended early, letting his fly ride the current down. At this distance, it was a white speck. It drifted twenty feet without incident. Adam cast again. "Wylie, you know that April Holly is America's biggest winter sports star, biggest money earner, a true showcase athlete, as the Austrians like to say. Salonne shampoo pays her three million a year for the ads and the helmet space. Her equipment makers come in at about that, too. Her apparel makers pay her roughly another two million just to wear the stuff. They pay and pray she won't start her own line — though April has told them she might want to do just that. Her appearance fees are in the high five figures for no more than two hours of her time. Those amounts will double or even triple if she stays healthy and wins in Korea. Ah, a fish!"

Wylie watched as Adam played the fish, got it onto the reel, and brought it in. Wylie netted it and worked the hook loose and held out the net for the old man to see.

"I love the dark browns," he said.

"That's a beauty, Adam." Wylie set the net deep in the water and the fish eased, then flashed away. Adam gave him his spot and Wylie fished the same run, but closer to the bank. The larger fish were assumed to lie along the cut, deeper banks, and in Wylie's experience, this was occasionally true. Adam's voice came from behind and beside him.

"Of course, Helene Holly has bent their ears," said Adam. "She told them that April is emotionally far younger than her twenty-one years. This, due to her meteoric rise as an athlete and somewhat retarded social development. Helene says April is extremely vulnerable, if not gullible. Helene says that April is given to pronounced highs and lows. She says that as competitions near, April becomes extremely focused on the event. She eats the exact same foods at the exact same time, wears certain 'lucky' clothes and uses certain 'lucky' gear. She sleeps up to ten hours a day, including an afternoon nap. She listens to the same songs and watches the same movies. April has a ritual that she does in her bathroom the evening before a contest, in which she arranges every grooming product on her counter in pairs, in a long procession, so that the front labels of each pair face each other, while their backs are turned to the backs of the coupled products on either side. Or something like that. Helene believes that this obsessive single-mindedness is what sets April apart. Helene says that when April loses focus, she is injury-prone. Helene's afraid — in a nutshell — that you're going to fuck everything up and April's going to lose the Mammoth Cup slopestyle to start her season. Which would be a disaster for her confidence. Or worse. April's never had a major injury. She's had minor ones, when she's lost focus. Helene predicts that the longer she's involved with you, the better are her chances for catastrophe."

"I get all that. And I'll go anytime, Adam. Far away as April wants. I've told her that more than once."

"The Olympic and snowboard mafias, and Helene, want you to make the move now. To get out of her life and let her win."

"She's happy to be free of her mother and the rest of the team. She's laughing off the pressure. I'm not wrong about this, Grandpa. I know her."

Wylie saw his fly vanish and felt the jerk on his line simultaneously. It was a small fish, and Wylie let it run until tired, then skittered it across the surface, knelt, and released it. He dried the fly and smudged some floatant onto the feathers, then cast it to the far bank. He gave it a quick mend and let it ride.

"Then the meeting got interesting," said Adam. Wylie looked over his shoulder at his grandfather. "These are not subtle people. So hear me out. They've got a reward/punishment offer for you. Ready? Their current thinking is that U.S. ski cross is a losing proposition for the Seoul Olympics. John Teller had that fabulous run through Sochi, but he was our only one. Looking ahead, they see you and Sky and Tyler Wallasch and a couple of guys out of Aspen, and that Bridger kid out of Colorado. They're impressed, but not impressed enough. So on a go-forward, the USSA and Olympic plan is to cut ski-cross support to a trickle."

"Ski cross is the best winter Olympic event there is!"

"The masses want boarding, not skiing. You know that."

"But ski cross is faster and crazier. It's a downhill blitz and a giant slalom and a NASCAR wreck waiting to happen — all rolled into one. Shit, Adam. Don't get me started."

"There's no accounting for what people want, Wylie. Or what they don't. But, of course, there's the reward side of the equation."

Wylie glanced back again. He couldn't keep the hostility out of his heart or his voice. *"Bring it."*

"If you break off with April, the USOC will put more resources behind ski cross. And the USSA will do likewise. They say they are offering you a chance to do something for yourself, and your sport. Not to mention theirs."

"Do you really believe they'd do much?"

Wylie glanced back and Adam shrugged.

"I can't vouch for what they'd do. They won't make any commitment that can't be denied, or at least modified. It's all CYA. This is how our sport is run, unfortunately. By organizations with their noses to the wind. But there are many winds. They change and die and start up again."

Wylie lifted the fly and false cast to dry it. He used a reach cast to create an upstream mend midair, and put the tiny fly close to the bank with a big loop behind it. "Okay, so what if I leave April and she isn't happy? What if I break her heart and mess her up?"

"Helene said it's worth the risk because April doesn't know herself. The boosters agreed."

"Buncha fuckin' pigs."

"Possibly."

Wylie saw the gliding, unhurried rise and felt the sharp tug, then nothing. He raised his rod tip smartly and the fly line whizzed downstream in a wake of spray. The fish was heavy and it found the fast water. Wylie knew he would either keep up with it or lose it. He splashed ashore and followed the narrow foot trail downstream, giving up line as he had to.

The foot trail was muddy and his boots slipped on the contours. It was like being on a ship pitching in an ocean. The fish exploded in a spray of red and silver, a kype-jawed rainbow, and Wylie heard the hard splat when it hit the river. Now it had most of his line, and Wylie felt no surrender, only an extra burst of strength as the fish tore into his backing and the reel screamed. He came to a chasm in the bank and leaped into it, climbing and slipping up the steep far side. The fish jumped again, and it looked so far away and alien, as if projected onto a plane that wasn't quite real, like an old Hollywood backdrop.

The next break in the bank was a shallow mud wallow, so he cut inland around it, busting through the brush, only to see that the trail would soon end at a gravel bar and a pool too deep to wade across. Once upon the bar, he dropped his phone to the rocks, lifted the rod skyward, and threw himself into the pool. He was instantly heavy and cold. Using one arm, he pulled himself forward, barely staying afloat in the deep, still water. It rushed over the top of his waders, trying to sink him. His boots were eerily heavy. The cold made it hard to breathe. Through the rod he could still feel the faraway fish muscling along with the current.

He tried to do the same, scooping himself with one hand toward the river proper. The current finally took him and he buoyed upright, running without his feet touching, as in a dream. Then he found bottom, a blessed rocky slope up which he clambered, pulling himself onto a shallow riffle, where he got his feet under him and renewed his trudge downstream. His heart was pounding, but he was breathing steadily and deeply and this was his mission. He retrieved the backing and a few turns of line.

Which was when the line jumped back at him, then went slack, the distant weight of his fish vanished. Wylie dropped to his knees, bellowing in agony, his voice puny in the world.

Adam caught up with him a minute later. He waded out onto the gravel and stood not far from the still-kneeling Wylie, whose teeth were already chattering. "Good effort," said Adam. "You did everything right that I could see."

"I'm not going to go until she asks me to."

"I didn't think you would."

"The only thing on Earth I'd trade April Holly for is that fish."

"Of course."

"Shit. Man. Christ."

"Well said. I picked up your phone."

Chapter Thirty-Four

Later that same day, Wylie looked through the Let It Bean window and saw Jacobie Bradford III traipsing across the lot in full fly-fishing regalia — waders snugged with a wide padded belt, gaitered boots, a rain jacket over a fleece, a thousand-pocketed fishing vest with gear dangling. He wore a light blue buff around his throat and a cap over his bald head. He stopped and patted the MPP possessively, like fingernails on a chalkboard to Wylie. Bradford then looked toward Let It Bean and marched forward.

"Look what's coming," said Beatrice.

"One-hundred-proof evil," said Belle. "Can't an avalanche just take him?"

Jacobie swung open the door and walked in, his cleated boots clicking loudly on the faux-wooden floor. It was three o'clock and Let It Bean was nearly empty. "Wylie, I'd like to have a word with you in private." He looked at a few of the customers to make sure they'd heard him. Belle turned her back on him and Bea marched away into the kitchen. Jacobie watched them, eyes on their butts in frank appraisal. "But first, whip me up a nonfat latte. Small. I should know what the competition is up to."

Wylie battled his desire to fling the man from his establishment. He remembered the Trout Derby pool, wished it was handy. "How'd you do today, Jacobie?"

"Stuck a sixteen-inch brown up in the Long Years section. Last fish of the day. And a bunch of little ones. You?"

"I farmed a big rainbow down on Hot Creek."

"Nothing worse than farming troutzilla."

"Some things are quite a bit worse."

"That sixteen-incher was my two hundred and forty-eighth trout in exactly ninety-two days of fly-fishing. Half days, mostly. So I'm averaging two point six-nine fish per day. Not bad for a beginner."

"That's a hundred dollars a fish, with the guide fees you're paying."

"A hundred dollars per fish. Guide fees. Gossip sure flies on this little mountain."

"It's not every day that someone exciting as you comes to town."

"True. And I'm happy to support the local economy. Because without my guide, I'd be out there flailing and untangling gruesome knots all day. But instead, I'm catching fish. I'm a real angler. Like you, Wylie."

Wylie finished making the coffee drink and one for himself, grabbed some napkins, then led the way outside. They stopped near the MPP, and Wylie used the napkins to wipe where Jacobie had touched. The storm was closing in and he could see the early darkness towering immensely in the north and west. The breeze was slight but cold. The streets were busier now than earlier, skiers and boarders coming into town for the first big snow. A commercial passenger jet eased down toward Mammoth/Yosemite airport. He could see his sisters' faces at the Let It Bean window, smudgelike.

"They're cute," said Jacobie.

"Fifteen and seventeen. Illegal."

"I wasn't even going there. Why would you think I was?"

"The way you look at them."

Jacobie shrugged. "It's the way I look at everything."

Wylie sipped the drink.

"You make a good product, Wylie."

"Thank you."

"Too bad Let It Bean can't compete."

"No. We can't."

"Which is why I have some very good

news for you."

"I'm ready for that."

"Gargantua wants to buy you."

"Mom and Steen would never sell to you."

"I told my superiors that maybe you could sway them."

"What's your offer?"

"One quarter of a million dollars cash buyout, and we'll take on fifty thousand in debt. That's enough for your family to make a clean start, maybe buy a Winchell's franchise. Of course, good carpet cleaners are always in demand in alpine climes. I only half jest."

Jacobie walked halfway around his black Range Rover, defensively considering Wylie from across the spacious black hood. "There's a personal component to the offer. Just between us. Because I like you in spite of our differences. If you take our deal, Grant Bulla won't ever know what I saw when I got to twelve Madrone that day. Which, just to refresh your memory, was you attempting to leave a garage full of stolen property and Belle hightailing it away in the snow. I think Grant could run far with that little tip. He told me he's lifted quite a few latents off that stuff. He'd certainly take yours and Belle's fingerprints for comparison. See, with prints, people think they wipe them all off, but they never do. I learned that on the cop TV shows I watch too many of."

"You are a pestilence, Jacobie."

"I try." He climbed into the SUV and the dark passenger-side window went down half a foot. "Just FYI, Wylie, Gargantua is known for its aggressive acquisition stance. The quarter mil is nonnegotiable, just to save us all some time. So give the offer serious thought. Talk to your tribe, pass around the talking stick, pick some fleas off one another's backs. You've got forty-eight hours. Oh hell — I caught fish today, so make it seventy-two."

The Welborn-Mikkelsen clan closed Let It Bean at the usual time, then convened, at Wylie's suggestion. Steen got the fire going strong and they pulled five leather chairs into a semicircle in front of the fireplace. Wylie told them of Jacobie's/Gargantua's offer, minus the stuff about twelve Madrone.

Silence.

Glancing through the windows, Wylie saw headlights far down Highway 203, and the steady stream of tourist vehicles pouring onto Old Mammoth Road. The snow had started, light and dainty, swirling capriciously in the down beams of the streetlights. To him, the snowfall from the first good storm had always been a fine thing, not quite sacred, maybe, but certainly to be beheld and thanked for. He looked at the flame-lit faces of his family and knew they all felt the same way. Or at least they used to. But he'd also known — almost since first walking back into his boyhood home ten months ago — that things were changing. And they knew it, too. There was always a point at which you had to move on.

Belle shook her head. "No way."

"No way for me, either," said Bea.

Steen sat up straight, as if someone had slapped his face. "That is not a fair amount for Gargantua to pay for a business that is strong. Or *was* strong, until Gargantua came here. Yes, it would pay off the eleven thousand dollars for the new ovens and walk-in of two years ago. As well as the time and materials for the Pastry Shed. And give us two years of the good profit we used to make and enough to pay for the new roof at home. But in those two years, we would have to create another business for supporting our family. We have seen how difficult this is. Our coffee and pastries are well known for quality in Mammoth Lakes, but still we do not make much money."

Kathleen had taken her work cap off, and now her face was shadowed by thick black hair. Wylie saw the gleam of her eyes within. "No. I won't take it."

"Good, Mom," said Belle.

"Way to go, Mom."

"Wylie?" asked Kathleen.

He looked outside again. The snow was coming down faster now, and the people on the sidewalks were hunched tighter in their caps and coats. He saw good things on this small-town street — community and progress and the passing of years. The streetlamps seemed to connect it to a previous age, though maybe this was just his young man's sentiment, but right now even the damned Gargantua banners with their inanely humanized gorilla faces seemed no worse than comic relief. What I was born into, thought Wylie, and what I am. But now what?

"Come on, Wylie," said Belle. "Gargantua can't do this to us. We're human beings and they're apes. I will not have Jacobie Bradford sitting in this chair in front of this fire a month from now, plotting his next move. I'll chain myself to the stove. I'll burn the building down. I will not allow this to become his."

"So totally," said Bea.

Wylie stood. "I need a moment with you girls. Back in the kitchen. Mom, Steen, we shall return."

He led them far back into a kitchen corner, where the walk-in hummed and the chill was heavy. They looked at him anxiously. He told them that Jacobie would go to the cops about twelve Madrone if they refused Gargantua's offer. The cops had taken fingerprints from the stolen property and a comparison would identify them. He'd read in *The Sheet* last week that the town council was publicly pressuring the PD for an arrest. Some of the council members were not fans of the chief to begin with.

Wylie crossed his arms and leaned against one of the stainless-steel prep tables. Beatrice had tears in her eyes. "It's our fault."

"*My* fault," said Belle. "My idea."

"I stole as much as you did."

"Think for a minute," said Belle. "The way things are right now, we can't say no to Jacobie. If we do, all three of us will be arrested and sit in jail until bail is set. After that, the criminal justice system will pauperize us with legal fees. Meanwhile, Let It Bean is still being strangled by Gargantua. And there's no staff. And Wylie gets DQ'd from the Mammoth Cup because of his arrest. Right, Wylie?"

"That's the rule for a felony arrest."

"But we would clear you," said Bea.

"It wouldn't be up to you," said Wylie. "My not reporting the crime is a crime, too."

Belle put a hand on Wylie's shoulder as she walked to the rear door and pulled it open. A flurry of snowflakes eddied in, and Wylie saw the silent, steady fall of snow and his little sister looking up at it, and she was him ten years ago, standing in that same doorway, holding the same door open, wondering what the first big storm of that season would bring to the mountain.

Belle looked out at the snow for a while, then closed the door and turned to her brother. "But there is one way we can tell Jacobie to shove it. And to pay a lesser price to keep our bakery. Wylie, back at twelve Madrone, you said Bea and I needed to go down to the cop shop and tell them what we did. You were right. It'll kill Mom and Dad to have raised criminals, but they won't have to sell for so little, just to cover us. And Wylie, you won't get caught up with what Bea and I did."

Bea looked pale and uncertain, as almost always. She stared at her sister for a long moment, then turned from Belle to Wylie. "I know I'm always, like, agreeing with people instead of thinking for myself, but I really do think Belle's right this time. You can stay focused on your race, Wyles. You can win the thing and shut Sky Carson up. We'll have a good snow year and Let It Bean will make it. Maybe we can borrow money for the roof. And maybe, because we didn't sell any of the stuff we stole, the owners can get it all back. And if we fully confess, maybe we get off with less punishment. And —"

Belle opened the door again and the three of them watched the snow, lessening now, smaller and sparser. It looked like she was saying good-bye to it. "I'll tell Mom and Dad," she said. "But first, I'll need a cigarette and a blindfold."

Wylie closed the door and brought them in close and they locked arms and bowed their heads together.

After dinner at home that night, Belle did what she'd said she would, even without a final cigarette or blindfold. ". . . you have raised two felons, but we're still good people," she concluded.

Kathleen stared at her daughters, mouth open and ready for speech, but no words came forth. Steen looked as if he'd been slapped and couldn't believe what had just happened. He poured another aquavit.

Wylie explained how it had all come to a head because of Jacobie. In the very long silence that ensued, Wylie listened to the syncopated plip-plop of melting snow hitting the three buckets that were now stationed in the living and dining rooms alone.

The girls and their parents commenced arguing about the best way to give themselves up. Steen suggested they hire a lawyer first. Kathleen vetoed it as a needless expense. Belle wanted to post the whole thing live on social media, maybe do a Kickstarter campaign to raise defense and new-roof funds. Bea hated that idea.

Wylie excused himself and went to the living room couch, where he checked his phone and found out that his beloved MPP had received a bid that doubled the existing high offer to twelve thousand. After paying Jesse, that would leave him $9,800 toward the new roof, on which work was set to begin in two days' time. He didn't know whether to raise a fist in victory or gnash his teeth.

Either way, it was *adios, MPP.*

He put more wood in the stove and used the bellows to stoke the flames, leaving the door slightly ajar. The fire popped and spit and lapped at the inside of the smoke-grayed glass. He wrote a text to April — "luv u miss u," wondered what a true poet would think of such an atrocity, then, before sending it, rewrote it as:

< 3 AM, the night is absolutely still;
Snow squeals beneath my skis, plumes on the turns.

> That's beautiful, Wyles.

< Rexroth. I do love and miss you.

> Then where r u?

< Tending to criminal females.

> Time for I more?

Chapter Thirty-Five

In the afterglow, they lay splayed and panting. Wylie lolled his head for an unforgettable view of April's moonlit buns protruding from a sheet. He pictured skiing down one. What a fall line that was. Looking out a high window, he watched breeze-scrubbed stars flickering in the sky. His Saber Fives stood propped against the wall, gleaming slightly, and Wylie thought he had everything in life he wanted. He crawled over and lay alongside April. She told him their lovemaking had allowed her to successfully image a back-side double-cork 1080 she was thinking about trying for the first time at the Mammoth Cup. It had never been landed before in a USSA competition, though there was an Austrian girl, nineteen, who had done one late last season in a FIS-sanctioned event. It would all come down to amplitude and good conditions. She had landed it in her mind just now.

Wylie fished his pants off the floor, opened his wallet, and handed April a neatly folded piece of white printer paper. "I wrote this for you."

She dropped her jaw histrionically and widened her eyes. "A poem?"

"A haiku."

"I love Japanese food!" She scrambled back against the headrest and pulled up the comforter. Unfolding the paper, she flattened it against her raised thigh and glanced once at Wylie. Then she read the lines out loud in the dry whisper of voice that he had come to love:

"The doors you open
And the rocks you lift reveal
Creatures made of gold"

She read it again to herself. "It's beautiful. The rhythm keeps its weight forward, like a boarder down a slope. It's about courage in dark times and me nailing that backside ten-eighty! And winning gold medals!"

"Precisely."

Wylie's phone rang. He swept it from the nightstand, sat up, and saw a restricted number.

"Yeah?"

"The south parking lot holds a reason for

you to take me seriously."

"Damn you, Sky."

Wylie looked to the curtained south window and saw a faint glow beyond the fabric, something small and round, like an orange wrapped in gauze or a distant campfire. He ran to the window, threw open the curtains, and saw the MPP roiling in flames in the parking lot below.

He told April to call 911, jamming into his jeans and a hoodie and a pair of shearling boots. He took the stairs down to the living room three at a time and ran to the front door. By the time he got to the MPP, the flames were high and bright, the smoke was black, and the smell of burning gasoline and resin was noxious. He threw open the propane hatch at the fore of the trailer and knelt to unscrew the fitting. He could feel the heat thrashing around him and smell his hair burning. When the fitting came free, he wrestled out the tank and flung it far into the lot. On his knees, he unhitched the trailer from the truck, then stood and backed away from the coiling heat to dig the truck keys from his pocket. It seemed to take much more than enough time for the truck gas tank to blow. Luck held. From the driver's seat, he could see the flames leaping in the rearview as he jammed down on the gas pedal and the truck screeched free, swerving on the slushy asphalt.

He got the fire extinguisher from the crew cab and charged back. Rounding the trailer to the windward side, he crouched and blasted away. It was a blessed standoff, flames versus retardant, and he saw there was true hope, but then the extinguisher huffed and spit and dribbled out, while the fire redoubled and took back lost ground.

April ran with a swaying bucket toward the MPP until the heat stopped her. She stepped back, braced, and heaved. By then, neighbors were spilling toward the MPP, some with buckets, some with extinguishers, one man dragging a garden hose in one hand and clutching a goblet of wine in the other. The hose stretched only partway, so the man stopped, arched the stream high, turned his head away from the fire, and drank some wine. Wylie saw the breeze-blown water droplets angling down ineffectually into the inferno.

An older woman shoved a small red fire extinguisher at him and he took it, wading in as close as he could get, then pulling the pin and blasting a load of retardant against the glass of a porthole. But he saw that the porthole glass was broken and the fire was raging inside the MPP. In the brief moment of chaos before the flames jumped back at him, Wylie saw the beautiful interior birch walls curling in the heat, the maple cabinets and table engulfed. Lying on a bench and still folded was the blanket that Jolene had given him, now ash black at its center, with its edges limned in orange-red, like a huge marshmallow left too long in the campfire. Wylie dropped the canister and backed away into the stink of his own burned hair, pawing at the pain on his neck. A wave of cold water crashed against the back of his head, and Wylie turned, to find April holding an empty white bucket.

"Outta the fire, Wylie!"

"Sky did this."

"Out!"

"It was Sky."

"I believe it. I believe it."

April pulled him away from the trailer, the fire now burning with a proud, percussive roar. Wylie wrenched free of her and stripped off his sweatshirt, running back into the conflagration, flapping at it uselessly as the fire unfurled at him and the flames licked his skin. Hands pulled at him and forced him back. He lost his footing and was borne away from the heat and into the wails of sirens and the rhythmic flashing of lights.

Soon the paramedics were there, but Wylie stood them down, wouldn't get into the van, batted away their well-intentioned blue-gloved hands. Shivering, he struggled back into the hoodie and zipped it clear to his chin. *"Christ, guys, I'm okay. Let me be."*

He watched the firemen swarm in with backpack extinguishers, waving clouds of retardant at the fire. As the flames shrank and sputtered, the MPP seemed to deflate, so that when the fire was out, it just sat there, nothing more than a small black shell from which rose random heat waves and thin coils of smoke.

"Excuse me just a moment," Wylie said to no one in particular. He squeezed April's hand. "Should move my truck out of the way, don't you think?"

He trot-skated across the lot, shivering and lifting the hood over his head. He could feel the burn on the back of his neck and hands, but the rest of him was soaked in icy sweat and water. His knuckles jumped with pain as he dug out his truck keys. He started it up and guided it cautiously over the slick asphalt, saluting April through the window. When he came to the road, he turned left and goosed the gas a little, bound for Sky Carson's condo.

■ ■ ■ ■

Nobody answered Wylie's knocks, so he stepped back, gathered his will, and crashed through the door. Inside, he hit the lights, barreled into an empty bedroom, threw the covers back to make sure Sky wasn't buried down in them. The idea came that he could burn the place down, tit for tat, but there were neighbors and it would be much worse than foolish.

He barged into Slocum's and checked the bar and the back dining room, where Sky liked to hunker, but there was no Sky. Sliding on the snow and ice, Wylie sped over to Cynthia's place, but Sky's Outback was nowhere in sight. Cynthia's pale face appeared in a window, backlit and ghostlike. Wylie stood on her porch, teeth chattering but dripping sweat, patches of his skin brightly hot, hair stinking, feeling as if his brains might scramble permanently.

"Sky burned my trailer to the ground."

"A simple apology is all he asked for."

"You Carsons can all go to hell."

"In due time."

"It's not going to work like this anymore."

"He's trying to be true to his word."

"You're all fucking crazy."

"So don't push our buttons."

Wylie slid his truck out of the lot, just about lost it when he hit Minaret, but mustered the self-control to downshift and plow his way safely up to Mountain High. A first-big-snow party was in progress, the street crowded with cars, the circular drive full. Wylie parked behind another truck and Croft met him at the door.

"Wylie. You look, like, burnt up."

"Sky here?"

"No. And neither are your sisters."

"I'm going to come in and look."

"I'm telling you the truth."

"Don't press me on this one, Croft."

"Don't you make me look bad."

The great room was packed with people and smoke. Music and voices wrestled. Wylie shouldered his way through the crowd to the kitchen, then to the downstairs theater, where *Chasing Mavericks* was playing. He was given a wide berth. On floor two, he went from room to room where the stoners were clustered, saw the bongs and little canisters of coke going around, the glazed eyes and idiot smiles, two people giggling under a bedspread with a flashlight, and a couple making out in a bathroom whose door was only half-closed.

Wylie hustled up the stairs, to find Helixon himself waiting atop the third-floor landing. The window on his glasses reflected the light in a compound, insectile way as he looked at Wylie. "Sorry. This is the forbidden floor."

"Give me Sky or I'll throw you down the stairs."

"He's not here. Don't know why not. But I swear to God he's not here."

Looking past Helixon, Wylie saw a long hallway and closed doors. "What do you do up here?"

"Pursue happiness. If Sky was here, I'd give him up. Go."

At April's, Wylie showered and washed his burns lightly with soap and water. The backs of his hands and fingers were the most painful — the skin pink and the hair burned mostly off — but no blisters. He finished with a cold-water rinse that sent shivers to his bones. After the shower, he and April sat in front of the fire, Wylie facing the flames, stripped down to his jeans so April could swab his burns with aloe vera. She brought him a large iced bourbon. She cut back his scorched hair so it was off his neck, then brushed more aloe gel onto his nape, blowing gently to help it dry. The gel went on cool and cut the pain. Wylie felt ambushed and fooled and primed for violence. He felt her cheek on his bare back and her hands on each shoulder. Her voice was soft and light. "Sergeant Bulla said you can come in tomorrow and answer some questions."

"Okay."

"He asked if I had any idea who did it. I said no."

"Good. Right."

"Are you going to tell them Sky called and what he said?"

"I don't know yet."

She rubbed his unburned shoulders for a good long while, hands small and strong. The fire lilted and popped. Her fingers brushed his chest and flanks, and the edges of his abs and the waistband of his jeans. He closed his eyes. "Should I just forgive him, you think, April?"

"It's all you can do. He's troubled. There but for the grace of God, and all that."

"I've forgiven him before. A thousand times. But finally, you are what you do. *You are what you do.* And you are responsible for it."

"We're not given equal things."

"Isn't that a bottomless excuse?"

"To be met with bottomless forgiveness. You can afford it, Wylie. You're more fortunate than he is."

"But it's my trailer that got burned to nothing."

"You'll get another one."

"There was only one MPP," he said, taken aback by his own pouting lameness. Wylie felt her fingers tracing *S*'s down his back, one fingertip on his left side and two fingertips in close parallel down his right, miming their run down Solitary, that second run they'd made, when they knew the mountain enough to relax and move together, then apart, then together again, as the run demanded. "I had this out-of-nowhere idea that you were the one who bid the twelve grand on eBay. For the MPP."

"Oh, really?"

A beat of silence while her fingers rode down his back again. He felt his goose bumps rising, tiny moguls on the course. The fire was hot on his face and chest and the aloe was still cool.

"It was going to be your Christmas present, Wyles."

"You shouldn't have."

"Why not? Tell me why I can't help your family have a roof and give you back something you loved?"

"It seems wrong. I know I'm being a stupid prick, but I can't help it." Wylie had never in his life felt this divided but pig-headed at the same time.

"I have something to say." She spread her hands across his thighs and dug in her thumbs, kneading the muscle. He felt her face and breath warm on his back. "We can stay in this house through the Mammoth Cup. We'll train all day, then lock the doors and draw the blinds and be together. We'll eat good food and get lots of rest. We'll read and watch movies and you can write as good as Rexroth. After the cup, I'm off to Aspen, then Europe for the FIS circuit. You will podium here in Mammoth and do well at the X Games, and make the World Cup tour, too. Adam so wants to sponsor you, to make it real for you. Now listen, it gets better. We can see each other on the FIS circuits, Wylie. There's some overlap at the venues. And a little time between contests. And when we're competing, we'll kick butt from one end of the tour to the other. We might fall sometimes, but we'll help each other even if we're apart, and we'll get up again and win medals and fight our way into the Olympics. We can do this. We can have each other *and* the world, Wylie. I believe it. I can taste it."

It was abruptly illuminating for Wylie to hear his Olympic goal analyzed in this clear, direct, can-do way. To have it sound possible. To consider a future tied to hers. To this April Holly. And it was wonderful to be nudged through the forest of his own doubtful pessimism, as if her hand were on his elbow. "Well. It . . ."

"Well it *what*?"

"Sounds impossibly good."

"Impossible? Banish that word from your vocabulary! It is your enemy. You win from within, correct? So we must live from within, too. I've seen you ski. I know what you're up against and what you can do. You have the tools. You have a gift. So you're right about this plan being good. Our success will give Beatrice and Belle a chance at something bigger. And when we're done with the competition, we'll open a ski and boarding school right here in Mammoth. I know Adam will help. He adores you. With our Olympic medals, we'll draw students from all over the world. They will flock to Mammoth Lakes. They'll buy their coffee and pastries at Let It Bean. I'll teach the boarders and you the skiers and we'll have babies and teach them, too. And we will gradually become plump and wrinkled by the mountain sun and we'll start repeating ourselves in conversation, but we'll be happy and together and nobody will ever, ever, *ever* be able to take it away."

A long moment passed. "I'm speechless, April."
"Step up to it, Wylie!"
"I think we . . . could do it."
"What does your heart say?"
"It says we can."
"I *know* we can. You have to believe in it. Everything follows from belief. Nothing exists without belief being there first."
"I . . ."
He felt her warm cheek on his back, her fingers walking his waist around to the front. His belt tightened, then went slack. He heard the dull pop of pant studs and felt cool air coming in. Brain and body on scramble.
April sighed. "Oh — just FYI and by the way, I made an offer on this place this morning. Cash, short escrow, low end of asking. Realtor says it'll probably go. I love it here. It will be our home on this mountain."
"You scare me."
"I scare me, too. Such a wonderful thing to do. I'd never dreamed of scaring myself until I met you, Wylie. It's like you got sent here by God. To undo my straitjacket."
"I make you crazy?"
"You just let me bean."
"Hmmm . . ."

"But serious, too. We're good for each other in different ways. You let me be free and I help you believe. You keep everything in and I let everything out. We're a good, good fit."

"I think I like it."

"He thinks he likes it. Thinks. Well, at least you're cute, Wyles."

"Never been accused of that."

"Want to, like, celebrate? Maybe on that fake bearskin rug?"

Chapter Thirty-Six

Snow stood twelve feet deep on Mammoth Mountain for the Gargantua Mammoth Cup men's ski-cross finals on Saturday, January 16. The temperature was thirty-one degrees, with a light breeze, and the sky was a hard pewter gray.

Wylie juiced his skis in the waxing area set up near the X Course starting house. His Sabers lay on the sawhorses and he waited for his secret concoction of waxes to reach the right temperature. He wore a respirator against the noxious fluorinated vapors. Some of the wax technicians stood by, drinking coffee in colorful steel mugs, waiting their turn. The techs were there for the Mammoth freeski team members only, but even when Wylie was part of the team, he'd always done his own waxing — part science and part meditation. His wax recipe was on the grippy side, because his racing style was for speed. He ironed it on in long, even strokes, the hot fumes wafting witchingly into the cold air. He was inwardly focused and borderline oblivious to things around him.

Later behind his starting gate, Wylie stretched, yawned as always before a race, felt that temporary standoff between fear and adrenaline. He glanced at the several TV cameras that would broadcast the start of the race to the big screens down at the finish. Thoughts careened through his mind as if on casters, suddenly changing directions, some linked and others rogue and random. *Claude's CR Fives the best. Invincible on them. Breathe deep. Patrol in Kandahar and racing down a mountain. Lose a leg, break a neck. Will and luck. The fall line is your bro. Boxes locked and shelved and you fuckers will not open until I tell you to. Good poachers for breakfast, pepper and butter on top. Start me up. Watch me go. Robert, Robert. April down there at the finish. April Holly. Ten thousand prize money. Ten thousand! Remember let mind go. Let mind wander. Worst loss was 'cause I thought too much, concentrated too hard, and made the body wait. Body knows best. Big picture only, eyes ahead, don't fight yourself, man. Miss the MPP, get another someday. Lucky on the burns and April's aloe vera. Love to kick Sky's ass. Going to kick Sky's ass, you just watch. Hope that wax was right, been a while. . . .*

Yesterday, Wylie's qualification and semifinal races had been good enough but imprecise, leaving him the fourth gate pick for this final race. For the cup, Mike Cook had outfitted the X Course with drop-in start gates to space the racers safely, and these gates were positioned fairly and evenly. Wylie was secretly pleased to get the least-wanted gate, number 1, on the far left. It would leave him the longest line into the first X Course feature — a right bank — but he would be making that turn on the strength of his dominant left foot, on which his best speed and balance had always been built.

Sky Carson looked at him from behind gate 4. Sky had smoked the qualies and semis to earn the first gate pick, and gate 4 would give him the shortest line into the first bank. Sky had already taken and held that line in both his qualification races and his semifinal run the day before. He was yet to lose a race, or even his lead. Wylie had watched, impressed. He did think Sky was taking some unreasonable risks, as if he were racing on the Imagery Beast instead of on a real course, but he was putting down the runs like he owned them. Bridger Burr and Josh Coates, teammates out of Crested Butte, Colorado, took gates 2 and 3, respectively. Wylie knew they could be expected to help each other if necessary. In ski cross, a racer might sacrifice his own run — and take out an opponent or even two — so that his teammate could win. Few spectators here on Mammoth Mountain today expected such teamwork from Wylie or Sky.

Wylie looked over at him. There had been no words between them since the MPP incident. Sky waved. His beard and mustache were blue, his helmet white, and his goggles red, with black lenses. Wylie smiled to himself. Then Sky held out both hands toward him, palms up, as if in question, ski poles dangling by their straps. He grabbed the poles and sidled around the start gate, backing up the slope toward Wylie. Wylie back stepped and they met behind the house.

Sky lifted his red goggles and fixed Wylie with the Cynthia stare — lake ice over unquestioned determination. "Good luck, Wylie. But I won't have any kind of mercy on you."

"None expected, Sky. If you make that first hole shot again, prepare for some genuine pressure."

"Keep your skis off mine, pal."

"Ditto your poles and my legs."

"The officials have been ordered to call a tight one."

"When you hear my skis in your draft, remember that I have twenty pounds on you and I'm going to pass."

"You remember that I'll punish you severely for unsportsmanlike conduct. Such as running me off the course."

"Good luck to you, too, then, Sky."

"My words mean nothing to you."

"Approximately."

"I can do no more for you. This is for Robert."

"For Robert."

They banged gloved fists and glided away from each other, Sky loosening up at the waist, Wylie yawning again.

The starter called them into their gates. Wylie slid forward until his ski tips touched the blue dye. He lifted his goggles again, then firmed them against his face, snugged the helmet and pushed the strap under itself and against his throat. Again he checked all his zippers and buttons, loops and hooks, cuffs and pocket flaps, and every small thing that could retard his speed. His bib was tight and he liked the big odd number: 77.

He looked down and saw the line for a hole shot of his own into that first right bank. First in, first out. Tempting. His route would intersect Sky's, without doubt. So Wylie considered a more cautious start, which would take him lower, ceding the lead to someone else, likely Sky. Then he'd play catch-up as he usually did, the Wylie play-book.

His heart boomed away and he heard the familiar roar of blood in his ears and his mind felt lighter now and damn if he didn't like the idea of a surprise start. Sky might well be caught off guard, and Wylie had his good left foot to count on through that first right bank. Sky would be flabbergasted, and Claude Favier, too, and, really, the whole mountain would.

He took three deep breaths, exhaling fully, then yawned again. He felt the vanishing CO_2 replaced by a cold surge of oxygen. Vision clear and ears sharp. Now I see. Make the shot. Take the lead. Yes. It's yours. For Robert. For April and the girls. For *me.*

The gates swung open and Wylie dug powerfully with his poles. He launched and dropped like a cannonball, hitting the steep half-pipe flank with a deep bend of skis, crossing the bowl barely ahead of Bridger Burr and Josh Coates, but already behind Sky Carson.

Through the first short run, they formed

a tight knot, skis rattling, poles digging. Wylie's legs felt heavy, and whoever was behind him was close indeed. He held his line to the first bank, but Sky got there well ahead of everyone. Wylie ceded the turn, then tucked in behind Sky on the short straightaway leading to Launching Pad. The course was fast and he was airborne before he knew it, soaring off the jump just behind Sky. Then Wylie was floating, weight forward and ski tips jammed downward to dig into the air as the vast Sierra peripheries slowly unfolded around him. Then the course rushed up. He landed well, closing fast on Sky, hearing the hiss of Sky's skis and the louder hiss of his own, and the steady grind of those behind him. He carved close behind Sky and into the welcome pull of his draft. Pressure, he thought. Pressure him off this mountain. One of Sky's poles flicked oddly and Wylie felt a sudden stab of pain in his left shin.

The four drafted tightly toward the first gate, a sweeping right. Sky took it high, above the track, where the snow was less trammeled by racers. Wylie followed, snow blasting his goggles and the rasp of skis close behind him, urgent and high-pitched. He tried to focus ahead, but all he could see beyond Sky was the course jumping crazily ahead of him. Then a maddening moment as Wylie carved too hard into the gate on the race-battered ice and had to check his speed. He shouldered past the panel as tight as he could, but coming out he heard sudden dread quiet behind him as Bridger Burr swept past.

Tucked into Burr's draft, Wylie held third position down the straight toward jump two, Goofball. The straight was wide but offered insufficient velocity to pass. He broke left of Burr for the jump, launched high and deep into the sky. Another long moment of motion frozen in time, then Wylie hit hard and tore into a gentle left bank leading to the next gate. He held third place through the panels and came out fast.

On Dire Straights, he freed his speed, hugged his fall line to come up tight on Burr, his thighs parallel to the snow, calves together, knees working like pistons. The heaviness in his legs was gone. He was thoughtless and automatic, arms and poles acting far ahead of his dumb authority. He felt no more in control than a sneaker in a washing machine. This straight was his bread and butter, the most profitable feature of the course for a large racer. Wylie felt huge. He tucked around Burr, made an easy inside pass, and found himself breathing down the neck of Sky Carson.

Tucking in behind Sky again, he *ooorahed* to rattle Sky's cage. They sped toward Conundrum, where Robert had had his tragic fall. Wylie moved deep into Sky's draft, but Sky was staunch, claiming his line for the commanding center of the Conundrum ramp. Wylie dropped back inches as Sky pressed ahead, loosening a blast of snow and ice into Wylie's face. Sky had the good lane and launched off Conundrum. Wylie shot into the air on Sky's right. Leaning into the sudden silence, Wylie pressed hard, driving his ski tips down so the wind wouldn't flip him. He heard the slash of Burr, then of Coates, both launching behind him. His altitude was good. He could see Sky fully extended, straining for inches. Sky landed past where Robert had hit the ice. Wylie landed right on it, but lightly — for him — and well balanced, and he felt the CR Fives arcing radically, their sharp edges carving around a wide right bank that suddenly dropped him onto the next straightaway.

Wylie closed on Sky again, tight to his draft. But again Sky was staunch and relentless, body and nerves stout, giving Wylie not one inch, nor the slightest hint that he was even aware of the threat behind him. Down the mountain they flew, rippling with speed, bound by a tenuous bond of velocity and blood.

Sky held the lead, taking the best and shortest line into Shooters. Wylie stayed hard upon him, inches off his fall line, heard the rattling hiss of pursuit just feet behind him. Wylie felt enemy skis crunching over the backs of his own, then the terrible shimmy of deceleration.

"Coming through, Wylie!"

He flew into Shooters two yards behind Sky, the world abruptly closing around him — tree trunks and branches flashing by in the diminished light, the snow frozen to ice here in this cloistered forest.

"Coming *through*!"

He felt the rough grating of skis riding over his own again, kept his poles forward and free, dug mightily after Sky, who by now had claimed an impassable line out of the first chute and into the next. Wylie came up hard behind him, heard the skis still rasping behind him. The chute was long and narrow, and Wylie shot through flashing spokes of shadow and sunlight. The chute resolved in a hard right bank and he sensed that Sky was going too fast to take such a high line into it. Risking much, Wylie checked his speed, inviting Sky to take a safer, lower angle into the bank.

More shear and grind behind him. *"Coming through, Welborn!"* Skis clattered over the backs of his own again; then he felt a nanosecond of wobble. Wylie jabbed behind him smartly, felt his pole point hit snow. Sky chose the lower line into the bank, tucked tightly and made his move. It took less than a second for Sky to sense his mistake. Wylie saw him glance back, then bunch still tighter, setting his left pole, driving his uphill shoulder into the turn. Wylie had the higher line. He saw that they would converge exactly on the apex of the curve — Sky on the downhill side and Wylie narrowly above him. Whoever took the turn would have the lead into the long final straightaway and finish.

Sky streaked in from the left. He glanced at Wylie again and Wylie saw the blue beard and the wild white of eyes behind the goggles. The gate rushed them. Wylie freed all the speed he had in him, drew his shoulders up and out, and bumped past Sky. Sky quivered upon contact, then drove over the backs of Wylie's skis for a higher line that would send him out of the turn first. At desperate speed, Sky came even with Wylie, then tipped up on one ski to speed alongside Wylie, poles out for balance but all physics against him. He went down like someone thrown from a train, then spun off into the trees and out of Wylie's sight.

Once through Shooters, Wylie hogged the fast middle course with fierce abandon. *For you, Robert.* He heard no one behind him. The seconds seemed eternal. He crossed the finish line alone and threw up a huge rooster tail of snow in the out-run before looking back uphill. Bridger Burr and Josh Coates followed a hundred feet back. Ten long seconds later, Sky came essing down in the slow sway of concession, waving one acutely bent pole to the cheering crowd, his right arm tucked weirdly up against his side.

On the middle podium, Wylie raised to the filled grandstands his first-place trophy and an oversized replica of his ten-thousand-dollar check. The trophy was cast in the form of a gorilla holding up a chalice that had *Gargantua Mammoth Cup I* engraved around its lip. The check's background depicted a gorilla's face coming up behind Mammoth Mountain like a sunrise.

Wylie heard the applause and the loudly amplified announcers' voices, saw the cameras flashing. He felt very strange. He'd never been so stuffed with gratitude and with belief in tomorrow and with strong love for what he saw around him. Could all of this really come from winning a simple ski race? It seemed unlikely. But what was wrong with winning a ski race? And what was wrong with setting your sights on the biggest ski-cross race of all, and winning that, too? Was being the best ski crosser in the world any less an accomplishment than being the best actor or baker or poet or doctor or the best anything else?

And speaking of life, did that have to be only about holding parts together, locking things in, keeping the memory boxes properly stowed? Couldn't it be about playing up? Dreaming bigger? Nailing it? He reminded himself that this moment was a beginning and he knew that the road ahead would be long and rugged. For an example, he glanced down at the blood-smeared hole in his snow pants, just above the left boot, Sky's doing at the bottom of Launch Pad. That hurt.

He looked out at April and Kathleen and Steen. Then at Beatrice and Belle with their beanies pulled snug for warmth over their shorn heads. At Jesse and Jolene. All his people sitting close together in the stands. He could see their smiles and puffs of breath as they pounded their gloved hands together and yelled to him. Falling snow muffled the sound. To the left side of the grandstand, behind the roped-off media area, on an asphalt walkway leading up from the lodge, stood Sky and Cynthia and Hailee, and a woman Wylie had not seen before. Robert sat among them in his wheelchair, bundled against the cold.

CHAPTER THIRTY-SEVEN

Twenty hours later, a drastically hungover Wylie Welborn sat in the stands with his family, waiting to see April's final slopestyle routine. She had already won the cup on the first of her two finals runs, untouched by any of her competitors. The common wisdom on a clinched competition was to play the second run safe and get yourself to the podium in one unbroken piece.

"Think she'll try that back-side double-cork ten-eighty, Wyles?" asked Belle.

"No reason to try it now. X Games probably."

"I want to see it. Never been landed by a chick. Not in competition, for reals."

The day was cold again, and both Beatrice and Belle scrunched close against their brother on the butt-numbing grandstands. They wore their heaviest parkas, and beanies with earflaps tied snugly down. It had been Beatrice's idea to shave their heads in partial penance for their thievery. After ordering them to write essays on why they had stolen, and why they should not have, an octogenarian juvenile court judge had sentenced them each to five hundred hours of community service — which would average approximately five hours per week over the next two years — spring and Christmas breaks excluded. They had done their first sixteen hours back in December, at town hall, apologizing and serving hot chocolate to people who were trying to reclaim their stolen bikes, skis, and boards at a well-publicized weekend open house. Belle had told Wylie that the judge, the Honorable Caroline Hoppe, had attended both days of the event, helping herself to the spiked eggnog and glaring at her and Beatrice occasionally, making sure they took their penance seriously.

As Wylie watched on the big monitor, April shook herself loose behind the start gate, slid in, crouched, and waited. Up top, the breeze was stronger, and April's well-known golden curls swayed below the rim of her turquoise-blue helmet. She wore the white and turquoise-blue colors that matched her eyes, had long been her signature uniform, from which she never varied.

Last night, the painless, wine-drinking

Wylie had cooked for April her "lucky pre-competition dinner" — a thin skirt steak done Mexican-style with onions and tomatoes, a baked potato buried in sour cream and bacon bits, asparagus, and chocolate pudding, served at 5:48 P.M., April's lucky preevent dinnertime. After dinner, he had watched her arrange toiletries and grooming products on her bathroom counter, each bottle, tube, and tub paired with its identical mate. The couples faced each other, front label to front label. The pairs stood in descending order by height, the tallest beginning back at the mirror and the rest winding out to the counter's edge, then along the front of the sink and back to the other side of the mirror. She hummed, her concentration was total, and she said nothing. Then a long shower.

Her lucky precompetition bedtime was 8:48. April told Wylie that all her lucky times ended in forty-eight because it had been lucky to her even as a toddler. So Wylie lay beside her in bed as she listened to music through earbuds. It was plenty loud enough for him to hear. At exactly 10:48, he nudged her, as instructed, and she pulled out the buds and turned over. For half of the night, she thrashed and called out through dreams that seemed disturbing even to Wylie, but he remained good to his word not to wake her. After that, she slept like the dead. Then, this morning, he had made for the seemingly refreshed April Holly her "lucky precompetition breakfast" of black coffee, scrambled eggs, and two packs of small waxlike chocolate doughnuts, served at 8:48.

Now the starting gate swung out and she launched, the crowd cheering. Studying her videos, Wylie had come to admire her unhurried starts, then how she built momentum into the body of her run, then closed with dramatic finishes. April now looked like she had just gotten out of bed and was easing her way into the day. After all, she had no clock and no opponents to beat down the hill. Why hurry? She put a little ragamuffin into it. But Wylie and everyone watching knew that she would need velocity — lots of it and soon — to get the big air she needed for her tricks.

She came off the start with a 50/50 on the downrail, held it long and casually, like a surfer having fun on a small but well-shaped wave. Wylie watched her with a smile. The crowd hooted and hollered as April, much larger than life, charged toward them on the big screen. She gapped to a board-slide switch out, then drove up the ramp with a sudden speed that seemed to be supplied from behind her, rocketlike. Then off the lip she flew, up and up into the blue sky, above the green treetops, the crowd *oohing,* Wylie agog. She twisted dervishly in midair, decomposing into a blur of board and body from which a favorable outcome seemed doubtful, then landed the cab-tail 270 in perfect balance, as if on springs. She scorched loudly across the trough and up the opposite flank, then launched back into the air for a switch backside 540 multiple body roll that seemed a defiance of time and space, a thing too complex and rapid to be clearly seen. She landed with the lightness of a leaf. The crowd was wild, and Wylie held his breath.

Then she flew into authentic view from the grandstand. Wylie watched as her compact white-and-turquoise form banked frontward off the edge and back into the air. Such joy in it. The crowd hollered louder as April carved down toward them, her dazzling speed seemingly given to her again. She banked high twice and laid down another 540, so much closer to him now that Wylie could hear the sharp carve and grind of her board.

She landed with a loud crunch and shot up the next bank toward her final jump.

Such wonderful speed now, even more than before, as if she'd been saving it. She sprang up over the blue edge paint and into the sky again — her biggest air so far — Wylie and the crowd sensing something new here, a raising of stakes. Higher and higher she rose. At the apex, she dropped her head and shoulders and the snowboard flashed upward, April tucking under it, board bottom to the sky, comets of ice falling, one hand on the rail for a long roll that accelerated to a blur of turquoise and white, woman and board, tangled and twisting. Then down she came. Wylie couldn't tell what part of her would hit the ground first. The crowd had gone silent. Suddenly, April's snowboard slashed into place beneath her and she landed hard. Her legs collapsed, springlike, and she wobbled slightly. Then she uncoiled into balance, raising her fists to the crowd and sending a wave of snow into the photogs. She carved to a stop in the middle of the out-run, beaming.

"I think I just saw, like, history," said Belle.

Chapter Thirty-Eight

That evening, Wylie and April drove to Village Square for the Gargantua Mammoth Cup Runneth Over Party. It was already in full swing when they got there, and Wylie had to park across the street in the pay lot. He and April walked arm in arm, leaning into each other. They both wore their winners' jackets, which had been handsewn by a local designer and underwritten by Vault Sports. The jacket bodies were Mammoth team blue, the sleeves white and red, respectively. Wylie wore a new blue shirt and his best jeans and black cowboy boots, recently polished. Under her winner's jacket, April dared a black miniskirt and leggings, black boots, and touches of lapis set in silver.

"I'm so happy and full right now," said April. "I want it to last forever."

He looked at her and found it difficult to believe that he was about to walk into a party thrown partially in honor of himself and his date — easily the most beautiful woman he'd ever seen. He knew that in no real way did he deserve her; in fact, pointedly did not deserve her. But if this was the flip side of life not being fair, he would take it. "Maybe it will," he said lamely.

"I had a long talk with Mom this afternoon. We're good. I'm sending her home. I'm going to travel on my own and learn to take care of myself. She'll still handle all the business arrangements. Logan's going to work with Sandra Brannen in Jackson, so he's covered. I'll train hard for the X Games and the FIS circuit, and spend every free minute with this Welborn guy out of Mammoth."

"He might like that."

"I hope I don't drive him crazy with all my habits."

"I hear he's just dumb in love with you."

Wylie looked out at the square, teeming with lights and people. Village Square was Mammoth Lakes' largest and most focused commercial development and one of its more recent. It looked like a Christmas card. The buildings were alpine-modern, the shops and restaurants upscale and expensive. Four-story condos lined the curving village walkways and a handsome Westin Hotel anchored one end of it. There were streetlamps and wooden benches and sculptures. A smooth, fast gondola whisked people up the mountain to Canyon Lodge. The square's focal point was a tall, peaked clock tower, which had become a key civic symbol of the city.

Tonight, the village was at its best. Eaves and roofs shouldered the heavy snow, and icicles dropped shining beads into the light of storefront windows. The snow had been blown off the plaza floor, and there were three bars and a dozen food stands spouting fragrantly competitive clouds of steam into the cold, clear air.

Walking up the steps to the plaza, Wylie was startled to see Cynthia Carson standing in the snow under a tall red fir, pointing a small camera at them. She was very close but scarcely visible in her winter-bark camo jacket and matching knit cap and gloves. The camera clicked twice, then dangled on a strap on her wrist. She held a pen in her camera hand and a small notepad in the other, her thumb marking her place. Her blue eyes looked backlit. "You won."

"Thank you."

"How did it feel?"

"Good."

She wrote deliberately, then looked up at April. "My name is Cynthia Carson."

"Yes, I know who you are," said April.

"Sky believes that your contact on the X Course went past incidental," Cynthia said.

"I thought he would," said Wylie.

"And what do you believe?"

"Neither of us gave one inch. The referee saw no infraction. It's part of ski cross."

Cynthia wrote again — carefully and slowly — then nodded, as if she'd anticipated Wylie's words. "Sky feels that he must follow through on his warning to you."

"I wish he wouldn't."

"I understand his position."

"I'll bet you do. But I'm not going to apologize to him for things I didn't do."

"His broken right arm has been set. He and his fiancée are up in Reno tonight. He feels humiliated."

"He ran a good race. I hope he lets us all be, Mrs. Carson."

"Don't escalate."

"I'm going to the party now."

"A pleasure to meet you, April. I never liked board slopestyle until today. I don't understand how you do it, but it's courageous and very beautiful."

Tonight, Village Square was overhung by a white canvas canopy outlined in strands of twinkling lights. Stainless-steel heaters glowed within and propane-burning fire pits threw up lapping waves of orange flames. Wylie guided April under the canopy, and as the revelers recognized them, they broke into hoots and shouts and glove-muffled applause. The DJ spun "Can't Hold Us," and suddenly phones and cameras were clicking and flashing. Wylie smiled and waved, then took April's right hand and raised it high. A platoon of reporters, photographers, and video shooters materialized from the crowd and made straight for her.

The winners' tables were bar-style, round and high, and spread throughout the canopied square so the guests could step up and talk with the athletes. Wylie joined the two Colorado ski-cross finalists, who pressed an open bottle of champagne on him, hugged him tipsily, and offered bleary smiles to the circle of ski-cross admirers. Wylie sipped a long, cold shot and hugged two girls who wanted him in their selfies.

Claude Favier broke away from a group and strongly shook Wylie's hand. "Never have I been more proud for Chamonix! I wish you all the good luck in Aspen. And in Europe, if you choose to compete."

"I'm taking those CR Fives on the FIS circuit, Claude." It sounded strange to hear himself say this in public for the first time. The World Cup circuit!

"It will be a challenge, but you are a good ski-cross racer. Do not let European snobbery destroy your confidence. I know the very best wax technician on the Continent and I will introduce you to him. He can read a racer's mind and reveal it in the waxing. He can improve any racer's speed."

"I'll send you a picture of me on the podium at Val Thorens."

"With the CR Fives prominently visible!" Then the Frenchman's smile dropped and he leaned in close to Wylie. "I saw your dramatic pass of Sky yesterday. Something in it disturbed me. Later, the chief of race allowed me to view the video. I watched it several times and decided that you did no wrong in the passing of Sky Carson. You raced honestly. But Sky is very temperamental, so you must be civil to him."

"I can manage it."

"His threats are, of course, nonsense. Ah — I see a friend I must welcome." Claude angled skillfully through the partygoers to intercept a tall and strikingly beautiful woman with a borzoi on a leash. The woman looked at the dog and the dog sat, and Claude cheek-kissed her three times in the French way.

Wylie talked briefly with a *Powder* magazine stringer who said he'd gotten a kick out of Wylie's "power pass" in the finals, though obviously Sky Carson had not. He told Wylie that Sky's broken wrist was a "green-stick fracture" and not serious. He said the FIS ski-cross circuit was much rougher than here — totally physical — then excused himself to catch up with a waiter bearing a tray of complimentary wines.

Next to Wylie, the Colorado guys had loudly begun reenacting key moments from their races, one of them snatching the champagne bottle back from Wylie. Wylie seized the moment to locate April, who stood at a middle table with the women slopestylers. The media troops had closed in again and her table had twice the crowd as any other. But, somehow sensing his attention, she looked over and found him and smiled as her admirers pressed in and the camera lights slapped her face. She had taken off her jacket and become even more beautiful.

Mike Cook brought Wylie a bourbon and they posed for pictures for *The Sheet* and *Mammoth Times.* As the photogs snapped away, Wylie saw Kathleen and Steen and his sisters yapping it up with Jesse and Jolene Little Chief. Beatrice and Belle did look penitent with their shorn hair and humble good manners.

Adam and Teresa made their entrance, to solid applause. Adam looked underdressed and bored, as he often did at social gatherings, while Teresa was radiant. The mayor and two council members stood with the chief of police and two Mammoth Lakes developers. Bart Helixon cut through the crowd, talking to somebody somewhere, wearing a trim navy suit, his window lens shimmering.

Grant Bulla and his son Daniel were engaged with the women half-pipe boarders. The sergeant looked over and Wylie nodded. Bulla had been persuasive in the legal proceedings against Wylie's sisters — urging leniency for their youth and good characters — and Wylie made a note to thank him again tonight, later. Coincidentally, Wylie spotted the Honorable Caroline Hoppe at the men's boarder-cross table. She was holding a steaming mug, nodding intently along with an animated presentation by the first-place medalist.

Jacobie Bradford delivered drinks to two young women Wylie didn't know. The women glanced at each other. Jacobie's head shined as if waxed and he had traded in his fly-fishing uniform for a tuxedo and a bold scarf in Rastafarian black, green, gold, and red. Wylie watched the snow falling in the darkness outside the canopy and heard his beloved Rexroth: *Believe/In the night, the moon, the crowded/Earth.*

He looked at April again, surrounded by her crowd and unaware of him. He pictured her last slopestyle run, the skill and abandon that she'd brought to a competition that she had already won. She's right, he thought, remembering the first long walk they'd taken together — from Let It Bean to her rented home in Starwood — when she'd told him she was at her best in the air, trying to do beautiful things. Impossible things. He admired that freedom. The freedom to be the best you can be. The freedom for it to be more than a job or a means or a contest or a way out. For it to be a way in, Wylie thought. *Thank you, April Holly.* Unseen by her, Wylie saw the flash of her smile, and he had never felt this full. He wanted to be closer to her.

Soon he was. The eighteen winners were herded onto a low stage set up near one of the fire pits. More photos, Wylie thought. The gold medalists took center stage, and the second- and third-place contestants squeezed in around them. Wylie arranged himself most happily next to April. Photographers both pro and amateur filled the floor in front of the athletes, and their lights flashed away as Jacobie rolled a wheeled, hooded object through them, stopping it at the stage.

With a flourish, he yanked on the shroud to reveal the newly redesigned Gargantua Mammoth Cup — a cast statue of a lowland gorilla with an almost human expression, standing upright and holding a chalice over his head with two stout arms. Hoots and hollers rang out. The trophy was close to four feet tall, and the winner's names had already been engraved. The medalists played it straight for as long as they could, then broke into impromptu aping. Wylie held a beer to the gorilla's mouth and the photographers fired away. April slipped her arm around Wylie and he felt the wonderful heft of her against his side and the beat of her heart. He knew this was one of the great moments of his life.

Sky Carson strode into the lights of the canopy. His right arm was in a red satin sling and his left was intertwined with the arm of a sleek young woman. He wore a tuxedo and his Mammoth Cup champion's jacket from four years ago. His colored hair had been restored to its yellow blond, and his blue beard was gone. The woman was sheathed in black leather and her hair flashed like obsidian. They stopped and Sky touched Claude's arm. It looked like Sky was introducing his date. To Wylie, Sky seemed like his usual old self — relaxed and happily the center of attention. Sky and the slender woman moved on then to another group, where he made a joking attempt to shake someone's hand.

A few minutes later, Sky looked across the room to Wylie and started in his direction.

Wylie was aware of the parting, now quieting crowd, but he was totally focused on his half brother. Sky's face was set. The photogs surrendered their ground to him. Wylie shouldered April behind him, noticing that Sky's left hand was empty. In his peripheral vision, Wylie registered Kathleen beginning to move toward him and Steen holding her back; the flames coiling in the fire pits and the snow swirling beyond; Cynthia and Adam drifting toward Sky from the rear of the canopy; cameras flashing; Beatrice and Belle unmoving, their faces puzzled. Jacobie's wineglass stopped just short of his lips, which rose into a smirk.

Sky stopped before the stage and released his good arm from that of the woman to point his forefinger at Wylie. "I couldn't have been more clear or honest with you. Account for what you did."

"I won't."

"I've tried very hard to accommodate you."

"Give it up, Sky. You've stirred things up enough."

"You decide whose mountain this is to die on."

Wylie tried to check his anger, but he was already moving toward Sky. The winners' bodies slowed him and he felt April's hands lock onto him from behind. But his adrenaline was spiking and he was stronger, so he dragged April hoppingly along. Then she swung herself in front of him with the same gifted lightness she used for slopestyle, dug in, and pushed him back toward the stage. "No, Wyles, this is when you let it go. You let it go right *now.*"

Looking past her shoulders and through her bouncing curls, Wylie saw Sky reach his left hand into the sling and withdraw a dull black thing. The sleek woman screamed and grabbed at it. Wylie powerfully swept April away as a gunshot cracked the thin alpine air. The crowd exploded as if a bomb had gone off. People screamed and charged away in all directions, while others fell flat and covered up. Wylie charged into another shot and another — feeling nothing — and he saw through the smoke and the riotous commotion that Sky's eyes were wide as he waved the gun. Then the horrified scream of someone shot. More screams, the sleek woman now hitting at Sky, the flare of her black hair in the lights. Fighting against the exodus, Cynthia Carson waded toward her son, and Steen tried to hold Kathleen back, and Adam barged toward Sky, and Sgt. Grant Bulla crouched in a two-handed shooter's stance, angling for a clear shot, his voice sharply audible through the gunfire and shrill panic: *"Drop it, Sky!"*

Wylie focused on the gun in Sky's hand. It went off again, muzzle flashing at the canopy overhead. Sky wheeled on Bulla. Two rapid concussive booms then, and Sky dropped heavily, as if the force that had held his body together had been yanked away.

Wylie turned and looked for April but couldn't find her. One of the half-pipe skiers headed toward the street, bleeding from his hand and escorted by two other medalists. Wylie barged into the big throng gathered to his left, where he had flung April to safety. People huddled and crouched, their attention drawn downward, their gestures frantic and emphatic, sending up a weird concatenation of questions and answers, orders and silence, outrage and consolations. In the middle of them lay April, spread-eagle on her back, with her head on

Belle's lap and a pile of coats and jackets randomly piled on, a swamp of blood loosening around her. Wylie knelt and leaned over her and looked down at her white face flecked with red and her wide blue eyes. Within the bloody garments, he got her hand and found her rapid pulse. Her eyes seemed to locate him at a great distance, and her pupils tightened.

"Hang on now," he said.

" 'kay."

"I love you very much."

"Good."

"What's going to happen is the medics will be here in a minute. And we'll get you on a gurney and to the hospital. It's a good one, here in Mammoth. I'll be with you every second and I'll never let go of you."

" 'kay."

"Think about Solitary Meadow, April. Picture the wildflowers and the creek. And the runs we made. And think about tomorrow and where we're going and what we're going to do together. We've got a busy schedule, girl. So much to look forward to." Wylie's throat clenched tight and he saw the frost trying to seize the blue of her eyes, saw the swoon of the black pupils, small to large to small.

"They robbed us, Wyles."

He touched his lips to hers and prayed for breath. Breathe April, please breathe. Do not stop breathing. No. Please. No. An immeasurable piece of time later, he pulled back and looked into her eyes and saw that she was gone. He lowered his forehead to hers and felt the hot outrush of tears. More time stole past, her face cold against his.

Belle touched him. He could hear her crying. "I saw you get her out of the way, but Sky was shooting everything."

Then more planes of chaos were intersecting above him — the ascendant screams of sirens, and hands and voices upon him. Mother and sisters. Steen and Adam. Teresa and Claude and Grant Bulla, ordering the people away, making way for the first responders.

CHAPTER THIRTY-NINE

I held Sky as his last breath quivered away. I felt a heartbreak I had never known, not even over Robert. Sky, my most talented and troubled. My most me. I tried to get him up into my arms and carry him away, but Sergeant Bulla would have none of that. I was thankful, because I wasn't sure I could lift Sky, or for how long, or exactly where I should take him anyway. I wanted to shield him from prying eyes. The worst is everyone watching you, after. So I rocked him until the paramedics arrived. They blitzed in, did their tests, hooked up the oxygen and saline, refusing to admit the obvious, which is their training. It is not theirs to pronounce.

I climbed into the ambulance after my son. Before the doors closed, I saw another crew racing April Holly into a second truck. Wylie, stone-faced and white, got in with her. I got just a quick look at April, that poor, sweet, talented girl. All her crazy grace and courage.

A shining star. Wylie had tried to get her out of the way, but Sky was shooting wildly because he'd lost his nerve, as he had in racing. So there was no safe place. Only chance. On the gurney, she looked lifeless, and I hoped that I was wrong, but I was not. Either way, my heart broke for her, a true innocent, like Robert. The doors slammed shut and the big boxy vehicle slowly ground along through the snow toward the hospital, lights flashing on the white world and the sirens howling.

What that *Adrenaline* show host never asked me, and what I've thought about all my life is, if I had it to do all over again, knowing what I know now, would I? Shoot Richard, I mean. I've had roughly a quarter century to ponder that question. Having walked my long, steep road, I must say that I would not do it again. Because there's no way to foresee the consequences of violence. You can't predict the many sad spokes that will branch outward from such a hub. But they will. I would not again burden the futures of my children, and their children, and so on, down the line. Of course, I knew none of that then. I knew only my own blind rage, and my betrayal by the man I had loved with all my heart.

Over my life, I've seen a pattern. But violence is not only a Carson curse. It is everywhere, within us and without us. The more I look the more I see it. The more I read, the more I find it — all the way back to when one of Earth's first two brothers rose up in the field against the other.

Rose up.

Why?

I'm not qualified to say. I have read the Bible and most of the so-called great books — plenty of time for that down in Chowchilla — and I have learned nothing decisive from them. Are we born to violence? Or forced into it? Scripted by jealous gods, or part of our nature? I don't know. But I do know that I am somehow not surprised that Sky rose up against Wylie. And Wylie against Sky.

The smell of Sky's blood still lingers in my nostrils after all these weeks.

I am finally learning to change direction. Of life's three great labors, this has been my hardest, regarding anything Welborn. I detested Kathleen and Wylie for taking what I loved from me. I do hear the towering selfishness in that statement. I always have. My change of direction began when I started watching the Welborn-Mikkelsen clan, which was not long before Wylie's return from the war and his travels. I had become curious about what I loathed. And a good reporter is always looking for new stories. So I watched and waited and gathered their stories, too.

Because of my observations of them, I was able to see why they had stolen the bikes and snowboards and skis. I'd seen their slouching little house in the forest, and their long hours in that bakery/coffee shop, and everyone in town knew that Gargantua was running them out of business. And everyone also knew that Beatrice's and Belle's mother had promiscuously seduced my Richard — a living legend no less — and stolen his seed from me to make something spurious of her own. So my heart went out to them. Somewhat. In their guilt I saw their innocence.

I admired those girls for enduring all that. And I saw that I could change direction without having to make some grandiose gesture of repentance. Without having to so much as look at that woman. To change direction is to change what you do, not what you feel. Thus I led Wylie to what his sisters had done — my first act of kindness to a Welborn. The beginning of atonement. Atonement. An overgrand word in my opinion. I remind myself not to get carried away with it.

Am I crazy, or simply the victim of my own temper? If crazy, was I born this way, or is it self-created? I do remember as a girl I had very dark moods and terrible headaches that would put me in bed in a dark room for several days at a time. Extravagant hallucinations. Like hell must be. When they were over, I would feel changed: lighter and emptier. And I would begin to worry about when it would happen again. The dark periods coincided with my social failures, defeats in competition, holidays, and with both the winter and summer solstices. I considered ending my life. So maybe it was in the blood. But so far as self-created madness goes, we all can cave under our own constructions when they are heavier than we can bear. Five bullets fired into my beautiful Richard, and thirteen years of prison, come to mind.

Jacobie Bradford III was fired by Gargantua after a video of him and two women appeared briefly on social media. The three were performing obscene and likely painful acts, but I have no interest in watching such things, so I can't be more descriptive. Jacobie's firing, however, did make page one of *The Woolly,* and I used a nice big head shot of him. I had lots of takers on that issue.

The buzz around Mammoth Lakes was that the women were prostitutes out of Reno and the activity took place on the third floor of Mountain High. The buzz beneath the buzz was that Croft, the bouncer at Mountain High, arranged the video without Jacobie's knowledge and sent it to Belle Mikkelsen, who did the anonymous posting. It's easy to see how a guy like Jacobie Bradford would think he could buy anything he wanted in our little town — a monopoly for his business, the fish in our rivers, a bargain mansion still empty from the Great Recession, two young women. And it's easy to imagine how hard a corporate gorilla like Gargantua would land on an expendable district manager caught with his pants way, way down. Since then, the town has lost its love of Gargantua and renewed its vows to Let It Bean. A complete flip-flop. Beware the fickleness of the mob. Howard Deetz over at Town Hall said there's talk that Gargantua may close the store here.

Wylie won the X Games ski cross in Aspen two weeks after April's death. I watched it live on TV and I will say that Wylie blew the competition off the mountain in the final that afternoon. As a downhill racer, I can tell when a skier is asking too much of herself, when the main thing she's relying on is simple-minded bravery. That's when you'll can up and get hurt, or worse. But I've seen Wylie race enough times to know that he was smart and measured and in command of himself at the X Games. He smoked the final schuss fifty feet ahead of silver. He did just a few interviews afterward, saying little. He looked distracted and bored. An obviously unhappy man before cameras. But he was in special demand, after what happened here on our mountain. You cannot underestimate the public thirst for shock and tragedy. The less he said, the more they asked. There was a dustup with a photographer in Aspen, whose camera Wylie destroyed in a parking lot. The video went viral, and in it Wylie looked a little crazy.

His story gets better. Two weeks later, he won the first FIS World Cup ski-cross event of the year in Tegernsee, Germany. Much was made of this upset, before which Wylie was ranked twenty-fourth in the world. Apparently, he knew the course well, having spent time in a Tegernsee monastery after the war.

Almost unbelievably, Wylie won the next World Cup race, too, early February in Val Thorens, France. Got himself lots of ESPN and network time, nice write-ups in the *New York Times, Wall Street Journal, Los Angeles Times, USA Today,* and a lot of other big publications. Plenty of magazine covers to come. They all want to talk about April and Sky and what happened here in Mammoth Lakes. He isn't saying much. So it's mostly Wylie's bearded, sullen face that the world has come to know. We'll see his expression when the endorsement dollars start to flow.

Wylie is on his way. Where?

I'm better now. Thanks for asking. I miss Sky very much. Every loss in life is different, every sorrow its own. He was such a happy little goof when he was little. Now he's a hole in anyone who knew or loved him. A hole covered by grass and marked by a headstone down in Bishop, near his father.

I have Robert and Andrea and Brandon and the two grandkids. I have Adam. Hailee and Antoinette and I are close. After some setbacks, we've gotten Robert moving his eyelids with volition again — once for yes and twice for no — either lid, we're happy with either lid. Soon as spring comes, we'll get him back outside in his chair, get some sun on his still-handsome face.

I consider myself blessed, though blessings are not always easy to detect. Some are secret. Some require faith. So I write my life. I'm my lone subscriber, my most attentive reader. We're all our own best audience.

This is my story to tell, mine to live and die with. They can't take it away from me.

Ever.

ABOUT THE AUTHOR

T. Jefferson Parker is the bestselling author of numerous novels, including *Storm Runners* and *The Fallen*. Alongside Dick Francis and James Lee Burke, Parker is one of only three writers to be awarded the Edgar Award for Best Novel more than once. Parker lives with his family in Southern California.

The employees of Thorndike Press hope you have enjoyed this Large Print book. All our Thorndike, Wheeler, and Kennebec Large Print titles are designed for easy reading, and all our books are made to last. Other Thorndike Press Large Print books are available at your library, through selected bookstores, or directly from us.

For information about titles, please call:
(800) 223-1244

or visit our Web site at:
http://gale.cengage.com/thorndike

To share your comments, please write:

Publisher
Thorndike Press
10 Water St., Suite 310
Waterville, ME 04901